Jana

Jana

Michael J. Sahno

Published by
SAHNO PUBLISHING
P. O. Box 46506
Tampa, FL 33646

First Edition
Printed in the United States of America

ISBN 978-1-944173-02-9

Library of Congress Control Number: 2015916579

Publisher's Cataloging-In-Publication Data
(Prepared by The Donohue Group, Inc.)

Names: Sahno, Michael J.
Title: Jana / Michael J. Sahno.
Description: First edition. | Tampa, FL : Sahno Publishing, [2015]
Identifiers: LCCN 2015916579 | ISBN 978-1-944173-02-9
Subjects: LCSH: Lesbians--History--20th century--Fiction. | Homophobia
    in the workplace--History--20th century--Fiction. | Discrimination in
    employment--History--20th century--Fiction. | Employees--Dismissal
    of--Fiction. | Day care centers--Fiction. | LCGFT: Humorous fiction.
Classification: LCC PS3619.A46 J36 2015 | DDC 813/.6--dc23

Cover Design by
Ryan Ratliff: RR Web and Print

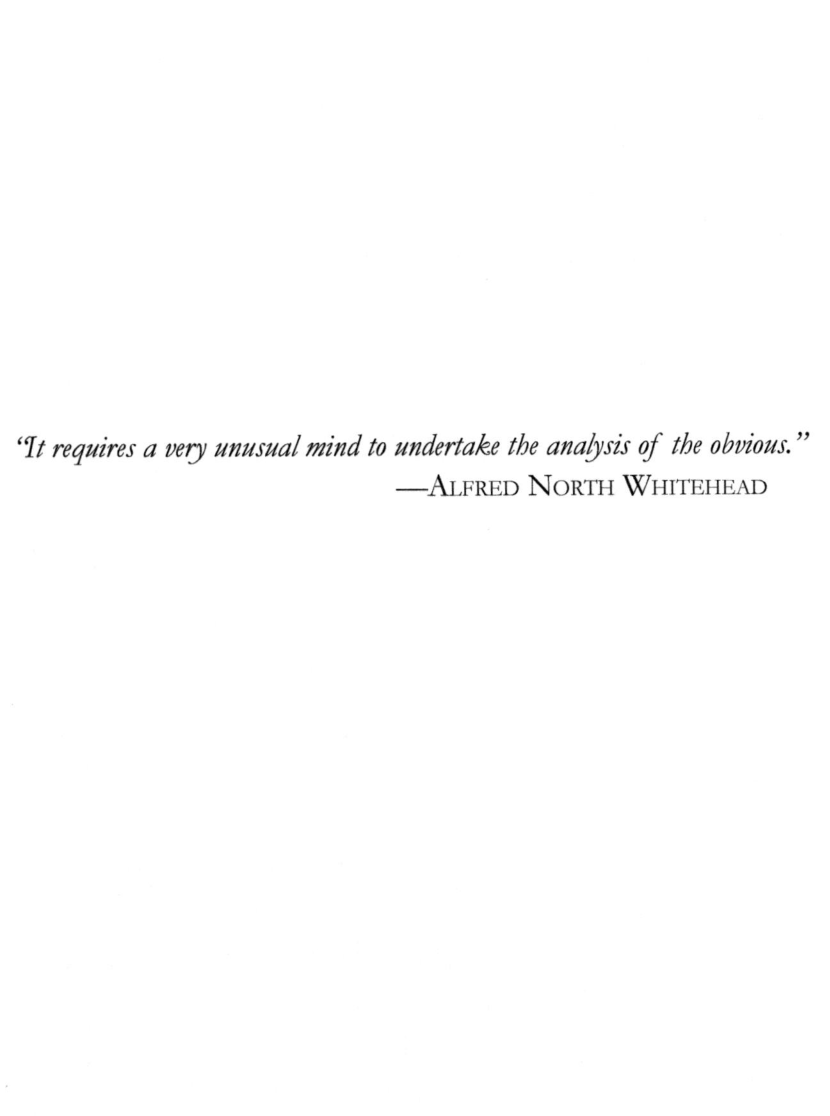

"It requires a very unusual mind to undertake the analysis of the obvious."
—ALFRED NORTH WHITEHEAD

Chapter 1

I'LL NEVER FORGET that conversation. We stand talking in the hallway of the Kiddie Korner Child Care Center, outside what we call the Day Room, Wendy Simpson and me. Wendy's blonde hair is bright from the sunlight behind her, and her eyes have the surreal glow of a hardcore caffeine addict. In her case, I think it's just self-absorption.

"You know, Jana," she says. "We could rilly do something with your hair."

I strain not to frown, and make sure to respond in even tones. After all, I'm a more recent hire than Wendy. "Excuse me?"

"We could rilly do something with your hair."

"My hair."

"Yeah, like have you ever gotten a perm?" She says *perm* the way another person might say *orgasm* or *diamond*.

"No," I say. "I've never gotten a perm."

"You should get a perm. I could help you pick out some eyeshadow that would rilly highlight your hair and eye color, too. You could have a whole new look."

"I think I like my *current* look, thank you." I smile when I say it, but my tone is no doubt like cold water in her face.

"Well…." Her eyes dart back and forth, and she looks down, like someone caught in a lie.

"Well, what? Are you trying to say something about the way I look?"

"Well…yeah." Her eyes meet mine. "I mean, I don't want to be *rude* or anything, but—parents don't like people who don't look… professional."

"You think I look unprofessional because I don't have a perm? Because I'm not wearing eyeshadow?" My voice goes up an octave.

"You don't have to yell at me. I'm just trying to say that people have a better impression of the center if you look nice." She brushes her hair back. Beads and baubles clatter.

"'Nice?' What does 'nice' mean? I mean, I'm clean, my hair's not messy…I'm wearing a blazer, for Pete's sake. Not that I'll keep it on while I'm working with the kids…."

She looks at me in frustration. Obviously a hopeless case. "Never mind," she says. "I can't explain it."

"Sure you can. You can explain it." I'm on a roll now. "You can look like someone who just graduated from junior high —"

"Oh!" she says with a gasp.

"— while I'm unacceptable because I don't put half a can of styling mousse in my hair or wear a lot of beads and bangles. Well, girl, I'm not about to try to become Miss Homecoming Queen, okay? I mean, I don't have to apologize for looking like a dyke and dressing like a dyke, because that's what I am: a dyke. Do you really think anybody has a problem with that?"

Oh shit. I wasn't out to her. Guess I am now….

While I speak, she looks angry, confused. But the word *dyke* really throws her. First she looks blank. Then her expression changes to one of abject horror, as if she'd just witnessed a murder. Her eyes widen.

"You mean you're…you're one of —" She takes a step back.

"Yeah, I am. Don't worry, you're not my type."

"That's disgusting!"

"Hey, maybe I think what you do is disgusting too. By the way, next time you decide to dole out fashion advice, call someone who cares." I walk away, my footsteps echoing down the hall, and I feel her eyes on my back like sunlight through a magnifying glass.

Chapter 2

SO, OKAY. CALL me weird. Call me anything (within reason, of course), but don't try to placate me by calling me normal; it's an insult. Call me weird or strange or the great euphemism, *different*; call me butch, a dyke, call me Jana Odessi, a twenty-four-year-old white American lesbian living here in Hartford, Connecticut, in the year of our Lord 1994, but do not—I repeat emphatically, do *not*—call me normal. It's such a copout, such a lame way of dealing with someone you might not understand.

You can call me an autodidact also, which just means that I've learned a lot of what I've learned on my own. I did a couple years of college (back in those glorrrrious George Bush the First days, when you could practically get a grant for being a lesbian, for Christ's sake), and in fact, I dropped out after my sophomore year as a result of sheer financial necessity. But I managed to learn a few potentially useful things, and although I was a Failed Musician at the time, I somehow gained an orientation for other areas of interest.

So when I dropped out, I educated myself in my free time. I read Kant and Descartes and Hiedegger and all those dudes, until the whole scene bored the absolute shit out of me. Then I did this women's studies thing—which my formal education had sorely overlooked—a lot of Emily Dickinson, and Anne Sexton,

Alice Walker, Toni Morrison, and so on, and so on, ad infinitum. Imagine Sylvia Plath and a bag of Fritos at three p.m. on a Saturday afternoon in August on the east side of Hartford. Eech.

After that, I discovered Radclyffe Hall, then Rita Mae Brown and May Daly, and whooo*ee*, let the sunshine in, babies! I was off into Literature Fantasyland, which led me to a final assessment of all the philosophers and sociologists and historians and biographers I'd been considering looking into:

To hell with 'em.

Eventually, I thought about adding one to the pile—a book, that is. I didn't exactly have the love stories of one of those pizzeria slut types, or some mall rat with leather jeans and a Jim Morrison complex. In fact, my intellectualization had been one of my relationship problems. I never fell into the stereotypical "you must be the dominant one" syndrome, but because I knew words like *ontological,* people assumed I was an Intellectual Snob looking for nothing more than lovely fluff in chiffon with the body of a model, the tail of a Bardot, and the brains of a small soapdish. (My friend Danielle has a great saying about such bimbettes: "She's like a cheesecake soufflé: light and fluffy, but bad for the heart, and with no nutritional value.") So, even when I wasn't *with someone*, I'd be having a conversation and the other party would be chatting me up about their best friend "Candy." Spare me, please.

Well, I needed some sort of material for a book before I could write one, and my relative celibacy had, for some time, kept me from collecting any real romantic stuff. It never occurred to me that a *major life crisis* would be just the thing, if only one would come ambling along.

And last year, one arrived, as crises will. It did not amble, of course. In fact, it bashed into my life like a renegade vigilante group on acid, and I'm still reeling ten months later....

I'm walking down Gold Street, on my way to my job at the fabulous Kiddie Korner Child Care Center, and this guy is walking toward me. Now, you have to get the picture here. It's a beautiful spring morning in Hartford—it's May, in fact. And I'm heading toward work and thinking about all the loverly-looking orchids opening up, when along comes The Guy. And he's, oh, I'd say thirty or so, and very, sort of, disheveled in a way; not dirty, but not perfectly clean cut, either. He has a real hideous blue collar look to him.

Now, don't get me wrong, I'm no snob—hell, I'm poorer than most blue collar workers in *this* state—but this bozo looks like he probably has duct tape on about half of everything he owns. Put it this way: if men were my bag, this dude would not be The One. And he's looking at me, real serious and pseudo-seductive, and I'm staring ahead, stone-faced, thinking, *Oh God*, when all of a sudden, as he's just about beside me, just about to pass me by, he gives me this *Sssssss*—*a* really long indrawn breath between his teeth, which he has, by now, with all the grace of a werewolf, *bared* for me—and then! Then! Like he's about to drop to the pavement in mute and desperate adulation of my nether parts, he goes, "Ooooooooooh." Just like that. Looking at me like I'm Little Red Riding Hood and he's the Big Bad Wolf and making a sound like he's either discovered the secret of fire or someone just checked his prostate.

I'm so appalled, so absolutely flabbergasted, and nauseated, that I can't even chuckle. I barely have the *cojones* to give him my best purse-lipped, vacant-eyed Betty Boop look. "Buzz off," I manage to tell him.

I mention this not to show you what I have to put up with, but to give you an idea of how bizarre life in Hartford, Connecticut can be. I mean, in New York City the bizarre is the norm and, ipso facto, not bizarre at all. Here, it's sporadic, and usually manages to be annoying in some way that, while perhaps not patently obvious, offends the sensibilities nonetheless.

So, how do I describe Hartford…poetically? (*The claustrophobic streets, the grim grey buildings, the shattered cement…*) It is a knotty problem. This is a city "in transition," and its new direction is not great. In fact, I read somewhere that there is now a 35% "occupancy deficiency" in Hartford. Translation: over one third of all Hartford office space is now empty. Is that good? Probably not.

There's also a sharp, acrid odor of pollutants in the air, although it's not noticeable to locals. The sky is never quite clear above the city—it's not Nebraska—but when it comes close, like on a day as temperate as today, the city itself is transformed: light gleams off the Gold Building, and the streets are filled with sleek-looking businessmen in paisley ties and lovely young bridesmaid-types in business clothes. (How uncool those squared-off padded shoulders look—a blatant bowing to male hegemony, although in a select few cases, it *is* a kind of improvement, giving at least the appearance of something other than spinelessness and "demure" acquiescence.)

Hartford has a strangely appealing quality on days like this, a kind of warped, limited ambience. Young black boys saunter down the street swinging gym bags, and elderly white women cross the street, with great tact and subtlety, to avoid them. On a clear day like today, there is a curious electricity, as if a passing rainstorm just ended, but of course, it is either the blood shaking off its winter torpor or the loud buzz of raging hormones.

Across the street from Southern New England Savings, a vendor sells natural soda, bottled spring water, and "frozen yogurt on a stick." He wears a turquoise T-shirt, and he must have a lot of turquoise T-shirts, because he wears one every day, and yet he always looks clean. I know him: his name is Carlos Pareja, and he speaks little English, or pretends to anyway, beyond "Thank you," "Have a nice day," and various prices from his list.

He grins at the nice lady from the daycare center. This does not necessarily indicate that he likes me, but, since his daughter is "a member of the Kiddie Korner family," he is diplomatic enough to be polite. Perhaps he's sincere, and I'm being ungenerous. He, at least, did not "come out" against me in the past year. (The irony of that expression is only too obvious, but I'm not trying to be cute here.)

I stand across the street from two young women, in front of Southern New England Savings, and I overhear their conversation. They have many things in common, starting with the face that they both want someone with a nice car to drop into their lives. It's okay if he's a yuppie, but even better if he's "really rich." And good-looking, of course. He must be loyal and faithful, apparently in a spaniel sort of way, but the most important prerequisites are the money, the expensive car, and good looks.

Both women are in their early twenties, obviously poorly-educated, and not attractive. They aren't clearly worthwhile in any apparent way (certainly their value system is lame, at best), but they seem quite confident that they will attract—*lure*, I should say—wealthy, eligible, loyal bachelors. Their calves are a bit on the chunky side, but their rear ends are plump, and clearly outlined through tight-fitting skirts. They would be comical if they were less pathetic.

Are they kidding themselves? Maybe all their talk of finding someone with a Lexus is just bravado, and beneath those heavily made-up masks are tormented creatures crying out for recognition, barely able to keep up the act. Maybe they know, deep down, that they will marry the first slob who comes along and offers them the inevitable gold and diamond cliché, then cheerfully abide whatever abuses "the old man" dishes out, until they are bloated from too many Hostess cupcakes, their legs as big as truck axles, their faces like the faces of Sharpeis.

Well, enough about Hartford. I'm supposed to be talking about myself, and I find it really hard to do that. In fact, the reason probably *isn't* that I have some big fear of intimacy or of being "revealed" for what I am (a *lesbian*, for Christ's sake). No, it's just that I have a hard time keeping the focus on myself.

So. I remember when I was seventeen, and my favorite song was *Thunder Island* by Jay Ferguson. I pictured a woman of about thirty when I listened to that song, a woman with marvelous blonde hair and a dusky complexion, a woman with the face of a Nico (or maybe more like Nastassja Kinski), a slender, taut body, small breasts, standing on the beach in a calico sundress, artfully displaced and undone in a provocative *deshabille*. She would have worn some subtle perfume, something mouthwateringly earthy, but not like those damned men's colognes that smell like some sort of failed Vietnamese dinner. This was something different, part "woods" and part "seascape," if that makes any sense.

And, of course, I used to fantasize about her, but then I had this recurring dream in which she stood above me, talking to me, and her face sort of loomed down at me, like I was seeing her through water. And she would be talking very loudly, and—well, how can I put it?—she would be *nagging*, I guess. She sounded like a scolding mother to a daughter, and I hated the feeling of that. It became, literally, a nightmare.

I never wanted to think about that dream, but I'd let it go around and around in my head until I had to push it out. I just had to push it away. I was afraid to analyze it myself, I guess, because it seemed like it probably meant I had some kind of horrible complex or something, some sort of reverse Oedipus complex (Reverse Electra?), and I sure as hell didn't want to know about it if I did.

I didn't want to think about it because I was uncomfortable, even then, with being a lesbian. I hate the word "gay," the way some people hate the word "lesbian." "Gay" just sounds like you're either willing to suffer fools gladly, or are eternally cheery. I am neither. Anyhow, I hadn't been comfortable with my sexuality since I'd discovered it, back in middle school.

The kids used to call me Janie Odyssey, which was a pretty clever play on Jana Odessi for a bunch of kids. "Janie Odyssey up in a tree, F-U-C-K-I-N-G, Dreamin' 'bout girls, Kissin' a boy, Buyin' expensive SEX TOYS!" Yeah, that was seventh or eighth grade. It's kinda difficult to convey the trauma of that sort of thing. Either you went through wretched stuff like that, and you have some understanding of the word *endurance* in that context, or you didn't, and you don't.

Let me give you the lowdown on a very basic level: I always loved women and girls, and never felt any particular affinity for men. They were okay, nothing to write home about, but not evil. I mean, my dad, for example—a nice guy, but sexy? No more than the average houseplant. I used to wonder, who *is* this guy? And why did Mom *pick* him, anyway? I couldn't help feeling they got married just because it was "the thing to do," and he was never a big part of my life. He was just sort of there, like the carpet and the television.

I was always somewhat distant from my parents, especially once I discovered that Mom did not think all that highly of the dangerous subculture known as The Gay Community. So, partly because of all that, I felt tremendous guilt and shame when I had my first sexual experience with another girl. Of course, I liked it so much I probably would have faced the death penalty to be able to replicate it, but I felt guilty just the same. I knew it wasn't "proper," and I'd heard people talk disparagingly of *lezzies* and *dykes*. Could I be one of those? It was unthinkable.

I should also mention that it stayed a big secret, as far as my parents were concerned, until I discovered, in college, whole groups of us in those phenomenal places called gay bars. After that, I became almost defiantly gay. That is, I made no bones about the fact that men were never to be anything more than friends. And it wasn't until I realized I felt alone in the crowd that I dropped out of that whole scene and avoided the potential relationships I could have formed there. More on that later.

A terrible image popped into my head the first time I was ever kissed by a boy; *really* kissed, that is. We were at Great Adventure, Jonathan Aparo and I, and had managed to escape from our parents under the pretext of buying some cotton candy. He took me along quietly and nonchalantly, then suddenly darted—with me still holding onto his hand, flopping clumsily along—behind a concession stand and against the blue shingles of the building. It seemed kind of strange that *he* was against the wall pulling me toward him, but Jonathan was never one for making fine distinctions such as "where the dominant one should stand."

When he tried to kiss me, I squirmed. Something was not right, and I wasn't sure it was just him. I glanced down while he was saying, "Please, please," and got a good look at all the filth on the ground back there: old sticky melted ice creams hardened into abstract sculpture, animal droppings, used condoms, torn candy wrappers, and, most grisly of all, the half rotted body of some furry animal, a cat or squirrel, maybe. The sight wrenched my stomach, and I got dizzy. I pushed myself back from him, one hand on his shoulder. "Wait."

"I can't," he said, lunging forward from the wall and kissing me hard on the mouth.

I yielded slightly, more out of a sense of compassion than anything else, but the thought of the dead animal had made me feel violently ill, and some weird association between the tongue that was forcing itself into my mouth like some fat tapeworm and the "Tongue" I'd recently seen in the supermarket deli made me gag. The smell of death filled my nose and, to my horror, I felt myself beginning to vomit. I pulled back, but Jonathan was pretty persistent—maybe he thought my grunts of mortification were the sounds of lust—and when my breakfast spewed out of me like lava, it was unavoidable that some of it would get him.

I don't think more than a tiny piece of it touched his tongue, since I had really ripped myself out of his grip, but later he would make a federal case out of it, saying I had blown chunks in his mouth "like a pig." He, in fact, *shrieked* like a pig, as vomit spackled his shirt while he backpedaled away from me. I was secretly a little glad that I had puked him—or in him—although I was more mortified than anything else. I would have to make many excuses—too many hot dogs, too much chili, the heat—and he would be a pain in the ass, I knew, the rest of the year.

But the real importance of the so-called heterosexual part of my background is that it enabled me to *play the game.* I learned how to be a lesbian in a world of straights, in probably much the same way a left-handed person learns to adjust to right-handedness as the norm. Of course, I'm sure it's no accident that lefties have a higher mortality rate.

What I mean when I say *play the game* can probably best be described as cultivating the false sophistication of the very young. We've all seen girls of thirteen or fourteen affecting a convincing display of apathy when dealing with boys. It used to be called *propriety,* and we were instructed to act as if they didn't matter, so that *they* would chase *us.* In my case, it didn't even require an acting job, though I did develop friendships later on.

The fact remained, I was *not* much interested in boys, and consequently they chased me. I even let a couple of them "have their way" with me before I turned sixteen, but I was in good company: Sally Chang, class president, Lisette Marquand, head of the cheerleading squad, and Jan Wysazki, who won state chess championships, were all getting banged regularly before they were fifteen. Comparatively speaking, I was a late bloomer. The important thing for me, I think, was that my true interests were playing the saxophone, woodworking, and running around town with a bunch of other wackos who also pretended, usually, to be straight.

Playing sax was a great release. It made me feel a little like I was about to hyperventilate, and not just because it demanded breath control, but because it was incredibly sexy. Maybe I had too much romantic nonsense in my head about smoky jazz joints and starving artists, or maybe it was just *better than trombone*. I don't pretend to know. But the fact remained that when I had an opportunity to be alone, and I made sure I had plenty of those, I was in love with sitting in my window and playing half-assed riffs for the whole neighborhood, establishing myself as a royal pain in the calzone to people who disliked my playing.

The second big interest, woodworking, merits some explanation. Why not metal shop, or concrete, you say? Frankly, I like wood. Mahogany, elm, oak, maple, pine and balsa, hickory, birch, cherry, and dogwood. I love trees, but once they've been destroyed, there's no consolation to be had unless something beautiful *and* useful can be made from the remains. That was always my credo.

So, much to the chagrin of my parents, at an early age I hammered together little coffee tables, sets of shelves, and magazine racks. Before long, my dad found friends generous enough to *buy* some of this stuff from me, partly to humor me, of course, but mostly just to keep the apartment from overflowing with the creations of "our little environmentalist." I'd lovingly sand it, and lovingly stain and varnish it, and *voila*! I'd have something saleable. The biggest problem was that woodworking—much more than playing sax—was a Tomboyish Activity, and that worried Mom and Dad. Were they ever in for a surprise.

My third big interest was running around with a bunch of other wackos, playing straight with a barely-concealed smirk and using the roughest language imaginable. This black kid named Leon and I used to hang out occasionally, and he was queer as pink Pepsi, but he liked to pretend he was my boyfriend just to bum out the local racists. Maybe people in Wichita, Kansas, or Tucson, Arizona, think of Hartford, Connecticut as some hotbed of liberalism, swingers, and public petting, but believe me, it isn't. They don't call it "The Land of Steady Habits" for nothing. In fact, it's more a middle-class-workers-posing-as-the-upper-class-type place. Sound uncomfortable? Right.

One uncool thing about hanging around with Leon was that he got aggressively "heterosexual" if there were other guys around who weren't in on his secret. It made me think he was a real sell-out, because they knew *I* wasn't his girlfriend—I was just one of the guys to them. When they asked him about his girlfriends, he'd launch into some wandering tale about his latest legendary fling: "Aw, yeah, man, you should see this chick. Sheila, her name is. Man, she be fiiiine. We went out this one Friday night, y'all listen here. We went—now, Jana, don't listen to none of this, okay?" (I would roll my eyes.) "Man, she was hot, hot, *hot*. I got me one 'a those…"

Here, he pauses for effect, until they fall all over themselves begging him for the end of it: "One 'a those what? What'd you have, man? Come on!"

He goes coy on them: "Naw, man, I can't talk about this *now*," gesturing in my direction with all the subtlety of a Bronx cheer.

"Aw, come on, she heard it all before," they say. "Come on, man." And then, like he really thinks it's inaudible, he says in a stage whisper, "French tickler."

When I wasn't hanging out with Leon and company, I generally hooked up with a girl named Lois Densmore, who was fifteen going on twenty-one to my seventeen going on seventeen. She had long blonde hair she'd let me comb until my legs shook, and eyes the color of honey in sunlight.

At times, I hated to listen to her, because she sounded like the ultimate Connecticut archetype of a Valley-Girl-cum-dental-assistant, but she was sexy as hell and loved French, and I don't mean French ticklers. She and I endured more unabashed stares from nineteen-year-olds with tents pitched in the fronts of their pants than I'd care to remember. We even flirted with them sometimes, because it was fun, and besides, it seemed like a good way to get them back for all that gawking.

Lois was a bit of an intellectual. Her older brother Don had gone to St. John's in Santa Fe, and he brought home every book he owned for her to check out. She was reading *Lolita* and *Lord Jim* at an age where it was uncool to *read*, period, and she listened to classical and jazz on the college radio stations. She turned me on to Billie Holiday, and I turned her on to The Doors. She thought it was way cool that the drummer was named Densmore like her, but she pretty much dismissed their first album as pretentious, except for "Alabama Song" and "End of the Night," the latter of which she called "a William Blake ripoff." She thought "Light My Fire" was overrated, and said that "The End" was "mostly gibberish." Wow. Having that much nerve at fifteen was admirable, even if I did disagree with her.

I fell absolutely in love with Lois: absolutely, achingly, and hopelessly. We rode around in her big blue Plymouth, listening to "Let's Call The Whole Thing Off" and "I Cover The Waterfront." The character in the latter song sings about whether the one she loves will come back to her. There in the car, with Lois' long blonde hair flying back like sea spray, I knew I was with the one I loved. I didn't have any illusions about guys like Leon or Jonathan Aparo. I knew where I stood, and I wasn't always happy about it, but I willingly accepted the inevitable: I was home.

It was funny driving around with her. Though she wasn't old enough to drive, and I was, there we were, in her car. It made no sense, but neither did a lot of things at that time.

My most memorable night with Lois was the night her father died. His prostate cancer had been getting worse and worse—it spread through his whole body by this point—and everyone knew he would not make it. But when he finally died, it still came as a shock, the way that sort of thing does. Lois called me, and I went over immediately.

She wanted to go for a walk in the woods for a little peace and quiet, away from all the wailing and breast-beating at the house. So we drove to Wethersfield, out to the pond by the old Solomon Wells House. It was summertime, June, I think, and a big thunderstorm loomed on the horizon. Purplish grey clouds mounted in the sky.

Hands in pockets, Lois walked by my side, never taking her eyes from the ground.

"Have you ever read a book called *Steppenwolf?*"

"No," I said. "I can't say I have."

"Well, it's about a lonely old man. He's getting old, and his health is gone. He lives alone, moves around a lot, and thinks of himself as a lone wolf, you know?"

She paused, and all I heard were the sound of our feet and of the wind turning leaves upside down.

"Anyway, toward the end of the book, the old man goes to this 'magic theater,' and ends up in this other world. And in this other world, which is really supposed to be a kind of game, people are shooting people in cars, everyone in cars is trying to escape from the people with guns, who are shooting *everyone*…mostly just *for the purpose of destroying the cars.*"

"Yeah…?"

"Well, that's sort of like what happened to my dad. He didn't get killed by machines, or for machines, but he died because of machines."

"You lost me," I said.

"Damn." She paused. "The machine got him just the same. He sat in that chair, day in and day out, cranking out useless information, and all the time his prostate cancer got worse and worse, because he couldn't *do* anything else. Don't you get it? *His fucking computer killed him.*"

For the first time since we'd started walking, she looked up at me, and the look in her eyes was terrible, like someone who's seen an accident. "His computer killed him," she said again, her fingers seizing my arm like a desperate old woman, and she began to cry. She cried and cried and cried, and I held her against the wind, rocking her, stroking her long blonde hair gently. Big raindrops pattered around us, darkening the ground.

"Lois," I whispered. "Sometimes, you just have to find the strength to get through. Sometimes you just have to have faith that everything happens for a reason. And maybe you and I don't know what the reason is, and maybe we never will know. But it helps if we believe everything's gonna be all right."

A fresh wave of sobs shook her.

"It's all right," I said lamely, patting her on the back. "It's all right." Beyond the stage of being comfortable comforting her, the effort made me tired, and the rain, which had at first been welcome, began to chill me. "Let's go home," I said.

That night, we made love for the first time. I felt guilty at first, but my guilt dissolved when she rose to my touch. I ran my hand down that long blonde body, guided by her and by my own intuition. So beautiful to hear her whisper, her lips crushed against my ear, and while that whisper thundered in my head, I pushed her back just enough to look at her. Never had I seen anything as fantastic as the sight of her face, darkened by shadows around us, eyes closed, lips slightly parted, her teeth gleaming like moonlight. I was home.

I found others, of course, after the "Lois" phase. But I don't need to talk about them all. Some were lesbians and some were just "experimenting," but they all had one thing in common with Lois, they were all cerebral in some way. One—we won't mention names—put on summer theatre groups; one was a student of Fellini; another, a student of Botticelli; another was a philosophy major at a local university, and another planned to be an ambassador, and was learning half a dozen languages. She drove me batty: *Que moi? Je ne sais quoi? Dominus fistulus. Chupa la mano.*

Another worked at a bank—and boy, did I get tired of hearing about finances in Hartford—and yet another worked for a mortgage company. Those two were always trying to give me financial advice—as if I could afford to use it. It was, "Oh, Jana, why don't you invest in some CDs," or, "Say, you know, mutual funds could really be beneficial for your future." Right, I'm making twenty grand a year, and I'm supposed to be able to *save* out of that? Oh, well, at least I've managed to stay friends with these people, which is more than I can say for some of my past friends.

I guess that brings me to my parents. I didn't want to talk about them yet, but I've already mentioned my father helping me sell some of my woodwork, and how that, in addition to other "tomboy" activities, was a sore spot for them. I can pretty much sum up my relationship with them in two activities: humoring me and worrying about me. Sure, they were always nice enough, and they tried to be understanding, even when I dropped the "L" word on them, but I could never get past their profound disappointment.

For a long while I felt as though I just didn't measure up. My dad would sit there, rubbing his eyes and blinking like an owl, depressed because he had "no one to carry on the family name" in the first place, and no one to even provide him with a grandchild in the second. At an age when most girls in West Hartford came out as debutantes (even though none of them actually called themselves that), I came out as something altogether different. Not exactly what they'd expect at the National Cheerleaders' Association Alumni Club picnic.

A couple years later, I heard a radio show about how some school in Seattle had a "Gay Prom" in addition to the regular prom, and I thought, Wow. Times have changed. But when I was going through it, I sure didn't know anyone else who was, and there weren't any gay proms in Hartford. In fact, I didn't even go to my prom; spent that night, just like a lot of other nights, wandering over the hills and fields of Wethersfield with Lois.

I stumbled across the phrase "come out" in the thesaurus one day, and it amused me to see it defined as a synonym for "debut." How ironic! Well, anyway, I knew I could have gone off and gotten myself knocked up by some UCONN student, but I couldn't stomach the hypocrisy and brutality of that. Soooo, I just tried to be grateful that at least I had not made the mistake of getting married. Considering the marriages of some of my friends, gratitude came easy.

I also knew I wasn't ready for some big Serious Relationship, so I just dated people whenever I found myself interested. Maybe that was kind of a strange approach, but it felt right. Except that I never brought anyone home to my parents.

So. My parents. What can I say? My father was born in East Hartford, and he was a full-blown professor of social anthropology before he married Mom. He always talked about "primitive" peoples, so I grew up thinking the Dobuans lived in the neighborhood somewhere. "The Dobuans wouldn't approve of that," he'd say, or, "It's a good thing we don't live with the Dobuans," which was his idea of a joke. Eventually, I learned from one of his books that the Dobuans lived on an island off the southern shore of New Guinea, and that they considered dourness and resentment to be among their primary "virtues."

Ethel just nodded her grey head in agreement, and continued picking at her bean salad. She never looked particularly happy. She never looked happy at all, in fact.

Not that she did anything good for herself. She'd started out as a receptionist in a small office of some sort, and wound up a legal secretary for a fairly respectable law firm. But she hated it, never got even a modicum of job satisfaction, and was burned out by the time she was fifty.

So, what was the lesson there? Be yourself. At all costs, do what you want to do, what you need to do, and to hell with compromise. Otherwise you might end up fifty, having not even a modicum of job satisfaction, and a dyke daughter to boot.

That's unfair, really. They tried. *She* sure as hell did. She used to go through this whole charade—*debacle* would be a better word—about me as a bride. I'd think how my little upturned nose would look so sweet beneath that white tulle veil, how the little baby's breath and burgundy roses would arch delicately over my breast, yes, and my husband's lovely herringbone jacket (a near-perfect imitation of the inimitable zoot suit) would match the hazel in my eyes…a tulle veil floating softly in the air-conditioned chapel with a lightness and delicacy surpassed only by the gossamer wings of a butterfly.

But I'm just having fun. It wasn't really all that bad, I suppose. And to her, not stupid at all. She was *so* damned sincere, too.

One thing I must say for them is that they always took care of me. I'm asthmatic, and my parents had to drag themselves out of bed at some pretty ungodly hours because I thought, and maybe they did too, that I was about to check out. After frequent visits to the emergency room and several hospitalizations, I grew intimately acquainted with fear. When an asthma attack hits, the feelings of desperation and suffocation—like a fish out of water, but ready to jump for the ceiling in search of higher realms of oxygen—are almost unbearable. Certain odors triggered attacks, and we often played a guessing game as to which ones they might be. Was it the pork chops or the beans? The lentils or the tomatoes?

Another thing about being an asthmatic: I started to try to overcompensate for my "frailty" by doing some pretty rough stuff—a helluva lot rougher than playing sax. I learned to play "kill the guy with the ball" at school, back when they still allowed boys to do that sort of thing. If you were flat-chested enough and kept your hair short, you could get into their game. I had no problem there, and I loved the dirt and sweat, the grime of it.

Talking about my parents and the safety and sanitization of that environment gets me right back to my roots. I needed to feel liberated from that, and maybe that was why I ended up doing something semi-dirty like woodworking, and something tomboy-ish, like like playing sax. These days I guess those things are sort of indigenous to both genders, but when I was a kid, it was a Big Deal.

I even used to work on cars with my buddy Leon. I remember this one car, a 1974 Chevy Malibu with a two-twenty-nine in it. When the starter went, I was lost. Leon and I went to the junkyard in East Hartford to get a used one for fifteen bucks, and soon I was standing staring down into the black and grey bowels of the car—the carburetor, alternator, belts, hoses, wires, gaskets—all lying inert, cruelly and silently imperious, almost hostile. They ema-nated a kind of vicious sub-atomic life of their own, the strange burnt-hot plastic smell of the car, its heat enveloping us like some invisible enemy, a vaporous disease.

A little kid named Mark came up and watched with a sour expression, pensive, all brown hair and strange multi-colored san-dals and dirty hands. He watched us almost furtively, then aban-doned the vigil to play with an empty shotgun shell on the drive-way. He scooped sand from the driveway with the shell, emptied it in small piles, scooped up more sand, empty and scoop, empty and scoop, ambling at last away, to lemonade, maybe, or a tricycle ride.

I spoke to him for just a moment. "Hi. My name's Jana."

He looked at me silently, with cancelled eyes. Has he been abused?

"What's your name?" I say.

"Mark." Just like that: Mark.

"Hi, Mark. That's Leon." I jerk a thumb under the car. "He's fixing my car." I smile.

He looks at me blankly, his face a wall of expressionlessness, impenetrable, like a stone or leaf. Maybe his father is drunk, or his mom smokes crack. Maybe flies swarm on his food every day. I return to holding sockets for Leon, handing him new ones. He is surrounded by sockets and adaptors, ratchets, extensions, wrenches. Mark watches, grows bored, walks off.

We are alone, Leon and me, with the clinking and scraping of tools and metal parts. While he works, I think about riding with him on his motorcycle, on a day when he is not reticent or aggressively "heterosexual," when he is just Leon. He lets out the clutch as we pull away from a stop sign, gives it gas until the tachometer redlines at eight thousand or so, then pulls in the clutch, shifts into second, giving it more gas. We are really flying now, wind whipping hair across our foreheads, his brown hands gripping the velvety-black big handles, the wind whipping harder now, so that even the slender leather thongs on his keychain flap back like tassels on a Wild Bill Hickock coat. The sun glints blindingly off the side mirrors, leaving spots impressed in my eyes, orange shifting moons.

Leon calls to me: "Start 'er up."

I rouse myself and climb into the Malibu. I turn the ignition key forward, pulling it back again almost immediately at the sound of the starter not working. A huge, grinding, rasping noise, like a metal hook against a wall of granite, booms out, I shut the car off, hearing Leon from beneath it: "Shit."

"What's wrong?"

Silence. I look under the car, seeing his mouth working in concentration, a wrench in his left hand barely visible.

"Try it again."

"Same way?"

"Yeah," he says. "Real quick, forward and back."

I try it again, the same sharp defiant crack of defeat scraping, splitting the silence, and —

"Whoa," he says from beneath. "Don't do anything."

I get out and wait, looking at the ground. I am respectfully quiet. A small metallic-looking piece of plastic lies on the ground before me. It catches my attention, and I pick it up: the grill from a matchbox Mack truck. I snap it between my fingers, a brief lapse.

Finally, he says, "Okay."

"Try it again?"

"Yup."

"Real quick, on and off?"

"Yup."

The car starts, VROOOM, immediate and clean. The smell of oil-rich exhaust fills the air like victory. Leon stands. "You're all set." He wipes his hands.

"Thanks, man." I smile and give him a bearhug.

"Anytime, Jana. Just gimme a call, and I'll come runnin', just like the song says."

I look at him curiously for just an instant.

"Didn't think ah lissened to dat *white* music, didja?" he says.

I laugh, surprised, and he laughs, too.

It's a beautiful autumn day, the kind of balmy afternoon that almost reminds me of a summer evening, and would, were it not for the scent of leaves in the air and the sound of geese barking across the sky. This kind of day always gives me that happy/sad nostalgic feeling I get whenever I think of certain toys I had as a child: the old Lincoln Logs, or the little red wagon with its rubber black whitewalls. I pull out of the lot, feeling free just because I have a car, like a teenager again. Leon waves at me in my rearview mirror as I drive away.

Chapter 3

I LEFT FOR Boston College the fall after my high school graduation. I'd saved a considerable amount of money, and though I wasn't completely paying my own way, I came damn close. I'd been accepted to the school's music program sight unseen—in my case, "sound unheard"—and had not even visited the campus.

I arrived in Chestnut Hill on a Saturday in early September, unprepared for my new home. I had my saxophone and my jazz records, my suitcases, a funny old lamp I intended to stand on a milk crate, and a lot of blue jeans and black T-shirts. I'd even brought some madras shorts and a really great jacquard shirt. I had hopes of going sailing nearby, and I was perfectly prepared to order the latest L.L. Bean catalog.

What I didn't realize until my arrival was that rock-climbing gear would have been more appropriate. Boston College is pretty much built on a huge rock, and, although the area is pleasantly woodsy, like some of Connecticut, it's hardly what I'd call a country club. I guess I'd been expecting Kennebunk or something, who knows.

One detail I'd missed was that the college was founded by Jesuits. I'd overlooked that bit of information in the catalog during my Research-Every-Good-School-With-A-Music-Program frenzy.

I didn't even know what a Jesuit was, to be honest, beyond the hazy recollection that they were Christians.

Now, I don't have anything against Jesuits, or any other sort of Christians, for that matter: I never have. But I think it's clear that anyone who wants to hang out with them should be prepared for what they're getting into. The Jesuits were quiet, gentle and patient. But everything they said sounded relatively metaphysical, whether it was or not, and relatively relaxing, which it sure as hell was. I spent many mornings beating back sleep, watching sunlight filter down in white squares on the polished hardwood floors as my first semester in Chestnut Hill emptied before me like a river into the sea.

One of the most bizarre things about B.C. was my first roommate. Eventually, I decided that God, if there is a God, works in mysterious ways, because this chick and I seemed to have been thrown together as some sort of mutual patience test. It could easily have been a scientific experiment. A black girl who didn't much like white girls, and a religious fanatic and homophobic to boot, I could deal with her standoffishness, and even the fanaticism, but the proselytizing got on my nerves, especially when she took to her knees at seven in the morning to pray out loud for Jesus to have mercy on my heathen soul and incite me to join the flock. *Herd, more like*, I would think to myself.

I always wanted to tell her, "Hey, Estelle, while you're down there, why don't you call Herbert?" Her boyfriend Herbert, who was from Waco, Texas, looked like someone you'd see on one of those forensic science shows about serial killers. I always thought of Estelle being on her knees when I contemplated the thought of her with Herbert. Also, I couldn't help thinking of Waco as "Wacko."

It amused me to listen to the two of them exchange insincerities. I wasn't exactly the most mature person on earth either, so I'm sure I was also kind of a pain in the ass, if only because I scared her. Plus, I was a raving lesbian, so that didn't go over real well. I think it would have offended her less if I'd been docile and milksoppy, or even just an airhead, so she would have been able to ostracize me without taking flak.

As it was, I didn't much care who knew about my sexual preference, or my preference for white chocolate, for what it was worth. I'd tell you that, and I'd tell you I wasn't a Christian or a Buddhist or anything else, for that matter, I didn't care, and if you didn't like it, then tough shit. This did not endear me to Boston College's authorities, by the way, but then I always did question authority, so this was nothing new. And even though Estelle's piousness didn't seem to match up too neatly with her and Herbert's noisy nocturnal activities, I tried to keep my mouth shut and secretly imagine that she actually had Bella Abzug in there with her.

I don't have any real serious interesting memories of the school, to be perfectly honest. They had a great jazz band there, very exclusive, called B.C. Bop, for which I had the dubious honor of auditioning—not everyone makes it to the audition stage—but I never got in. And of course, I could tell stories about the weirdness of the campus itself, like the infamous *Higgins' Stairs* part of the landscape, a seemingly endless set of steps that was the ruin of many a freshman's "hangover morning" walk to class. Mostly, though, I just did a lot of work and a lot of goofing around.

I played lacrosse, so I know what it's like to run around outside in shorts in the middle of February when it's nine degrees, and I spent time heading downtown on the old shuttle bus to Cleveland Circle, then the "C" or the "D" to downtown, hanging at City Side with some other students. Basically, I majored in lacrosse and saxophone, but my "real" major was Music. I had the big thrill of learning about the Great Composers, and was subjected to hours of Wagner and Debussy, when what I wanted to be doing was playing freeform jazz and blues.

Worst of all was the painful consciousness that my money was running out. I had to work, of course, and a few quick calculations revealed that my finances were in rough shape. I made less money every month, it seemed, mainly because the cost of living kept going up while my paycheck stayed the same—I believe economists call this a *downward trend*—and when the crisis finally hit, at the end of the first semester of my sophomore year, I had to bail out. Financial aid was not available.

Coming back was the worst. Slowly, over that last year and a half, I'd grown accustomed to living on that old rock, and found a kind of contentment that didn't exist in Hartford. I'd lived with roommates, several of whom were almost as scary as Estelle, and now, with the specter of my future looming like some implacable black monolith, the prospect of moving back in with dear old Mom and Dad made the taste in my mouth more bitter than ever. In a nutshell, things sucked, and I was depressed.

Things did not pan out quite the way I thought they would, but in some ways, that was okay. I didn't plan on working at Kiddie Korner Child Care Center for more than one winter, but it turned out to be what I needed, because I couldn't find anything else. And, as my friend Danielle says, "Ya get what ya need."

I'd wanted to work with children since I was a young girl. I could hardly stand the thought of teaching—so much stinking paperwork—and all the infighting among grade school faculty would drive me berserk. Daycare afforded me the opportunity to perch midway between babysitter and early childhood educator. It seemed perfect, and I was grateful to be gainfully employed in a sagging economy, but not grateful enough for my depression to lift. It hung on like a bad cold, making the first few days of December as grey as grey could be, as my mother herself might have put it.

The woman who hired me was the coordinator: Tillie Jones, a black woman in her late thirties with a master's degree in early childhood education, a wide smile, and a big heart. I liked her the instant I met her; some people just have a sense of rightness and sincerity about them. She also wore a big floppy hat that I liked immensely.

"Well," she said, perusing my application with a frown. "It looks here like you've got more experience playing saxophone than workin' with kids."

I smiled at the way she said "experience": *speeryince,* and took back the application thoughtfully, trying not to look offended. "I *have* worked with kids a lot, though," I said in my best interview voice. "I babysat a lot, and I've taken courses in early childhood."

Her eyebrows shot up. She sat back, folding her arms across her great chest like a sergeant. "What courses?"

I hemmed and hawed, trying to talk around the fact that I didn't remember their names. "Well, um, one of them dealt with primarily child psychology in an Ericksonian context, I believe, and uh, another was concerned with LD and SEM kids —"

My voice trailed off. She was looking at me like I was a crook and saying, "Mm-*hm.*" There was a long pause, but I could tell from her sharply indrawn breath that she was about to speak.

"You know something?" she asked finally. "Sometimes I think I liked it better back in the days when we just said a child was *slow* if he was 'developmentally delayed.'" She stood and walked around. "You ever try to explain to some poor immigrant mother that her daughter is 'developmentally delayed?'"

"No, ma'am."

She looked at me, hard. "It ain't easy."

I looked at the floor. There did not seem to be anything else to say.

Tillie looked out the window, her back to me. "This is a tough job," she said. "I could use the help now, God knows, and you've got some background—or, at least, enough to do the work." A pause. "You *like* children?"

"Sure," I said, too brightly.

"Well, I hope so." She wheeled on me, her eyes locked on mine. "Are you *sure* this is the kind of work you want?"

"I'm sure," I said. For a moment I could not help thinking that she'd planned this, that it was some kind of slick management technique to catch the new recruit in a dishonest moment. I was only being partially dishonest, of course—I wanted the job, after all.

One of the worst things about moving back home had been the way my parents acted. My mother told me, with great sympathy, that they understood it wasn't my fault, and that I wouldn't be living with them if I "didn't have to," but I sensed disappointment behind their veil of pity, like when I'd told them I was a lesbian and they'd pretty much said, "Oh, okay." Maybe this was just my imagination, or the residuals of some secret guilt lurking just beneath the surface, but the feelings were real enough.

So when I heard Tillie Jones say, "You're hired," I couldn't help being grateful. Any job was better than no job at all at this point, and if Kiddie Korner hadn't saved me from the burger joints, I don't know how I would have endured it. As it was, I still found myself every morning in the midst of two dozen children, wishing I were sitting on a window sill somewhere playing saxophone, low liquid notes drifting up above the neighborhood, making passersby smile up at me in appreciation.

It's tough to describe what Kiddie Korner, or "KK" as we called it, was really like. I wish I could say it had spacious sun-filled rooms and merry children smacking beach balls around, or quietly playing house and dress-up, speaking like adults to each other with great seriousness. What it was really like was a demilitarized zone: toys lay strewn across a multicolored carpet in the day room, which was in a slightly stuffy basement, the glare of fluorescent light overhead gave many of the children an almost ghastly appearance, even in the early morning when they were at their brightest and most bushy-tailed, as Tillie used to put it, and crack babies lay on special pallets in oversized cribs, trembling or twitching like children with chills and fever.

My first day there was like a harried dream that swept me along from task to task. Part of me was almost psyched that I was getting twenty-two thousand dollars a year, and the other part stood by, aghast, wondering why anyone would work so hard for so little money. Mostly, I just felt excited, fielding queries from concerned parents, fending off my own mounting feelings of insecurity, and running amok with the kids. We had treasured moments of play and instruction, and those made the fears and stresses bearable, if not surmountable, at least in my first week.

And during that week, I met the aforementioned Wendy Simpson.

At Wendy's request, I called her "Wen," and that's kind of what she was to me: a wen. Twenty and bubbly and superficially nice, she reminded me of the old Winto-green Twins on those TV commercials—too cute to have much character, and predictably plastic once you got to know her. However, I got the feeling that she would be endlessly cheery with kids, and no doubt a favorite with them, so I tried not to judge her too harshly.

"Hi, I'm Wendy," was her introduction.

"I'm Jana."

"Did Mrs. Jones tell you about the safety rules?"

I hedged a bit. What could this bird possibly know that Tillie would leave out?

"Well," she said, "you know you're not supposed to carry sharp objects, right? Or give the children anything small enough to put in their mouths?"

"Oh, yeah." I forced a cheerful smile. "She gave me some handouts on that stuff, one of those employee information folders like you probably got when you started."

"Uh-*huh*," she chirped. "That's it. So you're all set, then." She said it like a supervisor, and I almost chuckled.

"Yup."

"Cool," she said. I certainly hope that that meets with your approval, I was thinking.

Working with the fabulous Wendy got progressively difficult as time went on. Part of the problem, I think, was the contrast between us. I don't wear any makeup, and prefer my hair *au naturel*; Wendy was the exact opposite: bright lipstick, mascara that "highlighted" the green in her eyes, long sculptured nails…the works. Sometimes, I wondered if some of the wealthier West Hartford mothers looked at Wendy as an example of something I could aspire to, if only I would catch a clue. Unfortunately, even the kids picked up on this, and some seemed to have their value systems shaped, in part, by the baubles dangling from Wendy's scented wrists and the girlish ribbons in her blonde coiffure.

To fully appreciate Wendy, you had to see her in action, but I'll try to give you an idea: curly shoulder-length hair, hard green eyes, chiseled chin, heart-shaped mouth (lips almost the exact same size, just like a mannequin), high cheekbones, well-manicured lashes, and a decided switch to her walk. She had only been there a month herself when the center hired me, but already, she was an expert on everything. She even tried to convince me that the shortcut she took to work would save me time, if I'd just try it. I lived within walking distance, and knew the city better than she ever would, yet she didn't seem to hear me when I told her how close I lived. Consequently, I did a fair amount of daydreaming when the opportunity presented itself, especially when Wendy was talking.

I remember one particular cold day when I found myself drifting off into Fantasyland. It was January, feeble sunlight coming down into the day room. I'd started to imagine myself on a skiing trip—sitting in a ski lodge on a snow-covered mountaintop, John

Denver records playing in the background. Hot chocolate by a crackling fire, snow drifting down to earth outside my window….

"Victor!"

The sound of a child's shrill cry rent the air. "Shit," I muttered and stood.

And there I was again, this time with two kids fighting over some plastic eggs. Apparently, one kid's parents were vegans, and his strenuous objection to this fake food came as a surprise to little Darlene, who stood aghast while Vegan Victor threw the little fried eggs into the dust bunnies beneath the radiator.

I sighed, knowing I was going to have a splendid day.

Chapter 4

WHEN I LEFT my place in the morning I walked straight down Main toward Chelsea, then right on Chelsea and all the way to the end until I hit Prospect. After going left on Prospect, I walked down the ratty old sidewalk, then right on Arch, and all the way to the corner of Arch and Columbus Boulevard, where Kiddie Korner Child Care's white sign assuaged the senses every morning, like a sign in front of a chiropractor's or podiatrist's, white with black letters, homely and homey, swinging from a white wooden post.

That whole central section of Hartford always fascinated me, having grown up on the west side. My old neighborhood was a kind of tribute to white collar WASP suburbia, and contrasted starkly with downtown. Central Row had the nicest sights—the Gold Building, Wadsworth, the Old State House—but mostly there were old brick tenement-type apartments, and people milling about in T-shirts with cigarette packs rolled into their sleeves in front of storefronts with signs that said *Hay pescado* and *Part-time help wanted.*

There was Stowe Village, a four-block public housing project at Hartford's north end, best known as "The Projects." Hundreds of families lived there in the sort of squalor many Americans would associate only with Ethiopia or Bangladesh. *Dumpster* Village, we liked to call it, half-jokingly and half in despair, where the fifteen-year-olds look like whores and vice-versa, and perhaps this is no coincidence. On sidewalks and in driveways every sign of disrepair and grueling poverty assaults the eye: broken glass, torn-up mattresses, endless candy wrappers and cores of once-ripe apples and pears along the concrete steps that lead up to low-income apartments—huge rectangles of brick with fresh graffiti and yellowing grass—crazy wrought iron rails that look like pieces of plumbing soldered together loom out against the sunrise, along the storefronts the homeboys mill about or lounge against grey walls, smoking cigarettes and laughing, or looking at you out of canceled eyes. They call you *huevo*, "egg," when you pass them (if they call you at all), or give you a wolf whistle and obscene invitation. It's impossible to just ignore it all, and there's potential trauma in this scene of the young lady walking through the valley of the shadows. But you can't help being a bit philosophical about it all: the great grey city, with its half-baked dreams and endless inefficient machinations.

I became most familiar with the Park Street area in my Kiddie Korner days, and although it wasn't as bad as Dumpster Village, it sure as hell looked bad to anyone coming from the suburbs. Sometimes I found it hard to believe the neighborhood was just down the street from the Capitol Building, a gold-domed edifice of almost Victorian grandeur surrounded by plush, immaculate lawns.

The one end of the street is in West Hartford, a yuppified suburb with well-kept lawns. As the street winds out toward Hartford it becomes more a business district than residential: gas stations and Vietnamese markets, old houses and factories. Several arts bars, the best-kept secrets in town actually, feature local avant-garde bands, and other assorted arts types can bring in a few bucks on a Friday or Saturday night. People drive in from Fairfield and Ansonia and even Bozrah to check out some of the local talent.

One of the weirder bars in town sits on this little strip, a gay bar called The Green Parrot, which boasts some of the hottest local jazz bands at only a nominal cover charge. I call it weird because I had an uncomfortable experience there with some of my peers one night: about half a dozen of them sat at the corner table, all looking available, some of them very butch and some femme, but they had that "searching for romance" look. I could feel their eyes on me when I walked in, a host of eyes undressing me, and I simply did not enjoy the sensation. I'd been uncomfortable before in the straight scene, and now here I was uncomfortable in the gay scene, I could almost feel myself poised between two worlds, in limbo. The band was a classy jazz trio, the bass thumping out rich vibrato, quiet little snare drum riffs behind that, with the pianist kind of testing the waters over them, and it sounded pretty, but I got the hell out of there anyway before one of the corner table vamps took a liking to my neck.

Chapter 5

WHEN I FIRST started at Kiddie Korner, I found that the warmest, most comfortable person to be around was Tillie Jones, which was fortunate, since she was my direct supervisor. She had big arms and big hips and a big smile, and I just knew she was one of those soft-hearted people who always draw me in. She played down her supervisory role after that first moment at the window when she had wheeled around and hit me with, "Are you *sure* this is the work you want to do?" I first realized she liked me when, toward the end of that first hectic week, she asked if I'd be able to help her carry some old files back to her Arch Street apartment.

Tillie's apartment was sandwiched between a brick apartment complex that looked like the old YMCA and a string of storefronts with name like Ken Foo Convenience and Laundro-Rama. We climbed the battered stairs and Tillie opened several locks before we lugged the files into a spacious room with olive-drab walls and wooden furniture of an understated luxury that contrasted sharply with the hallway just outside.

I had an opportunity to look around and get the feel of the place while Tillie made us some instant coffee. I saw a bunch of coral-colored flowers in a stone vase, a wandering Jew plant, a cactus, an African violet, a set of books, including a World Atlas and World Book dictionary, an International Encyclopedia of Aviation, a cookbook, *Baseball's Greatest Moments, Britain in the Twentieth Century*. On the wall hung prints of an aerial view of a city and a painting of ships at sea. Pictures lined the piano too, a studio portrait of a black middle-aged couple and an old black and white of a young white woman in the thirties or forties.

We sat in her orange overstuffed chairs, sprawling with throw pillows and afghans, and drank our coffees. Tillie arched an eyebrow at me, unintentionally conveying some of that discomfort between people who barely know one another. If she'd been less familiar with my situation, I would have expected her to say something like, "So, are you still in school, Jana?"

Instead, she smiled almost shyly and asked, "What do you think of Kiddie Korner so far?" She put a funny accent on the name of the center, the type of half-joking tone that might indicate a lack of seriousness toward the topic, yet might not.

I was at a loss, trying not to blush *and* to sound diplomatic. "It's interesting work," I said. "How do you like what you do there?"

She paused. "There's a lot of political shit goin' on there. You stick around, you'll see what I mean." She sipped her coffee, looking for all the world like a black female Buddha.

"Has the daycare crisis in Connecticut had any effect on the center?"

She smiled, seeming pleased at the new girl's politesse.

"Well, to tell you the truth," she said, "it's *filled* the place." Again she sipped her coffee, dabbing at her lip with a napkin immediately afterwards, as if nervous. "You know that over two thirds of the children eligible for full-time daycare are *unable* to be placed in the state's formal daycare system?"

"Wow. Where do they go?"

She smiled bitterly—not really a smile at all. "Most of 'em have to be babysat every day: grandmothers, great-aunts and -uncles and all that. A lot of the rest, though, are in situations with a bunch of other babies in somebody's house, somebody not licensed, who doesn't have her place childproofed…maybe somebody drinkin' a bottle of gin in front of the soaps all day." She raised her eyebrows, cocked her head to one side, and looked hard at me, like she was waiting for a response. She fingered a mole on her lower left cheek.

"God," I said. "That's sad."

"Mm-hm." She looked off into the clouds outside her window, lost in thought. "But you know what?" she said. "We got it pretty good at Kiddie Korner. We got crack babies and all, and we still got it pretty good. You ever see a place that gets shut down?"

I shook my head.

"It's like somethin' out of a movie. People think, 'That doesn't happen in *America*. Not in this day and age.'" She chuckled. "But it does. It does."

"So what about Kiddie Korner? Why are we so lucky?"

"Well," she said, "I'll tell you what. You get a call from somebody, let's say. And they want to know, do we have space? No, there's a waiting list. But let's say there's an opening. We're there between 6:30 a.m. and 6:30 p.m., or at least someone's always there at those hours."

"Really?"

"Oh yeah. Do we have degreed personnel? Yes, myself and two B.A.'s. Plus you and Wendy, who both have some college and some experience. Do we have access to health care? Yes. Is a deposit required? No. These are all positives. We have the readiness program for pre-schoolers, we have a strong emphasis on verbal skills, reading, talking, constructive play. We have regular fire drills. The facility is childsafe. These are all pluses."

"What about the political thing?"

She looked out the window again for a long time, then sighed. "I don't know," she said, then turned back to look at me. "It's a business, you know? I can't say it ought to be run like a *church* daycare program, with sliding scale fees for single mothers and all that, even if I want it to. But it's hard havin' to turn away some of the applicants for strictly 'practical' reasons. I don't want to be a part of that."

"I understand," I said.

She smiled before she turned her gaze back to the window.

Chapter 6

MEETING PARENTS AT Kiddie Korner was a whole other trip.

I'll never forget Carlos Pareja. He had a three-year-old daughter named Angelica for whom he was solely responsible. Angelica's mother had been a crack addict, now deceased.

Carlos was twenty-six years old and had black hair and a black mustache and brown eyes that looked black. He had about the most V-shaped body I've ever seen on anyone outside of weightlifting. He was short and thin with a muscular upper half and arms like pistons with ropy veins visible even through the sleeves of his shirt, but his lower half threatened almost to disappear. It was skinnier than seemed possible, his flat ass unaided by the padding of his wallet, and almost atrophied.

Of the Latino men I met at Kiddie Korner, he was the only one who was both hospitable to me and also sincere in his attempts to communicate. Tillie was our translator.

"This is Carlos Pareja," Tillie said, and Carlos shook my hand, his teeth white in his brown face.

"Pleasure to meet you," I said.

"Mucho gusto enconocerlo," said Carlos.

I looked at Tillie for help.

"He said, 'Likewise.'"

Carlos nodded, as if to affirm Tillie's words. "Es posible que mi hija se puede con ella todos los dias?"

"Si," said Tillie to Carlos. She turned my way. "He said, 'Is it possible for my daughter to be with her every day?' I said, 'Si,' I mean 'Yes.'" She laughed.

I laughed too. "Great," I said. "Bueno." I smiled at Carlos.

"I'd say you've been paid a compliment." She lowered her voice. "He must have a good feeling about you."

"Gracias." I bowed to him, as if he was Asian and I was trying to make him feel at home.

"Gracias, gracias," he grinned, shaking my hand. "Gracias."

Tillie beamed at us like an approving mother hen.

"Ella parece muy…eh…competente," he smiled. "Tengo confianza."

Tillie grinned. "He says you look very competent. Don't let it go to your head."

"Gracias," I said, "gracias."

And Carlos smiled his white smile.

I only saw Carlos Pareja's apartment once, but it left an impression on me. I was with Tillie at the time, and Carlos was sick. To make matters worse, his car was out of commission and he had no one to take Angelica to the center, so, since he was a regular paying client, we agreed to stop by and pick her up that morning. In a way, it was nice to start out the day with an errand, and to be responsible for only one child for that brief period of time.

The morning was overcast and the grey light that filtered into the windows when we opened the blinds did nothing to improve the appearance of the Pareja household. The room was redolent with the neatness of poverty. Shelves with white ceramic figures of the Virgin Mary and baby Jesus. Glass jars of flour and sugar. A refrigerator with Pizza House and Milk-Maid Parmesan Cheese magnets, and a stove with a digital clock that was off by four hours and ten minutes. Straight-backed chairs with a flowered vinyl pattern and quilted seat covers sat around a rickety metal table, and on the table stood a bottle of Selsun Blue, an old General Electric toaster, and a plate with a few crumbs on it. A cheap framed print of "The Last Supper" hung on the wall next to a calendar from the local oil company. That was about it.

"Hi, Angelica." Tillie smiled.

Angelica smiled back and Carlos, looking sheepish in his thin bathrobe, managed a grin.

"Muchas gracias," he said.

"De nada," Tillie said. "That poor man," she said after we'd walked out with Angelica in tow. "You know he only makes about eleven thousand dollars a *year*?"

"That's not much," I said.

"No. Not in Connecticut, it ain't. Not for a single parent. You know, he told me that when this girl was an infant—you know her mother was a crack addict, right?"

"Uh huh."

"Well, when this child was an infant, Carlos got custody. The mother was unwilling to receive treatment for her addiction, otherwise Carlos might have actually *lost* the case. Anyway, he told me that when Angelica moved in with him, he had to share her baby food with her. He couldn't afford to take care of them both on his budget."

I let out a breath between my teeth. "How does he manage now?"

"God knows," she said. "God knows."

Chapter 7

WELL. I GUESS the next memorable parent I met after Carlos would have to be Harmony Stone. I don't think there ever was, or ever will be, anyone like Harmony Stone.

Some people drift in and out of your life and are soon forgotten. Were you to see them again even a year or two later, you might not recognize them, much less know their names. Harmony was the opposite: strong looking, dark-skinned, perhaps thirty-three, she stood about five feet seven, and weighed no more than a hundred twenty pounds. A Native American—of Mohegan descent, in fact—she *looked* Indian, in the classic beauty sense. She had high cheekbones, long black hair usually pulled back into a ponytail, and coal-black eyes. The mother of three, she worked at a telemarketing center in East Windsor, Connecticut, and was married to Frederick Stone, nickname "Flint," an ironworker.

I still remember the first time I saw her. She wore a loose-fitting outfit, some sort of Guatamalan or Indonesian thing, and carried a batik handbag. She looked like an Indian hippie, and she moved with a great steadiness and singleness of purpose—she seemed to float across the room. She stopped in to have us meet her three-year-old son, a prospect for the daycare center. She led him along by the hand, a black-haired boy with fair but tan complexion, like a mixed racial child.

I had a hard time concentrating on the conversation, mainly because she made me think of someone I'd met long ago, someone whose name and face were lost forever but who reminded me of an antique portrait of a great beauty, a mixture of innocence and charm wedded with sincerity, self-confidence, strength of character. Poise, I thought. She had tremendous poise.

I watched her while she talked about her son. She mentioned his name at least twice without going through the formality of introducing me, but I had not yet connected the name with the boy's presence. I only knew it was an unusual name, could not recall it to mind. Aghast, I suddenly realized how long I'd been spacing out, gazing dreamily at her and not giving a damn. Husband and kids? So what? She was beautiful, beautiful, beautiful.

"I'm sorry," I said finally, interrupting her. "What did you say your son's name was again?"

She looked blank. "Which one? I was just talking about Aaron and Roland a minute ago."

"*This* one." I smiled and gently touched the boy's left arm as it roamed along the chair Harmony occupied.

"This is Custer," she said. "Get it?" She grinned.

I blushed. "Custer?"

"Yeah, like 'Custer's last stand?'"

"Oh, okay," I said, laughing. "That's cute." Jesus Christ, I thought.

"Yeah, my husband and I have a lot of little things like that. Like I call him Flint, since our last name is Stone. And my oldest is named Roland."

I laughed, slightly more at ease. "That's good," I said. There did not seem to be much else to say.

"Oh, yeah, we have fun. After I had Custer, I went out and bought a Jeep Cherokee. Flint didn't think that was too funny, though."

We both laughed, and in that instant, I was able to recover my composure and see things in a rational light, and I realized she was extraordinary in her appearance and weird sense of humor alone. Beyond that, she was almost painfully average: working class, probably pregnant at eighteen, a regular viewer of several melodramatic TV programs, not much on conversation…the kind of woman you might expect the girl from the donut shop to grow into, or the waitress at the local burger joint. She didn't have a poetic bone in her body, or, if she had, it had been crushed out of her long ago by groping boyfriends, flat tires, kids with runny noses, feminine deodorant spray, and instant weight loss programs.

Not that that was *wrong*. I mean, there have to be people like that on this planet, and maybe they're better off than I am. All I knew, and know, is that the Harmony Stones of the world *aren't* my type. I think in the old days she would have been called "common."

"Anyway," she said, "about Custer. He's a great little kid. A real fighter. That's what I've always said about him, haven't I, huh?" She tugged on his hand as she questioned him, using the same babytalk voice you might try on a pet dog or kitten. Custer looked blank.

I smiled. "A fighter, huh? He looks like a fighter." I squatted down, grinning at him perhaps a little too broadly. "Hi, Custer. My name's Jana." He turned and clung to his mother's leg, glancing shyly away.

"I think he's still a little scared of women other than his mommy. He's not afraid of other boys, though," she chuckled.

"Well, no," I said. "He doesn't look like he would be. He's a fighter, right?"

"Right," she said, and launched back into the seemingly inexhaustible subject of Custer. I drifted again, studying the pattern of her batik handbag. It looked handmade, possibly by Harmony herself, and it occurred to me that the nineties were a lot like the roaring twenties: some prospered, but those who didn't had a harder and harder time of it.

I thought about my friend Susan, a twenty-three-year-old mother of two, sitting and working on her latch-hook rug. Not long before, a latch-hook rug would have seemed like the most abnormal thing for a twenty-three-year-old woman to be doing. I thought about the way I lived, how I rationed my water and used only as much toothpaste or shampoo as necessary. I thought of my small meals for one, how carefully I watched my diet, not only to avoid getting fat, but because nutrition was important, and healthy foods like fruits and vegetables were expensive. A little had to go a long way. I thought of my Aunt Frieda, who at forty-five was the youngest grandmother I knew and who taught neighborhood kids to reupholster furniture, patch jeans, and make dresses. Recycling was no longer trendy for these people, it was downright necessary.

Harmony Stone talked on about Custer, and I agreed that he might need special attention, then assured her that that would be no problem. The director came in, a woman named Barbara Helms, my boss's boss. She greeted Harmony Stone with the polished predictable smile she gave to all new parents, and they shook hands warmly. I was left with Custer as the two of them walked out into the hall. When it was obvious that we were alone, and I was just about to speak to him again, he looked around surreptitiously and said to me, baldly and almost with a smile, "You've got nice tits."

I did not react in the way one might have expected, or even the way *I* might have expected. My internal thought was something along the lines of, "WHAT??" But instead, presuming at least for the moment that he knew what he was saying, I looked coolly down at him, although my face reddened, and said, "Thank you. But we don't use those words here. All right?"

"All right," he said.

"Do you know why?"

He shook his head.

"Then I'll tell you. There are some words that are good words, and there are words that—that people feel hurt by. You don't want to hurt anyone, now, do you?"

"Nooo...."

"Good," I said. "Then you won't say that again to anyone, Custer. All right?"

"Uh huh!" He nodded, smartly.

This one is gonna be *big* trouble, I thought.

Chapter 8

ONE SET OF parents at Kiddie Korner lived in exact opposition to the Harmony Stones and Carlos Parejas of the world. Paul and Jeanette Robeson were both in their late forties, probably closer to fifty, so their daughter Ashley had obviously not been a planned pregnancy. I say "obviously" not just because of the age factor, but because Paul and Jeanette Robeson's other children were twenty-five, twenty-two, and twenty.

Jeanette Robeson made a much different impression on me than Harmony. For all her down-to-earth bluff and bustle, Harmony was still a warmhearted soul. Jeanette Robeson, on the other hand, was a dried-up looking thing, a weasel-faced matron with a face like someone who has spent much of her life sucking lemons. Her eyes were dark blue, always narrowed, it seemed, and white hair sprang from a brown mole on her cheek. Concentrating on the mole was less nauseating than her peroxide coiffure on the first day we met, at a luncheon sponsored by the center, or, as Jeanette herself called it, a "tea."

She stood by the pâté, I remember, eating gelatin salad with a long metal spoon. Sunlight came down through a chink in the clouds above—it was an eerily majestic overcast day—and light gleamed from Jeanette's garish pink lipstick. She stuck this long metal spoon into her mouth like a lollipop and pulled it down for an instant, so it clicked loudly against her teeth on its way back out of her mouth and made a grating, schlupping sound that turned my stomach. That violent lipstick of hers quivered in the sun as she dabbed at her mole with a paper towel.

That is one ugly broad, I thought.

We had to talk, of course, not because we had no one else to talk to—*I* certainly did—but because Barbara Helms, my boss's boss, brought Jeanette Robeson directly over to me and introduced us. I later found out this was because Barbara thought I would make a better impression than the unflappable Wendy Simpson, me being so serious and so…new. Also, Wendy's lipstick would probably have clashed horribly with Jeanette Robeson's, whereas the last lipstick I had owned was in 1988.

"Jeanette, this is Jana Odessi. She's new to Kiddie Korner, but we've been very impressed with her work so far." She put a heavy emphasis on the middle syllable of my last name—O-*DESS*-I—which wouldn't have bothered me, except that it reminded me of the way someone might say, "He's a real *ass* wipe." Barbara was so cool and condescending it made me want to clobber her. Also, she scared me.

"Hello, Jana," purred Jeanette. "It's a pleasure to meet you." She slipped a hand that was like a dead woman's into mine and shook my fingers briskly. The lines around her eyes contracted. I glanced at Barbara, for reassurance I guess, and she smiled plastically.

I smiled. "Pleased to meet you."

Jeanette looked quizzically at me. "Have we met before?"

"I don't believe so," I said in my most polished tea party voice. "Are you from the area?"

"Well, I'm originally from Boca, but my husband and I live in West Hartford." She said it "West *Hot*-ford."

What a fucking snob *you* are, I thought. "Oohhh," I said, "I live in Hartford. Perhaps one of your granddaughters or, er, daughters went to my school."

Jeanette let the "granddaughters" faux pas slide. But I did notice Barbara Helms' eyes widen a little.

"No," Jeanette said, "my daughters all went to Westminster Academy. You didn't by chance go there, did you?"

"No, not me. So, what brings you to Kiddie Korner?"

"Excuse me," Barbara interrupted. "I have to go see about some of the finger foods."

"Talk to you later," chirped Jeanette. "Well," she said, turning back to me. "To tell you the truth —" and here she lowered her voice "— all the daycare centers I wanted to get Ashley into were full. The waiting lists are just enormous for some of them."

"Sure," I said sympathetically. What did I know about it?

"And this was really the best we could do, given the circumstances. Not," she added quickly, "that Kiddie Korner isn't *nice*. It's certainly adequate, for now, at any rate." She said *Kiddie Korner* the way you might say *consolation prize*, and I realized she was embarrassed to be sending her precious Ashley to an ordinary daycare center.

"Well," I said, trying to play up my professionalism, "it's certainly an adequate facility in terms of things like safety." Then, conspiratorially, "Of course, we *are* seeing a lot of the latchkey children: minorities and so forth."

Her features tightened instinctively. "Mm. Naturally," she said.

"Not that that's bad," I added quickly. "After all, the school curriculum does put a heavy emphasis on multiculturalism these days. We wouldn't want these children to be growing up in an all-*white* world like you or I had to, after all." Part of me couldn't believe I was saying this stuff, but I just couldn't resist.

Her face registered dismay, but she managed to smile through it. "Well, certainly, it is good to have a child exposed to various… types, I'm sure." She looked distracted. "Where did you say you were from?"

"*Hot*-ford," I said, falling into her pattern of speech. I had all I could do to keep from batting my eyelashes.

"I see," she said. "Well, it was nice meeting you…is it 'Donna?'"

"Jana."

"I'm sorry."

"That's all right. Happens all the time." I tittered as she pressed my hand.

"Bye-bye now."

"Enjoy the day," I said.

She moved off into the crowd and I shuddered with relief. She is one cool customer, I remember thinking. I remember, too, that I had a bad feeling about her, a slight sense of foreboding. But I shrugged it off and turned my thoughts away from Jeanette Robeson as quickly as possible.

Chapter 9

I'D NEVER SEE the Robesons' place firsthand, but I did have a chance to see those of other parents: Carlos Pareja's, of course, and others. One of the most memorable visits was to Frederick and Harmony Stone's apartment on the lower east side of Hartford, a largely Latino neighborhood much like the one where Carlos lived. At first I thought the building couldn't possibly be an apartment complex—it was too square and modern looking compared to the broken-down efficiencies surrounding it. Potted plants perched on balconies, not all of the blinds were drawn, and the few windows opened onto the spring day emitted only a profound silence. Then I remembered: Harmony's husband was in construction, so they were not in the depths of poverty. They just had too many kids to afford a better neighborhood.

The Stones were an unusual couple, to put it mildly. I could see that from their wedding picture on the wall: Harmony looked like someone out of an Age of Aquarius poster standing next to Frederick, who reminded me of Popeye after a couple cans of spinach. He had all the right muscles, but somehow they seemed to be in all the wrong places. A giant American flag hung on the wall in their living room; that had to have been Frederick's idea.

Little Custer Stone lay on his belly on the floor, a painted toy soldier in each chubby hand. He'd ranged soldiers across the floor, placing them strategically into two very definite battalions. Of the two, the smaller battalion's soldiers had been painted a dark brown, presumably by Custer himself—they were little-kid messy. These were Iraqi soldiers. Armed against them, poised for eternity in mid-shot, and appearing to be the exact same shade of white—for what could a child be expected to know about historical accuracy?—the enemies of Iraq stood, the multinational forces of Operation Desert Storm.

"Boom boom," he said. "Boom boom."

"So," said Harmony, catching my eye as I looked bleakly up from the battlefield. "What can I do for ya?"

I looked around the room, probably seeming like someone who has lost her bearings. "Well," I said, "we need to talk, right?"

"That's what you said on the phone, all right," she said. She looked concerned. "Can I get you something to drink? We could sit in the kitchen."

"Sure, sure," I said. "Thanks." The question snapped me out of my reverie and we headed toward the kitchen table. "Water'll be fine."

"Are you sure? I have iced tea."

"That's okay. I actually prefer water."

"Boom boom," said Custer from the other room. He made a high-pitched screaming sound: definitely a death.

"Keep it down in there, Custer," she shouted, too loudly for the small apartment.

"Sounds like he's having a great time," I said, trying not to sound sarcastic. "Did he paint the soldiers himself?"

"Yeah," she said. "They were a baby shower gift from his grandfather during the Gulf War, and they got passed down to him. He's gotten into playing with them a lot. Of course, nobody ever hears much about that stuff these days, but we still have a lot of Desert Storm souvenirs."

"Souvenirs?"

"Sure, you know, hats, pins, T-shirts. You remember all that stuff, right?"

"Oh yeah." I felt my face get red, not wanting a confrontation. I had been antiwar all my life, had marched in peace rallies during that time.

Harmony talked on. "Yeah, that sonofabitch Hussein should have been assassinated by the CIA a long time ago. Did you know he tried to get control of the whole world's oil supply? Except what we have out in Texas and whatnot. But I bet he would have tried to take over the U.S., too. Don't you think?"

"It's an interesting question." Apparently, she was not aware of alternative media sources.

"Well," she said, "I guess we can thank God he didn't. Anyway, enough about that. At least we won, right?"

"Hmph," I grunted, forcing a smile. Right, we won. "Well, I know you wanted to talk to me about Custer—that is, *I* wanted to talk to *you* about Custer, but I felt it would be more comfortable talking here…it's less formal, of course, and —"

"What's he been doing?" she said abruptly. "Has he been bad?"

That threw me. I shifted in my chair. "I wouldn't say 'bad,' no, he's not *bad*. I mean, I think all little kids are good kids when you get down to it —"

"Wait a minute," she interrupted. "This isn't a normal procedure for you, is it? Comin' over parents' houses?"

"Well, no. I was concerned."

"You were concerned," she said. It was almost an accusation.

"Yes. Let me ask you something: is he a very aggressive child, would you say? I mean at home." Perspiration beaded on my forehead.

"Aggressive?" She looked over at him. In one hand, he held a soldier with a bayonet jammed against the body of the soldier in his other hand. "Well," Harmony said, "I don't know. No, I mean, he's not any more aggressive than any other little boys I've seen. I'd say they all like to play a little rough, but nothing serious. 'Snakes, snails, and puppy dog's tails.' Right?" She laughed, again a little too loudly.

I shifted in my chair, and wiped my forehead. "Sure," I said. I laughed a little, hoping to put myself, and her, more at ease.

A knock at the door interrupted us.

"Excuse me," said Harmony.

"Sure." I sipped my water.

The door opened and, from across the two rooms, I could see the man who entered, and hear the conversation, although at first he couldn't see me. Tall and dark like Harmony, almost like a male version of her, he seemed very much a businessman type, barrel-chested, with a broad nose, and vaguely Arabic-looking.

"Hey, Harm," he said.

"Stan," she whispered, "what the hell are you *doing* here? It's four o'clock in the afternoon."

"Ah, I figgered you'd be home, and I just got outta work, you know? What are you whisperin' for?"

"Sh, I'm not." She held up a finger to silence him.

"Got any blow?" he asked, a stage whisper, at best.

"No, of course I don't," she said. Then, back to her normal voice, "Come on *in* here, brother dear, and meet your nephew's teacher, Jana *Odyssey*." She grabbed him by the wrist and began to pull him into the room.

"Oh, shit," he whispered.

I stood as if to greet him, or to prepare to leave. "Hi."

He smiled uncertainly. "Hello. Say, you didn't—did you—I mean, uh—you knew I was just joking with her, right?" he laughed. "I mean, did you hear what I asked her?" He laughed again.

"Sure," I said, "no problem. It's cool." It was none of my business. I just hoped they weren't doing drugs around that child.

"Standing Free Ibsen." He grinned and shook my hand.

"I—I'm sorry?"

"Standing Free Ibsen," he repeated. "That's my name. Call me Stan."

"Jana Odessi. Pleased to meet you…Stan."

"I'm sorry," said Harmony. "I told him your name was 'Odyssey.'"

I smiled. "That's all right. Happens all the time."

"Well, anyway," Stan said, turning to his sister. "What was I gonna say…? Oh, yeah. I had a horrible day today." He seemed to forget my presence almost immediately. "We ran into mondo problems at the plant."

Harmony's eyelids dropped to half-mast. "Really?"

"Oh, unbelievable. Well, it's that brilliant goddamn system they've got there now." He turned to me as an aside, saying, "They've got an integrated system."

"Integrated?"

Harmony said, "Stan's an engineer."

"Oh."

"CAD/CAM," she said.

"CAD/CAM?"

"Computer-aided design, computer-aided manufacturing."

"Oh," I said, feigning interest. "I don't know *any*thing about engineering."

Stan glared at me as if to say, "No shit," then tried to smile through it. "Right," he said. "So anyway," turning back to Harmony, "this crapola system that ol' rocket scientist Pete Maheu decided on —"

"Why is this system so bad?" she interrupted. "I mean, I thought it cost like a kazillion dollars."

"Well, that's the thing," he said. "The problem with an integrated system is certain aspects of your operation don't *require* it. Plus, it's not as flexible as interfacing standalones. Of course, some people would argue you make less mistakes with integrated, or that it's more precise, but I don't know."

"Oh," Harmony said. "I think you just like the sound of 'standalone' 'cause it sounds like 'Standing Free.'"

"Well, in a way you *are* 'standing free' when you're dealing with PCs." He cupped his chin in his hand. "But on the surface, I suppose a fully integrated system could look attractive to management people…."

"Stan, nobody here gives a shit about computers. You realize that? Nobody."

"Hey, this is important stuff," he said. He looked genuinely offended.

"Where do you work, Stan?" I asked, hoping to defuse what might become an unpleasant scene.

He dismissed me with a wave. "Ah, it's technical."

Harmony turned to me. "He works for the government."

"Shut up, Harm," he said.

"Don't worry, *Stan*, I'm not going to tell her anything else. Besides, we were having a meeting before you barged in here."

"A meeting?" He looked back and forth between us, trying to piece it together. "Yeah," Harmony said. "Jana teaches at Custer's school."

"Daycare," I said in response to his puzzled look.

"Oh," he said blankly. "That's great." He looked distracted. "So, uh, are you gonna be at the party Saturday night?"

Somewhat awkwardly, I said, "N-no, I don't think so."

"Oh, we're having a party here Saturday night," Harmony said. "Why don't you come? It'll be fun. You'll get to meet Fred—my husband—and it'll give us a chance to talk." She glanced at her watch. "Today's gonna be bad, I can just tell."

I didn't know whether to feel flattered by the invitation or blown off after driving all the way over for nothing. For now, I accepted the invitation and decided to just get the hell out of there and sort the feelings out later.

"So great, we'll see ya then," said Harmony, ushering me to the door.

"Okay. Nice meeting you," I said to Stan, who shook my hand warmly, his white smile gleaming.

"A pleasure," he said.

Chapter 10

WHEN I ARRIVED at Harmony Stone's party, I was surprised to find most of the crowd several years older than me. In fact, I was obviously the youngest of the bunch, with the possible exception of Harmony herself, who was a close second at best. To make it even weirder, I felt a little like I'd walked into a scene from the sixties—incense burning, a folk song on the stereo (something about *Castro*, for God's sake), and even one of those lava lamp gizmoes. I saw no sign of Harmony's husband Fred.

As if being the "young one" and arriving alone were not awkward enough, I was also seriously overdressed. I had on earrings, a nice blouse and a longish skirt —which was patterned, fortunately, or I would really have felt like a loser. I used to think it was cool to wear that sort of thing everywhere, but these days it's such a cardinal sin to be overdressed in this town that even the most moronic gum-chomping cheerleader/majorette/Junior Miss-type can make you feel like a bozo with one simple "What are *you* all dressed up for?" And predictably enough, I got the full treatment from Harmony.

"Where are *you* off to? You goin' somewhere after the party, or did you just come from the *opera?*" she asked in perfect innocence and with embarrassing effusiveness.

"Oh, no —" I said, grin locked in place, sweat beading up on my forehead "— no, I'm always in such doubt over what to wear when I go out, I just try to compromise. Of course, I wouldn't have wanted to wear *my* jeans —" eyeing hers and taking in half the room with one sweep of the arm "— they're such ratty old things, I'd be embarrassed to wear them out of the house, unless maybe I was headed for the laundromat or something."

I dabbed at my forehead with my handkerchief, feeling like an absolute phony and knowing I must sound like one, too, but Harmony laughed with apparent good humor and introduced me to several of the people standing nearby. Afterward, Harmony's brother Stan flagged me down from across the room the way you might signal a bartender: a single finger held up, very direct eye contact, a sudden lift of the head, the upward nod that most people reserve only for those with whom they're well-acquainted.

I waved back, smiling and feeling the *oh-shit* sensation characterized by mild nausea and a tightness in the sternum, usually accompanied by a slight tic in one or more of the facial muscles, that comes with being approached by someone you don't particularly want to know. I followed Harmony into the living room, and Stan tracked us through the crowd, a strange fixed grin on his face. The look in his eyes was slightly crazed, impish, as if he'd just told a dirty joke, or sold a lemon of a car to an elderly woman. Remembering the other day, I wondered whether he'd been doing coke.

"Hey, I remember *you,*" he said as he came up to us. He had put on a very broad voice—the type adults sometimes use to address kids they don't know—for the purpose of sounding funny and, I guessed, of being friendly.

I smiled. "Hello."

"You're the teacher-lady," he said. "*Custer's* teacher, eh?"

The slight traces of powder at the edges of his nostrils confirmed my suspicion. I wondered whether anyone else noticed.

"Yes," I said. "Custer's teacher. And you're the engineer, aren't you?"

"Yeah," he said, surprised. "Did Harmony mention that?"

"No, no —" I waved a hand, reassuring "— you mentioned something about it when I met you before. I tend to remember stuff like that."

"Pretty eerie, if you ask me." He smiled, but the look in his eyes betrayed pure fear.

"Okay, Stan," said Harmony, "you can act like a normal human being again. The *teacher-lady* doesn't bite." She put unusual emphasis on the words, obviously to razz him.

"I'm sorry," he said, looking at Harmony, then turning to me. He put out his hand. "Standing Free Ibsen is my name."

I shook his hand, laughing. "I remember."

"Oh," he said.

"*You* told me that," I said. I tried to chuckle good-naturedly, conspiratorial, as if I understood perfectly, it was no big deal. "I'm Jana."

"It's a Native American name," he said.

"I thought so," I said. "Although I must say 'Ibsen' comes as a surprise."

"It was originally something else. Something long and relatively unpronounceable. Good old Uncle Sam changed it for us back during our great-great-grandfather's time or something." He caught Harmony's eye and she nodded. "It's not exactly the only thing we've had done to us, of course, but, uh, I don't exactly see things getting better. You remember all that bullshit about Columbus a few years ago? Or, better yet, the big Foxwoods Casino scandal?"

"Um —"

"Stan," Harmony said, "don't get on the soapbox, okay? Please. And wipe your nose."

"Hey, this is important stuff," he said to her, then turned back to me. He softened his tone a bit and wiped his nose with a handkerchief he'd drawn from his breast pocket. "Did you know," he asked me, "that there is not one single Native American member of the senate? There never has been. There's never been a Native American presidential candidate, a Native member of the Supreme Court, or a Native state rep…not one." He sniffed, looked offended.

"Wow." I wanted to say, "That's sad," but thought better of it—I had a feeling it might encourage a tirade.

"Not only that," he added, "these are *not* well-known facts. But if they ever did get into the newspapers, they'd be on page seventeen, under some article about Polish produce prices." He spat out the words, the *p*s deliberate, like a little kid repeating *Peter Piper*. "And to make it worse," he went on, "look at the people they *do* elect."

After a weighty pause, Harmony said, "Well, shit is shit."

Stan exploded in laughter, and Harmony laughed too. I laughed along with them mechanically, feeling I'd missed an inside joke.

"You'll have to explain that one," Harmony said to Stan.

"Tell her about Jewel."

"Stan had this friend named Jewel who was a Zen Buddhist," Harmony said. "This was a guy, unlike Jewel the singer."

"What do Zen Buddhists believe?" I asked.

"I don't know. He always said nothing mattered more than anything else, and comparisons are odorous."

"Odious," Stan corrected.

"Whatever."

"So I guess he meditated and stuff?" I asked.

"I think so. He drank Chinese tea all the time, and he used to play this little game called *Television I Ching*."

"I Ching?"

"I don't know what it means, but Jewel used to sit in a chair in front of someone's TV with the remote in his hand, skipping from channel to channel."

"Everyone does that…."

"Yeah, but he wouldn't stop to watch anything for more than two seconds," she said. "That was the game, see."

"Oh."

"Well, he always said, 'Shit is shit.'"

I laughed. "So that's where that's from. Was he a college student?"

"I don't think so." Stan shook his head. "But he hung out on campuses a lot, always making jokes about all of the 'punko/new wave/artsy-fartsy students' at Wesleyan. Maybe he audited some courses there."

"Maybe he was just jealous."

Harmony paused. "I don't think so. I met some of the people he was talking about once, and they sure as hell didn't seem as happy as he did."

"Jana," Stan interrupted "— it *is* Jana, isn't it…?"

"Yes."

"Would you like something to drink? I'm sure my buddy Gus can fix you up with something appropriately festive."

"Actually," I said, "water will be fine. I'm going to the gym after I leave here."

Stan looked at me, smiling with his eyes only, disapproving. "You sure?"

I nodded, and he led me toward the kitchen, where several more people in jeans and concert T-shirts stood with mixed drinks in their hands. One or two glanced at me, then continued their conversations. Stan came to the rescue: "Everybody, this is Jana."

A chorus of greetings rang out.

"Jana, that's Steven —" he pointed to a youngish older man with a beard and mustache, balding "— that's Eve —" a biker-type, maybe forty "— and these four clowns over here in the corner are Syd, Jack, Michael and Gus." The four of them laughed when he said "clowns," and looked at me wolfishly.

I smiled and said, "Pleased to meet you."

Of the four in the corner group, three looked reasonable and normal. Only Gus, with his large frame, his strangely mottled skin and frizzy longish black hair, looked weird. He wore a goatee with what looked to be an elastic band from a retainer around it, and he had a huge belly, more oblong than round, looming out over his belt buckle like a ship being launched.

The doorbell rang. I heard Harmony saying, "Rich!" from across the room, and about three seconds later, Stan excused himself to go say hello, which left me standing in the kitchen with all these people I did not know. I assumed that the conversation had shifted to religion, as Gus was saying, "Maybe God is this Power that created the universe, okay? Or maybe God is Allah or Christ or Mohammed or whoever. Maybe God is part of our consciousness, like that part that tells us when we're doing something we know is wrong…or right, for that matter. Maybe God is love, I don't know. But there are definitely three things I know about God —" he hesitated, like he was waiting for someone to ask, then charged ahead "— there *is* a God." He jerked a thumb at his lumpy chest, his great belly rippling. "It ain't me, and He or She or It does not need my help."

"How do you *know* there's a God?" said Jack or Hank or whatever his name was. "How can you possibly know something like that?"

"I know there's a God just like I know I've been on this planet before," he said. "Because when you go somewhere, and you have this profound sense of déjà vu that's so heavy it blows your mind, and yet you know there's no possible way you could ever have been there before, then you know you've had some Previous Incarnation."

His audience was silent.

Gus raised an emphatic hand. "And it sounds weird, but that's the way it was for me. I didn't know there was a God, and didn't believe any longer that there could be. But then it was proven to me by people applying nothing other than logic and instinct and experience. See, I used to be agnostic, but looking back, I was like a little kid saying there's no such thing as love, because he's never experienced it. That doesn't make him a philosopher…just naïve.

"Now, don't get me wrong—I don't claim to be a philosopher, 'cause I know where *my* thinking can get me. But, you know, I just try to appreciate the value of simplicity, and that's where my head is right now. And to me, listening to the dictates of my conscience is better than giving in to every temptation. 'Cause if I listen to my conscience, and act accordingly, I don't have anything to feel guilty about. Now *that's* simple."

I couldn't believe this stuff was coming out of this guy's mouth, but I was completely engrossed in what he was saying, and it made real sense to me. Before Gus could go on, though, we were interrupted by Stan and his friend. Stan played the same introduction game he'd played before, except that this time, he included me. Harmony followed them, and soon we stood side by side as Stan and the newly-arrived Rich had an animated conversation about work, Rich obviously being a fellow engineer.

"Yeah, so they hired somebody new to replace the manager of the department," Rich said to Stan.

"Clancy? They replaced *Clancy*?"

"Yup."

"Who the fuck did they hire?"

"Some chiphead. *You* know, they get some guy who says he 'knows about electronic sub-assemblies ….'"

"What? Jesus, 'electronic sub-assemblies' is kind of a broad category, it could mean anything from power hybrid microcircuits to pyrofuckingtechnic. It's like saying 'components.'"

He turned to the group. "What does *that* mean? You could be talking about capacitors, potentiometers, resistors. Jesus, somebody starts talking electronic sub-assemblies, I don't assume he's a *senior engineer*. Now, we get into specifics—ceramic resonators, logic

ICs, memories —" he ticked them off on his fingers "— then *fine*. But any nitwit can scan the classifieds and pick out 'CAE/CAD' or something of that nature. And that's what I think some of these fucking management types do."

"Exactly."

"Uh, Stan," Harmony interrupted, "we're not gonna be treated to two hours' worth of computer-aided geek language, are we?"

"Chill out, Harm," he said. "Rich and I are just catching up on what's new in the wonderful world of electronic data processing."

Rich guffawed at the mocking way Stan said *electronic data processing*.

"What do you do, Rich?" I asked.

"I'm in engineering," he said, the way some people would say, "I'm an attorney."

I arched my brows. Do I kiss the ring now or later?

Then he added, "I make electronic sequencers for seat ejectors."

"Oookay," I said. "So, uh, what's a 'chiphead?'"

He and Stan both snorted, exchanging a slightly embarrassed look.

Stan said, "A chiphead is sort of a nickname for a wafer designer—someone who's basically nothing more than an electronic data processor, usually some windbag with a degree or two."

"Yeah, in sales and marketing," Rich added.

"Really." Stan straightened up, suddenly more formal, almost businesslike, as if the discussion of work made something in him snap to attention. "Refill, anyone?" He reached for the ice bucket, then poured himself a scotch on the rocks.

Several of the people held out near-empty glasses, and Stan said, "Well, what the heck. I might as well play bartender, since I'm the one throwing this party for my dear sister."

I glanced over toward Harmony, who had moved to the other side of the apartment.

"Really, Stan?" said Jack, or Syd, or maybe Michael. They weren't too memorable, those three.

"Yeah." Stan tried to look a bit humble while he mixed the screwdrivers, and it was obviously an effort. "Even though Fred makes okay money, they're still kind of struggling with expenses, what with the baby and all. And, since I'm a respectable bachelor —" two of his friends burst into laughter "— I figure I can help her out some."

"So, Stan, when are *you* gonna get married?" somebody asked.

He grinned. "When I find a wealthy blonde with a Lexus." They all howled then, except him, and he continued, "Or a Mercedes. Hell, even a nice Beamer would do."

"No shit," Rich said.

"That's the thing," said Stan. "You work hard, you make decent money, you kind of feel like you owe it to yourself. You know what I mean?"

Harmony came back over to our little group just as Rich answered him. "Yeah, it's a struggle all right. The fabulous battle of the sexes, eh?"

Harmony scowled. "What are you guys talking about?"

"Money," said Stan, and at the same instant Rich said, "Sex." We all laughed. "Well, you know how it is." Stan looked mock-sheepish. "It sure is tough sometimes."

I decided to put in my two cents. "A lot of people out there are trying to make a living and having a hard time just doing that."

"Yeah," Rich said.

We all nodded.

"Boy, that's true," Harmony said. "God knows I've spent my share of time looking through the classifieds and trying to find something worthwhile. I hate where I work."

"What do you do, Harmony?" I asked. "I never did find out."

"I work for a place that does *telemarketing*," she said, beaming sarcastically. There were groans and noisy shouts of "Yeah" from the others.

"Yeah. It sucks," she said dolefully. "I sit there doing these goddamn business-to-business calls, getting people's voice mail all day. I call it Voice Mail Heaven." More laughter. "Sometimes you go all day without a sale, and usually you're on hold for probably a third of your day, at least. Even the music people have on hold is boring these days. About the only interesting thing I've heard on hold was when I talked to United Overseas Air Freight or something, and they had all this walkie-talkie stuff going on in my ear."

"What do you mean?"

"Well, like 'pilot-to-tower' stuff." She pretended to hold a microphone to her mouth, imitating two men on their systems: "'Ah, Delta 1684, prepare to land, Santa Monica 620.' 'Delta three.' 'Data three wilco.'"

We all chuckled, but Rich said, with a sympathy that was almost cruel, "God, that must be boring."

"It *is* boring," she said. "But what can you do? Not everyone has a real career they want to pursue, even some of the people I know with degrees. You look in the papers, you don't find much you're qualified for, unless you're in medicine or you're a tekkie. And I don't want to work as a stripper."

Several people cracked up, but they turned serious again when they saw her face. "Hey, don't laugh. I've thought about it. Not too many people can live in this state on six bucks an hour."

"You ever see those 'easy money' schemes in the backs of magazines?" I asked "I even thought about trying those at one point."

"Oh yeah," she said. "They have that crap all the time in *The Sentinel*. 'Read books at home!' 'Make up to three hundred dollars a week assembling products in your home!' What a crock."

"You ever answer any?"

"Nah. Why bother? They're all scams. Have to be."

I pondered it. "You have to admit, though, it is tempting. Just for the sake of checking it out, you know?"

"Yeah," she said, "but not that tempting."

"I wonder if people do get roped into really horrible scams," I said.

"No doubt," Stan said.

Harmony nodded. "I know someone who had the next worst thing happen to him."

"Really? What happened?"

"It was this guy named Carlos Pareja —"

"Carlos Pareja?" I said. "He has a daughter at the center, doesn't he?"

"Yeah," she said. "That's right, of course *you* know him."

"That's weird. I'm surprised you know him."

"Yeah, he got into this multi-level marketing deal, trying to sell all his friends and neighbors on this financial services thing— mutual funds, or whatever. Can you imagine people on fixed incomes actually *investing* in stuff? God, it nearly wiped him out."

"Wow. He didn't lose a lot of money, did he? I mean, he didn't have much to lose in the first place, right?"

"Well, yeah, this is it. Actually, he almost lost his existing business, 'cause he was spending so much time and effort trying to get this other thing off the ground. You know he has his own business, right?"

"Yeah, he's a sidewalk vendor."

"Right. Well, he was investing a lot of himself in this financial services deal, and they really had him hook, line and sinker."

"It didn't pan out, huh?"

"Myself, I think he got ripped off. He doesn't think so, he just claims he's not a born salesman, and that that's why he couldn't get it to fly, but I don't buy that. I mean, he *is* a salesman. What does he think being a vendor is?"

I realized Harmony and I were now having an essentially private conversation, and other people in our part of the room had broken up into twos and threes. I decided it might be an opportune time to discuss her son, since that was the main reason for my being there. I didn't know how to broach the subject, so I just launched at her more or less directly.

"Say, not to change the subject, but I meant to ask you about Custer."

"Yeah?"

"Well, he's having something of a problem with, um, aggression, I guess you could call it. I wanted to talk to you about it."

"How do you mean, 'aggression?'"

"Well —" I faltered "— he's not exactly a mean child…that is, he certainly doesn't intend to be hurtful to others, but a lot of his behaviors *have* been pretty harmful to other children in the center."

"Well," she said, "I mean, who's at fault, though? I'm sure he wouldn't instigate any serious trouble, he's very well-behaved at home." Her tone was defensive, and her manner had turned decidedly cooler.

"Let me try to explain," I said gently. "It's not as though he's being *bad* or malicious." I drew her toward a pair of chairs, almost without thinking.

"Well, give me an example of the problem," she said.

"Okay. One of our rules is that children aren't allowed to physically assault one another, even in a structured way. In other words, conflict resolution has to be by mutual separation, intervention by an adult, time in the 'timeout' room, and so on."

"So?" She crossed her arms.

"Well, Custer and another boy were playing this little war game one day, and it got out of hand." She cocked her head, listening intently. "Custer chased after the other boy with a toy gun. He waved it around like a club, see, and the other boy, Eric, had a toy gun, too, and when Eric held up *his* gun, and said, 'Bang, bang, you're dead,' Custer clobbered him."

She chuckled, not quite silently. "That just sounds like a typical thing kids would do."

I forced a smile. "But the thing is, he hit Eric in the head with the gun."

"Okay," she said, turning serious. "Doesn't this stuff happen all the time? I mean, seriously, I'm sure Custer isn't the only one there acting like a boy."

"No," I said, "you're right. Kids are kids. But with most of them, they get out of hand periodically, hitting someone, or being disobedient, or whatever. I'm just afraid that, with Custer, we're seeing a pattern."

"What do you mean?"

"Well, it's not the first time his behavior has been on the… outrageous side. Do you know what his first words to me were, the first time I ever saw him?"

"I don't think so, unless you mentioned it to me before."

"I didn't want to make a big deal out of it then, because it might just have been an isolated incident."

"Well, what did he say?"

I glanced to the left and right, and leaned forward in the chair. "He said, 'You've got nice tits.'"

Her expression went blank for an instant, then her brow furrowed. "What??" Her mouth hung open.

I leaned back, nodding. "I'm serious. I thought I was hearing things."

"Where do you suppose he'd pick up something like that? TV?"

"Could be." I shrugged. "It's not necessarily a big deal, but it was pretty bizarre. Now, since then, he hasn't said anything along those lines, but he has been pretty aggressive with some of the other kids."

"Well," she said. "I'll have to talk this over with Fred."

"Where is he, by the way? I thought I'd get to talk to you both."

"Oh, he had to work." Her gaze slid away as she spoke, and for an instant, I wondered whether she was telling the truth.

"So, do you expect him back soon? You think he'll make it back for the party? 'Cause, I mean, I'd like to be able to speak with you both about it. I want him to understand, as well as you do, that Custer isn't being 'bad.' He just has some things that need to be resolved."

"No." She looked distracted. "No, I don't know when he'll be back."

"Okay," I said. "I don't want to be rude, but I really don't think I should stay for too much longer, if that's the case." I smiled. "Not that I don't appreciate being invited, because I do, it's just that…well, in any event," I felt my face redden, "I have some other things to take care of tonight, and I wanted to make sure to leave time for them."

"Well, sure," she said. She looked almost as embarrassed as I felt. "I don't know when to expect Fred back, but I *will* talk to him about this. And I'll make sure I explain what you said, that it's not a matter of Custer being bad."

"Yeah, I don't know if I'd mention the 'nice tits' comment to him," I said, nudging her in a way that implied we were buddies, co-conspirators.

She smiled. "Men tend to overreact to stuff like that," she said.

"It's possible," I grinned. We were buddies now, the look in her eyes told me.

"Let me walk you out," she said.

"Oh, I'm sure I'm going to have to get through Standing Free," I said. "I doubt he'll let me out of here without an explanation."

We maneuvered our way through the crowd. "Don't worry about Stan," she said.

Sure enough, Stan had drifted over to another group, and was talking heatedly, his hands cutting the air as he pressed some point. I couldn't help pondering whether he had more of those little white crystals dangling from his nose.

"Okay," Harmony said when we reached the door. "You're safe now. You can make a quick exit if you just say 'bye' from here."

I turned to wave. Like a scene in a movie, the picture would stay fresh in my mind always: Stan in the background, his lips moving noiselessly; groups of people standing with glasses in their hands; the American flag on the far wall hanging down like some quiet, benevolent presence over these people resembling beatniks from thirty or forty years before.

I waved. "Bye, everybody," I said above the noise of the crowd.

Bye, Jana, I heard, surprised that a couple of people actually remembered my name. Mostly I heard, *Bye, See ya.* I turned to take Harmony's hand, but she was already giving my arm a quick squeeze, the kind of mock-embrace you give to someone when a handshake seems too stiff and formal, and a hug is presumptuous.

She ushered me out the door, motherly, as if to protect me from Stan's voice (*Bye, Jana*) as it rang across the room. But her eyes betrayed her relief to be rid of me. The door clicked shut and I headed down the hallway.

Chapter 11

AND NOW, THOUGH I've only touched on the subject superficially, it becomes necessary for me to talk about the one person I've most dreaded contemplating: the obtuse, the impermeable, the one and only Wendy Simpson.

Ah, Wendy Simpson. Windy Sempson, Wendy Simpleton, how I do loathe thee, let me count the ways. I wish I could somehow convey the bottomless, gut-wrenching vicious sensation that crawls up into the back of my throat and hammers at my eyeballs when I think of Wendy Simpson, every normal human being's nightmare vision of a fatuous bimbo, a brainless wench with a sickening sweetness, an aggressive artifice, a timeless tackiness, a veneer of veneers. I know I'm being unkind and uncharitable...*but I like it.*

Even today, when I think of Wendy, the hair on the back of my neck starts to rise, my stomach still gets the same appalling sinking sensation I get whenever I have an overheated radiator, and a chill seizes me that makes my entire body twitch, like someone with an uncontrollable tic.

I find it difficult to speak of her at all, but I have to try, as she plays a small but pivotal role in the saga of my life at Kiddie Korner Childcare Center. She it was who paved the way toward my ultimate and unjust dismissal from the center. She it was who, perhaps without even malice aforethought, tried to tell me how to dress, how to wear my hair, how to comport myself with the parents of our little Kiddie Korner kiddies. She it was who stood, looking sad but smiling, and waved to me, that last day at the center when I said my goodbyes.

Of course, I've already mentioned her: the baubles, the lipstick, the imperturbable hair. The flawless fingernails. And I know that, stereotypes aside, she made me question my own definition of femininity all over again, almost making me feel like I needed to reassess my own value system, like she knew something I didn't. But in the end, "my side" won, my strength, my convictions, my willingness to be true to myself, and I knew she was just what she seemed to be—predictable as a soap opera, lighter than light beer. As harmless to me, in the end, as a raindrop splashing the tip of my nose.

What I have yet to recount, however, is the impact she had on me. Because, brainless homophobic bimbo or not, she had an impact. And since part of her little speech was a "parents-don't-like-your-type" kind of thing, I had two reactions: first was gut-level anger and rage, the kind that made me want to go out and get a big can of mousse and shove it up her nose. Or worse.

The other reaction I can only describe as immediate excessive self-appraisal. I thought: do I look like a jockette? Am I really a non-conformist in some extreme sense of the word? Do people actually look at me and think, "Boy does *she* look like a dyke?" And if so, should I start making attempts to look like a magazine cover?

I answered all of these questions the same way: I don't think so.

Still, doubts lingered. It made me angry to think that all this crap I thought I'd resolved by the time I'd finished high school was still an issue.

Fortunately for me, somewhere around this time, I began seeing my friend Danielle Marshall. I started talking to Danielle about the whole Wendy thing, and she was a good sounding board. I'd known Danielle for years, and she's just a normal person, not one of those plastic dolls like the Wendys of the world, so I knew she'd understand. Our little exchanges were intense, and I soon found a strange intimacy growing there. Time and again, she would fetch me up sharply when I took Wendy's point of view too seriously, stopping me in the middle of a sentence in a warm, direct way, like a counselor or mentor would.

"Aren't you enough?" she asked me once while I was with her in a café talking about this stuff.

"What?" I said, taken aback.

"Aren't you enough?"

She'd really thrown me. "What do you mean?"

"Aren't *you* enough? Don't you think you're okay the way you are? Or do you really need to make some sort of artificial adjustment to the way you look just to feel better?"

"No, I don't, goddamn it." I slap my knee. "That's the whole point!"

She looks up at me from beneath long eyelashes, blue eyes flash behind the single shock of blonde hair falling over them. "You and I both know your self-image doesn't depend on what some prissy bimbo thinks of your hairstyle. To hell with her opinion." She smiles. "Why acknowledge her at all?"

"I don't know why I do," I say, and sit back. "Damned if that doesn't beat all. Why *do* I let someone like that get to me?"

She shrugs. "What can I say? *I* don't know: after all, I'm only twenty-three." The inside joke, based on my busting her ass about me being a full year older and wiser, sends us into hysterics.

"You're such a smartass," I say when our laughter subsides. "But really, how do you account for a thing like that? I mean, I don't look like a dyke, really. Hell, *you* look more like a dyke than I do, with that short blonde hair with the big long strand hanging down in your face. You look like someone in a band. One of those guitar chicks with a leather jacket. That's what you should have, a leather jacket."

I'm smiling, half-teasing the whole time, but Danielle seems to take it seriously. "Maybe I *should* get a leather jacket."

Our eyes meet before hers slide away from mine, and I blush to the roots of my hair, realizing that I have been unconsciously flirting with her. I try to cover. "You're not even a les, though, for Christ's sake," I say. "You don't have to be one to look like one, you know." I'm talking nonsense now, I know, but am too embarrassed to do anything else.

"I am bi, though," she says quietly, not looking at me.

"You keep saying that, but every time I see you, you're either alone or with that big galoot of a boyfriend. I never see you with any women."

"Well?"

"Well?"

"I'm not sure I understand the implication," she says, and smiles a little smile.

My heart skips a beat. "Well, I mean, he's a *nice* galoot, but what's the deal here? Are you getting engaged? Are you ready for the two-point-five children and the picket fence?" I'm still smirking, and feeling like a real shithead, but Danielle remains as level as the Buddha.

"No," she says. "No, in fact, I was thinking about—well, never mind," she says abruptly, her tone changed.

"What?" I say. "Don't do that. What were you thinking about?"

She stares off in another direction. "Nothing, really. It's just… well, all right. Have you ever spent any time with a friend where you wanted to be more than friends but somehow felt that anything other than friendship might ruin the whole thing?"

"Sure," I say, tumbling into a fog, plunged into some strange new world that is both terrifying and lovely to behold. "Sure, I've been there," I say. "Many times. It's a dilemma."

She looks directly into my eyes. "That's where I am now, Jana." Her expression changes, and for just an instant, I think she is about to cry.

"What do you mean?" I say. "What do you mean, that's where you are now? With who?"

"With you," she says. "Who else?"

The veil drops fully away. I see it all, see her in a thousand sidelong glances, simple smiles, those long sincere looks that only spoke—or so I thought—of genuine affection, platonic, uncomplicated.

"Me?"

"Of course, with you." She shakes her head, her lock of blonde hair bobbing. She brushes it away from her eyes. "It's not any *big news*," she laughs. "I've wanted to spend more than a little time with you ever since we met —"

"That was years ago," I say, sounding mildly doubtful.

"True," she says. "But I've always thought of you as more than a good friend."

I teeter on the brink of something beyond my range of understanding, swinging between elation and a kind of giddy fear that something is terribly wrong, or going to go that way. Nonetheless, I smile and lean back casually. "Danielle," I hear myself saying, "we *are* more than good friends. We're best friends. But let's not —" I lean forward "—let's not fuck up a good friendship with sex."

I let the words hang in the air, then tilt way back in my chair, balancing it on two legs, back away from the table. I feel as though there is no earth beneath me.

"What are you afraid of?" she asks.

"Afraid?" I sit back down. "Are you kidding? I'm not afraid. I'm pretty floored, actually. But don't you think—I mean, don't you feel—that there's an incompatibility issue here?" My formality makes me feel guilty before the words are out of my mouth.

"Incompatibility? How do you mean?"

"Like your *boyfriend*, for instance." I smirk, but I know my eyes betray something different.

"He knows," she says. "He's known I'm bi from day one."

"So what if you told him you were going to run off with another woman? Could he handle it? I mean, would you still be friends? Would you still want to be? Or would he? I mean, seriously, don't you feel like this is something you should think through?"

"He already knows all about you," she says quietly. "I told him."

"You told him about me? Told him what?"

A pause. "That I lusted after you in my heart." She looks up at me again, grinning.

I laugh. "Oh, that's good. That's just great." I shake my head, smiling, and try to picture him as she says such a thing. Cripes. "So where do we go from here, Ms. Lust-In-Your-Heart? Eh?" I laugh again.

"I don't know," she says. "But I absolutely don't want this to ruin our friendship."

I lean forward. "I don't either." I touch her hand across the table. "And I hate to say it, but I think for now we had better not even think about being anything more than friends. And I really do hate to say that."

I give her a look she seems to understand, but it's hard to be sure. I want to spare her feelings, knowing at the same time that my own feelings for her are so strong I almost cannot bear ignoring them. I know that, for her sake, we can be nothing more than friends. I have to stand by that; my conscience will not allow it to be any other way. And yet....

"This is just too surreal," I say.

"What?" She looks momentarily bemused, blue eyes twinkling.

"This whole conversation." I wave my hand in the air, as if a simple gesture could somehow embrace or define, *confine* the situation. Or make it disappear.

"Well, at any rate, it certainly got your mind off Wendy Simpson, didn't it?"

We both burst out laughing so loud that people at other tables in the café look at us.

"Jesus Christ," I say and shake my head, looking into those blue blue eyes. "Jesus Christ Almighty."

"Listen," she says. "I think I know how you feel. You don't have to say anything more."

"I won't." And I smile a little smile at her.

"It could be so great, Jana," she says.

"Sto-o-op," I say, laughing through the word. *Staaahp.*

"I'm sorry. You're right. Let's just not talk about it, and then it won't be an issue. Okay?"

"Okay."

"Really."

"It won't be an issue."

"Right."

"Right," I say.

A pause. "Not!" she says, loudly, and cracks up again, while people at nearby tables look and look away.

Chapter 12

AND YET IT would have been easy that day to get myself back down to earth if I'd only thought for a moment of Sybil Gerard.

I read an article in some magazine at the doctor's office last week about biodiversity and exemptionalism, which, as I understand it, is basically the opposite of environmentalism, and it basically said that we, as a species, are rapidly making ourselves extinct—mainly by squandering our natural resources. When I read the article, I thought of Sybil Gerard, who found a much faster way of squandering her own resources: crack cocaine. She managed to do some serious damage in a very short time.

Among the many underprivileged parents I met at Kiddie Korner, Sybil Gerard's case was the most wrenching. She lived the streets, knew the streets, worked the streets. She *was* the streets. I didn't know she was an addict when I met her, but I instinctively disliked and mistrusted her. She struck me as very tough, but somehow always on the defensive; if I'd thought about it long enough, I would have said she seemed defiant, though what she defied in the first place I couldn't have told you for all the yachts in Old Lyme.

At one point, she lived in an apartment, not on the streets or in a shelter. She'd had to get off welfare and get a job, and her daughter Cherise—who was not yet a ward of the state—was at Kiddie Korner. I was still pretty green, still in my visiting-parents-at-home stage, which was never recommended protocol, but it just so happened I'd gotten away with it in the cases of Harmony Stone and Carlos Pareja. I just couldn't help caring about those kids, more than I should have.

I went to visit Sybil after I'd heard through the grapevine that she was going to pull Cherise out of daycare. I knew that somebody like Sybil was driven to extremity of some kind or other, and given her history, it sounded downright drastic. So I went over.

Sybil lived in the north end of Hartford, in an area usually described simply as "a bad neighborhood." To my way of thinking it was, and still is, a ghetto. Now, that word may have some sort of loaded racial stereotype connotations for some people, but for me, whether you call it a slum, a barrio, the projects, or a ghetto, it's all the same: every imaginable sign of poverty is manifest. Sybil's place sat on the edge of "Dumpster Village," and I was nervous even going there at one in the afternoon on a Saturday. The fact that I didn't know whether she'd be home at all heightened my apprehension. First, of course, I had to find the place, and that was a nightmare in itself.

I approached the apartments nervously. Some pretty ugly customers hung around the front steps, black and Hispanic kids in muscle shirts and shorts, all with dark or mirrored sunglasses and pierced noses or eyebrows. One of them wore a shirt with the word NIGGA spelled out in about the biggest letters you can imagine. He spoke to me first as I approached, following a whispered conference with his buddies.

"Heeeyy, pretty lady," he said, "what you doin' *up*town? Slummin'?"

His buddies cackled.

"I'm here to see a friend of mine, Homey," I said drily. "Excuse me." I made a move to pass him, but he stepped in front of me. I tried to look merely annoyed without betraying any fear, and sighed.

"Heeeyy," he said, "you say that shit to me real familiar-like. Do you *know* me from somewhere?" He leered at his friends, and they laughed some more.

"I sure as hell don't think so," I said. "Now, if you'll excuse me —"

"What's the hurry, what's the hurry?" he purred. "Let's talk."

He'd made a move to touch my shoulder, and I shrugged his hand away, furious now. "Don't fuck with me, junior, or I'll have your head on a stick. Excuse me." I pushed him aside and headed for the cement skips. My heart pounded like it was trying to escape my chest.

"Ooh," said the others, and "Man, she dissed you, Irving."

"Bitch," he said under his breath. He turned away.

"Hey, who you goin' to see?" asked one of the others. "Maybe I can help you find him."

"Her," I said. "I'm going to see a her. And I don't think you clowns could find your asses with both hands."

"Ooh," they said in unison.

"They's only one bitch here, and that's Sybil," one of them said quietly.

I turned back. "Who?"

"Sybil," he repeated.

"Sybil Gerard?"

"You got the wrong building," he said.

"Well, which one is it?"

He looked at me coolly, sizing me up. "What you want with Sybil?"

"I need to talk to her."

He came closer, lowering his voice again as he did so, looking left and right. "You wanna cop?"

"Do I want a cop? No. Why should I need a cop?"

"No, do you *want to cop*?" he asked. He was right in front of me, my face level with his chest.

"No," I said. It dawned on me that he was talking about drugs. I felt naïve, in over my head, way, way over my head. "No," I repeated, "I just want to talk to her."

He seemed to sense something. "Well, that's good," he said. His tone had changed. "That's real good. She the middle door in that building." He pointed to my left with a bony finger.

"Thank you," I said. I felt about four years old as I walked away from them, my heart thudding.

I knocked on Sybil's storm door three times. Rap rap rap. No answer. I tried again. Rap rap. Still no answer. I was about to walk away, thinking maybe she was out or asleep, but my self-consciousness about the boys across the way, the weight of their eyes boring into me as I stood there, made me give the door a final rap with my knuckles. When I did, the inner door jerked open a crack. I almost leaped off the steps.

"Who is it?" demanded a voice.

"It's Jana Odessi," I said loudly, trying to make myself heard through the thin plexiglass of the outer door. "Jana, from Kiddie Korner." A bad silence, long and ominous.

"What you want?" the voice said petulantly.

"I want to speak to Sybil Gerard." I was not yet certain this was Sybil on the other side.

The inner door swung open to reveal a gaunt white female form with greasy black hair in a sort of pageboy cut, dark circles under the eyes. It was Sybil all right. "*Who* are you?" she asked.

"I'm Jana," I said. "Jana Odessi. From Kiddie Korner…?"

She glared at me.

"May I come in?"

"Yeah, all right." She moved back, eyeing me, sullen and suspicious. "What are you doin' here?"

I looked around briefly and wondered the same thing. What was I doing in such a place? It was probably just a little sicker than it looked, and it looked unhealthy. The room was stifling, a bad smell in the air, a combination of cheap macaroni and cheese, instant soup, and the smell of a mildewy bathroom. For a moment the sick feeling I got from the atmosphere made me forget why I *had* come there.

"I don't know," I mumbled. It occurred to me that I had just gotten a wicked head rush, and the blood that had gone to my head slowly drained back down into the rest of my body. I felt almost dizzy. "I, uh…I wanted to talk to you." My head began to clear.

"You did," she said matter-of-factly. "About what?" She folded her arms across her chest.

I looked her dead in the face, and at that moment, I knew she was under the influence of something, which couldn't be good. Without thinking, I continued on. "I wanted to talk to you about your daughter."

"Not much to talk about," she said. "She only a baby. She ain't big enough to do nothin' bad."

"No, no," I said, holding up one hand. "I didn't mean like that. I was just concerned that, well, I just heard that you might be considering pulling Cherise out of daycare."

"You think I don't know how to take care of my daughter? Is that it? That about right?" She stepped toward me.

"No," I said again, "I didn't mean to imply that at all. I just —"

"I'm too messed up to have her, huh? Like maybe, we should get DCYS in here? Look at this." She showed me her arms: needle scars.

"I know you've been through a lot," I began.

"You don't know shit about it." She moved toward the door, as if to shut it, or to leave.

I floundered. "Look. You're very sick. You need help. If we could maybe find a way to get you into a treatment center —"

She exploded. "I'm not gonna join some goddamn *cult* just to get everybody off my back! Get outta my way."

"Listen," I said, "I'm sorry. I'm sorry. I didn't mean to —"

"Get out of my house," she whispered hoarsely. "Just get your ass out of my house right this goddamn minute."

She stood in front of the open door now, gesturing with one hand toward the entryway. Her hair hung in her eyes and her breasts heaved from the effort of yelling. Her hand shook, just a bit.

I looked at her for a moment in silence, her blotchy face and bony hands. Then I looked into her eyes, and they were the eyes of a dead woman. I knew I was defeated.

"Goodbye," I said quietly.

She studied me without saying a word, still pointing toward the front steps, and shaking, her ragged breath the only noise in the room. I walked back into bright sunlight and the door slammed behind me.

Tillie

Chapter 13

ARE YOU LISTENING to me? Okay. It's like this: I got a fifteen-year-old daughter wanted to have an abortion, see? Well, she told me about it instead of just going out and doing it, which is good, but I didn't feel like that bit of comfort was going to be enough to *sustain* me for long, you know? And I couldn't exactly tell her I'm an expert on being a single parent, because Darlene's old man did marry me when he found out I was pregnant. Of course, he split three years later, but that was the longest three years of my life.

Still, I got to say Darlene had been with this boy a long time, almost two years, which is one hell of a long time in the life of a teenager, and he *is* pretty damned responsible for a seventeen-year-old boy—though apparently not responsible enough to take certain precautions on a consistent basis. The fact of the matter was, I wasn't comfortable with telling her I don't approve of the abortion idea, but couldn't make myself tell her anything but that it was her body, and ultimately had to be her decision.

And to tell you the truth—much as I hate to admit it—I couldn't help but think that somewhere in the back of her mind was this idea that she had to "break the cycle," so to speak, because, after all, I was only eighteen when I had her. And although we've always had the best relationship, she knows that it put certain limitations on me, and that it required a pretty superhuman effort on my part, for example, to get my Master's in Social Work, what with raising her all alone. I didn't know if that kind of fear preyed on her, but it did bother me, especially if that was why she said she didn't want the baby. I mean, she was already referring to it as *the baby*, for God's sake, it wasn't like she was thinking in terms of an eight-week fetus. At least it sure didn't sound like that.

So I got all this stuff in my head already, and then along comes this girl at the center: Jana, her name is. And wouldn't you know, she reminds me of Darlene so much, it just about breaks my heart. She's a white girl, in her early twenties, but she's still got that free and crazy sort of openness and self-confidence that always made Darlene such a joy in my life up until her pregnancy. Darlene got damn quiet with the abortion thing weighing on her mind.

I knew I was going to hire this Jana Odessi as soon as I interviewed her, but I didn't feel like I could show my positive reaction right away. So I stood looking out the window, which probably made her nervous, and then suddenly and very deliberately I just kind of whirl around and hit her with, "Are you *sure* you want to work here?"

She looks at me, real shocked-like, but trying to maintain her composure, and I almost burst out laughing and blow the whole thing. All I can think is that the next words out of her mouth are gonna be, "Are you *serious,* lady? Are you for real?" Instead, she just looks at me very serious—like a curtain came down over her eyes or something—and she says, "Absolutely. I'm sure."

I was thinking about all this stuff last night when I was heading home from my evening jog. Now, don't think I'm a fitness nut just because I mention it, but I did start jogging a couple of years ago—not because I wanted to, but because the doctor said my cholesterol level was too high and I wasn't eating enough cruci-ferous vegetables and a lot of other malarkey which somebody with a doctorate probably just sits around dreaming up to scare people who like cheesecake. But anyway, Okay, I said, I'll lay off the sweets, and I got me a nice pair of sweatpants and practically a guarantee from the saleswoman that I'd be able to put on a bikini the following year and not look like a Cadbury egg with two rubber bands on it. But it's been a long, slow, uphill battle, and even last night I felt my little jelly belly jiggling around as I was crunching through the fallen leaves on the sidewalk along Stanley Street.

I was looking at all those windows I always see at night with the blue light in them. That's gotten to me more and more since I started running, those blue-light houses. I guess it always bothered me some, knowing about the kids out there, even the ones who aren't as "disadvantaged" as some of the ones at Kiddie Korner, sitting there at home with that damn box blaring away at them day and night, filling their heads with all kinds of nonsense, while they *could* be reading stories or building with blocks, playing dress-up or hide and seek. It's sad, that blue light. It's got to be about the saddest light in the world. The only thing sadder, maybe, is the way it looks in the windows of lonely old folks who don't have a friend in the world, not even a companion, nothing but that damn blue light in the window, and a skinny old dog, maybe.

I try not to think about any of that stuff when I'm out jogging, because I want to be thinking positive, and especially thinking about the positive things jogging has done for me. One of the best is it's helped me lose weight. I looked down at that scale one day and saw that, sure enough, I'd lost three pounds. Now, when you're my size, three pounds may not seem like a whole lot, but at that point, I was so overjoyed to see some results other than a sore back, stiff calves, and soaking sweatpants, I just about cried.

After a while, I started to notice other benefits, too, like when I came back from a run, I seemed to have a sort of a heightened sense of awareness. I'd trudge into the apartment, gasping loudly after those three flights of stairs, a pounding pulse in my ears like crazy drums, my face wet with perspiration. I would have to sit down right away, and my cat Taft (named after the president, shaped like her owner) would always come sniffing around me.

At first, I'd get nervous when she did that, since she went right for the shoes, and I'd think, Oh no, did I step in something I didn't want to step in? But after a while, I realized she'd go for the shoes no matter what; she was just sniffing whatever there was to sniff, and being a housecat like she was, it could have been a little bit of a leaf, a speck of mud, or a blade of grass.

And then I'd get into the shower and really blast myself good with hot water until the steam rose up into my face like steam from a warm apple pie on a winter's day…maybe better. I'd put this lilac bath oil I got on a big loofah sponge and just rub myself down real slow and thoughtful, trying to soothe myself down and hoping I hadn't pulled a muscle or anything. And I'd think to myself, Damn, it has been one hell of a long time since you had a man, girl. And I'd smile and think, Well, that's all right. You're all right just the same.

That may sound a little improper, talking about showering and all, and it sure would have shocked my grandmother thirty years ago, but the way I figure it, folks all do it—bathe, that is—and if they don't, then they've *really* got something to be ashamed of. But I don't worry about mentioning people being naked or whatever anymore, no more than I worry about their love life.

Which brings me back to Jana. Now, if you're like me, you probably assume that people are straight unless they tell you otherwise. I mean, I don't make any assumptions on purpose about people, but if their behavior is pretty bizarre I might start to wonder. I guess what I'm trying to say, without digging myself any deeper, is that I don't think about a person's sexual orientation unless they give me some reason to, so I guess that if they *don't* give me one, then I'm pretty much operating under the assumption that they're straight. Not that it's any of my business.

So I made that assumption with Jana, and since she didn't mention it, I never gave it a thought. With her, I mostly thought about the fact that I'm only about nine or ten years older than her, and that she made a good contrast to Wendy Simpson, who's very pretty, and good with the kids, but kind of an airhead. I mean, she's pleasant enough, don't get me wrong. Real bubbly, I guess you could say. But still kind of an airhead. Well, Jana's very sharp, which is an obvious contrast, and not ugly by any means, but not pretty in the way that will turn heads like Wendy Simpson.

I guess what got me started on this is just thinking about Jana, and all she went through because of her sexual orientation, and the fact is, I just miss her. I mean, it's not like she's been gone from the center all that long, but I do miss her. And I got to thinking about her today because I was passing Carlos Pareja's place and I remembered having been there with Jana when she was new at Kiddie Korner.

She says to me one day, just like it was just casual, you know, she says, "Hey, Tillie, what's it like to be a black woman in your position?"

I was standing on a ladder trying to fix a heating duct, so I look down at her real serious and say, "You mean, what's it like to be a black woman standing on a ladder?"

She laughs and looks embarrassed. "No, no," she says, "I mean, seriously, what's it like to be a black woman in a position of authority? Do you think it's less positive for you than what people would assume?"

"I don't know. I think that, since I don't know what it's like to be any other sort of woman, being black doesn't seem to have much to do with it. But maybe I'm just kidding myself. Maybe my race makes the responsibility even bigger in my head than it ought to be. It hasn't helped the paycheck get bigger, that's for sure."

She smiles, and I smile back.

"At least it keeps me motivated to do a good job."

She laughs. "I probably shouldn't say things like that to my boss, huh?"

"Honey, just because I'm the supervisor doesn't mean we don't talk to each other like human beings. After all, we are *all sistuhs*." I make a fist with my thumb tucked in at an angle, the old "power to the people" sign, and she giggles.

"You crack me up," she says. "You said that just like what's-her-name in *Gone with the Wind* would have said it."

"Ole mammy?" I say this in my best "yes, massah" voice. "Chile, that woman was the classic white person's idea of a gooood nigga."

A pause. Jana looks serious. "Hey, what is the deal with that word, anyway? Did it suddenly become cool again a few years ago? I always learned it was something *never* to say, but I hear black people using it all the time, like it's no big deal."

Very broadly, I say, "That's *African-American* people to *you*, child."

"I'm sorry," she says, "African-American."

I laugh. "I'm just kidding. I don't know what it is with that word. People banned *Huckleberry Finn* from schools for that word, but it sure gets a lot of harmless usage. I don't hear too many white guys using it, though."

"Ah, that's *Caucasian*," Jana says. Her voice is serious, but when I glance down, she's trying hard to keep a straight face, and I laugh and laugh. Almost fall off the ladder, too.

"Careful," she says, also laughing. "Careful, Miz Tillie." That's how I like to remember her. Laughing, looking up at me with that crazy grin, and saying, "Careful, Miz Tillie."

Chapter 14

I GUESS SHE had a tough row to hoe from the start, that Jana. She came from a family where there wasn't a whole lot of talk about problems, she told me, and it kind of made me wonder exactly what sort of problems there were. Maybe that's a natural reaction for someone in my line of work, and I like to think it's reasonable as a general rule, and that I don't automatically assume the worst, but I don't know. Maybe sometimes I do.

I got to thinking about her and her family one night, shortly after she started at the center, and I started to worry. She'd said something about family that triggered a memory from therapy, way back in my twenties. It had to do with that 'Don't Talk' rule that seemed to show up in so many families I knew growing up, my own included. Whenever one of those things that we *really* needed to talk about came up, my old man would always break out a Duke Ellington record, or start a conversation about Uncle Joe's thrombosis; anything to change the subject fast and get everybody thinking—or pretending to think—about something else.

I got the feeling that, at Jana's house, a profound silence reigned, the kind of silence that takes over in a house where family secrets are so well-protected that no one even talks to himself or herself about them except for a few moments at a time, maybe, feeling guilty or disloyal somehow for doing even that.

And then I started to wonder whether she'd been abused maybe as a child. Not sexually, necessarily, or even physically, although I wouldn't rule that stuff out, but emotionally, at least. It wasn't until I found out she was a lesbian that I started to imagine the way it must have been for her, with her parents never really outright rejecting her, but by their very silence making her feel somehow defective, or a source of family shame or disappointment at least, that she didn't quite measure up. I couldn't say I even *knew* all this, really, only that I felt it must be close to the truth. And so I was scared for her.

I didn't find out about her sexual orientation right away, of course. When I did find out, it made sense that she hadn't trusted me at first. I thought to myself, Would you tell *your* supervisor if you were? And I said, Hell, no, what possible reason could I have?

But Jana had this little falling-out with Wendy Simpson over hairstyles or some foolish thing, and it had all come out. So she said she needed to talk to me about something personal. Words to that effect. She didn't make any apologies, and she seemed to want to impress upon me that she didn't think it had any bearing whatsoever on what kind of job she did at the center.

I agreed, but at the same time, I was quick to caution her against telling other people, because they might try to use it against her. I mentioned I'd have a talk with Wendy before I made any decision as to whether someone was owed an apology. I also told her I'd make sure Wendy understood that any discussion of other employees' sexual proclivities was inappropriate. In other words, it was something spoken about between the two of them and should not go any further. Jana seemed concerned about working with Wendy, and I assured her I'd keep them as separate as possible for the time being and maybe longer, and then I mentioned that our own conversation would be strictly confidential, and that was that.

But of course that was only the beginning, and it's only now, looking back at the whole thing, that can I see how all these events eventually got woven together like some big tapestry. It wasn't just this crazy random stuff happening, which was what it felt like, the way life tends to do, you know.

Around this time, when Jana was just starting at the center, we got in a little girl named Ashley who had two real gems for parents, Paul and Jeanette Robeson, and they were rich folks. Not that there's anything wrong with folks being rich, it's just that these two weren't just rich folks, they were snobby rich folks. I think they were the only people I've ever had come into the center who not only asked about my educational background but specifically asked what school I went to.

"Where exactly did you *receive* your Master's degree, Ms. Jones?"

I wanted to break out an emery file and sit back in the chair, studying it off-handedly and say, "Actually, it wasn't conferred upon me. Ah stole it from some dumb rich cracker in Queens!" But of course, I could do nothing of the kind. In fact, I had to try to keep up my most professional demeanor and smile through it all, while I was thinking things like, "Lily-white yuppie scum," and "I hope your child hasn't learned too much from you, because if she hasn't, there's still hope for her." They treated me with a very phony reserve, the kind that has *bigot* stamped all over it, like they were probably going to go wash their hands right after shaking mine.

I mention the Robesons because they played a big part in what happened to Jana, and it wouldn't make any sense to go on without talking some about the particulars. I just want to paint as accurate a portrait of them as I can. Paul Robeson was a tall man, kind of good-looking, I guess, in an Ivy League sort of way. He had terrible taste in clothes though, for someone with money. He used to wear these long plaid shorts, like something you'd see some Scottish guy wearing on the golf course, just real nerdy and old-mannish.

His wife wasn't much better. She had a real starched-and-pressed look to her, like butter wouldn't melt in her mouth, you know, real swanky and exclusive-like. Like you expected her to say *dahling* a lot.

They invited me to tea one day, not long after Ashley started at the center. I had a good look at part of the living room and all of the kitchen while Jeanette prepared coffee and tea that she carried over on a little silver tea tray. The house was incredible, a big Cape Cod with a lawn like that "astro" stuff they have on football fields, and about the biggest hedges I've ever seen. I always liked nice trimmed suburban hedges—they seem real friendly or something to me—but I didn't like these. They were too big and perfect, sculpted into this weird big block like a fence, that obscured most of the house from view, which was obviously the intent.

The inside was fancy, too, from what I saw, because I didn't see all that much. I mean, they didn't give me that nice informal "nickel tour" so many regular people give you when you come to their house the first time. Of course, theirs would've cost a dollar.

Still, the house didn't seem unlived-in, like some rich folks. In the kitchen, there was a small walnut desk with three drawers and, on top, a knitted pincushion embellished with "Give us this day our daily bread." The refrigerator was covered with red and blue magnets and photographs and news articles. I noticed a small figurine of a doe, a breadboard with two swans on it, an antique lamp, green with black florets painted on it, high-backed wooden chairs, a calendar with a boy and girl Hummel kissing, and a framed wall hanging with the inscription "A house is made of brick, but a home is made of love." Some of it wasn't even that expensive— like the Hummel calendar, which couldn't have cost much more than ten dollars—but overall, there was a real palpable sense of something cold and dead, but still having to do with money—kind of a wealthy sterility, if that makes sense.

Jeanette came in with the tea, made a fuss over mine—I did not, and will not, take milk or sugar in mine, so the fuss was over pretty quick—and then went to the window and waved at her husband, real cheery, to get his attention. I don't know why she didn't just open up a window or door and call him in the first place, but she didn't. She stood there and waved her arms, but he didn't see her, so eventually she rapped on the window with the middle joints of her fingers, the way people rap on a door that might be heavier than it looks, and she motioned to him to come on in.

He sat down, a bit heavily. "Well," he said, "this is sort of a nice little interlude for a late Sunday afternoon, isn't it?" He smiled at me, almost charming, but I could tell it was forced.

"It was very nice of you to invite me," I said in my most diplomatic tones. "You have a lovely home."

"Thank you," Jeanette said.

Paul smiled greyly, looking complacent as he leaned back in the chair a little. "It was my father's," he said. "He was in securities."

"Oh, goodness. I hope he wasn't involved in all that S&L business. I don't know too much about money."

"No, no," he said lightly. "He died about five years before all of that. Colon cancer."

"I'm very sorry."

He waved it away. "That's fine. He was long overdue. Actually, to be truthful, the old bastard had it coming to him." He laughed, a hard dry bark.

"I'm sorry to hear that. You must have had it pretty tough."

"Not really," he said. "He was just a ruthless son of a bitch. All good business people are. Heartless. He wasn't mean to *us*."

I glanced at his wife, her face blank and trance-like. She looked just past me, almost my way but mostly out the window.

"Anyway," Paul continued, "we didn't invite you here to talk about my old man. What we really wanted was to have a chat about the center. Maybe find out a bit more about where our little girl is spending so much of her time." He smiled hard, turning up the charm, and his tone did a total one-eighty from when he'd talked about his father.

You really are full of shit, my friend, I thought. Just what is your angle? To him, though, I said, "Well, that's understandable, and it's certainly considerate of you to have asked *me*." Two could play at this game. "One thing that occurs to me, though, is that Barbara probably gave you two quite a lot of information already. Did you have any particular concerns, just so I'm not giving you redundant information?"

"Well, of course, we went through a whole *seminar* with her, for goodness' sake," Jeanette smiled. "She answered many, many questions, and in fact, came up with quite a number of things we wouldn't have thought of ourselves. So we know all about the safety issues, and all the procedures, and the enrichment and recreational activities. I think that Paul and I were thinking more of looking at the…minutiae. Not that we want to hold up a magnifying glass to the center, but—well, we wanted to make sure, for Ashley's sake, that we took a look at some of the more subtle issues. Staffing, for example."

I must have looked confused. "All right," I said evenly.

"What Jeanette means," said Paul, "is that we want to have a better idea of *who* is working with Ashley on a day-to-day basis as her primary caregiver. Who those people are, and what they're all about, what their backgrounds are, maybe, if that isn't proprietary information. We both want to feel comfortable that person upholds the same *values* we do. You understand." And again he smiled his charming snake smile.

"All right," I repeated. "What exactly did you have in mind— just a basic overview from me, or did you have some specific questions prepared?"

"Mainly, as Paul was saying, we'd like information on the girls working there. Not to pick on any one person, but let's say I wanted to find out more about the young woman I met at the tea. Jana, I believe?"

"Oh, sure, Jana Odessi. She's relatively new. *Very* nice."

A curtain seemed to fall over her eyes. "Well," she said, "she seemed very pleasant, but kind of…unusual."

"How do you mean?"

"Well, she said something about the two of us being from the same types of neighborhoods. Actually, she seemed to think we had a lot in common, but I'm not sure how she would have *known* something like that…." Her voice trailed off, as if she'd lost her train of thought momentarily. "In any event, she was very sure to point out something to me about the cultural diversity among children at the center, and I'm not certain why. But she seemed to take great pleasure in doing it."

Hmm, I thought. That is unusual. "Well," I said, "she's quite proud, apparently, of that aspect of the Center. It is a positive thing, we think, that not all of the children are *black*, for example, or *white*." I gestured toward myself and toward them, respectively, but they looked blank. "Either way, I'm sure you'd feel confident having her work with Ashley if you saw her in action with the children. She's very good, very professional. In fact, it would be great if you could come in and spend an hour or two with us."

Jeanette nodded slowly. "I suppose my main concern with her is that she seems somewhat —" she searched for the right word, her hand in the air "— well, somewhat masculine, I guess you could say."

"Masculine?"

"Maybe that's not right. She reminds me of a girl I used to know in boarding school who played field hockey. She's not—I mean…well, you wouldn't happen to know whether she has any boyfriends, would you?"

"No, I wouldn't," I said, taken aback. "I'm not sure I understand where this is going."

"Well. I'd just like to feel that I can assess the situation accurately, really, that's all."

"But I'm not sure how something like Jana's boyfriends, or the lack of them, would be germane to our conversation."

"Well," she said again, and now she looked very cagey, "I can see where you wouldn't be aware of whether she's ever even had boyfriends." She smiled falsely.

"Well, yes," I said. "Exactly."

"But then again, if she—and I'm not saying she is, or, or even could be, but if—if she were one of those types who never had boyfriends because she didn't like men...*you* see what I mean. Wouldn't the center know that?" She smiled again.

"I don't think we would, necessarily," I said slowly. "I don't think it would be an issue. We don't screen employees with questions based on sexual orientation."

"Why on earth not?" she asked, now openly alarmed.

"Well, there was legislation, actually, passed some time ago, which prevents us from asking that sort of question on a job application. But in any event, we've never asked such a thing of potential employees." I looked back and forth between them. Her face strained to compose itself, his shifted into an expressionless mask.

"But in a daycare center, for goodness' sake," she said, her voice trailing off.

"I'm sorry to be the bearer of bad news but legally, and logistically, it's a non-issue. In fact, I read that there's a daycare center somewhere in Massachusetts entirely for the children of lesbian mothers. And I would presume it's staffed by lesbians, although I don't know for sure."

"That doesn't seem possible."

I shrugged and worked hard to look sympathetic. "Times have changed. But that wasn't what you wanted to talk to me about, was it? Whether or not we might have lesbians at the center?"

I directed the question to Jeanette, but Paul leaned forward in his chair. "Well, it's a concern. That is, if you had someone like that at the center, we would certainly not be comfortable having that person be with Ashley on an ongoing basis."

"As I said, I don't know that it's something I would be aware of. I mean, no one's ever come to me and said, 'Tillie, so-and-so's a lesbian.'"

"So," Jeanette said, "you're saying that no one there is?"

"I didn't say that," I said. "I'm just saying that I have no need to discuss my employees' sexual proclivities."

"Well, then, do you know whether you have any there?"

Shit, I thought. I knew she had me. If I said I didn't know, I'd be lying. If I said no, there aren't any, I'd be lying. And if I said yes, there are, it would be disastrous. The silence felt unbearable.

Very carefully, I said, "I don't presume to say that we do or don't have any lesbians at Kiddie Korner. What I do say is that I feel it's inappropriate for me to have discussions with employees about their personal lives, and that it's just as inappropriate to discuss those kinds of subjects with other people. I just don't feel it's any of my business." Sweat trickled down my forehead.

Her eyes narrowed. "It sounds to me like you're covering up for someone."

"I don't have anything to hide." I smiled and pulled out my handkerchief, trying to look casual as I patted my brow. "The law prevents us from asking employees about these issues, as I mentioned, and frankly, there's probably only one person at the center who might take the initiative to circumvent the law."

"Barbara Helms?"

"Barbara Helms, yes. She's the director. And I certainly don't think she'd do that."

There was a silence. "Well," said Jeanette. "If there was a question of that sort, she might be the best source of information as to how to proceed."

"She very well might," I said. "She has the authority."

A look passed between the two of them, but I couldn't quite decipher it.

"So," she said, "how long have *you* been at the center?"

I answered that question, and a number of others, all equally harmless and superficial. Before long, I was on my way home, and not another word about Jana or about sexuality had fallen. I had an uneasy feeling about the way things had gone from a near-confrontation to nothing more than small talk. Mostly, though I hate to admit it, I just felt relief about being out of there, of not having to deal with them for another day. But part of me was alert enough to know that I had to warn Jana about these people.

Chapter 15

NOT LONG AFTERWARD, I had my little talk with Wendy Simpson. I'd been mulling it over for a few days, wondering what would be the best approach to letting Wendy know I'd already spoken to Jana. But then Wendy spared me the trouble.

She came in on a Monday morning. I sat in the office going over some paperwork when I heard the knock at the door.

"Come in."

"Morning," Wendy said.

"Good morning," I said. "How are you?"

"Okay. Can I talk to you for a minute?"

"Sure. What's on your mind?"

She looked around secretively. "Are we alone?"

"Yes," I said, surprised. It hadn't ever occurred to me to be concerned about someone overhearing any conversation I might have with another employee. "Pull up a chair."

"Thanks." She sat down in a chair opposite mine, looking nervous. "Tillie, I need to talk to you about a problem I'm having with one of our other employees." She gave a nervous laugh.

I held back, in case she was also having problems with someone else. "What happened?" I asked. "A disagreement with someone?"

"I'll say." She tittered nervously again. "I don't wanna make a big deal out of this, but…well, I'm really more worried about the children than anything else. That's why I had to tell you."

"Maybe you'd better start at the beginning," I said.

"Well. It all started when we were having a little talk about fashion —"

I stopped her in midstream. "Would you mind telling me who this is?"

She sighed. "It's Jana." She looked at the floor.

"All right," I said. "Go on."

"The thing is, it's not like we were having some big argument. I mean, I think we were just talking about *hair* or something."

"Mm-hm."

She looked up and when our eyes met, the light went on in hers. "She already talked to you?"

"That's all right. I want to hear both sides of the story," I said.

She sighed. "What a relief," she said. "Did she tell you…I mean, well…you know, did she tell you what she said to me?"

"Wendy, just tell me your side as best you can, and I'll think it all over. I'm not going to tell her any of what you say, or tell you any of what she said. So don't concern yourself with that. I just want the truth as near as you can recall."

"Okay, let's see." She was almost breathless. "We were talking about hair. And I said, 'You should get a perm, Jana.' Not to be mean or anything like that, but just to make her look more professional. That was how I put it, I think." She seemed to think about it. "Yes. Professional, that was what I said."

"Oookaaay…."

"And she got so ticked off! And she says, 'Well, who do you think you are, little Miss Priss? I don't need any fashion advice from *you.*' And then she told me—I know I'm not remembering exactly how she said everything, or exactly what *I* said, but—well, anyway, she said she was a—she said—said she—I don't want to even *say* it!" She buried her face in her hands.

"It's all right, sweetheart." I touched her arm gently as I leaned over. "Just tell me."

"I don't wanna get anybody in trouble," she said between her fingers.

"Don't worry about that. Nobody's in trouble. Just tell me."

She put her hands down, her face streaked with tears, and looked me in the eye. "She said she was a *lesbian*." Right like that, she says it, all the fear and rage and hatred in her eyes and voice. I could see she was trembling ever so slightly.

"Mm-hm." I nodded. I was almost enjoying myself.

"Well," she said, "what are we going to do?"

I leaned back again and crossed my arms. "We're going to keep you two apart for a while," I said. "And soon, down the road, we'll have to sit down together and have a little talk to help figure out what you both can do to get along with each other a little bit better."

"B-but—what about the kids?"

"What about them, Wendy?"

"Well, I mean, aren't you concerned, I mean, I don't mean she would harm them intentionally, of course, but just to be on the safe side, I mean —"

"Wendy," I cut in, "I don't think Jana's sexuality is an issue in relation to what she does here." My dander was up now. "I don't think it's a work issue, I don't think it's a safety issue, and for that matter, I don't think it's a morality issue. It's a *non-issue*. The only issues here are a conflict between the two of you, and how to resolve that, and the fact that what went on between you is to go no further than yourselves, and this room. That much is clear, I think?"

She nodded sullenly.

"That's good," I said. "I don't think discussions of this nature are appropriate among other employees. It's a personal matter. And because of Jana's situation with you, we need to be aware that this could be a sore spot with her. Now, I don't want you to have to be thinking about it all the time, so I would suggest you avoid speaking with her about it. And of course, I'm going to keep an eye on your schedule and hers. All right?"

"Sure," she said, falsely bright.

"Good," I said. "We'll talk about it again later."

"Okay," she said. There did not seem to be much else to say.

"Thanks, Wendy," I said, rising to dismiss her. "I'll be talking to you."

"Okay," she said. "Bye." And she was out the door.

I didn't think much about it then, but her attitude was more than just the typical homophobic attitude of "grin and bear it" or "don't ask, don't tell." And the implication that "lesbian equals child molester" was so egregious that, in retrospect, maybe it should have occurred to me that she'd go over my head. But I never thought about it from her point of view, really, except maybe to imagine what it would be like to be bigoted in that way. Bigotry always appalled me so much, I guess, that I just shrank from it. I tried to think about something else, and tell myself it would all work out for the best. I never imagined the series of events that began after that little Monday morning conversation.

Chapter 16

ON THE DAY Barbara Helms called me into her office, I knew something was wrong. I had a feeling when I woke up that something bad was going to happen. Not that I'm psychic or anything like that, you know. I just get a bad feeling sometimes, and it seems to always be connected with some serious event. I guess I think of it as intuition.

I was carrying my newspaper back to the apartment, scanning the headlines, when this wave of fear came over me. The first person I thought of was my daughter. What if she'd miscarried? Or what if she was hurt? Or both?

But I knew somehow it wasn't her. Still, I called the school just to make sure when I got to the center, and she was awfully surprised to hear from *me*. I think she even accused me of being superstitious.

When Barbara Helms paged me on the speakerphone, that fear-feeling jumped back up in me out of nowhere. I knew it was something bad about to happen, and I thought, What if I'm going to be laid off? They'd already had to lay off one of the staff because of "budgetary constraints." It wasn't out of the question.

I walked into her office and tried to read her eyes. She might as well have been a mannequin, though, her face blank as a sheet of paper. I tried to smile as I gestured toward the chairs in front of her desk. "Shall I have a seat?"

"Please."

"What's up?" I said lightly.

She looked squarely at me. "We've got trouble."

"What happened?"

"I don't know how to tell you all this, so I'll just start from the beginning. You know the little girl named Ashley Robeson we have here?"

"Uh huh," I said. "Sure."

"You've met her parents."

"Oh, yes," I continued. "Jeanette and…Paul, I believe his name is."

"Exactly," she said, very business-like. "You remember meeting with them briefly several weeks ago?"

"Sure," I said, "I went to their house. Why?"

"Well," she said. "It seems they've uncovered a little problem with one of our employees." She paused, as if to weigh my response.

"A problem?"

"Yes. They've given me reason to believe that Jana Odessi is a lesbian."

In that moment, everything seemed to hang in the balance. I had no idea what Barbara's reaction would be to anything I said, other than the fact that she used the word *problem,* which made me speculate she would not exactly champion gay rights. I got scared, and all I could do—instead of feigning surprise or saying, "I know," or staying silent—was to repeat, "A lesbian."

"Yes," she said, looking beyond me to a point at some immeasurable distance. "She saw her with someone—I mean, she saw her with another woman."

My head swam. "Another woman?" Now I was determined to defend her. "That doesn't say much. Most women have women friends."

"I know, I know," she said. "But she saw them…together."

"What does that mean, together? What were they doing?"

"She saw them at a shop in Hartford. I guess they were leaving, and she saw them hug each other."

"So?"

"And kiss each other."

I bristled. "On the mouth?"

"I don't know," she said, exasperated. "I know it sounds nebulous, but Jeanette Robeson sounded pretty agitated."

"Who was the girl with her? Anyone we know?"

"No. No one from here. Jeanette Robeson described her as pretty blonde, with a short, 'punky' kind of hairdo."

"I'm sorry," I said, "but I don't see that hugging or even kissing some girl in a shop somewhere makes Jana a lesbian."

"Well," she cut in, "that's not all. I had a talk with one of our other employees yesterday about Jana. This is the other half of the story."

My heart froze. I didn't want to confirm or deny the conversation I'd had with Wendy Simpson. I was suddenly afraid of being caught in a lie, afraid more for my own security now than for Jana's, although I feel ashamed to admit it now.

"Okay," I said. "What's the rest of it?" I folded my arms.

"Apparently Wendy Simpson and Jana had a little falling out recently, and Wendy came to talk to me about it."

I looked at her, but she was not watching for my response. She fixed her eyes on a point on the wall beyond me. "Okay," I said. I guessed Wendy had not mentioned me to Barbara.

"And, according to Wendy, Jana told *her* she was a lesbian."

I continued to look at her, and when she finally did meet my eye, I gave her the most doubtful look I could. If there was ever a moment in my life when I actually appeared cynical, this was it.

"Look," she said after a short silence, "I know that Wendy is probably not the most reliable source of information. But I can't think why she would make something like this up, and the timing is just too much for it to be coincidental." She paused. "We've got a problem on our hands."

I shifted in my chair, abstractedly saying, "Wendy Simpson."

"Wendy Simpson," she said.

I looked at the floor. "I'm still not sure there's any *problem* here," I said carefully, "other than a perceived problem."

"Well, I don't want some big political thing going on that gets us into the news and brings Kiddie Korner a lot of notoriety for being 'the first daycare center in the state to have an openly gay staff member.'" A pause. "You see what I mean."

I didn't know how to answer, so all I said then was, "I'll talk to her." I think I wanted to convey that I'd make an attempt to alleviate the situation, and that talking it over with Jana might clear things up. But what I meant deep down was that I'd have to warn Jana to prepare for a witch-hunt.

"No, that won't be necessary," she said, and in that moment, I saw the curtain close down over her eyes. "I'll take care of it," she said. "I just wanted you to be aware of it. Okay?" It was not a question, but more of an, *Okay*, like, *That's that.*

"All right." I forced a smile. It occurred to me later that maybe, just then, she'd made her decision. "Is that all you wanted to see me about?"

"Pretty much." She shuffled some papers on her desk.

"Okay," I said, rising, "I'll talk to you later."

"Okay. Thanks, Tillie." She did not look up as I went out and closed the door quietly behind me.

I walked back to my office, the sound of children playing just beyond me. I closed my door behind me quietly, the way I had just closed Barbara Helms' door, and sat down behind my desk. "Damn," I said. "Damn it."

And then I began to cry.

Chapter 17

SO NOW I had to warn Jana about the Robesons and about this whole ugly situation. I didn't know what to say, or how she'd respond, but I felt the urgency. If she wanted to stay in the closet, I thought, now was probably a good time to do that.

She gave me two opportunities to talk to her, without even knowing it. The first time actually came on the same day I had my little talk with Barbara. It was late afternoon, almost time for the last of the parents to arrive for their kids, when Jana bounced into my office. She said something about recreational therapy for a young boy with a severe spinal disorder, and she was so obviously charged up about how much he was benefiting from it, I didn't have it in me to take the wind out of her sails. I resolved to tell her anyway, but my heart sank, and I realized I'd have to wait: let her have one more peaceful night, I thought.

The second time was the following day. I'd just gotten off the phone with my daughter, who had made an appointment with a counselor at the family planning center and needed to talk to me about that, and in came Jana again. I got a strange feeling when I saw her, almost like I was suddenly part of a script I hadn't written, and had no control over. It was a strange sensation, kind of like being in a dream. A lot like déjà vu, actually.

She started asking me some questions, and I answered them, the whole time feeling like I was repeating words I'd said before in a situation I'd gone through before. Of course, I'd just hung up with Darlene, who Jana reminded me of in so many ways, and now here was Jana in the flesh, obviously listening more carefully to me than I listened to myself.

Somewhere in there I managed to say, "I need to talk to you about something. Remind me when we're through."

And when we were through, she did remind me, and then I had to search for words again. "Jana," I said, "I don't know how to tell you this, so I'm just gonna tell you. Okay?"

"Okay," she said. She still stood by my desk, one hand on her hip.

"Have a seat."

She sat down. "What's up?"

I shook my head, looking at her. "I don't know," I said to myself aloud. "I just don't know." It seemed so unfair, all of it, I still didn't know where to begin.

"Well, what's happening that *I* need to know about?"

I sighed. "That's the question," I said, my fingertips tapping the desktop. "That is the question."

A mischievous smile crossed her face. "Didn't Shakespeare say that?"

"What?" I said. "Oh, yeah." I laughed a little. Dear God. "Well, anyway, I do need to talk to you, and it's about something that concerns you directly, yes."

"Have I done anything I shouldn't be doing?"

I laughed silently, without humor. "No, I wouldn't say that. No." Nothing other than being yourself, I thought. I've gotten into trouble for that a few times myself. Seems that sometimes people get really ticked off at you for the color of your skin, but I just go right on ahead wearing it anyway. "Do you remember our conversation about Wendy Simpson?"

"Yeah, sure," she said. "It was only a couple days ago."

I shrugged. "More or less. Listen: did I warn you at all about the Robesons?"

"Warn me? No. You've never 'warned' me about anybody. Why? Who are the Robesons?"

"*Ashley* Robeson's parents?" I prompted her.

She assumed a false British accent, mock snobbish. "Ah, yes, the Robesons?" She laughed. "What would I need to be warned about? Catching a cold from standing too close to 'em?" She laughed again, then stopped when she saw I was not smiling. "*What?*" she said. "What happened?"

"Look," I said, "Barbara called me in a couple of days ago and asked me about you. Apparently you met Jeanette Robeson at the tea. Do you remember that?"

"Yeah. I didn't tell her I was a *dyke*, though. Is that the problem?"

I nodded silently. "I think so."

"What did she say?"

"Barbara? Or Jeanette Robeson?"

"Either," she said, waving her hand. "Both."

"I don't know what the deal is with Jeanette. She supposedly saw you *with* someone. A friend of yours…."

She paled. "Danielle."

"Is that her name?'

"I don't know if she saw me with *her*. Did she mention short blonde hair?"

"Yes."

"Well, it *could* be. But so what? I mean, I'm sure she didn't see us slobbering on one another. Not that it's any of her business."

"No. But she did see you give her a hug."

"A hug? Jesus, Tillie, why should *that* be any big deal? I mean, I've gone to open A.A. meetings with my friend Roxanne and seen straight women *and* men hugging each other, for God's sake! A hug, holy Jesus." She shook her head and stared down at my desk.

"And a kiss," I said, embarrassed now to force the issue.

"I have never kissed Danielle Marshall on the mouth in my entire life…not yet, anyway."

"Whatever, whatever," I said, waving it away. "I don't want it to be a big deal either, Jana, I don't. I'm on your side here."

"Well, what did Barbara say? She's appalled, she's going to have me sent to the gas chambers, what? She wanna meet my friend?" She was furious now.

"She didn't say much. But she doesn't want some big political controversy for the center. She's very conservative, *very* conservative."

"Hmph." Jana forced a smile, biting her lip. "So, now what?"

"I would say nothing, if I were you," I said. "Confirm nothing, deny nothing…if it were me."

"Well, she can't exactly fire me for being a lesbian. It's against the law."

"That's true," I said. "But she could come up with some other excuse and not be honest about it. I can't guarantee anything."

"Would you tell me if she did that?"

A pause. "I can't guarantee that either," I said.

I couldn't look her in the eye after I said that. My face burned with shame, and I felt her eyes bore into me. But I had to protect myself, my own position, I *had* to. For Darlene's sake.

"Thank you for telling me," she said. "Is that it?"

I nodded silently, not looking at her. "Yeah."

"Okay." She stood and, as she walked out of the room, she repeated, with less formality and something that sounded like forgiveness, "Thanks, Tillie."

Chapter 18

AND THEN CAME a time of something even worse: waiting. Waiting for the other shoe to drop, for Barbara to walk in and tell me to place an ad for Jana's replacement, or for Jana herself to run into my office, outraged at being fired, wanting to tell me all of it, or worse, blame me for it because I did not have the courage to stand up and say out loud, "This is wrong, this cannot happen, this cannot be allowed."

And even though I knew that silently allowing it to happen was like some subtle and powerful complicity, I felt powerless. I'd already done the most I could do, warning Jana was a calculated risk, and if she went to Barbara Helms and said, "Tillie tells me you're maybe going to fire me because I'm gay," I might lose my own job. I had to cut my losses and move on. But I hoped and prayed she would not be let go.

On the day Barbara Helms came in to talk to Jana, I was preparing for a presentation to a group of local professionals. I sat in what we call the Day Room, flipping through my notes and drinking an early morning coffee. Jana stood across the room, straightening out the mess of toys on a bookcase we used for storage purposes.

Barbara walked in. "Good morning," she said.

"Morning," said Jana.

"How are you?" I asked.

"Good, thanks." Barbara turned to Jana. "I need to speak with you for a moment."

My heart thudded, and I wondered immediately if this was it. My shoulders twitched convulsively in response: *Damn.*

"Okay," Jana said. "Do we need to go into your office?"

"No, we can talk right here. Tillie? —" she turned to me "— you should be aware of our conversation, too."

"Okay." I folded my hands in front of me.

She put her arms behind her back and, for a moment, seemed to grow taller, as if she'd pressed her fists into the small of her back and straightened to her full height. She looked at Jana without emotion and said, "I think it's time we ended this relationship."

Jana leaned forward, squinting a little, as if unsure whether she heard correctly. There was silence.

"Now," Barbara went on, "I don't want you to think that this is a result of Tillie, or myself, for that matter, being dissatisfied with you personally. I think you're a reasonable, likeable, intelligent young woman with good prospects for the future. However, sometimes positions require the establishment of a certain —" she paused, looking for the word "— rapport with others. And in our case, here at Kiddie Korner, it's essential to establish a rapport not only with the children, but with their parents as well."

She sighed, took a deep breath. "Unfortunately, I don't think that's something you're cut out to do. It's not a deficiency that couldn't be corrected or that would weigh heavily against you in other positions. But here in the Kiddie Korner family, it's critical that the staff all have this ability. And so, I'm afraid we're going to have to let you go."

Still Jana was silent. My eyes were on her, and Barbara's eyes, too.

After a pause, she said slowly, "So what exactly am I being fired for? I mean, what's it going to say on my pink slip?"

"'Failure to meet company expectations.' That's all, just as simple as that. Nothing more." She turned smartly to the right, away from me, and in that instant, Jana shot a look at me. *Is this* really *what I'm being fired for?*

I wanted to leap up. I wanted to say, "Wait a minute. Wait one goddamn minute, lady." But I was paralyzed, my folded hands getting tighter and tighter, and I only had one chance, in that one or two second turn of Barbara's, to arch an eyebrow at Jana and scowl my most dubious scowl. Just as I could not help knowing her question, she could not help knowing my answer: *This is bullshit.*

Barbara went on talking, of course, in that breezy way that made me want to jack her up against the wall and get my face right up in hers. She was still talking to Jana, but it was all PR, more of the same tired old nonsense she always spouted about Kiddie Korner Child Care Center. And when it was over, and she said, "I'm sorry, Jana —" with great formality, and feigned sympathy—she whisked me away, into the next room, making further discussion alone with Jana impossible. She quickly changed the subject, gave me a series of things I needed to get done ASAP, and walked off with a quick thanks. Then I was alone.

What could I do? If I kept quiet, I'd have to go on feeling the way I felt, but if I said something, although I'd feel vindicated, I was sure I would lose my own job. It felt like a choice between the lion's den and the piranha tank. Eventually, I told myself I'd just have to get over it, cut my losses and move on, but it gnawed at me. How it gnawed at me.

I went for a run that night and was able, for a few moments, to forget about the whole thing, but I didn't get that all-enveloping sense of well-being that came with a good mile. Instead, I huffed and sweated and whined, and my feet flopped on the pavement like those of some clumsy schoolgirl. When I finished, I felt a new pain in the arch of my foot that just came out of nowhere, and not even *while* I was actually running. Then thoughts of Jana came crashing back, thundering in my head like terrible news, and I was back to staring at my conscience in painful, bewildered silence.

Why couldn't I have told her the truth? I thought of my exact words to her: "I can't guarantee anything." Couldn't I have at least told her that Barbara Helms was undoubtedly going to fire her, that she could call up the State Commission on Human Rights and Opportunities if she wanted to file a grievance, that she might even have a case, even if I would not, could not, take the risk of testifying? Couldn't I have said that much?

And then, to my eternal chagrin, I realized that, if she *did* file a grievance, and the thing ended up in court, I might very well be subpoenaed anyway. And sister, I asked myself, how would that be?

I had to admit the thought scared me before I dismissed it. Jana would never file, of course, and if she did, why would it get to court? The center would offer a conciliation agreement, or whatever was done in those types of cases. And that would be that.

But then things happened that I did not expect, and life, like it so often does, took a strange and unnerving turn. Maybe for the better, maybe worse. Who could say, at the outset? Not me, certainly. No way.

Jana

Chapter 19

SO THERE I was, out of luck and out of a job during one of the worst recessions in the history of my country. Was I pissed. I wanted to lob hand grenades at Barbara Helms' Saab. I wanted to go and stand at the end of her driveway, catch her in the morning as she left for for work, and flash her a sign saying *Will Work For Food*. Most of all, though, I wanted to find out if I could file a complaint against the center, because I had a strong suspicion my firing was about something other than "Failure To Meet Company Expectations."

It took *so* long to get another job. God bless anyone who has to go through the hell of unemployment. Every day you have to just show up. Go through the classifieds, go to United Labor Agency, Job Search, the temporary firms, whatever.

In my case, it was "Unemployment." The week after I lost my job, I went into their office, logged onto the computer, then had to switch from a computer to *microfiche*—remember that stuff?— and sit down to look at the possibilities of driving a semi, picking tobacco, flipping burgers, making corn fritters, or any one of a hundred jobs I had neither the experience nor the desire to pursue. I used to call the place "Unenjoyment," as in, "I'm gonna go pick up my check from Unenjoyment."

And that check was a mere pittance…certainly not enough to live on…the job itself having been relatively low-paying in the first place. Meanwhile, I called my local government agencies to see if I could file a grievance for discrimination for Barbara Helms' firing me. I quickly found out from a friend of mine who had studied law that there wasn't any point in considering my case from the viewpoint of restitution or back pay on the part of the center. Though he had flunked out of law school, so at that point, I just hoped he knew what he was talking about.

The fact was, I'd been a trainee in my job—although no one had ever mentioned that word exactly—because I was only in my third month as an employee when they fired me. To this day I refuse to use the word *terminated*. It's a stupid euphemism, as euphemisms go, and besides, it sounds like you were executed by the CIA or something. So from a legal standpoint, the best I could get, according to my legal beagle friend, was either a conciliation agreement from the center—which, in my case, could only be getting my job back, since benefits and loss of income were basically non-issues—or some kind of financial payoff, by way of a lawsuit, which would stipulate that I receive reparations for emotional trauma, etc. etc.

But these were all long shots, he told me, because they assumed victory in the first place. Besides, I didn't actually have a lawyer to represent me. I couldn't afford one.

Since finding work took forever, I invested some time in researching how to file a grievance. First, I learned that in state governmental entities, as in federal ones, the left hand doesn't always know what the right hand is doing. Eventually, after the obligatory nineteen frustrating automated-attendant-voicemail-from-hell phone calls, someone steered me toward the State Commission on Human Rights and Opportunities, or SCHRO. I followed up a phone call to their office by going down to get materials from them under the pretense that I had a friend who thought he'd been fired on the basis of race. As it turned out, my instincts were good, because the law had just then gone into effect that made discrimination on the basis of sexual orientation illegal, so very little material was available on the topic. Oh great, I thought, I get to be the pilot test.

A visit to the library yielded nothing current or relevant, but they pointed me in the direction of the State Law Library. That Saturday, I hopped the E bus from Sigourney Street to Capitol Avenue. Once aboard, I was treated to the thoughts of a jock-ish-looking guy about three seats behind me as he had a loud conversation about nutrition with his friend.

"Bananas are good for ya," he said. "You get your potassium for solid shits. Nice solid shits."

Ah, the charm of public transportation.

Finally, we reached the State Law Library, an official-looking building with at least as many concrete steps as an average courthouse, and the kind of imposing pillars a more knowledgeable person would probably describe as Georgian or Doric. I climbed the steps, overwhelmed by the sheer size of the building itself, and walked through heavy old-fashioned revolving doors into a dark hushed antechamber, all wood and marble and gold railings. The whole place had the air of a law school, a collection of drawers and desks and cabinets, dark like cherry or mahogany. *Reverence* was the only word I could think of for what people who studied there might have felt for the place.

I decided to look through some books before I actually got up the nerve to ask for help. To tell the truth, I really hoped I could find what I wanted on my own. But the best thing I located was a book referencing the types of discrimination that were illegal in Connecticut. I learned that, in alphabetical order, it was illegal to discriminate on the basis of *age, ancestry, color, criminal record, learning disability, marital status, mental disorder, mental retardation, national origin, physical disability, race, religion, sex, or sex orientation.* There it is, I thought. It's official.

But I couldn't find anything specific on the law itself, and eventually I had to resort to a reference clerk, who coolly informed me that the *Labor Law Reporter,* a publication put out by the Bureau of National Affairs, would provide me with info on recent cases in a periodical format. Even that looked intimidating, and at last I decided that this whole thing was stupid, I needed to go back to SCHRO and talk to someone in person.

First I went home and took a second look at the materials SCHRO had given me. I found a reference to something called Public Act No. 91-58, subtitled "An Act Concerning Discrimination on the Basis of Sexual Orientation." This was buried in the text of a pamphlet entitled "Statutory Provisions Enforced and Administered by the State Commission on Human Rights and Opportunities," a compilation of laws and procedures, including how to file a complaint or grievance.

I'll admit I started to panic when I read this section. Words like *plaintiff* and *defendant* drifted into my head, and my heart thumped when I thought of court. This kind of nightmare wasn't supposed to happen to people like me.

The woman from SCHRO, Carolyn, remembered me when I went back. "I'd hoped you'd come back," she said. "So many of them don't."

She had known right away, she said, and apologized for the analogy but compared it to a teenage boy buying condoms—how they always said they were there for a friend. "It's like a rape," she said. "*You're* the one who's been violated, but you feel guilty. And if your case is legitimate, which of course I assume it is, there's no reason to apologize to anyone. What kind of complaint did you intend to file? I mean, what do you think was the basis of the discrimination?"

"Sexual orientation."

Her face changed slightly, as if a light flickered over it. "You're a lesbian."

"Yes, I am."

"Okay. Well," she said, "there's a relatively new law about that. I'm not all that familiar with it. In fact," she said brightly, "you'd be the first complainant to register that type of grievance in the county. Maybe the first in the whole state!"

I grinned sheepishly, comforted nonetheless by her tone of voice. "Okay." Yep, just what I feared – the pilot test.

"Now, here's the thing," she said. "Was the case within the past one hundred and eighty days?"

"Excuse me?"

"You were terminated from the job, I take it? Fired?"

"Right."

"That was within the past one hundred and eighty days?"

"Oh, yeah. It was, like, last week."

"Well, we're in business. Here's what we have to do. We need you to file your charge within one hundred and eighty days of your *knowledge* that the discrimination took place. You follow me?"

I nodded.

"No problem there. Okay, how strong is your evidence?"

"My evidence?"

"Yes. I'm not supposed to get into particulars, but do you feel you have a case strong enough to hold up in court, if it came to that?"

"I don't know. I'd like to think so, but I have my doubts."

"All right, then here's what you do. I'm going to give you all the materials we have. This handout —" she reached into a drawer and searched for the right one "— this outlines the new law about sexual orientation. It basically is a replica of the sex or race discrimination law, so there's no real rocket science to it from our viewpoint *here*." She pointed toward the floor to signify she meant the Commission itself. "What I'd recommend is that you take the materials home and familiarize yourself with them, then come back as soon as you can to meet with the investigator. Wait at least two days, since he's booked up solid now."

"The investigator," I repeated.

"Yes, an investigator will be assigned to your case. He'll draw up a formal statement based on your story, and it'll be as easy as pie."

I doubted that. But I smiled anyhow when I thanked her.

I had to give a sworn affidavit before the investigation could proceed. That's what they called my complaint: an affidavit. So I went back in later that week to meet with someone they called an Intake Officer, to give him all the information I could. When I left for home that day, I felt like a towel that has been wrung out a little too enthusiastically.

Chapter 20

SUBSTITUTE HOUSE BILL No. 7133
Public Act No. 91-58

An Act Concerning Discrimination On The Basis of Sexual
Orientation

*Sec. 3 (NEW) It shall be a discriminatory practice in violation of this section
for an employer, by himself or his agent, except in the case of a bona fide
occupational qualification or need, to refuse to hire or employ, or to bar or to
discharge from employment any individual or to discriminate against him or her
in compensation or in terms, conditions or privileges of employment because of
the individual's sexual orientation....*

I looked at the phrase "bona fide occupational qualification or
need." Could that possibly include heterosexuality?

I shook my head. For what conceivable reason could my sexuality have been used as a reason for firing me, anyway? Did Barbara
Helms really believe that my personality was such that I could not
maintain enough rapport with parents to be effective? And even
if that *had* been the case, would that be sufficient grounds for dismissal? Or did they think I was some kind of pervert, that I'd
molest little girls or something?

With a jolt, I realized that that might actually be the case. The statement I'd made to Tillie rushed back: "Well, she can't exactly fire me for being a lesbian." But she would if she thought that lesbian equaled child molester.

Why it hadn't hit me sooner, I didn't know. Maybe I was in denial, maybe I was just dense, but it never occurred to me that another person might view me as a threat. And then, with that cold light of bigotry shining in my face, turning outrage into rage, I remembered darling Estelle, my old college roommate, and her ceaseless prayers for my salvation, and I was suddenly aware again that there was no end to this bigotry. It was as deep and essential as marrow.

Maybe that was true for Barbara Helms, maybe not. Maybe it was all about Jeanette and Paul Robeson. Maybe there was even more to it. But ultimately, it didn't matter: I was there with a choice to make, and my fear and disgust couldn't prevent me from making it. I had to fight. I would make my rage work for me, not against me.

I read the materials over with meticulous care. Much of it was hard, if not impossible, to understand. In some sections, the law made reference to other sections, which I dutifully looked up, only to find more references. It was like looking up a word in a dictionary or a thesaurus and finding, instead of a definition, a reference to look elsewhere. And then, when you flip to the place it tells you to, you find a direction to look somewhere else. Fortunately, I was a quick study.

Two days before I interviewed for my next job, I went back to SCHRO. I met with Steve Torres, the investigator assigned to the case. He took my hand in his big warm palm, smiling behind a black mustache, and instantly I felt at ease.

"It is a pleasure to meet you," he said solemnly, in a rich Latino baritone.

"Thank you," I said, still shaking his hand. "I wish we could be meeting under better circumstances."

Again, he smiled broadly. "Undoubtedly."

I told him my story. I told him about Wendy Simpson and Jeanette Robeson and Barbara Helms. I told him about my conversation with Tillie, how she had basically warned me about my peril. And I told him about the way she looked at me on the sly when Barbara fired me.

"So," he said, his fingers drumming the desktop lightly, his eyes fixated on the point where the wall and floor met, "she intimated by a look that you were wrongfully let go?"

I cleared my throat. "Yes." I had to admit, at that moment, it all sounded pretty shaky.

"And was there other evidence of discrimination? Other conversations, other staff members involved?"

I had already told him about the incident with Wendy. "No," I said. "No, that pretty much sums it up."

His fingers stopped drumming, but he stared intently at the point ahead of him. I could only imagine what he was thinking, and there was a long silence, in which I almost believed he had hypnotized himself or fallen into some kind of dream state. Suddenly, he snapped out of it with a shake of his head and that flash of a grin. "Well," he said, as he rubbed his hands together and looked across the table from beneath dark, bushy eyebrows—"we shall have to work with what we have, won't we?"

I smiled uncertainly and bit my lip. I nodded. Yes. We shall have to work with what we have.

Chapter 21

MEMORANDUM

Re: Jana Mariana Odessi

It is the responsibility of the State Commission on Human Rights and Opportunities to present the following information about the complainant abovementioned. The complainant alleges that: on or about March 3rd, 1993, she was wrongfully terminated from her position at Kiddie Korner Child Care Center; and that, although she was informed at the time of said termination that the reason for termination was "failure to meet company expectations," it was apparent to her that her termination was a result of her sexual orientation; and that the abovementioned Kiddie Korner Child Care Center did intentionally, and with malice aforethought, terminate her position, with no severance pay or compensation beyond minimum requirements provided by the State Department of Unemployment; and that she is entitled to full and unrestricted restitution, either in the form of back-pay, reinstatement or monetary damages as sought in a court of law.

The Commission represents neither the complainant nor the respondent. The responsibility of the investigator in this case is solely to provide both parties with information, to collect documents and testimony where applicable, and to review them with the complainant. If the investigation shows that the alleged discriminatory act occurred, this agency's sole responsibility is to attempt to affect an agreement satisfactory to both parties, under the current guidelines for conciliation agreements applicable in the state of Connecticut.

In the case of failure of a conciliation agreement, or in any case in which the matter is not resolved to the satisfaction of both parties, a public hearing may be held as a means to affect a satisfactory resolution.

In addition to this type of statement—to be presented to Kiddie Korner—I had to sign and swear to a lengthy statement drafted, by me, with Steve Torres' help. The only part I felt good about, to be perfectly honest, was the *Statement of Remedy*, which said that the full remedy for the Center's "alleged" discrimination would probably include "full back-pay plus interest, minus interim earnings, including unemployment compensation and compensatory damages." This meant that, contrary to what my law student friend said, there was still a slim chance of receiving some financial compensation for my ordeal. Obviously, I didn't want the damn job *back*—how could I stand to go back? It was unthinkable.

I had one endless day between the day we sent the notice to Barbara Helms at Kiddie Korner and the day she replied. I don't remember exactly what I did for those twenty-four hours, but it seems to me I did a lot of pacing. When the response did arrive, Steve Torres said it was typical. I didn't keep it, but basically it said the Center was surprised and saddened by the accusation, but would be in touch soon by way of their attorney's office.

Immediately, I felt deflated. I don't know what I'd expected, but this made me aware of my own definite smallness—me against *them*, Jana Odessi against the entire Center. For an instant, although no one knew it but me, I wavered. I thought about retreating. But the injustice and outrage and humiliation came crashing back on me with such force that I never even opened my mouth. *Of course* I was going to fight. Besides, I didn't need a lawyer for the public hearing. And I knew it might not even get that far. Maybe a settlement was possible, though I didn't really expect them to offer one.

A lot of the details of the investigation remained to be covered. Part of the job, Steve Torres said, entailed gathering information from "both sides" of the complaint. He would collect documents from the Center—everything from my original application to my pink slip—along with statements from key people: Wendy, Tillie, Barbara, and so on. The thought of him talking to all these people made me feel defensive, although I was the one filing the complaint. I thought of what Carolyn said about me being the one who was violated, but still feeling guilty. Was it inevitable that I would feel like *I'm* on trial?

Then, too, I thought about the case I had to make. A lot rode on Tillie's look. She'd never actually said a word to me. Could I possibly have misinterpreted that broad, sarcastic glance? What else could it have meant? She would only use that kind of look to convey disapproval, if not of a person, then of something else.

Could it have been triggered *by* me, not directed *at* me? What could I have said or done wrong? All I'd done was ask what my pink slip would say. Could Tillie's one raised eyebrow and scowling lip have meant, "What kind of dumb question is *that?*" I couldn't believe it was so. Would she be subpoenaed? I hadn't thought to ask.

In the meantime, I'd had to get a job. I told each person who interviewed me that I'd been let go from my last position after only a brief probationary period, and they asked more about the position than anything else. I went so far as to mention the "failure to meet company expectations" issue, and the response was surprisingly sympathetic. In the end, I got a job based on my ability alone. I would be teaching music to kids, which was much more straightforward than my job at the Center had been. At Kiddie Korner, I'd been more or less an instructor, and music was only a small part of the picture. Here, it was the picture itself.

My first day on the job I had a rude surprise: I was going to have to teach students to play the recorder. This made perfectly good sense, and my saxophone experience certainly prepared me, but I'd brought my sax with me for the job, and I was disappointed it would have to sit there, unopened, in its case. Obviously, not too many of these kids were going to have saxophones. I don't know what I'd been thinking. I guess the stress of the discrimination case addled my brain.

I'll never forget that job. We did stuff like "Old MacDonald" and "My Country, 'Tis of Thee," and one great bit of classical music with accompanying lyrics:

Papa Haydn's dead and gone,
But his memory lingers on ....

The kids were great. They asked questions, they were good listeners. At the end of the session, they even liked to have me play some sax for them…just improv stuff, though sometimes I'd throw in a bit of a familiar tune just to get a reaction. After a while, I got acclimated to the job, and thought less about Kiddie Korner, which is to say I no longer thought about it *all* the time. I started to enjoy myself, though the pay was so abominable that I was forced to accept financial help from my parents. They'd been badly shaken by the firing, and were happy to see me get another job, regardless of the particulars.

One day, though, I had a disturbing reminder of the Center. We had these great radio commercials at Kiddie Korner, and one day while driving, I heard one. A woman's voice extolled the virtues of this great facility while cheesy elevator music played in the background. By the time I realized who the ad was for, I felt compelled to listen to the whole thing, and my blood pressure rose as the voice went on and on about what a great opportunity Kiddie Korner provided for "growth"—social, emotional, blah, blah, blah.

It was kind of funny at first, but by the time it got to the end, I was rolling my eyes and clutching my gut. A man came on and said, "Kiddie Korner Child Care: child care with a touch of class," just like some telephone company commercial. Then the music changed to those terrible sounds they always use for ads involving children, "bing, bong, bing," like somebody on Demerol playing a xylophone. I changed the station.

Eventually, of course, I had to deal with the case. Steve Torres from SCHRO called me one day to make an appointment with me. In the deep Latino accent that had become like a lullaby, he warmly assured me the appointment was just a formality: "We merely have to give you some information about the Center's official position, and about where we stand now, based on statements collected from several of their employees, and of course from your own statement."

He sounded like he was sitting back in his chair with a big Cuban cigar, smiling complacently, feet on the desk, his hands locked behind his head. He had me on speaker, which I hate, but I didn't protest.

"So when do I come in to see you?"

"—en do you do *what?*"

"When do I come into your office?" I said loudly. Damned stupid speakerphone.

"—ell, that is up to you. What does your schedule permit?"

"I'm always home by 3:30," I said. A pause, then a hiss.

"Okay. Why don't we meet at four on Friday?"

"Okay."

"—ill that be convenient?"

"Yes," I shouted, "that's fine."

"—see you then, okay?"

"Okay, great. Bye now."

"—eye-bye." Click.

I sighed. It was only Wednesday, and I had a whole two work days to go through before the meeting. The suspense would be excruciating.

The following day, I got two hang-ups on my answering machine. I had no reason to suppose they meant anything out of the ordinary, but it *was* kind of unusual. For some reason, it made me think of Wendy Simpson, which got me nervous. I tried to dismiss the thought that she would harass me, but it wouldn't go away. I tried to think about anything other than the case—work, my parents, Danielle, even good old Leon from high school—but as soon as I had my guard down for a while, my thoughts again raced with possibilities of subterfuge, coercion, conspiracy. I got paranoid.

Finally, I did something productive. I called Danielle.

"So what's the real issue?" she said, after hearing my woes. "You're afraid that Wendy, or some other person from the center, is going to start harassing you? I mean, do you think even if you got a few rude phone calls, it would escalate after that? You think there's really a chance of that happening?"

"I don't know. I don't *think* so, but I don't know."

She paused. "Look," she said, "you're under a lot of pressure. I mean, you're beginning a big battle. And *of course* you're concerned, and *of course* you're afraid about what might happen. But I don't really think it's gonna benefit you to try to predict the future. You'll do better if you reserve your strength for the battle ahead."

"I know," I said.

"You're a strong person, Jana, you don't need me to tell you that, but, y'know, if you let this preliminary part sap all your energy, you're gonna have a hard time." Another pause. "Can we get together later?"

"Okay," I said. "Wait a minute. Should we?"

"Why not?"

"Well, I don't know. I mean—I don't want to be dragging you into this whole thing—and if we're out in public —"

"Oh, Christ, let's not even—I mean—goddamn, you know, you're not on trial, your lifestyle's not on trial. These people would like to conduct a witch hunt at old K.K.C.C.C., but the issue, if I remember correctly, was some nonsense about 'failure to meet company expectations.'"

After a silence, I sighed, and said quietly, "I know." I stared down at my feet with the phone in my hand, then slowly closed my eyes. "I know," I said.

"I mean, after all, we are just *friends*, right?"

We both burst out laughing suddenly, and my shoulders relaxed a little. "Yeah, right. In practice, at least."

"That's right," she said, "you've never kissed me on the mouth in public in your entire life!"

I caught the reference, my words to Tillie, and laughed again. "Okay," I said. "I'll go. Give me a call after you eat, okay?"

"Sounds great. We'll go to Elizabeth Park and look at roses for a while."

"I'll talk to you later."

We both hung up, and I sat back in my chair and slowed my breathing, like I was doing a yoga exercise. I realized I was already very tired. Tillie's words rang in my head: "I would say *nothing* if I were you...confirm nothing, deny nothing...I don't want this to be a big deal, either...I'm on your side here."

My brain reeled. Silence equals death. What martyrdom from coming out in a public way? Well, hell, people come out every day. Even teenagers, these days. Still, I felt an awareness dawning slowly within me, an inevitability of which I could only be dimly aware, like a faint snatch of music almost remembered, some sense of being drawn into a fate over which I had neither control nor influence.

I remembered a movie I'd seen in which a woman was stuck on a conveyor belt that pulled her toward a horrible shredder. Melodramatic orchestral music shrieked in the background, and the hero of the movie struggled to save his heroine, but the conveyor belt pulled her relentlessly on. I felt as if I were on some sort of metaphysical conveyor, a fast track to Hell, and I was not sure that friendly hands would save me at that last cliffhanging instant before a grisly end.

Not that the whole struggle would actually destroy me. It was just this sense of *fait accompli* that unsettled me.

That night was the first in weeks where I had a good time and actually managed to get my mind off the case for a few hours. Danielle and I wandered around the park for a while, looking at the vast floral arrangements only the wealth of West Hartford could supply, probably purchased with profits from Dow Chemical or the Aetna or something. Eventually, we went to a coffeehouse thing at a place called The Burning Brassiere run by a couple I always referred to as "diesel dykes." Terrific ladies, actually, but very tough-looking customers, if you get my meaning, with beefy arms and spiky haircuts. They were originally going to call it "The Burning Brasserie" as a pun, but they didn't serve alcohol, and had no desire to mislead potential clientele.

On this particular night, it was filled with a lot of people I presumed to be regulars. Danielle and I looked like kids next to a lot of those women, but we were probably not all that noticeable considering the heterogeneity of the crowd. It was "open mic" night, so guys with acoustic guitars came in, along with high school bands complete with bongos, electric basses, all sorts of crazy stuff.

One trio of women did a group of songs ranging from techno-folk to blues, and then a bunch of young guys performed some very bizarre music over which one of them, wearing a white magician's hat, recited a poem about a murder. Then a guy got up and sang an old protest song about Vietnam a cappella, after which Danielle actually had the courage to sing a song by Swinging Porters called "Pop Song."

He was tired of taking chances
And she was looking for romances
They were waiting for advances
But the chemistry wasn't right.

So they sat like statuettes and
Studied both their silhouettes and
Felt like they were marionettes and
Probably they were right ....

She sang in a little-girl voice, almost like a put-on, that sounded to me like how Elton John might have sounded if he'd been a woman. She was great, actually, but I felt extremely nervous for her the whole time, which surprised me a little. I admit I was relieved when she finished and came back to our table on a wave of applause.

"Wow," she said. "I was having a cow up there."

"You did great. You didn't even look scared."

"I moved my leg once a little, and I felt it shaking like my knees were knocking together." She took a gulp of her soda, her eyes shining.

I smiled at her. "I'm serious. That was really good."

She looked dazed. "Jesus," she said. Her jaw trembled.

"I didn't know you had so much talent."

She returned the smile. "Actually, my real talents lie in other areas."

I looked at the floor. When I looked back up, her eyes met mine slyly and blazed up for a moment like fire. Then, just as suddenly, we both looked away. I knew I must have had the same flurried look of coquetry on my lips that I saw on hers, and I felt myself floating into that dazed combination of lust and confusion, which, mingled with complete respect, isn't really lust, only a kind of desperate infatuation and deep longing so much like a drug it leaves you not only discomposed but breathless with anxiety about losing your bearings. You worry about smashing your car, falling down stairs, and when you go to bed at night, your heart pounds as your thoughts race down tunnels of confusion and fear so fast that you forget to breathe. And when you finally do fall asleep, it is a fitful, dream-ridden sleep, more impoverishing than satisfying, and you wake and know that you are not at all satiated: you are bewitched, entranced, smitten, enamored, crazy. But not satiated.

And so I sat there, wishing for the peace of satiety but feeling the emotional connection, the pull toward her, and not knowing where to take it, whether or not to fight it, wanting more than anything else *not* to think about the Center and the affidavit and all the rest of it. And in that longing to forget, and its accompanying desire to stay in the moment, I surrendered.

Chapter 22

I HAVE TO admit I was a little shocked when the Center didn't offer to settle out of court.

Steve Torres had warned me. He'd said that, most likely, given the Center's response to the complaint—"We are grieved, shocked, dismayed, saddened"—whatever bullshit they'd thrown back, they would most likely not offer me a settlement. Undoubtedly, they would bide their time, and see what sort of result that brought about.

In theory, they had nothing to lose. If the decision went in my favor, *then* they might offer a conciliation agreement of some sort, which, to me, meant a kind of settlement. So they had nothing to lose by not offering to settle.

So why was I surprised? I don't know. I guess some weird form of idealism—foreign, I must say, to my nature—weaseled its way into my consciousness. I just couldn't help thinking that, surely, they'd see the error of their ways and offer to make amends.

As it turned out, they wound up having to contend with a decision in my favor. They surprised me this time by offering a conciliation agreement; however, my idea of being conciliatory was a little different from theirs. Mine was based on the "statement of remedy" concept: full back-pay, including unemployment compensation *plus* compensatory damages for the severe humiliation and pain of the whole ordeal. What they actually offered was the thrilling option of *getting my old job back.*

Unbelievable or what? I took one look at the letter and felt rage boil up inside me so fast and furious I was afraid I'd explode. I hadn't felt that outraged at the firing itself.

"Oh, those dirty…," I said. "Those dirty…dirty…."

"Calm down," said Steve Torres. "This may be a big break."

"How?" I shouted. "How might this be a break?"

"Well, it brings us to the point of a public hearing. And the decision, remember, in your favor, was brought about by a, uh, how you say, compilation of evidence, or rather, testimony, given by people at the center. And so, in effect, you will now have your day in court, eh?" He smiled broadly beneath his dark mustache, dark eyes twinkling.

My day in court. My day. Of course I'd have my day. It had been building toward this all along. I saw the sinister design, saw it in all its infernal corruption. Saw Barbara Helms, her soricine face masklike beneath the perfect coiffure, gazing coolly across the courtroom with mock sympathy.

Poor Jana! These poor girls, these poor tortured lesbians with their perse-cution complexes! If only we'd spent a little more time with her, she would have been able to see that she just wasn't up to snuff. Just wasn't up to the demands of the job. But we're willing to take her back, if she'll concede; we'll be able to get her up to speed somehow…it just means a little more work for us, and just a teensy bit more effort on her part….

And my argument? Ah, God, it was so frail, as frail as a crystal globe. It rested entirely upon the glance of Tillie Jones, and on a private conversation in which she'd "warned" my weary ass about the Robesons. One tiny nudge, one good breeze, and my argument would shatter on the concrete. Unless Tillie was holding an ace for me. *I can't guarantee that either*, she had said. There were no guaran-tees. And yet the decision had been in my favor. Why? I suddenly snapped back to attention, back to my conversation with Steve Torres.

"You said that the decision in my favor was brought about by the testimony of people at the center."

"Certainly. And by your own statement, of course."

"Why was it in my favor? Who at the center provided testimony that influenced the decision in my favor?"

Steve smiled his imperturbable smile. "Jana, if I told you that, I would be doing the justice system a great disservice. As it stands, I may say nothing, not even about the issue of whether anyone at the center *did* in fact provide influential testimony. Remember, I am not a lawyer. My allegiance must be to neither one side nor the other."

He took a breath. "I am a functionary, whose sole purpose is to gather facts and make objective assessments. Which is not to say," he added, looking at me from beneath those black eyebrows, "that I am wholly unmoved by the situation. My official position prevents me from disclosing where my true sympathies lie."

The look in his eyes was unmistakable, and I felt a great surge of gratitude as I took his hand. "Thank you," I said. "I understand. And thank you."

He nodded and gave my hand a slight squeeze before withdrawing it. Then he bowed, as always, and walked from the room, the papers that might determine the fate of my case stowed in his briefcase.

"Ah," he said suddenly, stopping in the doorway, "I almost forgot to tell you —"

"What? What?"

"The hearing," he said. "It has to be scheduled. We will be in touch to let you know when the date has been set." He paused. "*Try* not to think about it," he said gently. "Enjoy yourself." Then he was gone.

Enjoy yourself. The tone was almost reproachful. And yet he was right. The weekend beckoned to me, and here I was in an office.

I opened the door onto a sunny morning, stepped outside, and looked up into a sky blue with promise. Enjoy yourself, I thought. Have a good weekend.

That afternoon, I called my friend Roxanne. Roxanne was an alcoholic, or had been one, or whatever. She was in A.A., and hadn't had a drink in three years. We'd been in touch on and off for a long time, and I decided to call her and see if she wanted to get together. She'd become, in her sobriety, one of the mellowest people I knew, and I felt like I could use some of her calming influence.

"Hello?"

"Hey, Roxanne."

"Jana?" she said uncertainly.

"One and the same."

"Holy cow," she said, sounding awed. "How *are* you?"

"I'm all right. What's up with you, kiddo?"

"Not much," she said, still sounding as if she'd been struck by lightning. "Oh, this is bizarre."

"What? Hearing from me after—what's it been …?"

"It's been months," she said. "That's the thing: I was *just* thinking of you…like ten minutes ago. I can't believe it."

For a moment I was afraid she might try to attach some huge cosmic significance to this, so I pressed on, tongue in cheek: "Well, Roxy, apparently you're psychic. Your brain always did have some strange tendencies."

She laughed. "Jeez, I've never been psychic before. But they say there are no coincidences. How's it going?"

I told her everything, about the center, about Wendy Simpson, the Robesons, Barbara Helms. It took a long time.

When I finished, she breathed out a long sigh and said, "Wow." She paused. "Hey, Jana," she said. "Can I ask a question?"

"Sure."

"When you were talking about that woman, your ex-boss, you sounded pretty angry. Is that a safe assumption to make?"

"That I got ticked off at Barbara Helms?"

"Yeah."

"To tell you the truth, I really think I wanted to kill her. I mean, like, I could have done it, I think, quite cheerfully. She is such an incredible bitch, Rox. It's incredible, it really is."

"She's a sick woman, Jana."

"Sick? She's a megabitch."

"Sick," she said. "I'm serious. A person with that kind of hate needs professional help. Therapy would be a good thing for her, I think."

"Therapy? How about long-term mandatory institutionalization? How about manacles and—and valiums —"

"And a body bag?"

I exploded with laughter. "Yeah, a body bag! That's great. *I'll* give her a body bag, all right…."

"I'm serious, though, Jana. She's sick. That kind of hate, that level…." Her voice trailed off.

"Yeah, well," I said, "I've been hating her in return for a while, you know? I mean —" and I laughed, tittered, really "— I mean, uh, that doesn't exactly mean *I* need therapy, right?"

"*I* don't know," she said. "I wouldn't presume to say whether someone in your situation needs therapy or not."

"Let me see if I have this straight. This woman hates me. Hates me and 'all my kind.' She fires me. So now I hate her. We both hate each other. So therefore we're alike? We both need to go to therapy?"

"Well, if the shoe fits," she said. Then she laughed, as raucously as I laughed when she'd said "body bag."

"Now I think *you're* the one who's sick," I said, laughing myself.

"Hey, listen," she said, "in all seriousness: I don't want to take an inventory of you *or* her. I'm suspending judgment on the whole thing. But just for the record, all I have to say about therapy is I think *anyone* can benefit from it. Whatever their reasons for going."

"You think I need that?" I asked. "All kidding aside."

She paused, as if she'd shrugged over the phone. "I dunno. Couldn't hurt." And then she said something that really threw me. "Why do you think you made this call?"

I jumped. Why had I made this call? Wasn't it just to talk to my old buddy Roxanne? Which is what I said, of course. "I just called to talk to you." But I was in a daze, suddenly.

"But why me, Jana? I mean, like you said, we haven't talked in *months*. I didn't know all this stuff was going down. And now, out of the blue, you just call me? Pretty freaky."

"You mean I called you because I wanted you to tell me to go to therapy?"

She laughed. "I don't know. I mean, no, not necessarily, but who knows? You were looking for something, I think."

"And maybe I found it?"

Another pause on the other end. "Maybe you have."

"I never really thought about it," I said. "Therapy, I mean. For Barbara Helms, maybe. Not for me."

"Well, like I said before," she said, "I'm not suggesting any-thing, but if you're considering it, I'm just saying it's not such a bad idea. I mean, it couldn't hurt."

"But would it help? I mean would it be worth the money?"

"I have no idea. Is this whole business gonna end up in court?"

"It might, I don't know." It *will*, I thought.

"So you would have to face this woman in court?"

I thought about it and I realized that yes, I would, and probably I'd still want to kill her. Dead. "Yeah," I said. "I'm sure I'd have to see her."

"Okay. How well do you think you'd handle yourself in that situation?"

I admitted I didn't know. "But my heart beats a little faster just thinking about it," I said.

"Do you think you could remain calm? Like what if the defense came up with some wild story about you having a grudge against her, some bullshit about you making up the discrimination charges in order to get revenge for the firing? Could you act cool about it?"

"I don't think so," I said.

"Then you really might want to consider some therapy."

"Therapy's gonna help me not be *nervous*?"

"No. But it might stop you from sitting there in court, shaking with rage and thinking about homicide."

"I think you're right, Rox," I said. "No matter what happened, I'd be sitting there 'shaking with rage,' as you so succinctly put it."

She laughed.

"And if I run this by my parents, and they go for it, maybe they'll help —"

"Atta girl."

"— Because, right now, just thinking about her makes me shake a little bit. Just on the inside, but that should count for something, you know?"

"Yeah."

"Do people do this, just decide-all-of-a-sudden-to-go-to-therapy? I would expect anyone who does go would struggle with the decision for weeks. Maybe months. People don't just *go*."

"You may be the first," she said with a smile in her voice.

"Are you busting my ass?" I asked in the same tone. "Are you giving me a hard time?"

"I'm just kidding around," she said. "You *may* be the first, for all I know. But regardless, you have every reason to be proud of yourself."

"Thanks," I said after a pause. "And I think you're right. I do deserve to be proud of myself. I'm daring to be different."

"Not the first time…."

"And not likely to be the last!"

We both laughed.

Chapter 23

I GOT TOGETHER with Roxanne that night, and we talked about it some more. She didn't want to recommend her old therapist, because she felt biased in his favor. "Besides," she said, "you might do well to consider a woman first." She actually had two people to recommend by word of mouth, both of whom were therapists of friends of hers. She promised to get the names and numbers and call me with them.

I thought about the prospect of therapy. It sounded so goofy, like I'd be lying on an old leather cliché of a couch, with the therapist—a brown-haired bookish woman, with glasses on a long chain and a clipboard in her hand—sitting behind me at a slight angle, saying all the therapist-type things you'd expect: "How do you feel about that?" and "Go on," and "Let's explore that."

It gave me the creeps, to be honest, though a part of me got a kick out of it, too. What was it that compelled me to want to do it, anyway? Surely my background, with its traumatic "rite of passage," made me a prime candidate.

But there had to be something more, something behind the curious mind-numbing ambivalence. I thought of my fantasy woman from the days of *Thunder Island,* my woman in white. Had she been a signpost, was she emblematic of something in me I would not want to understand, something only the rigors of therapy would force me *to* understand? Oh, if I could just be seventeen one more time. To see the gauzy image in my mind, to stand on the shore in that summer afternoon dream and breathe the breath of summer one last time, and dance and drown in a riot of perfumes.

But summer was over, and youthful dreams had turned to the realities of adulthood. My gauzy dream was gone.

One incident spurred me into action more quickly than I'd planned. It happened shortly after my get-together with Roxanne. She and I went to see some friends of hers who were going to an A.A. dance at the Knights of Columbus hall, which they referred to as the KFC as blithely as if it were a Kentucky Fried Chicken franchise. At least I *thought* they did, but later on I would learn, after hearing it about twenty-five times, they were actually saying K *of* C.

That night, I got the phone numbers of two therapists in Hartford who might be of some assistance. I'd planned to call one or both the following week, but as it turned out, I was on the phone within forty-eight hours.

It started when I went out with Danielle, the night after I saw Roxanne. Danielle said she wanted to tell me something, and she seemed to take great precautions to ensure I wouldn't get upset, overreact, go berserk, and so on. This made me nervous. What could possibly have happened that she should feel compelled to walk on eggshells with *me*?

"I just want to make sure you don't take this any more seriously than necessary," she said as we walked through West Hartford center.

"What?" I said. "What's the big secret, Danny? Are you getting a sex change? Running away to join the circus? What?"

"It's this." From her handbag she pulled a copy of *The Alternative Voice*, the local gay/lesbian paper handed out free in health food stores and coffeehouses.

I looked at the headline: DAY CARE BIGOTRY. My heart rammed against my ribcage as I began the first paragraph....

"Local day care facility Kiddie Korner Child Care Center recently became the center of controversy as a former employee, Jana Odessi —" *Oh my God* "— filed a complaint against the facility for unlawful termination based on sexual orientation...."

My face must have gone white, and I felt Danielle's hand grip my wrist as the sidewalk rocked beneath me.

"Jana." Her voice seemed to come from somewhere far away. "*Jana.*"

I scanned the article, waving her back like a drunken soldier bent on fixing the enemy in his sights. The article went on to describe the story in full detail, championing me as a courageous, though reticent ("Reticent?" Where the hell did people get this stuff?) victim who had since found employment elsewhere. Barbara Helms, whom the paper had tried to interview, refused comment.

That set me off more than the shock of the article itself. "No comment!" I shouted, crumpling the paper in my hand. Heads turned. "I'll give her no fucking comment. Yeah, no wonder, Jesus Christ, the reason she has no comment in the first place is because anything she says can and will be used against her in a court of law, *so help me God.*"

Danielle made a valiant effort to silence me, but I raved for another fifteen or twenty seconds. I almost blacked out, I think, or "whited" out. Everything got very, very bright, brighter and brighter, until the world disappeared behind a ghostly grey-white curtain of haze. I felt myself swaying forward and backward. Danielle was holding my forearm with both hands, I suddenly realized. She thought I'd fainted after the end of my last sentence, which I believe ended with the words "scum-sucking bat-tle-ax," though Danielle recalls it being more along the lines of "weasel-faced bitch." I tried to focus on the space in front of me, wondering how in hell this stuff could have found its way into this paper, what friend or enemy had seen fit to pass it on. Then I realized it didn't matter. The damage was done.

Several people stopped right there on the street, some of whom obviously thought my abusive epithets were directed at Danielle, and stared as she led me away, docile as a kitten and looking shamefacedly back at them while whispering apologies in her ear.

"Forget it, forget it, forget it," she said, apparently hellbent on getting me off the street with all possible speed.

We ducked into The Burning Brassiere, where Danielle felt certain a cup of espresso would calm me down. Why anyone would expect caffeine in vast quantities to work as a sedative is beyond me, but that's Danielle for you, God love her.

"I can't be*lieve* this!" I said, slapping the paper with one hand as I sat down. "Who the hell would send this story in to these guys? And for what purpose? I mean, Jesus, it's not like I'm some famous person. What the hell is going on?"

Several people nearby heard my remarks and turned to stare at me. Before Danielle could respond, our waitress came over. Danielle ordered espresso for both of us, and I cooled my heels while we waited, muttering under my breath and shaking my head periodically. If it's possible to feel flattered, outraged, scared, angry, embarrassed and proud all at the same time, then that would pretty accurately describe me at that point.

"Listen," said Danielle. "I don't think this is part of some evil plot. I think somebody saw a scoop, and decided to go for it. Maybe they thought the publicity would help the case."

"Shit, are you kidding me?" I buried my head in my hands. "This is enough to put me over the edge," I said. "It really is freaking unbelievable."

"Well, the whole thing is that you took a stand, and someone is applauding it." She took my hand across the table. "I mean, they're on your side, right? Look at the headline: 'Day Care Bigotry.' They obviously believe your complaint is legit. So it's not *all* bad."

"But why me? And what could possibly prompt someone to get this story into the public? How would they even find out?"

She looked at me. "You've been outed, Jana. Face it. I don't know how or why. Maybe someone thought you'd try to keep it private."

"Yeah, but Jesus Christ, that makes no *sense*. I'm filing a complaint, I'm—I'm taking a stand, like you said."

"You are. But a stand isn't necessarily public. And who can say whether this thing will ever see the light of day? Even in a public hearing scenario? Nobody goes to those things."

I sighed. "Well, yeah, okay. Even a public hearing is not necessarily gonna be considered newsworthy. I mean, I don't think it would wind up on the front page of the *Hartford Courant*."

"Well, there you go," she said. "And what the heck. Like I said, maybe they thought it *would* help your case, rattle some cages, *you know*."

"I'll bet it sure rattled Barbara Helms' cage when they called her. 'No comment.' Ha." I laughed, suddenly, and with real humor, for the first time in what had seemed a long while.

Danielle smiled. "That's more like it," she said. She let go of my hand, sliding hers back across the table, and I felt the slight sense of loss that went with that gesture. "And hey," she said, "if nothing else, it lets Barbara Helms know that this whole thing doesn't exist in a vacuum. There are interested parties out there, other people who aren't involved personally, but who are interested anyway."

"Mm," I said, as something else occurred to me. "You know," I said, "I definitely think I need to get some counseling ASAP."

She cocked her head to one side and looked at me. "Why?"

"Because…thinking of Barbara Helms again…." My voice trailed off.

"Yeah?"

I paused and studied Danielle. "I think I'd still like to kill her," I said quietly.

To my surprise, she smiled slightly again. "No doubt," she said.

"I'm serious," I said. "I need to get over this stuff on some level before I face that woman again. I'm liable to just jump on her face or something. That's all I need, an assault charge."

"Your parents would freak."

I laughed out loud, and she laughed a little herself.

"Maybe you do need a counselor," she said with a smile.

"Could be." I sipped my espresso. Several heads had turned, and some of them continued to stare our way. I felt very self-conscious all of a sudden. I wanted to fade into the woodwork.

"What's wrong?" she asked. "What are you thinking about?"

"Oh, nothing much —" I snapped back to attention "— I was thinking that I just drew a hell of a lot of attention to myself. I was being pretty loud, and now I feel like I've made a spectacle of myself."

"Don't worry about it," she said. "What they think isn't important. It's what *you* think that matters."

"I know, I'm just tired of this nonsense. And it's nowhere near being over. I mean, it's barely even started, you know? Jesus Christ." I buried my face in my hands again. "Do you realize that? It's barely even started."

She reached across the table again and took one of my hands. She didn't have to say a word, but after a moment or two had passed in silence, she did.

"It's gonna be all right," she said.

Chapter 24

FOR THREE OR four days after that, I didn't see Danielle at all. I remember them as some of the darkest days of that year, almost a complete blank, a grey spot in the midst of great turmoil. She really held me together for some time there, just being there in a way no one else had in a long while. Even today, it's hard to believe our relationship was still platonic at that point, but like I'd said to her before, we were 'just friends' in practice, but deep down, we both knew better.

Those few days were a blur not only because of Danielle but also because of other events. Still reeling from the shock of the *Alternative Voice* article, somewhere in the middle of that terrible week, I then found myself in a situation that made me feel as if I'd been put on top of the highest building in the land naked, with nothing to wrap around me but a banner reading *Gay Rights*.

Here's what happened: I was on my way to my car after work, walking down the sidewalk toward a parking garage on Main Street in a part of Hartford so congested with big buildings you could almost forget the appalling level of poverty just a few miles across town. I was not in a great frame of mind. Work had been unusually stressful that week, and I felt like I was functioning on auto pilot as my anxiety level hit critical mass. Cranky and overtired, my body ached from stress.

Three women stepped into the street with me as I crossed the intersection of Main and Gold. I still recall what they looked like, though I'd hardly noticed them at first. The tallest one, a brunette with a short pageboy hairdo and a long plain black dress, had skin as pale and translucent as milk. The other two were of middling height, one a heavy redhead with a skirt and hiking boots, and the other a blonde, thin and delicate-looking, but tanned. They could not have been a more diverse trio.

As we crossed the street, the tall brunette pulled fairly close, with the other two bringing up the rear. I heard her say, "Excuse me," and "Pardon me," before I realized she was talking to me.

I continued walking, wary of strangers on the city streets, but I glanced back and caught her eye. "Yes?" I said, still walking.

She caught up with me. "Excuse me. I'm sorry, but you're Jana Odessi, aren't you?"

I stopped and looked at her. "Have we met?"

Her friends stopped short behind her, and now we all stood on the sidewalk. "No. No, we haven't met, I saw you in The Burning Brassiere with a friend of yours." She shrugged. "I'm Lynn," she said, "and this is my friend Lisa —" the redhead "— and Catherine." The blonde smiled nervously.

"Hi," I said, feeling like I was wincing. "How do you know my name?" But I knew.

"You were in the paper—*The Alternative Voice*? I thought it was great that you did that. Not everyone would."

"I had nothing to do with that," I said curtly. "They didn't even try to interview me. Maybe they thought that, uh, my filing a complaint as a *private citizen* meant trying to stay in the closet. I don't know. But I'm not exactly happy about it." I tried to modulate my tone, but I still felt myself color.

"Well," she said. Her manner toward me cooled significantly, but she still smiled a friendly enough smile. "I hope I didn't embarrass you. I just wanted you to know that there are plenty of people in your corner."

"Well, thanks," I said, "but to tell you the truth, I just wish none of it had ever happened."

"Maybe it had to," the redhead piped up. "Maybe we need more incidents like this to mobilize people into action."

"Action?"

"Yes," she said, "action. Maybe this is what it's gonna take to get all the little fluffies, with their nail files and styling mousse, off of their complacent little asses and out into the public domain with the rest of us!"

"Lisa, please," said the brunette. "This is neither the time nor the place."

"There's always a time and place for the truth." She pointed to me. "She should be proud to have someone champion her fight in print. She should —"

"Excuse me," I interrupted, "but who the hell are you?" My voice rose. "Do I know you? Do you have any business on God's green earth sticking your nose into my life? Who are you? Who. The hell. Are you?"

"My name," she said flatly, "is Lisa Myerson. I'm —"

"I don't give a flying fuck who you are," I screamed. And I got right up in her face. "Leave me alone. Do you understand? Mind your own goddamn business and stay out of mine. You are not in my life, and I don't want you in it. Goodbye!" I wheeled around, about to storm off, but the sound of her voice made me pause.

"Your gay and lesbian brothers and sisters outed you for a reason. You're a public figure now, Ms. Odessi."

"I am *not* a public figure."

"Yes, you are, whether you like it or not. And you have both rights and responsibilities —"

I exploded. "Don't read *me* my fucking rights, lady." I crossed the sidewalk back to her. "I have no desire whatsoever to go out on a platform and yell, 'I'm a dyke,' and that's *my business*, not *yours*."

"You have a responsibility, not only —"

"Mind your business —"

"— not only to other lesbians, but to all the HIV-positive —"

"Good day! Goodbye! Have a nice day."

I stormed across the street, heels clicking, my breath coming in short bursts. I didn't pause to get my bearings until I reached the parking garage, and even then I had to sit in my car for several minutes before I felt okay to drive. The words "gay and lesbian brothers and sisters" rang in my head like some terrible clichéd mantra. And how I wished it all had never happened. Feeling wrecked, I drove home slowly, meticulously, my vocal cords shredded, my eyes blinking against the brightness of the afternoon sun.

About this time, I remember, I started to think in black and white terms. I'd always been more into shades of grey, but now I saw I had only two choices. First, I could become a spokesperson for the LGBT community, and become a VPL (Very Public Lesbian). Or, I could keep my head down and bear straight ahead, quietly attempting to see justice served without making a big splash.

I remember a friend of mine named Jean once told me that everyone on earth was actually composed of many people, so that one part of me was an old woman and one part was a young man, and so on. It made sense to me at the time, and I felt strongly that this was true, that yes, I was more than the sum total of what others perceived. Now, that was nearly gone. I was Jana Odessi, twenty-four-year-old white American lesbian. That was all.

Chapter 15

FORTUNATELY, JUST BEFORE the incident in Hartford, I'd made my first appointment with a therapist named John Wagner, recommended by Roxanne's friend Lisa Pelton. Lisa was also an old acquaintance of mine from before I'd gone to Boston College, and she remembered me as a smartmouth kid, but had always been friendly. I called her a couple of days after seeing her at some friends' of Roxanne's. "Listen," I said on the phone, "I know I've never really known you all *that* well, but Roxanne gave me the number of someone who's supposedly a good therapist, and she said you'd recommended him. I hope that's okay."

"Is his name John Wagner?"

"Yeah."

"He's a *great* therapist," she said. "He got his Ph.D. from Rutgers, I believe, about twenty years ago, and he's been practicing ever since, as far as I know. In fact, he was recommended to me by a woman who knew him when he was a child, and *she* had gone to him."

"Sounds like high praise indeed."

"Oh, yeah."

"So you do recommend him." Like she hadn't already.

"Absolutely. Yeah, I've been to three different therapists, and I have to say that he's the one I'd recommend first. Not that the others weren't good, but…."

Three different therapists? I wanted to say, "Okay, thanks," and get off the phone, but I didn't know how to end the conversation. Finally, I just said, "Well, I guess I'll give him a call."

"Yeah, I do recommend him," she said again. She sounded preoccupied. "Have you been in therapy before?"

"No...."

"Oh, he's perfect, then. You'll love him; he's great with newbies. There's just nothing phony about the guy. I mean, he's very non-threatening for someone with an advanced degree."

She laughed, and I laughed with her. The notion that the guy was down-to-earth made me feel better.

So I called. But I have to say, I really sweated it out. I mean the whole thing, the phone call, the conversation with the receptionist, the first drive over there. Still, everything kind of fell into place. Lisa Pelton was right—there was nothing phony about John Wagner, Psy.D. From day one, he insisted I call him John. He would have "none of this *doctor* stuff." At some point in our session that day, I specifically remember thinking, *This guy is cool.*

Of course we talked about a lot of things. It would take forever to tell it all, but the main work focused on my anger. I found out pretty early that John believed anger to be what he called a *secondary emotion*, something with another emotion invariably beneath it. "Usually fear," he said. "Fear of not being worthy, fear of being abandoned, fear of death, fear of life, fear of love, of hate, of... whatever."

He gestured in the air, a flick of the hand that was more a shrug than anything else. I got to know that gesture well, and behind it, I always saw his open admission that there were mysteries to be fathomed and that he didn't claim to know all the answers. I could almost see him in my mind's eye, shrugging philosophically and saying, "What the heck."

But we got to the bottom of that anger, all right. Beneath the rage, beneath the desire to strangle Barbara Helms and all the rest of it, wasn't the fear of losing my job. I'd already lost it. Beneath lay a true fear, one I can hardly describe, and hate to even discuss.

Somehow, deep down, I believed that I was not all right, that I was not only *not* all right, I was not going to *be* all right. In some obscure, indefinable way, I believed that I could not be myself, and be all right, *and* be happy. I believed that pain and suffering and humiliation would be my lot in life, and that the firing from Kiddie Korner—as devastating as it had been—would be merely the first in a stream of traumatic events extending into perpetuity. Maybe they wouldn't all be events related to my sexuality, but certainly a lot would. Certainly I would be made to pay the price for my pleasure, again and again.

I don't know where I got this belief, or why I had seemingly no power over it, but there it was. And when I finally admitted that, yes, not only did I *feel* this way, but also I believed it, I began to think it wasn't simply because I was a lesbian. I think I would have had it regardless, male or female, straight or not. Something in me insisted that I did not deserve to be me and still know peace and joy and love. And I learned that the belief caused me to replicate these situations with other women in which I would get involved only to a certain extent, with only a particular degree of intimacy I found tolerable, and then that was it. And sometimes they moved on in peace, and sometimes I was the one who moved on, and sometimes there were fights, though not always, but inevitably the result was the same: moving on.

So now came this time of examining beliefs, re-forming emotions I hadn't felt for a time, and seeing that, yes, even the relationship with Danielle was an issue. I had taken it only so far, and instead of some consummation, it remained an intangible, like a shared secret, this fragile bubble of a relationship that was platonic and yet not platonic, always floating just out of reach. It frightened me to think I might never have the kind of love I truly wanted and deserved if I continued down these avenues.

John Wagner helped. John Wagner let me see I could change my thinking. He taught me something of the utmost importance. I don't know he got it from his books or from experience, but I couldn't help thinking of it as a spiritual teaching—he taught me that the solution to my problems was ultimately love, and not just of myself, but of others. And the key was to begin with forgiveness.

Tillie

Chapter 26

PROBABLY WASN'T EVEN any rational reason for me to go on thinking about that Jana Odessi, but somehow I couldn't help wondering what I could have done differently. When you second-guess yourself like that, you get uncomfortable, you know, and I just couldn't let it go, because I felt I'd done something wrong. Like one time, I clipped a car in a parking lot—caught the tail light with my bumper while going around it—and I never stopped. I mean, I stopped and looked, but I didn't leave a note or anything, and I knew it was wrong, but I did get over it…eventually. I didn't lose any sleep over it, because I wasn't well off, you know, and I had a daughter at home to feed, and I guess you could say I rationalized it.

But this thing with Jana…she was special to me, like my daughter, and I felt like I'd sold her for a bag of silver. I felt like Judas and a mean old snake and I don't know *what* all. I told myself I'd have to get over it, but some time went by, and I couldn't. And then we got word at the center she'd gone and filed for discrimination, and right away I felt like, All right, you go, girl, and then the next thing I know, I'm panicking, My God, I'm going to get called on to make a statement. I sold her down the river, and now I'm going to have to make a statement.

My dilemma became real clear when I realized the spot I was getting squeezed into. I could keep the security of my job and income by going along with Barbara's story, whatever that happened to be. Or…but I couldn't think about the alternative, because the risk of losing my job was so real.

Certain periods of your life have more stress than others, and in that period it seemed like stress was a constant companion. Things were stressful at work—Jana hadn't actually been replaced, and all her job responsibilities had been distributed among several people, who ultimately reported to me, and who had a real propensity for slacking off. So I had to watch them all the time.

Plus, Barbara Helms was running around like a maniac, acting cool but looking more and more pinched up as she flew from one meeting to the next, put out fires, did her usual damage control, and then filled me in on all the details. And things were stressful at home, too. My relationship with Darlene had deteriorated to the point that she wouldn't even talk about her abortion, and I began to wonder what the point of it all was. I don't mean what was the point of her considering having an abortion, but I really wondered about the point of life, of going on, if things were always just going to be so damned *hard*.

I remember this one Sunday afternoon when I sat downtown reading the paper. I'd decided to go to the coffee shop that day, mainly because of the weather. I don't usually go anywhere on Sundays, but this particular day was overcast and a light mist filled the air, like a fine drizzle, all day—the kind that drives you crazy if you don't have one of those "delay" functions on your windshield wipers. It was a miserable day, and I decided I'd be better off with *some* human contact than sitting alone in the apartment, since Darlene was working all day at the QuikMart, and the coffee shop seemed as good a place as any, so off I went.

I sat down at the counter and ordered me a large decaf before spreading the paper out across the counter. Two old men sat across from me wearing old men hats and old plaid jackets that looked like they'd been stored in moth crystals for about forty or fifty years. One of them had one of those torpedo-shaped cigars in his mouth, and about a four days' growth of beard; the other one looked relatively clean. They were talking about off-track betting.

"Jesus Christ, Ange," says the clean one. "What'd you have to plunk down fifty on that sonofabitch for?"

The cigar goes slowly down to the ashtray. "Listen," says the man in a voice like gravel, "you guys are always after me to play my hunches. Well, now I played my goddamn hunches, and it's time to pay the piper. I didn't tell you guys to pool your money."

I spread my newspaper out and glance across the headlines. This, I think, may not be the best place to be on a Sunday. Cigar smoke drifts across. Maybe church would be a better plan.

And then my eye falls on an article with the phrase "civil rights" in it. Before I've even read the phrase completely, I am thinking of the sixties, of Dr. King, and Mississippi, and what went down when I was a little girl. At the same time, my gut churns because I'm realizing the article is about someone who classifies herself as an active participant in the "gay and lesbian civil rights movement." The phrase rings in my head, *gay and lesbian civil rights movement*, and I hear Jana's voice in the back of my mind saying, *Careful, Miz Tillie. Careful now.*

I sit and look at my cup of coffee for a long time. Part of my mind is running fast, like a clock wound too tight, but I can't hear what I'm thinking. Not really. It's like all the blood has rushed to my head and now I'm trying to listen to these voices in my mind arguing and fighting in the background, but all I can hear are the accumulated noises in the shop, and even they aren't clear, just a distant roar, something heard under water. I put my head in my hands and look at the brown surface of the decaf sitting there in front of me, little rainbow-like patterns like an oil slick.

All of a sudden, everything seems to fall away, and I emerge almost as if I'd fainted—I never fainted in my entire life, not one single time. The sounds in the coffee shop come back clear, feet scuffing against the floor, spoons clinking in coffee cups. I smell the cigar smoke again as the man with the four-day stubble says, "These guys are all the same. When the chips are down, they take off like bats out of hell," and when I glance up from my coffee, I see that he is talking to himself: alone, his hand in the air, in a gesture of defiance, or despair. Like a jilted lover in that Sunday afternoon gloom.

Chapter 27

SO THAT WAS a turning point for me. I realized that the only way I could survive and retain my job was to keep my mouth shut, because I knew that what was going on truly was a civil rights movement in the most basic sense. My silence was a type of complicity I would find hard to live with, but I couldn't jeopardize my future for the sake of acting "heroic." And even if I did act heroic, it did not guarantee that Jana would win anything. It only guaranteed that I would jeopardize my own future for the price of her possible gratitude.

I don't know why the civil rights article pushed me in the direction it did. Maybe it was like reverse psychology. In any event, it solidified my position. If someone asked me questions, I'd answer in monosyllables wherever possible. I would cooperate on a superficial level only. It would be obvious I had no vested interest. I could convey that attitude of sullen disinterest as surely as if I'd been born with it.

And I felt guilty, God knows, knowing I was going to do that, but I planned to just the same.

I used the phrase "according to Barbara Helms" a lot when Steve Torres from SCHRO came to do his investigation. I remember he asked me flat out if there was anything in the center on paper to indicate Jana had been fired because of sexual orientation.

"No," I said. "To the best of my knowledge, there is nothing here that would indicate that." This was true.

"Ms. Jones, Jana received a pink slip when she left. Is that correct?"

"Yes."

"May I see it?"

"Certainly." I found the file and handed it to him. He held up the pink slip when he found it, and read aloud: "*Failure to meet company expectations.*" He put it down slowly, and looked at me. "Could you describe in your own words what that means, Ms. Jones?"

"Failure to meet company expectations?"

"Yes."

"In Jana's case only?"

"Yes."

I paused. "According to Barbara Helms, Jana was not cut out for the job in that her relations with parents were…less than exemplary."

"Can you elaborate on that? That is, from your own experience?"

"No."

He looked quizzically at me. "No?"

"According to Barbara Helms, Jana had spoken to parents who then seemed to have reservations about her."

"About Ms. Odessi?"

"Yes."

"Could you elaborate on that?"

"No."

"Is there someone who could?" Then, in unison, we both said it: "Barbara Helms."

We chuckled, sizing each other up.

"Forgive me," he said. "I do not wish to seem as if I represent Ms. Odessi. I will have to speak with Ms. Helms, obviously. Just one more question, if I may. Is there anything —" he paused, as if searching for a word "— is there anything you would say in Ms. Odessi's behalf?" He looked at me, eyes challenging.

I tried not to wince. I looked back at him, as levelly as I could. "I miss her."

When I went home that night, I thought about it for a long time. Darlene was at a friend's house—she'd left a note on the stereo in the living room—and so I had no need to cook us dinner. I popped a TV dinner into the microwave and ate it while watching the news. The apartment was dark except for the blue TV light, and I thought about how it must look from outside—how it would look to someone passing by, looking up at my apartment window. Sad, I thought. That sad old light.

Chapter 28

I THOUGHT ABOUT Jana Odessi for a long time, yes, but time has a way of slipping by, and the little details of our lives have a way of driving us forward—appointments with doctors and dentists, grocery shopping, the weekend laundry—and before long, I'd more or less forgotten about the whole thing. My daughter had the abortion, which was just as well, I suppose, but at the time, it weighed us down for a good three or four months. I forgot what Jana Odessi even looked like, in the way we will when someone passes out of our lives forever.

Five months had passed, I guess, since Steve Torres came to visit us, and Jana had not yet had her hearing. I hadn't known what would happen if she had a hearing, or even whether it would happen in the first place, and would have completely forgotten about it if not for a fax to our main office that said *Attn: Barbara Helms* at the top.

Later, I learned that the Commission found "just cause" in Jana's case, based both on Jana's complaint and on something someone at the center must have told Steve Torres. It could have been me, maybe even what I *hadn't* said. It ended up that the center was going to make some kind of settlement offer, which would be called a conciliation agreement if she accepted it. Barbara Helms eventually let it out that she was going to offer Jana her old job back. I thought this was foolish, an insufficient offer, but obviously, I didn't say anything.

One night, Barbara called me at home at about nine o'clock. When the phone rang I was surprised. It usually didn't ring after seven unless Darlene had car trouble. She was out with her boyfriend that night—they were spending a lot of time together, even after her abortion—and I assumed it was her. I wasn't thrilled at the prospect of having to go out in the rain to get her out of some jam or other, so I'm sure my voice sounded flat when I answered.

"Hello."

"Tillie?"

At first, I didn't recognize the voice. "Yes?"

"Tillie, it's Barbara."

My mouth fell open. "Hi…."

"The little bitch rejected the agreement."

"Pardon?"

I heard her take a swallow of something. "The little bitch rejected the agreement," she said. "Jana Odessi. The conciliation agreement." She swallowed again. Her voice was heavy, like someone with a cold or a heavy smoking habit.

"She rejected it?" The only response I could muster.

"Yeah. Flat out. Now I have to go to court. Can you b'lieve it?"

"Well, uh, I don't —"

"Tillie."

I paused. "Yeah?"

She laughed, a terrible sound that was not a laugh and yet was. "Tillie," she repeated.

I strained to keep my tone neutral. "Yes."

"Tillie, the little dyke rejected the *goddamn* agreement."

"I know, Barbara," I said.

"Listen," she said. She seemed to sober up just then, her voice resuming its regular authoritarian tone. "Listen, Tillie. If we have to go to court here, I may need you to go to bat for me. You know what I'm saying."

"Yes."

"You know what I'm saying?"

"Yes," I said.

"I may need you to go to bat for me. For the center. I won't volunteer you as a witness, I wouldn't do that to you. I don't want you to go through with it unless they ask you. But you may need to go to bat for me."

"I understand."

"You understand?" Her voice seemed to slide back down again.

"I do."

"You understand."

"Yes."

"Are you sure you understand?"

"Yes," I said. "I'm sure."

"Okay," she said. "You understand. That's good. I'm not going to take up your time now. We'll talk at the office, if we have to. I mean *my* office. Okay."

"Yes," I said.

"Thank you, Tillie," she said. "I'm counting on you."

"I understand, Barbara," I said, and for the first time ever, I think, I felt completely equal with her. Her authority over me evaporated, and I saw her as she was, no better or worse than anyone else, just another human being chicken-scratching for her existence. She said goodnight and we both hung up, and I sat back in my chair and looked at the phone. I had to take the receiver from the hook again and wipe the sweat off it, and off my hands and forehead.

"Goddamn," I said beneath my breath. "Goddamn."

Jana

Chapter 29

WHEN STEVE TORRES told me I would have my day in court, I remember feeling a mixture of dread and anticipation. In a way, it was like the feeling I got before going to college. I mean, I still felt this profound sense of excitement, but also definite fear. I brought a lot of that fear to the offices of John Wagner, Psy.D.

It's hard to say why, but I had a real feeling of inner peace when day one finally arrived. For one thing, in addition to Dr. Wagner—John—I had the full support of Danielle Marshall, who has my eternal gratitude. To be honest, I think I'd already put her through the emotional wringer at that point, and she was either brave or crazy, and possibly both, to stick around so long.

She was sitting in her favorite blue chair, reading me something from *The New York Times Book Review* one sunny day that year, when I realized for the first time that I was in love with her. I'll never forget it. I can still see her face. Sunlight was making bright squares on the hardwood floor, and I found myself staring blankly into them while Danielle's voice lulled me into a dream.

I blinked, and the room seemed brighter than it had been the moment before. When I looked at Danielle, I was suddenly aware of every aspect of her physical presence in a way I'd never been before. Her feet, long and slender, with their rounded curves across the tops, and her legs—crossed at the ankles—boyishly supple and strong-looking at the calves, but by mid-thigh, where her terry cloth shorts made all further surmise impossible, her form undeniably female. I saw the faintest trace of down along thighbone where she had neglected to, or chosen not to, shave. The rest, except for the twentieth century hairstyle, looked like a sculpture from some museum of Anglo-Saxon idealism, a perfect form neither too round for youth nor too angular for adulthood. She could have been in acting or modeling school, the slight nose and honeyed lower lip just a shade too subtle for Hollywood. Old fashioned, unexotic beauty.

On and on she read, punctuating phrases with a periodic smile that made her gorgeous, dimpled profile light up like a flare in a dark sky, her lower lip drawn across the white of her smile. I felt an aching deep within me, an unmistakable longing that could not be ignored, and a warm glow ran up through my thighs and arms and breasts, making me tingle deep inside. Before I'd thought about what I was doing, I was standing and walking across the room until the newspaper was almost within reach. And when she looked up and said, "What?" I was already bending to kiss her lips and draw her down from her chair to the knitted rug on the hardwood floor in front of her.

I kissed her there for a long time, and then we moved, shuffling and stopping and turning, into her room, always kissing, our eyes closed but still with me leading her into the room like some unseeing ballroom dance partner, and she was making soft little expressions of surprise and excitement even through the kiss, and it wasn't until we finally separated for a moment on the tangle of bedspread and blankets that I heard the long slow breath that fell from her as naturally as a smile.

Later, we lay in a silence unbroken except by the sound of a light breeze outside her window, my face curled into the hollow of her shoulderblade. After a certain point, she said, in a whisper just above my head, "Why did you do this?"

"What?"

"What we just did."

A pause. "I didn't want to listen to any more of that article you were reading, but I couldn't think of a polite way to tell you."

She sighed. "You don't really expect me to believe that, do you?"

I smiled to myself. "Not really, no."

We stayed in bed for a long time, not doing anything but talking in whispers, the sort of hushed tones you sometimes hear at pajama parties when you're a kid. Though it seems somehow secretive, in reality, it's just that you feel you've created some magical space impervious to outside forces. Adults' troubles, wars, responsibilities. In a way, a kind of sexless place—the green world. I think that's why we stayed there so long that day, and why we spoke in such hushed whispers, to keep from breaking the spell.

I nodded off eventually, though it was only midafternoon. I began to dream, and I always dream in color: a beach and deep sky blue water and palm trees wavering a little in the wind, with spiky fronds like punk hairdos. Everything looked placid but surreal.

A woman stood near me on the beach, just out of my range of vision. I lay in the sun, and as I tried to look at her, she receded just beyond my peripheral vision. I thought she was wearing a white robe or dress, but I couldn't tell, because I could never get a real look at her. I just knew she was there.

Finally, I closed my eyes and gave up, and when I did, I felt the cool touch of a hand on my wrist. I opened my eyes and looked into the eyes of the woman in white from my dream when I was seventeen. Her face and hair kept changing, blurring, she was never, even for an instant, a recognizable person, yet somehow she was beautiful. I knew she was. Every change, every face, was beautiful, yet I could see her only through a haze.

Then suddenly, she was Danielle. I saw her as clearly as if the thin veils had fallen from my vision, and she was as clear and real as a beacon of light, looking deep into my eyes, searching them with a troubled look. "No," she said, "don't," and her voice sounded very far away, the voice of someone on the other side of a wall, someone in another room. I woke with a start, bolt upright in the bed, the upper part of my body going from horizontal to vertical so fast and hard it was like being pushed. I gasped for air, drowning.

"Jesus Christ," I said under my breath. What a jolt, like simultaneously coming out of a nightmare and having an asthma attack; something I hadn't had for a long time.

Danielle wasn't in bed with me, but I heard her running water in the other room. I remembered the bronchator in my purse, a device I use sometimes to enhance my breathing. I grabbed it and took a hit before sitting back in bed and taking a minute to calm down.

Okay, I told myself. You're all right. You're going to be okay. Everything in my life came rushing back as the dream receded, like it so often does upon awakening: the case, Steve Torres, my new job, the newness of having made love with Danielle.

What time is it?

I couldn't have slept that long. I was surprised she hadn't woken me up. The bathroom door creaked and made a little banging sound against the doorstop. It kept repeating, getting fainter, and then she came back in.

"Did you call me? I thought I heard something."

I smiled, not wanting to look as serious as I probably did. "No, I don't think so. Although I just woke up from a dream like *that*," I said, snapping my fingers.

She knelt on the bed. "What did you dream about?"

"You."

"Oh, boy." She flipped over on her back, bouncing down beside me. "You, of all people, you're getting corny. I can't believe it."

"Hey, I can't help what's in my dreams," I said, nudging her. "Besides, it wasn't that kind of dream."

"What'd you do? Hook me up with Barbara Helms or something?"

I laughed. "No, it was just you and me on the beach —"

"Sounds corny."

"— I was lying down and you were peering into my face. And very seriously and businesslike, you said, *No, don't.*"

"No, don't?"

"That's all you said."

"What were you doing? Trying to untie my bikini strap?"

"I wasn't doing anything. And you weren't wearing a bikini. You were wearing a long white dress. Like a sundress."

"Weird. Are all your dreams like that? I mean, do you always have really strange dreams?"

I thought about it. "Yeah," I said. "Yeah, I guess I do."

Chapter 30

NOT LONG AFTER that, I had my day in court. So much preparation for such a small event. A public hearing, of course, is not exactly court. At least one lawyer is always present—the one appointed by the commission to sit, judge-like, and oversee the proceedings—and sometimes, as in our case, there are lawyers to speak on behalf of the complainant and defendant.

For whatever reason, Barbara Helms chose to go that route, and her lawyer spoke entirely on her behalf. She never said one word. She had a hell of a good lawyer, too. Well, Kiddie Korner Childcare Center had a hell of a good lawyer, to be accurate.

I don't know if he was her personal lawyer, too, but he was definitely defending The Center. His name was James Kahn. I thought that was funny at first, because in my mind I pictured his last name as *Caan*. Like the actor.

I found out later he'd been a district attorney, and was now basically a "corporate lawyer." He'd made a big reputation for himself throughout the state by winning a case for some major manufacturing company that had gotten nailed for violating toxic dumping regulations because somebody blew the whistle. They had literally dumped tons of toxic waste into local waterways. I don't know how he got them off, but everyone thought he was a great lawyer. The whole story made me think he was just a scumbag. Eventually I changed my mind; he was a great lawyer, too.

Genteel-looking, almost to the point of being slick, Attorney Kahn weighed about two hundred pounds, but was just tall enough to only look large-boned. He had black hair, glasses, and a receding hairline, the kind of tall forehead that makes certain men look smart, like Shakespeare. He wore the best clothes I've ever seen on someone in real life, and he was always pulling at the ends of his sleeves, adjusting them, looking down at nothing, like he was studying his cufflinks. More than anything else, that's what I remember about the hearing: watching Attorney James Kahn study his imaginary cufflinks. It annoyed the hell out of me, to tell the truth.

The Law Offices of the State Commission on Human Rights and Opportunities are at 119 Lincoln Street, a stone's throw from the gold-domed Capitol Building, tucked away in the uppermost floor of what used to be a three story mansion. The windows are large and dirty, and the foyer when you enter looks like something out of a Hitchcock film—spooky marble stairs curving up out of sight to the second and third floors.

The public hearing is in room 331 on the third floor, and it happens to coincide with the case of Jerome Hopkins vs. Technical International Technologies, which is scheduled for room 330. I know this because I see it beside my own entry on the docket. "Jana Odessi vs. Kiddie Korner," it says in its impersonal dot matrix print.

I cannot help feeling that my name sounds bland and ineffectual next to the center's cute, overtly marketable name. Kiddie Korner Child Care Center. Next to that, Jana Odessi might be some sort of ogre, a psychobitch with a personal vendetta, a crazed vengeance campaign. Most of all, I feel small. It is me against *them*. I wonder how good old Jerome Hopkins feels, going up against a company whose middle name is *international*; probably no better than me against a company whose middle name is *child*.

So, here I am in court. Well, not court, exactly, but it sure feels like it.

I do not expect anyone to be there, really, but sure enough, there are three or four people with cameras and microphones and clipboards with legal pads: a genuine press corps. I try to look invisible, but of course, inevitably, Steve Torres will be there, and he will greet me loudly in his charming Latino accent. He does. I smile and proffer my hand, which he takes between his own big hands like an envelope he is pressing shut. And while we exchange this brief moment of surreal quiet in the midst of the hum of voices, I'm aware that anyone in the room who was unsure of my identity a moment ago undoubtedly knows now that I am the plaintiff. I say the word in my head and think: *plaintive*. Yes, that too.

Eyes fix upon me, many eyes, though nothing has happened yet. I feel myself coloring, and attempt to counteract my rising panic with a breathing exercise learned from the great John Wagner, Psy. D. At the same time, however, I chew the nail on my right index finger.

Steve Torres speaks, his voice low. "The man in the grey pinstripes is James Kahn. He is the attorney for the defense. Never, *never* let him intimidate you. Remember that *you* are not on trial here. The woman next to him, with the microphone, is Camille Tattaglia. She is editor for the local gay and lesbian paper."

"*The Alternative Voice?*"

"The same." He nods smartly, looking pleased.

"I've got a word I'd like to have with her."

His eyebrows go up. "Whatever you do," he says, "you must remain cordial. They may be among your greatest allies."

"Swell," I say. "Who are my enemies?"

He turns back toward their group, leaning in closer in order to keep from having to raise his voice. "The woman with the dark blue blazer," he says, inclining his black head in her direction ever so slightly, "is Annie Rozetta. She represents a religious group called Friends of the True Way. Arch-conservative."

Now my eyebrows raise themselves. "You're shitting me."

"No," he says slowly, "I am very serious. "The Friends of the True Way are vehemently anti-homosexual. One might say *virulently*. She will no doubt be looking to write you up in their newsletter as a threat to children's welfare, or a menace to society in general. If she could make you out a prostitute, it would probably give her a thrill of self-righteous pleasure."

"Maybe I'll go over and pretend to hit on her."

He chuckles silently for a moment, his shoulders shaking. Then he turns serious again. "She, too, is important from a PR standpoint. *If* I were your attorney —" he spreads his arms wide, as if in protest "— which of course I am not—I would advise you to work at least as hard at charming Annie Rozetta as you work at charming Camille Tattaglia. I would say you must be a model of propriety. But," he says suddenly, "I am not your attorney, and of course you will act as you wish." He smiles his little mysterious half-smile.

As if on cue, the attorney assigned me by the commission, Wilson Carr, walks in. "Morning," he says to us.

We exchange greetings.

"We will be with you in a moment, Wilson," says Steve. "I am briefing Jana on the *Who's Who* of Odessi vs. KKCCC."

"Ah."

I turn back to Steve: "Anyone else I should be aware of? Any serious threats, other than The True Way?"

He looks around. "Well, of course," he says, "there is *her*."

I look where he has indicated, and my stomach drops, like the first big hill on a rollercoaster. Barbara Helms sits among a small group of very proper-looking women, matronly in her blue business suit and light blouse with its ruffled collar. She looks like she could be a child psychology expert on *Oprah*. Her gleaming teeth shine out of the soricine face, a false smile that reveals nothing and gives no quarter. Somehow, I can tell already that she will not be saying a word during the proceedings. She will be a stone, revealing only expressions of deepest sympathy for yours truly.

Steve Torres sees all this, or seems to, and touches my wrist with great tact and delicacy. "She is only as harmful as you allow her to be," he says.

I meet his steady gaze. In that moment, he is like a Zen master.

"But surely," he says, "she will never be an ally."

Ally. The word rings in my head. No, she will never be an ally.

"Okay, Wilson," I say to the great bear of a man beside me. "What's the deal?"

Torres has prepared him well. He arrives with nothing more than answers; no questions for me. His briefcase is like a small brown trunk, rectangular when opened. He lines up file folder upon file folder on the extra chair beside us. Within moments the files are stacked like battalions against the red leather of the chair.

"Our best defense is a good offense," he says. His tone masks his implied belligerence, soothing and level as a minister's. I find it difficult to picture him employing any kind of offense. Throughout our meeting, two days prior to the hearing, he sat and listened quietly to Steve's and my presentation, bending a watery eye on us in his fatherly way, and pausing only at the very end to ask, "Anything else?" Today the bags under his eyes attest to the time he's spent preparing.

Steve says, "It's very unusual for the media to be here." He runs a hand over his black hair. "Ordinarily, the press are no more interested in public hearings than they are in figure skating." I arch an eyebrow and he smiles. "Ordinarily," he says.

Before long, he and Wilson are conferring quietly, and I am left to my own devices. I need the time, really, to blank myself out, to engage in not-think, and I look around the room. With ridiculous clarity, my eyes fix themselves on small details.

A bleak-eyed woman, the court monitor, sits at the front of the room reading the advertising section of a newspaper behind a wood finish desk. Beside her stands a table with two microphones flanked by an American flag and the flag of the state of Connecticut. There are other microphones, including a pair for the commissioner's desk, and they are all plugged into a kind of central apparatus on the court monitor's desk, the long black cords tangled along the floor, and taped down with masking tape to prevent the kind of swan dive that might lead to other types of litigation.

Two obvious camps divide the back of the room: ours and theirs. At their table, where Mr. Kahn stands studying his cufflinks, two other people, a fortyish blonde and a bearded man of indeterminate age, sit exchanging folders and underlining things with thin blue markers. I wonder if they are lawyers. Virtually everyone drinks coffee from paper cups with plastic covers. Against the far wall on the left side of the room are two copy machines. For the moment, none of this means anything to me. I might as well be at the Burning Brassiere.

And now another older blonde woman, one with a pageboy haircut, walks in and says, "Good morning. Shall we start?" This is the commissioner. My anxiety level rises when she announces to the court monitor that she's forgotten her glasses. How the hell will she read anything? She acts like some sort of spacey bag lady before she finally gets down to business, and I notice that this seems to make the attorneys even more deferential, as if she were an absent-minded sage to whom they pay homage with each "Yes, your Honor," "No, your Honor."

She chooses the court monitor to read things to her.

"Have you received any further papers from the defendant?" she asks Carr.

"No, your Honor."

She turns to the court monitor. "Are we on the record?"

"Yes, your Honor."

She changes her tone, suddenly formal: "This is the case of Jana Odessi vs. Kiddie Korner Child Care Center, SCHRO case number five-seven-nine dash six-two-seven. I'm Hearing Officer Melody Haver. Will the people in the room identify themselves, please, starting with the table on the left side of the room?"

We do.

At one point, she asks to have a pair of giant folders labeled for her with a large *one* and *two*, since she has forgotten her glasses. These are "exhibit files" and "commission files."

After the introductory rigmarole, Attorney Kahn stands and makes the first motion. He says Kiddie Korner Child Care Center would like to have their employment records put under protective order, so that their salary policy—and other policies, I would presume—are kept confidential, that is, out of the public domain.

"Motion granted," the commissioner says.

"I would like to ensure that the complainant can share documents with counsel, as well as with Attorney Torres," says Wilson Carr.

"Also granted," says the commissioner.

"It is also understood then," says Carr, turning slightly toward Attorney Kahn's table, "that when this case reaches a court of law, the complainant reserves the right to her own counsel." It is almost a question.

The commissioner appears to hide a smirk. "Mr. Carr, this is an administrative procedure only, as you know. We are a long way from determining whether or not it will be necessary for *any* one in this room to appear in a court of law. Be that as it may, we will go on record as stating that if and when this case reaches a court of law, the complainant will of course be allowed to avail herself of whatever counsel she desires."

"Thank you," says Wilson Carr.

The commissioner does not smile as she says, "You may be seated."

My brain goes on hold, like I'd had a lobotomy for breakfast. Kahn and the commissioner and Carr are talking, but I've lost the sense of what they are saying. I begin to panic, and John Wagner's deep breathing exercise helps, but it does little toward restoring my brain to any sort of competence. Fortunately, I have nothing to do for the moment except sit and look composed, but the sense that I am missing something—and that it will come back later to haunt me—overwhelms and frightens me. Knowing I'm frightened, and may *look* frightened, causes me to force the look of composure, and the effort, as I ride the big wave of "overwhelm," drains whatever inner resources I've got left. Worst of all, I suddenly realize this is the exact condition I was in when I had my run-in with the three women at the corner of Main Street in Hartford: cranky, overstressed, and then, mind gone blank. Out of that condition I exploded into a towering rage, embarrassing, potentially dangerous. I can clearly see that, today, here at the first session of my own public hearing, I might actually be a danger to myself. This does nothing to alleviate my anxiety.

At length, I realize I will have to give some extremely detailed testimony. Not just give. I will be required to withstand a great deal of questions, required to look at a great quantity of documents and answer whether or not I recognize them, even read parts of them aloud for the group. Much like an actual court case. The first document is Exhibit One, the next Exhibit Two, and so on. Exhibit One is my job application, which Wilson Carr holds aloft at the end of his opening remarks.

"I'd like to mark document one for ID," he says, lifting the paper high in the air.

Defense attorney James Kahn says he has no objection. Admitted, says the commissioner.

Carr hands copies of the application to the court monitor, the commissioner and myself. I have been summoned to the front of the room, where I sit at the table with the microphones, under oath.

"Do you recognize this document?"

"Yes."

"What is it?" he asks. He is almost sarcastic, as if he didn't know himself what it was.

"My application."

"For employment at Kiddie Korner Child Care Center."

"Yes."

"Tell me—are there any questions on that form that you found to be extraordinarily personal?"

"No."

"Nothing about your having ever used drugs, for example, or having committed crimes?"

"Not that I recall."

"Nothing about your sexual history or sexual orientation?"

"Objection," says Attorney Kahn. "Relevance?"

The commissioner turns to Wilson Carr. "Mr. Carr?"

"Your Honor, the commission's entire case rests upon the issue of sexual orientation. We would like to first establish that of course the day care center has no official policy on sexual orientation, and one clue would be the fact that there is nothing on the application suggesting otherwise."

He appears to be about to continue, but the commissioner says, "I'm going to let it stand." Then, to me: "You may answer the question."

"No. Nothing about sexual orientation."

"Or sexual history?" Wilson Carr asks.

"No sir." I put the paper down.

"Let Exhibit One go on the record," he says, and hands my copy to the court monitor. Almost inaudibly, the commissioner sighs.

This goes on and on. Exhibit after exhibit goes into what they call my *dossier*, as Wilson Carr presents to me documents I recognize, documents I do not entirely recognize, and documents I never knew existed. Ultimately, many of them—the one dealing with a visit I paid to Harmony Stone, or the one describing my role in assisting an accident-prone child—are meaningless, as far as I can tell, and I begin to wonder just exactly what Attorney Carr is up to. Is he just working to present a picture of me as a model employee? Perhaps. Occasionally, there is an objection from Kahn, but he does not question the ones *I* would have. So I'm left to draw my own conclusions about "relevance."

One hour into the hearing, Carr brings forth Exhibit 19A. "Do you recognize this document?"

"Yes," I say.

"What is it?"

"A copy of my pink slip. What a thrill to see *that* again." The room erupts into laughter, and I blush, trying not to smile.

"What does it say under 'reason for dismissal?'"

"'Failure to meet company expectations.'"

"What is your understanding of those terms?"

"What do you mean?"

"The expression, 'failure to meet company expectations.' How do you understand it?"

"Very poorly," I say. More laughter.

"Was it ever explained to you?"

"Not formally."

"Was it explained informally?"

"I suppose, yes."

"Who explained it?"

"Barbara Helms."

"Was this at the time you were terminated, or before?"

"At the time."

"Do you recall what she said?"

I hesitate. The room is hot and tense. "She said I hadn't been able to establish a rapport with parents, and that it was critical that employees be able to do so. She said she didn't feel I was cut out to do that."

"She didn't feel you were 'cut out' to do that?"

"Objection," says Kahn. "I fail to see the relevance of repeating Ms. Odessi's remark."

"Sustained."

"Very well," Carr says. "Ms. Odessi, why do *you* think she felt you weren't cut out for this line of work?"

"Objection!"

"*Sustained*. Mr. Carr, you're going to have to make your argument in a manner more congruous to the protocol of this hearing. Bear in mind, please, that this is an administrative procedure only, not a performance for a jury." Then, turning to the court monitor: "You may continue. However, strike the above remarks from the record."

The court monitor nods, and starts the tape rolling again.

"One last question," says Wilson Carr. "Do you feel that *you* know the reason for your termination?"

Pause. The question throws me, big time. Of course I know, idiot! What's the follow-up question, what *is* that reason? Kahn will jump on that like it's an ambulance he's too out of shape to chase, shouting, "Objection! Objection!"

I look at Wilson, and we size each other up, it seems. I can see by his eyes he is merely waiting for a cooperative complainant's reply, a simple yes or no. A simple yes, in fact. *Yes, because I am a lesbian.*

"Yes," I say.

"I would like Exhibit 19A to go on record." He hands the copy of my pink slip to the court monitor. I am glad to see it go.

I am aware, naturally, that plenty more will follow. Nonetheless, I'm surprised and pleased to see us end the morning on such a strong note. Exhibit 19A is the last document before we adjourn. We will not return until tomorrow morning, at which time the defense will make its case.

That evening is like torture to me. I call Danielle, then remember she will be out of town for these two critical days. My need for someone to talk to, anyone, grows after I make two more nonproductive calls—one busy signal, and one that rings and rings. I pace, looking out the window but seeing nothing.

This is probably the worst part of the whole ordeal, waiting and pacing before the window like someone expecting a wayward spouse or child. It's hard to believe I might have to submit to two more days of this, and not resolve anything. I realize my jaw has been clenched for hours, my face set in that phony look of composure. The entire lower half of my face aches, and now that I think about it, I notice my neck and shoulders are also sore. I need to slow down. And I do, taking in a long slow breath and heaving an exhausted sigh. As my head clears, I can't help thinking about tomorrow. What they'll say, what type of case they'll make against me. The overwhelming sense that the whole thing is my word against theirs.

What baffles me is that they think I've even got a case to begin with. What ace does Steve Torres have up his sleeve, or Wilson Carr? Tillie Jones? Impossible. Wendy Simpson? Beyond impossible.

There just doesn't seem to be anything behind it; from a legal standpoint, the whole thing is smoke and mirrors. The Wizard of Oz. Except for the obvious fact that I am telling the truth, that what I know happened in that room, that day, did happen. There was no *failure to meet company expectations.* I know that much.

I cannot believe I've been tense all day. I ought to have calmed down during the long downhill slope of the afternoon, but apparently the period of decompression would not come until now, so I'm left only with this utter exhaustion and a head reeling with thoughts I wouldn't wish on anyone. Tonight, my mind is like a bad neighborhood—I shouldn't go in there alone—but I go, and when I finally reach for my pillow and pull the covers up to my ears, I am too tired to fall asleep right away.

Chapter 31

TEN A.M. WE sit in the hearing room waiting for Barbara Helms, James Kahn, and all the rest of that crowd. Steve Torres and Wilson Carr are once again quietly conferring.

They enter briskly, all at once, a minute after ten. Though I am in an agony of stress, the atmosphere in the room is surprisingly casual today. The commissioner chats up the court monitor, and yesterday's press corps are conspicuously absent. It feels as though something has already been resolved.

"Shall we get started?" asks the commissioner. I notice she has found her glasses.

Attorney James Kahn stands, shuffles some papers. "Your Honor, on behalf of my client, I would like to request that we move for a dismissal."

She weighs it, looks puzzled momentarily. Obviously, she expected a more considered line of attack. "On any particular grounds?"

"Your Honor, my client—and I—still believe the plaintiff has no case."

I look at Steve and Wilson. Their faces impassive, but beneath the masks a genuine consternation.

Kahn launches into a speech about the case. So, he does have an opening argument: not only a lack of compelling evidentiary documentation, he says, but a lack, even, of sufficient motive. Nothing beyond the circumstantial and anecdotal, and so forth, he goes on, on, on, the sonorous voice bringing a lull to the proceedings almost immediately. Every syllable seems to contain a hidden kindness, like a doctor giving the bad news to a cancer patient's family: no hope.

He is so persuasive, so overwhelmingly gentle in his argument, that the harshness of the conclusion is almost lost even on me. I am nearly convinced he is right. I have no case, it was all in my head. And the look Tillie Jones used to jolt me, to galvanize me into action? Just a misunderstanding, or, even worse, maybe even something I *imagined*.

I shake myself out of that, of course, in time to hear the pronouncement of Hearing Officer Melody Haver, who has been sitting very still behind her desk, looking concerned.

"This is not the ordinary procedure in a case like this one, but this case has been anything but ordinary. Particularly the media circus yesterday. Given the fact that I've had little opportunity to deliberate, and would still prefer to follow the usual protocol of allowing both parties the third day of hearings to present closing statements, I'm going to adjourn for today. I will have all of you return tomorrow morning at the same time. Ms. Odessi," she turns to me, "I regret having to put you through another twenty-four hours of waiting, but the fact of the matter is, you would have had to wait until tomorrow morning for a verdict anyhow. This way, I still have the usual amount of deliberation, which I feel is certainly reasonable in this case. Fair enough? And with that, we will go off the record."

The court monitor takes her cue and shuts off the recorder.

"Now, Mr. Carr," says the commissioner, "do you have anything we need to take care of before we close for the morning?"

"No, your Honor."

"Mr. Kahn?"

"No, your Honor."

"Very well. We will adjourn until tomorrow morning at ten a.m. sharp." She stands and walks briskly out the door behind her on the left, the one I always think of as "the back entrance." Her comment about "ten sharp" strikes me as a parting shot in light of Kahn and company's 10:01 arrival this morning, and I try to hold on to that as I leave for home. It's the only good feeling I have so far from the morning.

Now I can see that Wilson Carr and Steve Torres have nothing whatsoever up their respective sleeves. They've worked to make the best possible case for the commission and, by extension, for me, and have come up with nothing Attorney Kahn thinks is concrete enough to warrant an action. Of course, I'm aware that, even if I win, the defense will appeal the decision. Then, perhaps, would be the time for Kahn to break out the heavy artillery. As it stands, I feel as if he's already made his closing statement, and the sense of closure is almost palpable. I don't believe I'll win, and neither does he.

But something in me fights the pessimism, and I feel the old anxiety build anew as I debate the question on the drive back home. I know I have a case, however circumstantial the situation, however inadequate the evidentiary documentation. Would there be any evidentiary documentation for racism? No. Would there be a memo about homophobia? I don't think so. Would there be recorded phone calls with Barbara Helms indulging in gleeful dyke-bashing? Of course not.

The fact is that most discrimination cases of this sort are based on facts known best, and often *only*, by the main perpetrator and the victim of the discrimination. Two individuals. My word against hers, hers versus mine. My case is so typical, it makes me squirm.

And now I have to sit at home for another night and stew about all this, wallowing in my knowledge of the inner workings of our wonderful judicial system. I know how these things usually come out; I have taught myself as much as possible about law in these past weeks, discrimination cases in particular. Most discrimination cases are either simply lost, then abandoned, because the plaintiff is too scared or broke—or both—to pursue the matter in court. Or they are won, but then abandoned by the plaintiffs when the process of going through hearing after hearing—and listening to the defense try to run their credibility through the mill—proves too costly, frustrating, and time-consuming. Many are just broken and beaten down by the hideous bureaucracy of it all, and in the end it becomes impossible to "win" anything. The only consolation prize is the old "well, you proved your point."

So I brood on this, anxiety mounting in my breast like some monstrous disease my body is trying to reject. I'd throw it up if I could, anything to be rid of it. Piles of bills and other pieces of mail I have not taken time to open lie on the kitchen table, and of course, I know that more are on the way. My new job will not provide me even with sick days or vacation time, so every hour of public hearing time is another hour subtracted from my next paycheck. Which translates to another bill to pay.

I brood on the job, too, as I stare out the kitchen window at the lines of traffic below. What kind of future can I expect from teaching music to children five days a week? I know I'll have to line up something else during the summer months. Tutoring? It seems only vaguely possible that it would be sufficient. I can't help the little wave of self-pity that washes over me. After all my training, after my years of playing jazz, am I really supposed to be teaching a bunch of kids to play the *recorder*? It's not even a real instrument, for God's sake. And the pay is abominable.

But if I can't do anything with my music for now—that is, anything that pays well enough to keep me alive—what the hell am I supposed to do? I can't take handouts from Mom and Dad indefinitely. Get a roommate? I'd really like to live with Danielle, if she'd be willing, but why should it have to be *here*? The more I think about it, the more I realize I want to blow this town, just get out of here as fast as possible. And I know I'm not alone; Hartford is one of the fastest-shrinking cities in the whole country.

Of course, this whole line of thinking creates an intolerable paralysis. Maybe the periodic sound of sirens in the distance, the piles of bills, the prospect of the dead-end job, the amazing shrinking paycheck I'll get as a result of the hearing…any one of these could be the proverbial straw on the camel's back. Whatever the case, I need someone to talk to, and since Danielle isn't an option, I call my other friends. Everyone is out though, and I get answering machine after answering machine. When I finally decide to call Dr. Wagner—tonight he is *Dr.* Wagner, not just "John"—the phone rings and rings. Not even a machine.

So I turn on the radio.

"The reason so many women today seem so angry is because for years they've been subjugated to what is commonly perceived as this white male power structure, and now that they've won some power, they're tending to use it in the same types of self-serving or even coercive ways that men have for centuries. It's really kind of discouraging to see. Typically, one thinks of women as more likely to recognize the superiority of cooperation over competition and of community over control and mastery, and yet women in the public eye today seem to be exhibiting the same kinds of predatory, acquisitive behaviors that have supposedly made men their oppressors since the beginning of time. It really just clearly demonstrates, I think, that everyone has an ego —"

I have had enough of that. *Click.*

Not what I wanted to hear right now. No simple solutions to complex problems, though, no way to get through all this without some sort of plan, some shifting of gears. I imagine the situation like a set of Chinese boxes: open the box and there's a smaller box inside, open that and another box, another and another, until you reach…what? A fortune cookie? With a tiny slip of paper in it that says, *You have been fired from your job; you're screwed.*

My mind begins to drift. And then the dream: like an old ghost, the ghost of a friend, white gauzy dress, the beach, that hazy gorgeous face beautiful and indistinct looming down at me, *Thunder Island*, the salt breeze. An ecstasy of perfumes, seascape, forest, my hands wet with everything, myself disappearing, me, my body, a wisp of light, a shadow from clouds, song of birds across the sky, birdsong gullflight wings flapping in my sleepy ears. Daylight sparkles on water forever endless light and warmth and…yes.…

I am startled awake.

A brief nap, not even a catnap, really, merely dozing at the kitchen table, slumping slowly down in the chair after falling into the kind of reverie that always strikes at times like this. I need a creative outlet, I realize. It's high time I picked up my saxophone.

Long low notes, heavy and rasping as a blues singer. Liquid sounds, scale upon scale, my best attempts to imitate a Coltrane, Parker, Rollins. My poor attempts, thankfully private. But comforting nonetheless. Long low notes, squeaky high ones. Mother's milk.

And so on, until sleep. And then morning again.

Chapter 32

THE ALARM BEEPED steadily from across the room. I lurched from my bed to a spot on the floor halfway between bed and bureau, unsure at first whether I was still asleep. I had slept the sleep of the dead, so deep that it felt like coming up from the depths of some watery cavern.

I'd been dreaming again, and in my dream, Barbara Helms was offering to adopt Danielle. Already it was a long way away as I shuffled out to the kitchen, and the whole thing receded from my consciousness like the water I'd emerged from, draining back and disappearing, gone. It dawned on me that the Danielles of my dream, the Barbara Helmses, whomever they might be, existed only in my mind, were confined there forever, not to be confused with the real thing.

The morning of that last hearing stands out in my mind very clearly, even more so than the first long day, when things took on that surreal clarity usually reserved for exceptional crises or the lucidity of the mad. The sun was shining, and I remember having an old Duke Ellington tune in my head when I went into the hearing: *Take The "A" Train*. My spirits were high, if only because I knew that this was the final day of the proceedings. I can't think why else I would have been so cheerful. I wasn't even anticipating victory.

And yet, something happened when I walked into the commission. Somehow, everything took on a purpose and meaning, and I felt sure I'd win after all. Intuitive, that's the only way I can describe it. The commissioner walked in and said good morning, pleasantly enough, and all the pain and suffering I'd gone through became irrelevant, just part of a natural process. I looked around, then sat back comfortably in my seat and smiled. And felt good.

Steve Torres and Wilson Carr didn't arrive until close to ten, nor did the defense. Kahn arrived, of course, along with some other people from their side: another lawyer, no one memorable, and someone from the center's board of directors. Barbara Helms was nowhere in sight, which surprised me somewhat, and made me a little relieved. I didn't want to deal with her at all, regardless of the outcome.

"Due to some scheduling restraints," the commissioner said, "we'll have to limit any closing arguments to one half hour each, so that we can adjourn by eleven o'clock. Will there be a problem with that?"

Both sides said no.

"All right. Are there any further closing statements, then? Mr. Kahn, any closing statement from you?"

"No, your Honor."

She turned to Steve and Wilson. "Mr. Carr?"

"No, your Honor."

"Very well, then. In light of the evidence presented against the center, and the lack of eyewitnesses or other substantial testimony, I must tell you I am obliged to deliver a verdict of not guilty."

Not guilty. I did not hear another word after that. Not guilty. I think she actually said, *I'm sorry, Ms. Odessi* at some point, probably in response to the look of anger or disappointment or outrage in my eyes, or the way they filled with tears and threatened to overflow but did not. I think I went into shock, overwhelmed by a feeling of deflation, an upward surge of despair at the time and effort wasted, the loss of income, all for nothing. Only when I felt anger rise in me again did I realize what was going on around me.

I had to deal with some formalities, of course. Steve and Wilson, talk of an appeal process, going to Superior Court. I heard very little, or rather, I tried to listen but heard little. Nothing registered beyond that one reference to Superior Court.

For the rest of that day, I might as well have been sleepwalking. I remember I went to Elizabeth Park afterwards—I sometimes liked to go there with Danielle—and just wandered around looking at flowers. I had a strong sense that this was all unreal, the bright sun and blue sky made it seem like some strange nightmare, like the feeling you get when someone dies and you get the news. Everything shifts, becomes somehow hellish, the sounds of rustling leaves in the trees or birds chirping make it all seem untrue, impossible. He can't be dead; it's too nice a day. I can't have lost; look at the sky!

I would have to tell my parents, I realized, and the thought filled me with dread. They'd been there since the beginning in sort of a peripheral way, basically as a functional support system. They'd made overtures toward hiring hotshot lawyers, that kind of thing. Nothing had ever come of it, of course, just "maybe this" and "maybe that" and "if it becomes necessary to." I never pushed it, because inserting reminders into their consciousness always made me feel like a kid who'd rejected her parents' religion or something.

Any talk about the case was exactly that, a reminder of my sexuality, and the whole business with *The Alternative Voice* and the three women from The Burning Brassiere was something I preferred to keep private. I guess my mom drilled it into my head through the years that it wasn't a good idea to "worry" my father, so most of my struggles—if I'm honest, probably all of them— were only made known to him in the most oblique terms. Jana's little troubles. If a relationship with someone ended, it was, "Oh, I don't see much" of *that* person; if I went to a shrink, it was "a little counseling." So on and so forth. And all that minimizing made these situations feel like they really were not big deals at all. It wasn't merely mom keeping stuff from him—his blissful ignorance was somehow more important than my petty difficulties.

Not that we had kept the case from him. Far from it. But I think his perception of it was more a mild tolerance of a daughterly whim, something to smile over rather than tell the boys at the donut shop, or the local mailman. I could no more picture my father doing that than juggling flaming jackknives while smoking cigars and whistling *La Cucaracha.*

I suppose that's why I dreaded telling them I'd lost the case. It wasn't so much that I'd have to deal with my mother's fatuous exclamations—"Oh, *isn't* that awful, those people just don't know what they're doing, do they? Oh, well"—or even the encumbrance of putting a brave face on it, as if I *weren't* devastated. I just knew it would gall me unbearably to see my father sitting there, nodding sympathetically, thinking it all a minor inconvenience for me, a little glitch in life's computer program. Like the wrong boy asked me to the prom, for Christ's sake.

So I chose not to tell them right away. I knew if I went home and checked the answering machine and found a message from them that I was obliged to return the call, and there'd be no postponing it. But I had no messages on my machine, and they did not call that night. I had a two-day reprieve if I spoke to neither of them until the weekend.

Danielle was back, so I called and told her. She was outraged too, her anger so unexpectedly fierce that it actually gave me some perspective about the case, some distance. I even found myself mildly amused at the severity of her reaction. Of course, she'd been away for the first and second days of the hearing, so I hadn't had a chance to prepare her for the outcome. After her relatively pleasant trip, getting this bad news no doubt felt like cold water in her face. Still, I couldn't help smiling a little at the fact that she sounded angrier than me, and I actually had to console *her*, calm her down with more minimizing—it's okay, not that big a deal, I'll survive. She managed to alleviate that by insisting we get together that same night.

"I have to see you," she said.

"Tonight?"

"Absolutely. I haven't been around for three whole days. If you include today. And I feel guilty, not being able to be there—at least at the end of the day, if not in the hearing."

"Well, you didn't miss much."

"Apparently not." She paused. "But I did miss you. If that counts for anything."

"Ditto for me. And yes, it does."

"Oh, Jana, I'm really sorry. Did you feel like you got something out of it, even though you didn't win? Like you proved your point, made 'em think? I mean, I guess I'm wondering whether there's any good side to this whole ordeal. Did you take *anything* away from it?"

"An image," I said.

"An image?"

I closed my eyes, picturing it. "Attorney James Kahn studying his invisible cufflinks."

"You'll have to explain that one to me."

"I will."

Chapter 33

DANIELLE AND I spent every possible minute together after that day. Not in sympathy, but from the simple naked desire to be together like never before, to be present for each spring morning, summer evening, twilight rain, for languid August afternoons and boring Sundays at the mall and PMS days and bad hair days and fantastic dinner days. For the whole enchilada.

I don't think we really made a conscious decision, either. It simply happened. One day, she was just recently back in town and my case had just ended, and the next, we were inseparable. I'd almost call it bizarre, some weird circumstance you don't plan for, that simply *happens*.

And we began to speak of staying together.

In my humble opinion, moving in together is more of a Big Deal for a gay couple than for a guy and girl. Straight people have come to expect the cohabitation thing from their kids, and in fact, sometimes encourage it. But for the gay and lesbian community, the step is truly a dramatic and major one, and often gets disguised as a roommate situation, either to assuage someone's guilt, or to feed someone's denial system. I'm sure there are other excuses for the Roommate Lie, but to tell the truth, I don't know, or give a damn, what they are.

Probably the denial system one is the major one. If no one in the family is really willing and able to acknowledge that little Bobbie Sue is a raving diesel dyke, then the Roommate Lie is going to appear attractive. Maybe even inevitable. I mean, think about it. To some people, the words, "Mom, I'm gay" are like, "Mom, I have cancer." Or even worse, actually. With cancer, you'll probably die, but if you're gay, you might live on and on. So if the Roommate Lie proves to be the only way to keep grandpa from having to have that big quadruple bypass, then it certainly does look attractive.

Maybe even inevitable.

But the Roommate Lie was not for me. My parents had known for years, and I'd be damned if I let fear of disapproval keep me from making a new choice in living arrangements. The real issues were Danielle's parents, the work/career scenario, and some obvious stuff that went along with it—"vocational rehabilitation" versus the search for a career path in the early childhood and/ or music fields versus a series of dead-end jobs providing only anguish, heartbreak, and rent money. In that order.

Danielle's parents, first of all. Nice people, really, but very staid, a sort of old world version of my own parents, but with an edge. Danielle's father was a child psychologist and her mother was a CPA, which may or may not have made things weird around the house…like, which did they fight about more, money or how to raise the children?

But the main deal was with her father. He was old school, like pre-Freudian or something, which meant that, in the Marshall household, the word *homosexuality* was synonymous with the word *perversion*, and that sexual preference, instead of being governed by genetics, is strictly a result of enculturation, and therefore anyone who *deviates from the norm*—and the key word there is "deviates"—is a *deviant*. Is sick, as a matter of fact, undoubtedly a product of childhood sexual abuse, poor parental role modeling…whatever. Which had a lovely irony to it, since, if Mr. Marshall found out his daughter was a dyke of all things, he'd be not only horrified but, according to his own doctrine, he'd have no one to blame but himself.

With malicious glee, my inner child was delighted by this.

On the other hand, I also saw it as tragic, especially as a practical matter. It meant that the Roommate Lie would be necessary for an indefinite period. And it rendered meaningful communication with the Marshalls impossible. As far as the practical end of things went, it would necessitate the shamelessly dishonest practice of "de-dyke-ing" the apartment whenever they came over to visit. Can't have erotic art lying around when the 'rents show up, after all: it might cause a Family Brouhaha.

We did have one possible solution, of course, which I was more anxious than Danielle to consider—leaving the area altogether.

Several issues converged here, and it's hard to say in retrospect what stood out in my mind most. One obvious advantage was that we'd never need to worry about de-dyke-ing the apartment. But that was hardly a primary consideration. Mostly, I think, the three issues I've already mentioned proved to be critical: first, "vocational rehabilitation," also known as starting over from square one—not my favorite choice, but not completely unacceptable— second, the search for a career path in either the early childhood or music fields—equally unpromising, actually, given my background and the concomitant risk factor; third, the prospect of a series of dead-end jobs so bleakly unrewarding that euthanasia would begin to look pretty good by contrast.

That's what finally clinched it, the problem of employment. My income wasn't sufficient, and Danielle hated the job she had in a retail outlet. So, beyond all reasonable doubt, our prospects within our local area were painfully limited. I'd found this out on a trip to the local Unenjoyment Office to look for another job, and had also searched in vain for something for Danielle. So I began to think in terms of, "Well, hey, we're young, we're both single, we have no kids…can't we just split?"

I couldn't simply blurt the idea out, though. For some reason, I was afraid she'd react with hostility to the notion of leaving dear old Mom and Dad behind and heading into the unknown.

I first broached the subject one sunny afternoon in Elizabeth Park. We were walking among arbors heavily laden with thorny vines—they would be roses in the summertime—over wheat-colored sod damp with the moisture of a long winter. We had to walk with care to avoid sinking into the turf in some spots.

We'd been talking about the hearing—now over and done, so what's next for us? That kind of thing. Which was basically what I asked: "So what do we do now?"

"I don't know what I want," she said. "I mean, what else is there?"

"Move to Northampton and find an enclave?" A smile. "Maybe not, huh?"

I took her hand and we walked along, silent. Not a soul in sight. "Have you ever wondered what it would be like if all this could be normal?" I pressed her hand slightly to show what I intended by "all this."

"It is normal," she said, "in some places, I guess. P-town, San Francisco. Northampton, from what I hear."

"But those are like exceptions to the rule. Almost like they aren't real. I mean, if you went to Disneyworld and stayed a week there, wouldn't you still realize you're just on vacation? That you can't keep that temporary feeling of freedom, you have to return to the real world sooner or later?"

"I guess that's why I was wondering, what else is there?"

"That *is* a good question." I thought about it. "I don't know. Go out west, see the country. Live a little. Get out of this rattrap town. Maybe head somewhere where there's a little less gunplay?"

"I have relatives in northern California."

"There ya go."

"And some of 'em may even know who I am." She paused.

"Well, if they don't, they can get to know you, right?"

"I suppose. I don't know if I'd want to travel that far, though. But I wouldn't mind a nice long road trip." She smiled.

"What if we just packed everything we own into the old Malibu, sold what wouldn't fit, and headed west?"

"Are you serious?"

"What's stopping us? You hate your job, mine is totally insufficient…even if we lived together, we'd still be pretty miserable here, just based on those factors alone."

She mooned at me, mock starry-eyed. "But we'd have each otherrrrr…."

I laughed and gave her a dry look. "Well, misery may love company, but…."

"I guess you're right," she said after a silence. "If we can't make ourselves happy, how can we possibly make each other happy?"

"Exactly."

"And if we can't make each other happy —" She stopped.

I sensed a need in her to process something still not spoken between us, and held my peace.

"— *Then* what?" she said.

"Well," I said. "I think we need to do whatever we can to make ourselves happy." I looked ahead, but from the corner of my eye, I saw her watching my face. "And I don't think anyone can actually make someone else happy. So, maybe if we both just work on making ourselves happy, we'll succeed individually, and be happy as partners, as a direct result."

"That's very wise."

For the first time since I had taken her hand, our eyes met. I wanted to see whether she was being ironic, but her expression was serious. I studied the ground as we walked on.

"I don't exactly have it all figured out. I just know I need to do whatever I need to do to take care of myself, and you're going to have to do *your* thing, too, whatever that may be, and if we can be together through it —" I fell silent.

Danielle shook her head. "I don't know about you. You're so serious sometimes."

I glanced over and smiled. Her manner was playful, but I saw something more underneath it. "Isn't life serious sometimes?" I said.

"You bet," she said. "But I'm gonna have to think about all this."

I nodded.

"I don't mean staying with you. I don't have to think about that. I know I want there to be an *us*. Not just you plus me, but *us*. Do you know what I mean?"

"I think so," I said, my tone an assurance that I *knew* so.

"But leaving everything behind for the great unknown…I don't know, it sounds kind of like it'd be fun, but it sounds scary, too. Don't you think?"

I was slow to respond. "Maybe. Yeah."

"You really want to take that chance?"

"I've been thinking about that. I took a chance when I filed that discrimination complaint. And I know I lost the case, but I'm still glad I took the chance. Hell, you took a chance when you told me how you really felt, and look where we are now. I mean, you took a *huge* chance. Especially with that old *boy*friend of yours."

She laughed. "The big lug."

"Well, it's risk-taking. Sometimes you have to."

"But heading west, just like that. Why?"

I thought about it. "I guess it's just a part of my spirit. There are no whys in the realm of spirit. Just action or inaction."

"We sound like we're having an intellectual conversation. Shouldn't you be smoking a French cigarette or something?"

I burst out laughing, and so did she. She had such a magical way of bringing me down to earth, making me smile at my own high seriousness yet somehow bringing me back to myself. "It's good to be home," I said.

"Did you want to head back?" she asked, misunderstanding.

"No, no," I said, swinging our hands together up and down, looking ahead into the sun. "No, this is fine. This is home."

Chapter 34

SO, THE ANSWER to the question, What do we do now? became Let's split, get outta Dodge, hit the road, jack. Take a freaking hike. The whys and wherefores became less and less important, eclipsed by more concrete and practical logistics, like when and how. We discussed utility bills and phone companies, furniture storage, yard sales.

I don't recall who first mentioned the idea for the joint yard sale, but if it turns out it was actually me, I'm willing to take the blame. In any case, it wasn't the brilliant scheme it appeared upon first glance.

On a prematurely warm New England Saturday in March, one of those first miraculous days of spring that actually *feels* like spring, I go for a morning hike in the park, and the sun warms my face as I walk. For the first time in I don't know how long, I cannot see my breath. Mounds of dirty snow from the latest blizzard still line the streets, eaten into by uneven rays of sunshine, lumpy with the upswell of thawing earth beneath. The sky is an old-fashioned blue, even close to the sun where usually it would be that chloro-fluorocarbon white that makes days like this seem too painfully glorious to be real.

I exhaust myself walking, passing all the people who have come out to push their babies around in strollers, sniff the warm air, talk politics in Spanish, get fifteen minutes of exercise. And when I've finally grown tired, and the lull of the day seems to match the lull in my blood and bones, I sit on a stone bench and watch pigeons flutter down from a huge gnarled oak and strut before me like peacocks. Women in shorts and windbreakers push baby strollers—so many babies!—and lovers walk slowly along holding hands; old people sit in cars with windows rolled down, reading newspapers, smoking cigarettes or eating pastries, gazing coolly through windshields at snow banks lining streets.

I sit on the stone bench and contemplate those in contemplation and those just in a hurry, and the sun beats down from the cerulean sky, and it feels good. It's such a beautiful day that all I want to do is sit back in a lounge chair and let the warm spring wind drift over me, bringing the sounds of Big Wheels scraping and skidding on pavement, the high-pitched laughter of children, the chirping of larks and sparrows. I do not want to work, and I certainly do not want to have to deal with a yard sale.

But eventually the hour arrives, and I wander back to meet Danielle. We're at my parents' house—her parents have a condo in a deed-restricted community, so this is the only choice we have for a site—and my parents and Danielle's father are helping out with our first big adventure in salesmanship. Her mother will be arriving on the scene shortly. Meanwhile, we've revealed to the sun our bags and boxes stuffed with everything from old textbooks to teddy bears, along with a pile of used furniture to rival the Salvation Army Thrift Store.

Of course, we have told our parents all about our plans to head for the great unknown, and they were duly distressed. Now they are in "supportive" mode, and I feel genuine gratitude, knowing how miserable they *could* have made it for us. My dad is better at playing the affable host to his arriving guests—potential customers—than at trying to be a moving man. He stands beside Danielle's big white sofa, talking animatedly with a grey-haired woman in a designer dress. He looks pleased but tired, pouches under his eyes and cheeks flushed an unhealthy color, like someone with high blood pressure or a tendency to hit the sauce. One hand lays on his great distended belly, the other periodically brushes back that white forelock hanging almost into his eyes.

From where I stand, I think I can see him perspiring, whether from the day's unseasonable warmth or the anxiety of pitching to the grey-haired woman, I don't know. I wander their way to eavesdrop a moment on the sales pitch, if that's what it is, and maybe put my two cents in. But as I get nearer, I realize, to my unmitigated horror, that Dad is apparently delivering some sort of educational lecture.

"The problem in our culture," he is saying, "is that we have this compulsion to mythologize everything. I mean, I would hope no one would mythologize *my* life when *I* die. I wouldn't do it to someone else."

"It's the *con*struct," says the grey-haired woman. "The hierarchical construct." She pronounces the words very carefully, as if reading a script she has never seen before.

"Sure," says my dad. "It's a cultural construct. No one would ever think to do it in *some* countries. Are you familiar at all with the Dobuans?" He grins, watching gamely for her reaction.

"No."

"Small island off New Guinea. What many would call a primitive culture. Their virtues, or their ideas about virtue, are much different from our own. They're an awfully dour people, and they consider mistrust and fear as admirable characteristics."

"How very odd," the grey-haired woman says.

I drift away. I have heard all this before, and it looks like it will be a while before an opening presents itself to interject something about the sofa, or any other yard-sale-related item for that matter.

My mother brings out a tray with cups of hot apple cider, apropos of the still somewhat brisk weather, and offers some to a stout, sixtyish woman in a long pale blue coat, who looks and acts like a bag lady. Probably an eccentric millioniare. Mom smiles a pasty plastic smile, chatting her up, while the bag lady nods attentively, sipping at her cider and idly examining some old ink bottles and other knickknacks, as if she has actual intentions of purchasing something.

I stroll back toward Danielle, looking as though I'm aimlessly making the rounds but, in reality, hellbent on getting away from my parents. Danielle stands behind an artificial potted palm, about twenty feet from her own father. I am visibly annoyed.

"So," she says in a low voice, "do you think we're actually going to be able to get rid of all this junk?"

"That's the least of our problems right now. My dad's over there talking cultural anthropology with some other academic type, and my mom's serving apple cider to the homeless."

She gives me a mock look of horror. "Jesus," she says, laughing.

"It's not *that* funny," I say. "I'm thinking we might even do better if we could somehow get them all to go out for a pizza and then you and I just stand here and limit our conversation to 'Hi' and 'Hello,' and quoting prices."

"You have a point," she says. "Don't worry, though. My mom'll be here soon, and she makes used car dealers look like amateurs."

"Oh no."

"No, really," she insists. "She's like one of those people who sell skin and hair care products. You know, the *Your Skin* people?"

"You mean the ones who skin *you*?"

She laughs.

"Yeah, I'm familiar with them," I say. "Unfortunately."

"It's hilarious," she says. "She'll stand there talking forever about how wonderful something is until the person actually believes that *she'll* buy it if they don't, so they'd better, like, seize the opportunity. That kinda crap."

"You really think she'll do that with our stuff?"

"What's so bad about our stuff?" Her look is reproachful.

"It's not like we're selling a bunch of Ethan Allen," I say. "I mean, it's all serviceable, or decorative, but will your mom really do that?"

"Trust me. She'll be here a matter of fifteen minutes before she has the whole yard looking like a *Better Homes and Gardens* display. And she'll be trying to sell the bag lady on that sofa."

"Even though she doesn't have anything to drive it away in," I say, and we laugh.

"Or a home to take it to," she says, suppressing a chuckle. "God, that really isn't funny, is it?"

"It really isn't. I mean, we'll be without a formal home for a while real soon, but we won't be homeless."

"Hopefully."

I frown and, as if on cue, Mrs. Marshall now arrives.

Danielle's mom is in her late forties and, of the parents, the youngest in the bunch. She's a CPA, a very good one if I can believe the family hype, and an intimidating figure for the uninitiated. My own mother—dour as a Dobuan—gets along with her just fine, but if she did not, she would undoubtedly describe her as an "Ice Queen." Mrs. Marshall is slim and of medium height, though she looks taller, and she has a certain primness to her movements that suggests she's a force to be reckoned with, someone you want on your side. Or at least, someone you do not want as an enemy.

She steps out of her Saab and onto the street with the look of a woman who has had a bad morning. She waves to my parents with a wan smile and brushes back dark brown hair from her forehead, yet, by the time she reaches the front yard, she looks as cool and unruffled as someone in a pantyhose commercial. In the time it takes her to step from the car and walk toward us, a series of freeze-frame images imprints itself indelibly in my mind: Danielle's half-inclined head as she acknowledges her mother's arrival, my own mother's toothy grin and animated wave, my father and the lady professor chatting amiably. It is all so apple-pie, so *family*, with the four parents in one place, I could almost believe for a moment that Danielle and I could be a couple, our parents just as embracing and tolerant as they would be of a new hairstyle, or a choice of college. My own parents' tacit silence about the whole situation makes it only too clear that they have no serious objection to feeding the Marshalls' denial system, and I feel both guilty and grateful for what they are willing to endure for my sake. The cider has cooled, and I feel a twinge as I remove the tray from in front of my mother and the bag lady. Nostalgia, a sense of lost possibilities, I don't know what. *Je ne sais quoi*—that's what that means, right?—I don't know what. I've come to so many crossroads before, with school, with the center, with Danielle…and as I balance the tray on one hand and walk, waitress-like, across the front lawn and into the house to warm up the mugs with fresh cider, I have a sense of precariousness about everything in my life. With the cider tray before me, I sit down in the kitchen and stare blankly at the kitchen table, a moment's respite.

Danielle appears and breaks the spell, standing before the table with her hands on her hips, Mae West style. "Hey."

"I needed a moment away from all that."

She gives me a dry look. "Well, now, don't ignore my mom too long, she's liable to get suspicious."

"I don't think she has a clue I'm actually doing it with her daughter."

"Not *that*. Suspicious that you're mad at her or something." She comes over and kisses me on the mouth, just for several seconds, but enough to get my attention. My hands grasp instinctively for the nape of her neck, the back of her head. She pulls away.

"God forbid I should have a problem with *her*," I say and flash a little smile.

She looks like she considers something for a moment. "They really aren't that bad. They just have…limitations."

"Which they'd like to transmit to you."

"I suppose." She stretches her hands out. I take them, and she pulls me to my feet. "I suppose they don't even consider it any more, to tell the truth. At my age."

"You might be surprised."

She draws me toward the window and stands behind me, her arms wrapped around me. The tomatoes on the windowsill have little bruises on them. From where we are standing we can see the whole scene outside—Danielle's parents, my mother with the bag lady, all of it—and I understand the instant sense of comfort it brings her. We can see them, but they don't see us; our few stolen moments together don't stand a chance of being interrupted by the intrusion of their reality.

"It's tough sometimes," she says.

"It's a tradeoff either way. I'm not exactly on the cover of *Lesbian National.*"

"Not this week, anyway."

"No," I laugh, "but I'm not in the closet either."

"Sometimes I like it in there," she says slowly. "It's so…I don't know. Peaceful. And quiet." I hear her exhale.

"Dark," I say, knowing I'm on dangerous ground—not my business.

"Dark, yes. Usually. But not scary."

"A closet is still a closet." In spite of my best intentions, I say this, and I feel her warmth around me relax. "I'm sorry. I only —" I let it trail off.

"You're right," she says after a moment. "I know you're right." Then comes a long silence that I don't know how to fill. "It's… well, time."

"All the time you ever need. You know that."

"I know. It's just the way you say things sometimes."

I lean back into her arms, wanting suddenly to cry. "Don't take me too seriously when I do that. Sometimes I'm just babbling. I might as well be making barnyard noises."

"You weren't making barnyard noises just now. *A closet is a closet* is pretty clear."

"Well. Big mouth, you know."

"It reminded me of something you said to me recently about action and inaction. Sometimes that's what I think I am: a woman of inaction."

"You want some action?" I say it seriously, but she catches the pun, and when she shakes me slightly, I can't help but burst out laughing.

"I'm serious, Jana. Sometimes I think everything in my life is based on either something happening to me or something being decided for me."

"Even heading west?"

"It was *your* idea," she says.

"And my decision?"

"You know what I mean. I never would have dared to consider it if you hadn't sold me on the idea."

"Oh, now don't blame me…."

She laughs, exasperated a little, and I realize how funny it is, peculiar, that I'm taking on this ironic tone with her when she's being serious; a reversal of roles. Her humor is the one thing that brings me down to a level playing field when I'm at my most dramatic and self-absorbed.

She twists away and we face one another, still close, all fingers interlaced. "You sound like me," she says. "Smartass."

"You know, it's funny. I was just thinking that. And that you sound a lot like me right now."

She smiles. "I don't know if that's good or bad."

"What's weird is that I was thinking along exact opposite lines from you, right before you came in."

"How do you mean?"

I look down. "All the choices I've made, the paths I've taken. Everything from the hearing to playing sax. Or not playing sax, I should say. Wondering if the decisions I've made were the right ones."

"How will you know? Or *when* will you know?"

"If I could tell you that, I would."

"But aren't you at least glad you took the chances you did?"

I look back up and into her eyes. "Not half as glad as I am that you took yours."

"Mine?"

I pull the hem of her blouse gently in response, pulling her toward me. She understands, leans into my kiss.

My father's voice suddenly interrupts. "Jana, I—oh, excuse me, girls…."

We separate, trying to look calm but no doubt looking foolish after the monstrous adrenaline jolt that rocks us both. Danielle flushes a deep scarlet, and my heart pounds like a bass drum.

"Hey, Dad. Is mom still talking to that bag lady?"

"What?" He looks puzzled.

"Oh, I keep calling that woman the bag lady, because she sort of looks like one. We've got to get Mom away from her, or she'll hang around all day shooting the breeze, and nothing'll get *sold*." I keep babbling—my parents have never seen anything even remotely resembling a P.D.A. between another woman and me. And while I ramble about nothing, my father looking more and more confused, Danielle pours cider, trying to recover herself.

"Well," he says at last, "why don't I take this out to your mother?" He moves toward the cider tray awkwardly, all three of us aware that what he's really saying is *I'll leave you two alone*. I'm still trembling from the shock of his entrance, the fact that we somehow overlooked his absence from the scene on the lawn.

Danielle takes his offer as a cue. "That's okay, Mr. Odessi. Let me."

"No, no, don't trouble yourself," he says.

I can see a struggle about to ensue, like the comedy of two polite people trying to let each another through a doorway, but I feel powerless to intervene.

Danielle solves it by retreating. "Okay. Thanks."

"No trouble," he says. "We can't be putting the guests to work here. Besides, you've got enough cut out for you out there, what with all these fantastic things for sale." He whisks the tray away, smiling and disappearing into the living room, and I realize belatedly he was probably at least as mortified as us, just much more skillful at hiding it.

"God, I'm so embarrassed," Danielle says.

"Isn't it ridiculous? It's like being a teenager again."

"It practically *is* being a teenager again. I've never had anything like that happen to me in my life."

"Plus he scared the shit out of us. I hadn't even noticed he wasn't out on the lawn."

"I know. Thank God it wasn't *my* dad."

"Or your —"

"Don't even say it." She shudders. "Girl, I don't even want to contemplate that."

I pause a moment, looking at her. Of course she's more shaken than me. "We'd better get back, I guess."

"I know." A last kiss, all too brief, almost frantic in the urgency of secrecy. Then we head back out to warm March sunlight.

My father stands behind a table of silverware and glasses, knickknacks, vases, and kitchenware. The academic woman is gone, replaced by a short, fat man in a brown old-fashioned suit, whom Dad warms up with all the laidback polish of someone at a car dealership. In this *post interruptus* moment, he looks insufferably pompous. His smile is all-knowing, and he blinks his owlish blink and displays price tags for the newcomer; as if his protection of our secret confers upon him some special sanctity, and he will henceforward be an honorable member in the Benevolent Protective Order of Friends of the Gays or something. In spite of all his tact and delicacy, or perhaps because of it, I feel like I owe him one.

Danielle spends some time talking with her mother, who, true to form, is busy arranging certain items so that they will presumably look more appealing. The entire scene suddenly makes me feel desolate—perhaps it's the sun having just retreated behind a cloud, the urgent quality of Danielle's kiss before she flits away to play straight with her mother, or even what just happened with my father; maybe the simple combination of all these disparate elements.

Whatever the case, I'm left with an overwhelming sense that everything is grey. Futile. I am very tired all of a sudden. It occurs to me there's some lesson here I'm failing to learn, some obvious truth about myself, my life, perhaps about my relationships with Danielle, my parents, something that might benefit me if I could just *get it*. But nothing comes within my grasp, and even the few ideas that pass in and out of consciousness are as ephemeral as the handful of clouds above us.

I have no idea which is more important: the question—whether I'm suffering some early spring doldrums—or the answer—whatever actions I must now take to alleviate them. But I think of my comment to Danielle about action and inaction, and I decide the solution is "change a thought, move a muscle." I head over toward Danielle and her mom.

"Morning, Mrs. M."

"Morning, Jana." She checks her watch. "Afternoon, actually."

"Let me give you a hand with some of those boxes." I unpack some of the items we had postponed unpacking, thinking them less important than other items, and second-rate to boot. I now realize that we will no doubt sell most or all of them, since the yard is filling up with strangers. A pang of reluctance strikes me, the pointless, acquisitive feeling that prevents me from throwing away even the most worthless junk sometimes.

Maybe this accounts for the melancholy, the sense of lost possibilities. Inwardly, I rebel at this business of having my possessions on display, subject to the petty, undignified haggling and the scrutiny of strangers. I look around, realize I have things of relatively high sentimental value: dolls I've had for twenty years, my first tricycle, a Red Rider wagon, all with price tags of two, three, at most, five dollars. They are worth thousands to me, if only I would admit it. And, as if a little girl crouches within me, heartbroken, in need of comfort, I picture myself going and buying back my old toys, returning them to this four-year-old version of me, who, in her gratitude, throws her arms around my knees.

Of course, I ignore the feeling of self-betrayal as I continue to unpack boxes. A woman comes over with her small son, holding a wooden plaque with Sylvester and Tweety lacquered on it, a kind of découpage thing I made in the third or fourth grade.

"How much is this?"

The tag has apparently fallen off. "Fifty cents."

She pays, and I watch it go. The momentary satisfaction the plaque seems to give the boy is only partial consolation for me; the sensation of having sold another piece of my childhood still clamoring within.

But I put the fifty cents in the changebox and unwrap another piece of glassware.

The day is not the disaster I have probably made it sound. We do end up selling almost everything, and what we don't sell is mostly junk that our parents will cheerfully keep in the attic until such time as we might relieve them of it. But I still have feelings of sadness, and a sense of having sold out, along with a certain measure of relief. The relief is not the strongest of these elements, which explains why I walk away, at five o'clock that afternoon, thinking this whole joint yard sale deal was not the brilliant scheme it first appeared.

Then we have our preparations for moving—or, as my parents put it, "taking off," as in, "So, when are you two going to be taking off for the wild, wild west?" They love that one, that and, "So, you're really taking off, eh?" They act pretty cheerful, though I sense behind their smiles some genuine disappointment, fear, sadness…something. It's as if, just as they have put on a brave front at the yard sale, resisted the temptation to confront the Marshalls' denial about Danielle and me, so it is with this: a pair of smiley-face masks, pulled taut over their usual masks. Subterfuge added to tact, duplicity upon duplicity, all for my sake. And Danielle's, I suppose.

Surely it must give Danielle no small measure of comfort to know they are supportive of us, and, by extension, of our plans to leave. Yet I sense the truth withheld, and to protect Danielle from my doubts, become a silent partner in the deception. It actually seems natural, since we never have any opportune moments during the days we are preparing to move. So many things to do—we have lists and lists—everything from having the electric company shut the power off at the right time to getting back our security deposits, which we will need for the expenses ahead, motels, food, fuel. And souvenirs.

We prepare to leave on March twenty-seventh and, amazingly, we are ready by then: everything packed, the utilities taken care of, bills paid, mail forwarded to our parents for the time being. We say our goodbyes in bunches: some separate, some together. Danielle says goodbye to her parents while I'm out on an errand—just as well, for my money. I make the rounds of old friends—not as many as I'd hoped, actually—and Danielle does the same. On the Saturday morning we leave, my parents arrive at my apartment to give us a big sendoff, the last of the goodbyes.

We stand in front of the house in the wind. There's a smell in the air like scorched metal, and as I turn away from my parents toward the car, it makes my eyes water slightly.

"When do you think you'll be back?" My mother's face is serious, and with the wind blowing her hair back, almost severe.

"I don't know. Maybe a few months. We may decide to get a place somewhere." I look to Danielle for confirmation—my co-conspirator in this wild goose chase for comfort and security. She shrugs good-naturedly.

"Are you sure you wouldn't prefer a P.O. box? You could send us a monthly check for it."

"I'm sure. We'll be in touch often enough."

"I'm just thinking of the possibility you'll get mail you want more immediate access to, because you'll have to be calling *us*, and she'll have to be calling *her* parents." She points to Danielle.

"It'll be fine, Mom. Well, I guess it's time." We have been through all this already, and no need to prolong the agony.

"Take care of yourselves," my father says.

Hugs and kisses. Somber waves as we back down the driveway.

Into the metallic wind.

And then we are gone.

Chapter 35

WE ARE HEADING west on Interstate 84 toward Danbury when we see the truck: an eighteen-wheeler, red with white stripes and a big gleaming silver grille like a metal grimace, painted more like a racing car than a semi. Two guys sit tall in the cab, and when we first pass them, we think nothing of the truck, or the guys, for that matter. Only when we notice them catching up with us do we get a little nervous.

"Relax," I say to Danielle after she comments. "We're gonna have that happen all across the country. Truckers are always passing and then falling behind. I think it's because they allow the truck to coast down the long hills, and then when they build up enough speed, they don't even bother to use the brakes. They just build up momentum for the next hill."

But the truck is rapidly approaching from behind, and even as I speak, I hear its horn. *Hwonk hwonk.* Like the blast of a train whistle.

"Oh, shit," she says.

"It's all right," I say. "Look, they're trying to signal us. Maybe there's a *Smokey* up ahead." I grin over at her.

"Huh?"

"Cop," I explain, but the train whistle is already blasting again. *Wonk.*

"They want us to pull over," I say. "Maybe there's something wrong with our trailer hitch. Maybe your signal isn't working."

"*My* signal?" It's my car.

"You know what I mean. *The* signal. Look. They look serious. They aren't even smiling."

It's true. They get off at the next exit, motioning for us to follow. Danielle curses again beneath her breath.

"Go ahead," I tell her. "We don't have to get out of the car, even. Just crack the window and see what they want."

She says nothing, pulling off behind the big semi as it lumbers down the exit seven off-ramp.

"Looks like there's a truckstop up ahead. Looks like they know where they're going."

Danielle says nothing.

"That's good," I go on. "They're heading somewhere public. Their intentions are obviously good." But my voice trembles.

"I'm just gonna crack the window enough for them to hear me," she says. "Don't crack your side, okay?"

"Okay." I watch as she eases the window down an inch.

We swing in behind them, our car and trailer absurdly small among the eighteen-wheelers.

The driver comes toward us first, his friend dawdling a little in the cab and then loping along behind like he's a bit on the shy side, or nervous himself. The thought that *he* might be nervous strikes me as ironic. The first one, the driver, has short, neatly-trimmed hair with a beard and moustache, and he wears a baseball cap. He looks like a trucker. His friend is less easy to pigeonhole, tall and thin with a slightly sinister goatee and an evasive look about the eyes.

"Something wrong?" Danielle shouts through the crack.

"Best coffee in all of Fairfield county," the trucker says. "Nothin' wrong with that."

Suddenly and incongruously, part of an old John Coltrane saxophone solo scurries through my head. Pentatonic patterns, F minor and B major, and a sound like a scratched balloon. Is my life about to pass before my eyes?

"Why did you signal us to get off the highway?" Danielle asks, ignoring the trucker's comment.

"You looked thirsty," he says. He smiles, boyishly flirtatious.

I roll my eyes. Jesus Christ, I say to myself. "You want to get out of here?" I mime to Danielle.

She looks at me, smiling strangely. "No," she whispers. "Let's have coffee with 'em. It'll serve 'em right."

I laugh. "You sure?"

Danielle nods.

"Okay."

She laughs with me, a fake, throaty laugh intended to seduce truckers with its adolescent pitch. It works. They tense, turning a little serious. Testosterone courses through their veins like salmon swimming upstream.

"*I'll* have some coffee," she says, swinging open the car door while the truck driver backs out of her way. "Best coffee in Fairfield county?"

"Yes, ma'am," he says. He touches his hand lightly to his cap, like a small informal bow. I think of a baseball pitcher giving a signal to the catcher, and it registers a little late that his accent is faintly Southern.

We introduce ourselves on the way in. The driver tells us his name is Steve, and his silent partner, he says, is named Otto.

"I'm Danny, and this is Jana."

"Danny?" Steve asks.

I chime in: "Short for Danielle."

"Aha." He holds the door open for us, and we walk in as a group. I am already uncomfortable with the implicit deception, though I have to admit I'm still a little amused. Once we are all seated—"Danny" and I on one side of the booth and the truckers on the other—I look at them seriously and say, "Listen, fellas, we're a…a couple."

Danielle flashes me an incredulous look, her mouth open. For a moment I can see her weighing it. Should she go along with me, or continue her game? Then she closes her mouth, understanding me and trying not to look disappointed.

The driver is nonplussed. He looks back and forth between us. "Y'all are *dykes?*"

"We prefer something a little less graphic—like, uh, 'alternative lifestyle practitioners,'" Danielle says.

"Huh?"

I say, "Or how about just something less formal, like 'renegade bitches?'" We crack up, but they do not.

"Naaaw, come on," says the trucker. "You're putting me on."

"Honey," says Danielle, "I wouldn't put you on if you were a mink coat." This gets a good laugh even from Otto, the silent partner. Old Steve sits there looking irritably at us, like he's thinking it's a crying shame, and says, "God damn." He shakes his head. "God damn." But he purses his lips in a little rueful smile.

"May I help you?" asks our waitress.

The intrusion makes everyone lapse into phony informality—like we're all pals. Steve and Otto slouch down on their side of the booth, cowboys in some hometown saloon.

"Coffee."

"Same for me."

We all order coffees only, no food, and when the waitress disappears again with a scowl, the conversation resumes. "What are you doing in *Dan*bury, *Dan?*" Steve asks. "That is your name, right? Dan?" He's smiling once more, still flirting with her.

"We're going cross-country together," she says. "Sort of a lesbian *On The Road.*"

"Aw, now, come on," he says. "Y'all aren't really serious about that, are you? You're just tryin' to fend us off. I understand. A couple of pretty young ladies like yourselves —"

"We're telling you the truth, dude," I say. "Sorry." I am smiling now, amused more by his denial than anything else.

"But how do you…I mean, what can —?"

"Oh, we shoot the works, babe," I say. "You name it: strap —"

Danielle, laughing, clamps her hand over my mouth.

"— canes, nylon bungee —"

She wrestles around with me in the booth, shutting me up, shutting me *off*. We're laughing like crazy by now, and Steve looks at us like we're demented, but still with a bit of the gleam in his eye.

Danielle looks like she feels as reckless as I do. "Listen, buddy," she says. "Didn't you ever see *Thelma and Louise*? You gotta watch out for strange women. You never know what they're gonna do." She sits up straighter, almost primly, and gives me a mysterious look.

"But *shit*, man," says Steve, giving full rein to his irritation. "Y'all can't be dykes. There's no way —"

"Why not?" asks Danielle. "Why can't we be?" She's turned serious.

"Well…just *look* at ya!" He gestures with one hand in apparent despair. Otto sits like a henchman beside him, expressionless.

The waitress brings our coffees, so there is another brief respite before Danielle answers. "What are dykes supposed to look like?" she says. "Overweight? Big biceps?" She sips her coffee. "Mustaches?"

Steve looks confused. "Well, no, but…but not like that!"

"We don't look like *dykes*, huh?" Her eyes meet mine. "We don't look like dykes," she says and she shakes her head.

"Apparently not," I say.

"Help me out here, buddy," Steve says, nudging Otto. "What do you think?"

Otto looks at us, then shrugs. "I dunno. They look like they could be dykes."

The two of us laugh again, and Steve says, "This conversation ain't goin' anywhere."

"Well, Steve," Danielle says coolly. "That is your name, isn't it? Steve?" He nods. "We may not look like what you'd think of as your ordinary run-of-the-mill dykes. But like my friend Jana here says, we are a couple, and if you can just accept that about us, we can all probably enjoy this cup of coffee a lot more before we get back on the road again." She smiles: "Know what I mean?"

Steve purses his lips and nods. Finally, one side of his mouth curls up into a kind of half-smile. "Aw, hell," he says. "I guess I was just disappointed is all."

"Well, now, don't you fret," she says, picking up the cadence of his speech, and I wonder whether he thinks she's making fun of him. "I'm quite sure," Danielle says, "that there are plenty of nice young women out there who you can lure off the road for a little cup of the old java."

He smiles.

"But don't you have somewhere you need to be? All these delays are probably costing you money."

"We're coming back tomorrow, actually," he says. "Just making a quick run to Pennsylvania. Then Thursday I have to be in San Antonio."

"No kidding. Texas?"

"Yep. It'll be time for us to put on our cowboy hats and cock-roach-killers. Right, Otto?" He sips his coffee, and Otto nods, reflective.

"Well," says Danielle. "To tell you the truth —" and here she nudges me a little beneath the table, secretively "— we aren't really both dykes. That is…well… I'm bi."

"Whaaat?" He scoots forward in the booth about an inch.

"See, I had a boyfriend back home," she says.

I lean forward and try to catch her eyes. What the hell is she doing?

"And I left him to come out here on this cross-country trip. With Jana."

"But you do like guys?"

"Well," she says coyly. "Obviously, I have my preferences." And she nods toward me.

Something seems to have snapped in him at the word *obviously*. I see it happen, like a light's gone off in his head. "Y'all are nuts," he says, standing. "Come on, Otto, let's get the hell out of here." He slurps his coffee, then rattles the cup down again onto the saucer.

"What about the coffee?" Otto says.

"Take a rain check. Here." He throws a five-dollar bill down. "That oughtta take care of it. Let's go." He walks away, shrugging himself into his jacket.

"Sorry, girls," Otto says as he slides out of the booth. "He ain't been laid in awhile."

Danielle bursts out laughing, but I just shake my head. The whole scene has just become very unfunny, the air in the room heavy and thick with tension. It feels like a funeral's been announced. Danielle sips her coffee, looking unruffled.

"What did you do that for?" I ask.

"What, tell him I was bi?"

"I mean, why did you do it like *that*? Like you were torturing him?"

"I don't know, he was just kind of irritating, you know what I mean? I don't really think I'm gonna miss him all that much." She scoots a little closer to me in the booth and smirks.

I give her a sidelong glance, shaking my head. "He was right. Y'all *are* nuts."

She laughs.

"I mean, he *was* kind of a redneck, but he seemed harmless enough. That was like borderline cruelty."

She continues to look down into her coffee cup. "You're right," she says softly. "I'm sorry. I just—I don't know, men sometimes…." She lets it trail off, thinking. "Sometimes I think men just don't get it. You know, I still like men, I can't say I'm not bi…it's just that sometimes it isn't even about sex. Like with you—don't get me wrong, the sex is great, but the emotional connection is the key to the whole thing. Shit, did that guy really think these two women were going to just come in and have coffee with him and his buddy, and be so overtaken by their charisma we'd all jump in the back of his rig for some rockin' sex?"

"Maybe he did think that. Or hope it. Maybe you're just reading more into it than there actually was."

She waves it off. "I mean, just his whole approach. *You looked thirsty*," she mimics, sneering a little in imitation.

I laugh. "Well, maybe that's what works for him."

"Jesus," she says, "I don't know. I'd feel pretty disillusioned about people in general if I thought that. I don't think that guy could ever *understand* the connection you and I have, much less become capable of having something like it. Even trying to explain it would be like discussing metaphysics with a two-year-old."

"Hey, who knows—maybe two-year-olds are really in touch with metaphysics."

Now it's her turn to laugh. "Y'all are nuts."

"Maybe," I say. "Listen, you want to get out of here?"

"We ought to wait, maybe, until we can be reasonably sure Heckle and Jeckle are back on the road."

"Heckle and Jeckle? More like Larry and Moe."

She laughs again. "Yeah. You still want me to drive? I seem to get us into trouble."

"You can drive at least as far as Ohio. I want to be well-rested, and this coffee's probably not gonna help."

"Well, we haven't gone that far yet."

"No. I could probably wait until tomorrow to drive, to tell you the truth."

She looks at me and smiles. "Okay, let's make sure they're gone."

Chapter 36

I CURL DOWN into the seat a little more, hugging myself into a potentially comfortable position for sleep. Danielle sits behind the wheel, the old green Malibu bumping along Route 84 on our way into Scranton, Pennsylvania. At that point, the highway is layered with those small, speedbump-like metal tiers that create a steady, irritating rhythm: *Boomp-boomp. Boomp-boomp.*

My head wobbles loosely a little on my neck at each *boomp-boomp*, and my eyes are heavy with fatigue and burning a little from the cigarette smoke at the truckstop. The Supremes play tinnily on the only decent FM station we can find, and I can just hear Danielle, who probably thinks she's too quiet for me to hear, whistling along softly beneath her breath. I notice she's braking a little more than normal for a straightaway

I open my eyes. "Traffic jam?"

"Little bit," she answers quietly. "There must be some construction ahead."

"Oh, well," I yawn. "It's not like we have to be somewhere any special time."

"True enough."

The traffic slows to a halt, and we begin the kind of bumper-to-bumper, stop-and-start inching forward that always drives me crazy, even more than being at a complete standstill. I'm glad she's driving.

"Wow. Something must be wrong up there." I sit up in the seat.

"It may just be construction," she says.

But it isn't. I see the flashing lights on the horizon, and at that distance, I know we might actually reach the accident scene before the ambulance. A state trooper is already there, and as we get closer, I see he's alone. Morbid curiosity being what it is, people in passing cars stare wide-eyed at the scene: a shattered van and a small compact car so absolutely collapsed it looks like it hit a Jersey barrier at a hundred miles per hour. With a terrible shudder, it strikes me that the odds of someone surviving that crash are nearly impossible.

Blood and glass are everywhere. The trooper, on one knee above the man on the ground, holds tightly to the hand that grips his from beneath the blanket. We pass the scene just as the ambulance pulls up, waved on by the trooper, and when I see the spreading pool of blood, and hear a howl through the closed window like the sound of a tortured child, a wave of pain within me brings tears to my eyes. Only then do I notice Danielle's white knuckles on the steering wheel.

"My God, my God, my God, my God." Tears stream down her face, and in the paralysis of this moment, I can only reach over and put my hand on hers.

We say nothing. Eventually the traffic picks up speed, and we look straight ahead, away from the scene of the accident. I hear only the sounds of our breathing, heavy from crying, and the drone of the car engine as we ease into the middle lane and our speed levels off at sixty-five.

Still, we say nothing. What can we say? I'm sorry you had to see that? (*Me too.*)

I'm sorry that had to happen? (*Me too.*)

So we remain quiet, and in the silence, our breathing returns to normal. We wipe our tears and try to look recovered. I take my hand from the steering wheel, and now we sit like people miles apart. Eventually, we speak, of course. Tame words, the kind of clumsy small talk you make while visiting someone terminally ill, or recently widowed. I remember nothing much about Scranton, Pennsylvania. A rest stop, maybe, square white houses, street lights. A convenience store.

I am as numb as if the man in the road had been my father, or a brother. Only after several hours am I able to admit that, beneath that blanket, his legs had undeniably been reduced to pulp. There was simply nothing visible there.

I wish I could say more about Ohio, but I remember very little, just a couple great night spots in Cleveland. But a whole part of the trip is a blur. It seems we have plunged into the depths of winter at that accident scene, and we do not emerge into sunlight until we've wandered around Ohio. We feel so bruised from the experience that we decide—on a whim of Danielle's—to head south instead of west.

And so, we travel directly south, like some sort of wacky migratory animals with a green Chevy. We burn through Kentucky and Tennessee and Georgia, and we do not stop until we reach Florida.

Chapter 37

IN 1513, PONCE de Leon discovered what he thought was the Fountain of Youth. All it was, of course, was a section of the Florida flatlands. The main town of the area, St. Augustine, was not actually founded until 1565.

St. Augustine may be old, but people from New England are often horrified at the newness of places in Florida. We are accustomed to living in towns *incorporated* in the 1600s or 1700s, and though our existence is often confining, cramped, and conservative, *it feels safe*. Homey. Old fashioned.

Visitors describe small New England towns as *quaint* and *picturesque*. We may not think that way ourselves, but certainly we are always struck by the terrible newness of a Las Vegas or a Fort Lauderdale. We New Englanders sniff out commercialism and a sense of the temporary, and we transmogrify it into a lack of safety and history, a lack of permanence and character and…morals. We look at these towns like art critics and perceive a lack of serious intent.

On the other hand, "new" towns create an infectious excitement. After all, in New England even a lot of the younger people seem old, hopelessly status quo, locked into the circle of IRAs and mortgages and PTA meetings like desperadoes surrounded by a posse. They are fortified by Dow Jones, the Wall Street Journal their sole source of morning meditation. Maybe those of us who feel differently aren't appalled by the newness of dynamic small towns or younger cities because we see bright possibilities in the ethnic diversity, the hectic clash of retail and grocery stores, laundromats, salons and spas. We may even feel a bit of the pioneering spirit, a hankering after that old time Gold-Rush-fever-man-on-the-moon American dream thing. Not manifest destiny or the divine right of kings—just a sense of exploration, a newer path. And no matter how out of touch we are with the present, there's always the comfort of knowing we can find some ten-year-old to tell us what's new and noteworthy.

The first place in Florida I actually see from outside of a moving car is Tallahassee. For me, the most memorable thing in Tallahassee is not sun or sand—it's not a beach town—but a TV talk show that Danielle and I catch while stopping over at a motel called the Dutch Inn just off Route 27. The hostess stalks guests with microphone in hand, throwing questions either at the dreary bunch seated onstage or at the audience.

The topic of the day is apparently lesbians, and I must admit that, although I don't usually bother with talk shows at all, my curiosity gets the better of me. I mean, hey, maybe if I were a black male heterosexual I'd be *bored* watching a show about black male heterosexuals, but I'm a white female homosexual, and I'm interested.

"I don't know," a guy on the panel says, "some of the lesbian separatists are kind of a pain in the —" they bleep him "— but I don't have a *problem* with it. Heck, it's none of my business."

"But it *is* your business," says the right-winger chick from a religious organization—P.O.W.E.R.? P.R.A.Y.E.R.? Something like that—"it *is* your business if your school has children in it being raised by these 'couples.'" She spits out the word with contempt, and you can see the hatred in her eyes.

I once knew a couple, "out" lesbians, who adopted a baby girl. I couldn't help but wonder if they would raise her in a radically different way than her friends. And if so, would it be more healthy? At least, in a spirit of loving tolerance? Or would they teach her to scorn her straight peers, branding them as "breeders," and making an outcast of her, in effect?

But then I read up on it, since no one I knew came from such a home, and found what I'd probably known all along, deep down: each case is different, each family unique. The children of gay couples weren't any more likely to be gay, and the potential for ridicule was not as bad as you might expect. Obviously, the parents wanted what was right for their children, and their priorities and feelings were pretty much the same as those of straight people.

"What do you mean, 'It *is* your business?'" Danielle says out loud.

I hate it when she talks back to people on TV; it's like something my crazy grandmother would do. In fact, it's something my crazy grandmother *did* do.

"Who the hell do these people think they are, judge, jury and executioner for the right-wing hate movement? Jesus Christ, man, this shit's gotta stop."

"I'll shut it off," I say and move toward the TV.

"No, no. Wait," she says. "I want to see this." She holds her arm straight out in front of me for several seconds, as if she's going to prevent me from getting to the television. To be truthful, I'm more interested in her reaction to the show than in the show itself.

"Okay," says the hostess. "Let's take our next caller. Caller, are you there?"

"Hello." A woman's voice, tinny.

"Yes, hello. Do you have a question for the panel?"

"I just want to make a comment," says the disembodied voice. "I think it's just contemptible that these so-called 'women' are actually the subject of your show."

Danielle gives a sharp cry of outrage.

"It's an indication of the sad state of affairs in this country when these people can even get air time."

The hostess cuts her off right there: "Okay, thanks anyway. Next caller."

A smattering of applause goes out over the airwaves, and a few of the panel members make sounds of approbation, but mostly there is a pleasant chorus of boos, groans, and laughter from the audience.

Danielle begins another tirade. "I can't believe I'm hearing this...."

I listen to her for a while with a curious mixture of calmness and indulgence. Part of me empathizes with her outrage, but part of me wants to tell her it's ironic. Considering her recent conversion to a more-or-less openly lesbian lifestyle, I can't help thinking she sounds a little like a newly-registered Democrat at a Republican convention. Well, of *course* this is what it's like, I want to say. What did you expect?

I've been living with this stuff for years. For me, this is just one of the basic conflicts central to my life, my identity as an individual. Yes, it's a conflict that could get me killed. Hearing her speak with all the fervor and outrage of a neophyte revolutionary makes me feel strangely divided, partly her equal in ideology, but ages her senior in practical application. And the arrogance behind that is not comforting. Babe, you ain't heard nothin' yet, I want to tell her. I just can't help it.

Later, we do some touristy stuff, and since March is nearly over, we get in on an annual festival called "Springtime Tallahassee." It's basically a month-long series of concerts and art shows, along with tours of some of the city's well-known gardens, which are absolutely magnificent. In fact, Tallahassee itself is a revelation. I've always thought of Florida as sand and palm trees; I had no idea there were acres of oak forest, rivers and lakes, rolling hills. But despite all that, the most definite thing that sticks in my mind is that crazy talk show. I guess it just goes to show how selective memory can be. It's like that accident we saw. I don't think I remember much else from that whole week.

From Tallahassee to Tampa is about 270 miles. Danielle and I take a route listed on the map as the 19/27 "alternate," which remains inland for the majority of the trip, only nearing the coast when we pass Crystal Bay, where we see signs for Red Level, Inverness, and, bizarrely enough, Beverly Hills. The highway then skirts back inland, but swings out again along the Gulf when approaching the Tampa area: first Hudson, Port Richey, Holiday, then Tarpon Springs, Palm Harbor, Ozona, and Clearwater.

At this point, we pick up 275 to 75 South, which runs down to Sarasota, Port Charlotte, and finally to Fort Myers, where it's just a matter of crossing the causeway to Sanibel Island. Farther down 75 South would take us into Naples, which is a straight line east across the state to Fort Lauderdale, the mecca of spring breakers.

"Screw that," Danielle says. "It'll be a zoo there."

Fort Myers Beach is also a little crowded with spring breakers, but we find a terrific place across the causeway out on Sanibel Island. And here I first really fall in love with the Gulf of Mexico. That blue-green water and white white sand, and the sound of gulls in the air. We snuggle down in the sand like honeymooners on our little beach blankets and towels, and it's heaven. A couple of guys try hitting on us, but we tell them how the land lies, and they are surprisingly mellow about it; nothing as tense as the scene with the truckers.

These days are probably my best Florida memories, seagulls wheeling above us, the most perfect beach weather we could want— eighty degrees and dry with a soft breeze like some occasional haphazard caress while we lie in utter repose and silence. For me, the sounds of the beach, the kids yelling and gulls crying, all drop away, it really *is* silence, and it's as if I can feel the earth turning beneath me, spinning ever so gently through space, my heart beating in slow and regular cadence, completely at peace, far from the Kiddie Korners and Wendy Simpsons and Standing Free Ibsens of the world, virtually alone in this transient paradise, alone with my beautiful Danielle, and if I could record all the minutiae of my experience, the raspberry Sno-cones, the sand on the backs of my ankles, the rich garlicky smells from Italian restaurants, the sounds of Latino rhythms from buildings, the sight of fat Puerto Rican boys in cars, eating calzones, fiddling with the radio—capture it all and put it somehow into some tiny amber prison, the way a person might collect beach glass, I would keep it always, sitting and turning it slowly in my fingers, like a locket in the fingers of an old old woman with a faded picture inside of a lover from days gone by.

All summer dreams pass eventually, though, and soon we have to pack up and leave Sanibel. The truth is, we are running out of money, and although we've done a couple days' work in Tallahassee to pad the portable expense account temporarily, it's clear that soon we will have to do more. We hear Naples has lots of jobs even toward the end of the tourist season, so off we go, leaving Sanibel with a slight sense of melancholy and vowing to get back there some day "in the off season."

Naples is great, although I still prefer Sanibel. We've time and money enough to do one last low budget version of a weekend getaway before we go to work as office temps for a couple weeks. As in most of our Florida stops, the first and last priority remains: hit the beach.

At the north end of Naples is Vanderbilt Beach, with a strip of upscale motels and, fortunately, some modest ones. The beach I like best, because of its relative isolation, is in northern Naples, the Delnor-Wiggins Pass State Recreation Area, or, as locals simply call it, Wiggins Pass, with its good mile or so of shoreline and its excellent shelling. Because it's a state park, no boomboxes are allowed on the beach, so it's nice and peaceful.

Danielle is not as much of a beach bum as me, though, and she makes sure to drag me through the Port Royal section of Old Naples, a wealthy neighborhood on the south side of town. The scent of hibiscus, the streets filled with sunbleached fan palms, old cottages and modern villas, the glow of whatever was in the air at Sanibel returns, and we prolong the languor with lazy sightseeing—Palm Cottage, The Pier, some nice random shops—before meandering back to our motel, where we sleep the sleep of the dead, awakening late only to return to the beach for more relaxation and great long rambling talks…probably the best, most important parts of the whole trip. I say "most important" because, in a very real sense, we get to *know* each other on this trip like never before, the way we've always wanted but were afraid to try. And above all, and especially in the quiet times in Naples and Sanibel and Tallahassee, we know that we're in love, and we are scared.

The temp jobs are slow. For one thing, the town is a lot more laid back than we're accustomed to, being from Connecticut, where practically everyone acts like they're in New York City. There's a certain measured quality in the office and, although in some ways it's preferable to the work I'm used to—hectic, chaotic, and highly stressful—the relative lassitude makes the days go slow.

We realize we have to make some decisions about what to do and where to go next. The motel is too expensive, and although we initially planned to go cross-country, we see that for now we won't be able to afford it. We live on the cheap for our two-week assignment, take our savings, and split for the north country again—Tallahassee, that is, where costs are lower and permanent jobs are supposedly more plentiful.

On the way back to Tallahassee, we visit Tampa, one of the few growing cities on the west coast we have yet to visit. Though the place has appeal, it is uneven at best: resonant sunsets, snarling traffic, friendly people, proliferant strip joints and pawn shops, palm trees lining boulevards packed with strip mall after strip mall, plaza after plaza, and big indoor malls crowded with restless teen-agers looking for expensive clothes and cheap thrills. Before long, we are careening through what might accurately be termed the Latino quarter, Ybor City, with its cobbled streets and strange art and sculpture, and its boutiques and bars, specialty shops and cof-feehouses, where the patrons spill out into the street like part of some crazed Mardi Gras celebration, a floating party on Seventh Avenue. We check out the Blue Ship Café, a blues bar where a great guitar player does a rocked-out version of "Goodnight Irene." On the dark concrete wall outside, I see a pink salamander with cold blue eyes who fixes me with a stare like a tiny demon, and I think *Tampa*, yeah, Tampa is all right.

Still, it's just one more stop on a trip that is taking longer and longer, longer than I thought it could, almost too good to last. Danielle finds work in Tallahassee first, waitressing in a place called The Grey Lion, while I spend a couple weeks going through the motions, trying to get some kind of tutoring assignment. I want to avoid daycare if at all possible, and yet I still want to use the résumé. But the other options, like teacher's aide jobs, all require some sort of certificate or another, or degrees I do not have or even want. The critical nature of our situation becomes very evident one day around the beginning of the third week, when Danielle and I are talking about her job as she prepares for the three-to-eleven shift.

"So, what did *you* do this morning?" she yawns. She has slept late, because of the work schedule, whereas I was up at nine.

"Oh, not much," I say. "Went into town, read the classifieds. Only about an hour at the pool."

"You went out to the pool?" She sounds testy.

I shrug, apologetic. "Well," I say, "there's not much in the paper. I'm hoping if I hold out one last week, I'll find something decent."

She sighs. Silence. After a few moments of poking around in a drawer, she says, "I hope you do find something, but if you don't, after another week of this crap, we're gonna need the money from somewhere. I can't do this alone."

"I know that," I say. My voice rises, and I know I sound defensive, but can't seem to shut myself up. "I said I'll find something. I don't want to have to go for some cheesy clerical work if I can get something better, that's all. It's hard to work things like *envelope stuffing* into a childcare specialist résumé."

"Or waitressing?"

"I didn't say that, Danielle. I meant nothing of the kind. I'll waitress, too, if I have to."

More silence.

"And the pool?"

We glare at each other.

"Oh, this really is *not* about the pool, is it?" I pause, watching her. "I mean, seriously, is it?"

She says nothing. I cross the room to where she stands, still rifling through a drawer, take her hands, and she allows me to lead her to the couch, where we flop down all in a heap. But she will not look at me.

"Let's not fight about money," I say. "Everybody fights about money. Let's be original."

She laughs and finally loosens up a bit. "Okay," she says, "we'll fight about something original, if that's what you want. How about the pool?"

"Forget the pool," I say. "Look, I know it probably seems like I'm goofing around while you're out busting your ass —"

"As a matter of fact...."

"— But wait a sec, just hear me out. I want to find a job that'll make sense on my résumé, but if nothing happens for me this week, I promise I'll take whatever I can get. That's a promise. Now, as far as the pool, what I was going to say is, I know it seems like I'm out goofing around while you're busting your ass, but I'm *really not*. It's just...well, it's been a slow couple of weeks, and I needed a little breather. So instead of taking a coffee break, I took a tanning break. I really am doing my best, though, Danielle. I really am. Sometimes I just feel a little lost is all."

Our eyes meet.

"You know, it's funny," she says. "I never once thought about you feeling lost. I mean, look at me. I'm waitressing in some place I have no interest in, I have no plans as to where to go or what to do next. I don't *have* a résumé, babe. Lost?" She sighs. "I'm feeling more lost than I ever have in my life. It's like being a kid again." She looks around the room bleakly. "Where are we, Jana? Where *are* we going?"

I hold her in my arms, and I feel her shoulders shaking. I cannot think of a word to say. My mind is as blank as an early-morning blackboard.

Chapter 38

SHORTLY AFTERWARDS, WE leave for Colorado. It isn't spontaneous. In fact, the plan is to head for California, where Danielle has a cadre of aunts and uncles, and even a few stray cousins.

Leaving Tallahassee is hard, but not as hard as it was to leave Sanibel. It's still April, so the tourist season is not quite over yet, and things are on the hot and crowded side. Nonetheless, the thought of heading to places relatively cold and miserable feels more than a little unsettling. We have some of our fall and winter clothes dry-cleaned before we leave, just to be on the safe side.

We sell the old Malibu and buy a van, so we're able to ditch the trailer, which cost an arm and a leg to rent. The van is big and white and clunky, but it has a nice anonymity—the type of van a serial killer would probably want, so big and white it's paradoxically almost invisible. We head back north into Georgia on a bright Saturday morning, our stuff packed into boxes piled up on the floor behind us.

That van becomes emblematic for me; it's *the cross-country van*, as white and anonymous as its passengers. When it pulls into towns in Georgia and Alabama and Oklahoma, no one seems to notice. It eases its way quietly across the borders like some big rectangular shadow, so unobtrusive that its navigators make the travels of beat poets look positively warlike.

Since I never did find work, we're on a shoestring budget all the way. We start to eat in cheesy diners now, instead of the family restaurants we'd gotten used to on the road. The first diner is just outside Columbus, Georgia, a tiny box of a place off route 27 called The Little Chicken. I think of Chicken Little, and sure enough, when we step out onto the dusty blacktop and look out at the blue and grey clouds piling up on the horizon, it looks as if the sky is falling. I say as much to Danielle.

"Yeah," she answers, running a hand across her brow. "It not only looks like the sky is falling, it feels like it."

We stretch and yawn as we stand outside the van, like people on the road always do. Before we trudge our way into The Little Chicken, we stop at a newspaper box, the old-fashioned kind with the little metal grate. It's the previous day's paper, but we don't much care. We're really just buying it for the funnies, the weather forecast, and national news.

Once inside, the harsh reality of the early hour strikes like some miasmic vapor. Bacon and eggs smoke away on the grill, and a one-eyed waitress leans over the counter and drawls, "Mornin', ladies. What can I get y'all?"

We ask quietly if they are serving lunch—we've been up since six, and it's now 10:30—and we're disappointed when she shakes her head.

"No, miss, I'm sorry," she says. "Lunch menu ain't in effect until eleven. They're late risers in this town." She grins hideously.

We settle for bran muffins and a pot of coffee, then squirrel ourselves away in the least conspicuous booth in the place. Even then, I feel like we have neon signs on our foreheads saying "Out-of-towners." All the other patrons at The Little Chicken are men in short sleeves who look like construction workers or parks department laborers. The waitress is the only other female.

"You know," I say, "part of me says this is the smartest thing we could possibly do, and part of me says we're out of our cotton-pickin' minds."

She takes another bite. "Eating muffins?" She tries to keep a straight face, but isn't able to manage it.

"Nooo." I shake my head at her in mock-exasperation. "*Moving.* Shuffling off to Buffalo."

"Ooh, that sounds like a bad idea," she says. "I bet you Buffalo would be cold right now."

"It probably would. You know what I mean, though?"

"I understood the *smartest thing we could possibly do* part. What about the *out of our cotton-pickin' minds* part?"

"Well, doesn't it feel a little crazy? Like when-we-left-Connecticut kind of crazy?"

She sips her coffee thoughtfully. "No, not really. Not to me, at least. I mean, what's so crazy about splitting for California? Plenty of people do it." She pauses. "We're going from one warm, sunny climate to another. It's not like we're heading for Alaska."

"Maybe it's exactly what you just said. *Splitting for California.* It sounds like the typical fantasy of every east coast adolescent. Or threat."

"You mean, like, threatening their parents?"

I shift in my seat, uncomfortably. "Exactly."

"But what other choices did we have? You weren't finding work. We had to do something."

"I suppose. Adventurers, eh?"

"Pioneers," she says, and lifts her coffee cup. We toast. "We're like Lewis and Clark," she says.

I laugh. "Yeah, right. More like Laurel and Hardy."

"Heckle and Jeckle?"

"Larry and Moe," we say in unison, and both laugh at the unintentional specter of the Danbury truckers rising from the not-so-distant past.

"I wonder whatever happened to those two clowns," I say.

"Our friends the truckers? Hey, if this rig's rockin', don't come knockin'!"

I burst out laughing, and a couple of backwoods/hayseed types crane their red little necks around and goggle. For a moment, I see the whole diner, everyone, all of it, like something out of a Sinclair Lewis novel. Banjoes duel in my head, and old alleycats meow to each other across a fence. I say, "Let's get our bill and get the hell out of here."

She doesn't question it. "Oookay," she says. "First I have to use the facilities, though."

She takes the majority of the newspaper with her to the ladies' room, and I pay our bill and sit at the counter with the comics and sports section while she's gone. I read an article in Sports about plans for the Oksana Baiul Skating Rink in Hartford, Connecticut, and for a moment, I have that unreal sensation of the tourist reading news about home. Home, I think. That's odd. I haven't thought of the place as home in some time. I rub my palms on the front of my jeans, as if I could somehow wipe off Connecticut, wash my hands of it, both literally and figuratively.

Danielle returns from the rest room. "Take a look at *this*," she says, holding the paper before her like a book report with an A-plus on it. She has left it folded over, the travel section showing.

"What?" I say. There are articles about Aruba, New Mexico, Pike's Peak in Colorado.

"This." Her fingernail traces the letters of the Pike's Peak article: *The View from the Top.*

"Well," I say, "we'll probably be going right by there. Colorado's on the way to California, unless you go straight west through New Mexico and Arizona, heading toward Los Angeles." I realize with acute embarrassment that I sound exactly like my father, and I hate that. Also, I don't see what the big deal is.

"Oh, let's go, Jana," she whispers urgently, her breath hot in my ear. "It'll be so great. It says here that from the top of that mountain you can see like fifty kazillion miles. You can see into Wyoming and New Mexico and I don't know what. Let's go there, can we? Can we?" Just like a kid.

I smile. "You sound like you're asking my permission. Why not? I'm game. We've got to go where the jobs are, though, ultimately. It may not *be* there; in fact, it might not be in California, either." My father, again.

"Oh, don't be a poop," she says, stretching for a swat on the arm. "It'll be like one great big vacation, just like the trip from Ohio down through Florida, before we got those jobs."

We walk back toward the van. "Well, it'll only really be like a vacation if we take turns driving."

"I know."

"And if we camp out some of the time. We definitely don't have the bankroll for hotels all the way." I smile again, a bit ruefully.

"Sure," she grins. Undaunted. "But it'll be fun. Have you ever camped out in the desert?"

"Can't say as ah have," I drawl. "Sounds scary, though, don't it? Awl them scorpions and rattlesnakes and cacti." I start to laugh, she smacks me several times on the shoulder. "And not only that, but no water atall, as far as the eye can see."

"Well, then *you* can camp in the desert, and I'll drive to a Motel Six." She says it mock-petulantly, pouting at me.

"Riiiiight."

We climb back into the van and start off, Danielle behind the wheel and sunlight beating down on the windshield so the heat waves rise off it like on a midsummer's day. It's hard to believe it's only April.

"Where are we going, then?" I ask. "Oklahoma? Kansas?"

The road atlas lies beside her on the seat, opened to Georgia.

"I don't know. Is there a map of the whole country in there somewhere?"

"In front," I say. "Let me see."

She hands it to me, and I flip to the map of the U.S. It's two full pages, like most of the maps of individual states. I feel a slight surge of pride, absurd, and a touch of childlike patriotism as I suddenly understand what a large country it is. The magnitude of our trip flashes open for me.

I trace with my finger Alabama, Mississippi, and Louisiana, into Texas, then north through Oklahoma and Kansas, and again west through Colorado. Just getting to Colorado will be amazing. Danielle follows the motions of my finger as it slides from state to state, and I see the same realization dawn in her eyes as she glances over.

"We really *are* out of our cotton-pickin' minds, aren't we?" she says.

I laugh. "Not necessarily. I don't know, though. Ask me again when we get to Kansas."

She smiles. "What do either of us know about Kansas?"

"I don't know…Dorothy, Toto?"

She laughs and scans the traffic ahead, changing lanes. "That's one thing I've never been able to figure out. Why would anyone want to leave Oz? Especially to go back to Kansas. I mean, I'd take my chances with those flying monkeys just to avoid having to go back to that black and white world."

"Well, it *was* only a dream, after all, right?"

"Only a dream." She grins.

We fall silent. It's the first time I can remember rocking along in the big white van, feeling comfortable with Danielle, even in silence, just as aware of my contentment as I have suddenly become of my surroundings. I see everything before me—the billboards, scrub oaks, sunlight glinting from the sidemirrors of passing cars—and I feel the warmth, that sense not of diminished experience but of fulfillment.

When I was younger, and even into my early adult years, there was always talk: my mom rattling on about bridge or broken fax machines, my dad expounding cheerfully about the Dobuans…but never a sense of peace, never a feeling that everyone could just sit in silence and be okay. Silence equaled tension, it only lay heavy in the room when someone, or everyone, was enraged, when talking could be nothing more than the flame held up to an already explosive situation. In my family, silence was like some self-inflicted punishment for our collective inability to communicate beyond a superficial level.

So when I experienced these long pauses that take place when people run out of things to say, I always found something to fill in that space. And when I began to spend more time with Danielle— that is, with the open, already-acknowledged fact that we were more than friends clear between us—I made sure that even the briefest pauses were cut short by more conversation. To me, it was radical to do otherwise.

Yet, when the moment comes, we are suddenly like some old married couple whose silences may even convey more meaning in the purest sense than any possible words. And I start to bask in that warmth, quietly looking out the window and glancing over occasionally at Danielle, who has just the hint of a smile on her lips. And taking her hand in my own.

Chapter 39

MONTGOMERY, ALABAMA: A Tuesday, somewhat rainy but pleasant, with the mid-spring pleasantness of a southern April day. Danielle is asleep in the passenger seat of the van, which is parked by a stand of pines in a rest stop where we spent the night, the decision to spend at least one night camping out and taking showers at the local YWCA in the morning precipitated by a brief flare-up about money: the cost of motels, the limited budget, and so on.

Danielle is a little freer with money than I am, and I feel sure we must economize strictly if we are to make it to California without selling our clothes or our blood or something. Or without getting jobs again, temporarily.

I think about that now, here in Alabama. *Getting jobs temporarily.* We've done something that seems both radical and radically old-fashioned: piling into a car and going all over the country, splitting like two beatniks for the great whatever. No permanent jobs, no mailing address, no medical bills, no rent or kids or mortgages. No trappings. And yet, I can't escape the feeling that the trappings will catch up, that eventually we'll end up with IRAs and dental insurance and all the other things that define the lives of the very people we sought to escape.

It's like television…I mean, could I live without one for an indefinite period? And even if I did, could I eliminate them from my life entirely? No, I'd still see them at bus stations and in store windows, above convenience store counters, flashing out the backs of minivans.

No matter what, unless I moved to a shack in the woods, I'd still see that hazy blue light reflected in the windows of houses and apartments if I walked at night down any residential street. I'd still hear kids on the street imitating things they've heard from favorite shows and adults talking about what they watched the previous night. I'd be unable to escape its pervasive influence.

And I can't help thinking that this other thing, this uniformity, hegemony, homogeneity, whatever the hell it is, is also inescapable. It's like being in a prison, and every time you dig out, you find you're just on a different part of the grounds, one you've never seen before. You haven't escaped at all.

But for now, the illusion of freedom, the radical will to self-responsibility and personal choice Danielle and I have adopted, is an attractive one, and I've chosen to forget what I know. I've decided to let the illusion shine. And I know that Danielle, in her dreams as she sleeps here beside me, dreams the illusion, too: the sunlight on mountaintops under blue skies, the clouds and stars, the freedom of the road. The dream. Like my old mystery woman dream, *Thunder Island*, the calico sundress. And yes, it is only a dream.

After camping out in Alabama for an evening, we realize we like its rustic appeal better than we expected, and so we decide to stick around for a couple of days. We discover the main hub of activity in the state is Tuscaloosa, a bit of a hike to the north and west of Montgomery. It takes us a few hours to get there, but proves well worth it.

For the uninitiated, it should be said that Tuscaloosa is not just a college town. Sure, the University of Alabama is there—with its pear trees and its early Saturday afternoon touristy "campus tour"—but Tuscaloosa is so much more than the university. At a grocery store, where we pause for deli sandwiches and idle chitchat, a woman in a grey blouse swings her Ford Escort around our van and into the street, her manner that of someone accustomed to comfort and security, the predictability of routine. Before she pulls out, her car is the nicest in the lot.

In the center of town stands a flagpole surrounded by flowers. People once held segregationist rallies here, an elderly black woman tells us. Today, the town is fully integrated, of course, but it wasn't that long ago, after all, her voice seems to tell us.

The pace here is so different from that of the Northeast. It takes longer for the woman to tell us about the days of Jim Crow than it would have taken someone up north to give a stranger directions to the other side of town, and *she* has initiated the contact, not us. Just shooting the breeze, like she's got all day, and knows we must too. No one up north would do that. It would be considered an imposition.

She directs us to a local spot of interest two blocks down, the Old Tavern. Once a stagecoach inn, the two story building—brick and not at all like a tavern—has become a museum open to visitors. Next door stands the State House, or what's left of it. It burned down in 1923, but the foundation was eventually restored, along with some pillars and part of a rotunda, so that the effect is vaguely like that of the Roman Colosseum.

Other downtown scenery is equally quirky and picturesque: lovely old churches, all stained glass, marble columns and Gothic spires, birds flying off them like some well-directed scene in a film; as startling, in their incandescent beauty, as if they had sprung from the ground overnight. As if the birds, to dazzle the eyes of people below, all flew backward.

We decide to have dinner at a restaurant called The Strand, on the recommendation of the elderly black woman, Martha. A place "for young people," she calls it, like there are places for old folks, too, and she's certain we would just as soon avoid them. As it turns out, dinner is shockingly cheap, and we find ourselves surrounded by college students celebrating happy hour with buffalo wings and nachos. They are an eclectic group of dudes with goatees, girls with pierced eyebrows or noses, and preppy kids with oversized sweatshirts, who look eerily northern and suburban, like Danielle and me; as if they were scooped up out of New Jersey or Maryland without a chance to streamline their wardrobes and lose the boat shoes.

I suddenly miss college and all its hodgepodge of great ideas, improbable romances, solitude and calculated ennui. I wish I could be back there for just a little while, maybe a couple of years—long enough to get my degree maybe, while I figure out what it is I really want to do when I grow up. I think vaguely about this while Danielle samples the Cajun stew, and can't help wondering about her take on the college scene. But I do not ask. Instead, I say, "How's the soup?"

Life is difficult, and often unfair. But, says Danielle, the soup— "stew," she corrects—is good, and that is enough.

Before we leave Alabama behind completely, we make one last stop on our trek west: Grandma Estelle's Museum of Miscellany, twenty miles west of Tuscaloosa, off Route 80.

Grandma Estelle herself is the curator of the rustic spread of buildings at the end of a badly-paved road ending, almost, at a riverbank. The location reminds me of an old junkyard and, indeed, the "collectibles" on display are what Fred Sanford might have sold if he'd been a woman. Down a hallway lined with hundreds and hundreds of old inkwells and soda bottles, Grandma Estelle leads her visitors, talking a mile a minute.

"This here used to be all polished up beautiful, you know, but I just can't keep it up the way I used to, what with my arthritis and all, not that I have any real desire to do a whole lot of cleaning, I've done my share of that in my lifetime, God knows. And now with my Leroy all growed up and ready to take over the museum, he don't want no part of it, nope, 'cause the place ain't a *business*, you know, the admission's free, and we don't even ask for donations, although we do keep a can for 'em right here in the room we're goin' to, what I call The Nursery."

And just as she says this, the hallway opens onto a room filled with miniatures in an almost completely omnipresent baby motif: tiny possums play cribbage at a tiny table, tiny kittens sleep in a tiny baby carriage—all real, taxidermied, their glassy eyes eerily lifelike in the dim grey light. They peer out at us from a childhood frozen in time, a creepy horror-movie-type nursery scene that seems capable of coming to life after the lights are off and the adults have gone away.

We wander through other buildings and look at the other junk, and after a while, none of it actually seems like junk at all. We look at a collection of sewing machines, some of which even work, and a collection of kerosene lamps. We look at marbles, old steelies and agates and glasseyes. We look at polished stones, houses of cards. We look at dolls and Tinkertoys and G.I. Joes, buttons, keys, pens and pencils, lava lamps and crockery. Everything and anything you can imagine, mostly plain old fashioned Americana.

The only things we don't expect to see, after the first few buildings, are pornography and art deco. But we even find some art deco items, real stuff from the twenties and thirties, and it finally dawns on me that the whole place is a monument to kitsch, a collection of the gaudiest trash and the most cloyingly sentimental everyday items, all stuffed into room upon room and given the reverent appellation of Art. In one way, it is funny, and almost quaint, to my culture-corrupted American brain, and in another it is pathetic, a testimonial to the crass blindness of our endless and inevitably conspicuous consumption.

Even so, when we leave, we put five dollars in the can. After all, it doesn't really seem like junk after you've seen enough of it.

Back in the van, moving fast up Route 20, we rethink that spontaneous moment of stuffing the five-spot in the donations can. It seemed like the right thing to do, especially given Grandma Estelle's complaints about Leroy and the high cost of living, but now, once away from the scene, the charitable moment seems ill-advised.

"We should've just given her a buck," Danielle says.

I arch an eyebrow.

"Well, maybe a buck apiece."

I hold the dubious expression.

She defends the thought: "Hey, we're not rich, either."

I slouch in the seat and close my eyes, affecting fatigue. "I know, I know." And I think about the venerable Grandma's poverty.

"We've got to hold on to every extra penny we can until we get to the coast, right? Aren't we on a tight budget?"

"Sure." I open my eyes again, and yawn behind my hand. "We are now reduced to eating at cheesy diners, and pretty soon we'll probably have to actually start cooking, God forbid. But didn't we just have this whole conversation?" I yawn again, as if for effect, and it causes her to yawn, too.

"Uh-huh," she says. "That we did. *Let's not fight about money. Let's be original.*"

I laugh. "Did I say that?" As if I didn't know.

"I believe those were your exact words."

"Well, let's *not* fight about money. We'll just have to be careful with our charitable contributions from now on."

"Right. None of 'em are tax deductible."

"Exactly." I close my eyes again and settle down in the seat. "We should be *taking* charitable contributions, not giving them."

"Well, you want to start begging? Go to the next Sally's Boutique we can find, buy some raggy clothes for fifty cents or whatnot, go a few days without bathing or cleaning at all?"

I make a retching sound.

"Then we can find some good oily dirt for our faces and hands, make signs that say *Will work for food*."

"You're sick," I say without opening my eyes.

"I know." She laughs. "I know it isn't funny, though. I mean, not *haha* funny. Do you ever think about how lucky we really are?"

"Sure. We talked about it the day of the yard sale, didn't we?"

She considers. "Yeah, I think so. Sure, I remember that woman who looked like a bag lady. That was the day you told me a closet is a closet."

I feel myself redden slightly. "I'm never gonna live that down, am I?"

"No, no, I didn't mean it as a zinger. I just realized that that was the same day."

"You're not pissed off about that, are you?"

"No...."

"Because you sound pissed off."

"I'm not. Honest. You were right. I mean, it was true then, and it's true now."

"Yeah, but you sounded pissed off. And *sound*."

"Not at all. When you're right, you're right."

"Come to think of it, you're not really all that 'in the closet' anymore, if you think about it."

"How's that?"

"Well, for one thing, practically everywhere you go these days, you're with me." I cannot resist peeking over at her, and when she catches me at it, I start to laugh. "Plus don't forget those truckers back in Danbury. *Danielle*-bury."

She cracks up. "Sometimes I think you're sicker than I am."

I close my eyes again. "Maybe I am. By the way, where are we going?"

There is a pause, as if she is deciding that instant. "Jackson, Mississippi."

I open my eyes again.

Chapter 40

"'THE GREAT MISSISSIPPI, the majestic, the magnificent Mississippi, rolling its mile-wide tide along, shining in the sun....'"

I'm back behind the wheel again, and Danielle is reading aloud to me from a paperback copy of Mark Twain's *Life On The Mississippi* as the big white van booms down the highway. A seemingly endless highway, Route 20 runs from Tuscaloosa to Jackson and beyond, curving down in a diagonal arc that hardly begins to even straighten into an east-west line on the map until the first big city over the Mississippi border, Meridian. Here, the bodies of water have names like Okatibbee and Chunky, and towns range from the picturesque—Toomsuba, Obadiah—to the bizarre: Prismatic, and, farther to the south and west, Hot Coffee, Improve, and Arm. We continue west on Route 20 through Meridian, past Hickory, Newton, and Decatur, then through Bienville National Forest.

What impresses me most about Mississippi is what I think of as its splendid decadence: cypress and gum in the bottomlands, pines and big-trunked oaks on the hills, the sound of whippoor-wills in the afternoon as we walk by a creek down a long sloping bottom near a rest stop, two-family houses with pillared white porches, and white and lavender jimson weed, wisteria, myrtle and syringa around us, all heavy with the burden of spring. It doesn't look quite the same as the bayou country of Louisiana, with its standing water, murky-brown and bleak with nearby willow trees, but it shares the same overripe quality…moss on trees, the rich earth fertile beyond belief, perhaps beyond need. And of course, the Mississippi River itself, or, as it is still simply known, the River—not Twain's Mississippi, but the River of today—draws us to its banks like the pull of a magnet.

Our romance with the Mississippi River begins at the State Wildlife Museum in Jackson, the state capital, where that week they happen to have an exhibit of early riverboat photography. Most compelling is a picture of a Mississippi passenger and freight packet from the 1800s, a sternwheeler with bales of cotton stacked twelve high, and people walking or standing around on top of it as if they were construction workers on top of a building. Huge smokestacks tower behind them, the captain at his wheel in the tower above it all, like a man in a raised pagoda looking downriver as people wave from the shore.

Everything in that time period, it seems, was dominated by the river. The photo exhibit features not only pictures of sternwheelers and other boats moving down its meandering course, but also pictures of men and women on its banks, working at loading-docks, waving bon voyage to departing passengers, posing under parasols in the noonday sun. Every aspect of life was clearly influenced by the ubiquity of cotton, by its relationship to the river. In picture after picture, I see the big dark bales, stacked like bricks or lying at odd angles, their tone in those old black and white pictures more like that of steel wool than straw or wheat.

Probably most striking to my twentieth-century eye is the lack of machinery, steamboats notwithstanding. Even those few buildings depicted look so structurally pure, so obviously creations of brick and stone, that it's hard to imagine how anything that sound ever got built at all without bulldozers, steel girders and plexiglass. It seems so radical I feel intimidated, sheepish about my relative ignorance. Of course, it's not a great revelation to say that there were no stereos or TVs then, probably no phones or toilets or electric lamps for most of these folks either. That's what makes me uncomfortable, that level of ignorance underneath all my comments to Danielle about "Fulton's Folly" and the human capacity to strive amid primitive conditions for better things.

Chapter 41

WHEN WE LEAVE Jackson, we head for Vicksburg, thinking it, too, is a huge city, based only on our map-knowledge, which is essentially *no* knowledge. In fact, Vicksburg's population is probably less than 30,000, much smaller than Jackson, and we are surprised. We are reminded in a vague way of old battles, the Civil War, and sure enough, a Confederate soldier statue stands in the center of town. There's also an exhibition called the Corps of Engineers Mississippi River Test Mock-ups, which we pass up, somewhat reluctantly. To my way of thinking, a mock-up is a full scale model of something, and how or why engineers would build a full scale model of the Mississippi is beyond me. I want to see the real thing.

And see it I do, in the best circumstances possible: totally unrehearsed, and from a serendipitous angle, without the benefit of a tour guide or strategic viewing point to "package" my impressions. And it, The River, exceeds my expectations. It is huge, bigger than any river I've ever seen, and it being springtime, running very high but slow. This is what the Nile must be like, I think, the Tigris-Euphrates, the Congo: magnificent, awe-inspiring, capable of making you both catch your breath and realize your own smallness, like a mountain range or tidal wave.

Eventually, we get back in the van and go west, but not before a little stroll along the riverbank, and a few moments in the sun. I think about those pictures back in the museum in Jackson, all those people on the shore. I wonder how many of them traveled on the same spot where we now stand, how many lifted bales of cotton onto steamers, waited for long-traveled relatives to come home from the river, only to wave goodbye again in too short a time.

So we cross over the Mississippi, essentially the state border between Mississippi and Louisiana, then on past Tallulah, Waverly and Delhi, past rivers with names like Bayou, Macon, and Lafourche, then the big town of Monroe, where factory buildings loom like squatters on the side of the highway. The interstate cuts straight west, past universities, Grambling State and Louisiana Tech, until finally, just before the Texas border, we reach the Shreveport and Bossier City hub, a busy metropolitan area dominated by colleges, universities, and hospitals. We stop in to see the Norton Art Gallery, an unassuming little museum with an impressive collection of art and beautiful grounds, after which we have a slice of pizza at a little one-stop, and then head for the big country: Texas.

Spring is definitely the time to be here, we have no doubt. As the names of towns go by—Harrison, Pritchett, Mineola—the rolling hills of timberland with their forests thick with pines, cypress and oak trees eventually give way to flatter and flatter prairie until, as Dallas gets nearer, the landscape flattens out enough so that the bluebonnet fields allow a view of the city from far away. This might be true even without tall buildings, since the Dallas metropolitan area is second in size only to Houston, and hosts a population of over three million, and having passed through those piney woods and small towns along the way, the metropolitan area feels that much bigger, the contrast that much more astonishing. It being April, temperatures are in the mid-seventies, so we still have no regrets having gone north again from Florida. We are not cold.

We take our time, losing our way in the vast city, and we just wander and explore, explore and wander. Probably the most fun is Fair Park: two hundred acres of museums, an amusement park, the Cotton Bowl Stadium…a city within a city. We visit the Dallas Museum of Natural History and the Dallas Museum of Art, the latter of which boasts an impressive American collection, then off to the amusement park for just a short while. Money worries resurface here—we could spend money in this town like it's New York, for God's sake—so we chill out, take a walk in the park, and enjoy some conversation, the best and cheapest entertainment around.

Danielle talks about the surprising lack of cowboy hats and cockroach-killers—she'd expected virtually everyone to be in western gear—and about visiting the site of the Kennedy assassination, Dealey Plaza, an unusual sort of tourist stop—standing on the *grassy knoll* and all that. I am more interested in kicking back and talking. Really talking. About the important stuff, the ground we've been covering, where we're going, what we're doing.

"Can I ask you a serious question?"

"What's that?" she says.

"We've been bopping around like this from town to town… how well do you think we'd be able to live together, if we were just settled down in one place?"

She looks at me in surprise. But her slow response tells me she is considering it. "Why?" She shrugs, a little nervously, it appears.

"I don't know," I say. "It just seems like, what with all this constant change and novelty, it's easy to stay entertained, and not have to really make any changes of our own. But when things get routine…."

"You think too much." And suddenly she kisses me on the mouth, a huge, brief embrace that leaves me flabbergasted when she dances away, laughing. Two old women stop and gawk a moment before walking on, shaking their heads. A brief moment of comic deflation, the kind of classic scene that could only happen in lives like ours.

She comes back over and whispers in my ear. "Did you catch the look on the two old dames?" She takes my arm, forcing me along the sidewalk.

"You're really incorrigible."

She laughs, out of control. "I bet you *they* were dykes, those two."

I can't help laughing. "Oh, of course. Two old-fashioned purveyors of the closet. Like Gertrude Stein and what's-her-name."

"Hey," she says, "I know. Let's go to the Lee Harvey Oswald Museum and look for the Onassis exhibit."

"You really have lost it today. Is there something in your root beer?"

"Shot of Cuervo. Scotch on the rocks...." She starts to giggle again.

"Let's just hold hands," I say, disengaging myself from her arm. "That's probably radical enough for this town."

We continue down the street and she swings my arm, forward and back, up and down, the way kids do when they play Red Rover. We walk on and on like that for a good long stretch, collecting a few more stares but not caring at all.

Chapter 42

WE LEAVE THE next day for Oklahoma City, traveling north by way of Fort Worth on route 35. It seems a long time since we were on a north-south route, and the change of scenery is refreshing. This trip has two main elements that differentiate it from the previous legs of our tour: first, we spend several days camping out, instead of just one or two; and second, we are painfully aware that we are running low on funds. We have to break out the good old gas credit card, and yes, we will have to find jobs before we ever attempt to reach California, because at the rate we're going, we'll be arriving in Colorado Springs flat broke—not a good thing.

This line of thinking brings us to another point—discussed at great length in the van while approaching the Wichita Mountains, a detour from the northern highway—which is that, as two women traveling alone in the big bad world, we still risk being raped, robbed, murdered, or whatever, even though the two of us always being together considerably minimizes the risks. I'm surprised that we haven't contemplated this more seriously before, although perhaps she has, and she's just stayed silent until now. I know my parents sure contemplated it before we left, but I'd been on my own so much at Boston College that, really, the thought of being with Danielle all the time made me feel a lot more secure when we were leaving than I'd ever felt alone in a major metropolitan area.

We cruise up 35 North, and even from many miles away we're able to see the improbable mountains rising nearly 2,500 feet at their highest point, set down in the middle of open prairie like some strange cosmic practical joke. They are so incongruous with the surrounding landscape that even at their most desolate points they are astonishing, beautiful and savage.

"Isn't that beautiful?" she says.

"I don't know. Somehow they seem—lonesome."

"Lonesome?"

"Desolate, in a way. Maybe because it looks like such a wild place from here, like there's no one out there at all."

She consults the atlas. "The map says there's a big wildlife refuge."

"Oh, I'm sure it's a huge tourist draw. It's just that, from here, they look deserted."

"Well, it probably wouldn't be the worst place to murder somebody."

I give her a look, and she grins at me, her little half-smile. "That's a pleasant thought."

She laughs. "Isn't it, though?"

"I'll tell you what. This may sound fatalistic, but I think we're lucky nothing's happened to us so far."

"Oh," she scoffs, "now, come on. Just because women are alone doesn't mean Jason is hiding somewhere behind a tree with a pitchfork!" She makes a monster face.

"I know, I know. There's safety in numbers. But sometimes I think we'd be better off out in the mountains, like up ahead there, than in another camping ground. Some of those places really give me the creeps."

"And being up in the mountains doesn't?"

"Look at them." We scan the horizon. "I bet you could get lost up there for days and not see another soul."

"Lost is right. And never get found again, either. Unless maybe by some coyotes or hyenas or whatever."

That cracks me up. "There aren't any hyenas up there."

"Well, whatever. I'll bet you there are plenty of coyotes."

"Maybe," I say. "Even so, if we just stayed on a well-marked trail, we'd probably be fine."

"Where would we sleep? We don't have a tent. We don't even have sleeping bags. That's why we've been camping at these places with cabins, you know."

"I know. We could crash in the back of the van, like in Alabama."

"We only did that for one night in Alabama. I mean, is that really what you're thinking? 'Cause too many nights in a row sleeping in this thing would probably about kill us. Or at least make us very, very cranky."

"Well, maybe two nights. If we go into Oklahoma City, we can probably sort of take it from there."

We head into the city for provisions, but not before taking the scenic detour through the lonesome mountains, where we get our first view of how grand a state Oklahoma can be. The Wichita Mountains Wildlife Refuge is immense, with buffalo—the first either of us have ever seen—and plenty of cattle wandering around, mostly longhorn steers. The only road in the place is on Mount Scott, so that becomes our main route for a short time. A camper we meet confirms Danielle's suspicion that coyotes do indeed thrive out here, along with skunks, beaver, fox and deer, armadillos, and bobcats. Yes, bobcats. We decide then and there that crashing in the woods will not be an option, van or no van.

In Oklahoma City, we get jobs, realizing that we don't want to arrive broke in Colorado. Fortunately, the weather is amenable to our camping, and for the two weeks before we get paychecks, we stay in a campground called the Lonesome Giant. Though far from the mountains and the bobcats, it is depressing as heck, a bleak wasteland of tents and mobile homes with drunk-looking mothers clutching dirty children as they stagger inside and slam cheap metal doors behind them. We're both tempted to try a boarding house, or the local YWCA, but decide to tough it out.

Danielle's new job—"waitressing and sometimes host-essing"—is at an Italian restaurant called Don Pepé Pizzeria Napoletana, one of those dark places where pizzas disappear into a brick oven on the ends of big paddles, and candlelit tables with white tablecloths and heavy silverware fill the dining room. The proprietor, of course, is Don Pepé, a thickset man with black hair going grey and a handlebar mustache, who talks always with one hand in the air: "Hello folks, I'm Don-a Pepé, welcome to-a the Pizzeria Napoletana!" I half expect him to say, *"Mangia, mangia!"* and sometimes, when I call Danielle at work and get *him*, he says, "Danielle? She's a no here! No, no, she lef'!" Nothing about him is understated, and I can't help but wonder if, God love him, he's ever spoken a quiet word in his life.

You might think I'd get a cushy office job in Oklahoma City, but my luck is not quite that impressive. I land a position that, if it bore a title, would be something like Assistant to the Field Supervisor in a market research company called WATS Bank, which is mostly just a big room with a lot of phones in it called, appropriately enough, a *telecenter.* My job duties include sending invoices, data entry, answering the phone, and a host of miscella-neous odds and ends, from stuffing envelopes to brewing coffee to photocopying advertising copy. I learn a whole new language's worth of fancy-schmancy jargon, phrases like multivariate demo-graphic analysis and qualitative consumer mapping, and none of it means much to me, but I retain some things. The job isn't exciting or glamorous, but it pays the rent, and for the time being that will have to suffice.

And now we settle down into a humdrum period, and the question of what things will be like for us if we settle down in one place—the echo of Danielle's *You think too much* in my head—is apparently getting answered, even though Oklahoma is only a stopover. We get up in the morning, shower in our little primitive campground shower stall, usually taking turns, although sometimes one of us will scoot in for the occasional backrub or to do the other's hair. We have mellow breakfasts and humble dinners, and in between, the vast gulf of the work grind. A hundred and sixty-eight hours a week, day in and day out, we live together, but the forty spent in work—more for us, really, Danielle's schedule rotating in some indecipherable formula—draw us together tighter when we have the chance to spend time together.

Although I don't have the experience to know for sure, I suspect we're like some young married couple, the honeymoon going on and on. I can't wait to hear her stupid stories of the redoubtable Don Pepé, and she asks me almost daily about the antics of the WATS Bank's field supervisor. Our lives are humdrum only in that we've been lulled into a kind of dream. The domestic chores are there—we divide them amicably—and the little leisure activities we allow ourselves on our limited incomes still hold laughter and a sense of adventure. Long shifts apart set up great twinges of longing that go off in my chest like firecrackers.

Day turns to day, night follows night, and everything glides along as smoothly as if we had nothing left to contemplate except putting some money away for old age and making an effort to touch base with the folks back home. Why do I call it humdrum? Because it *hums*. I'm like a beachcomber gathering stones, and it sings in my ears like the ocean.

We actually do keep in touch with the folks back home. My mother is distant—more so than in real life, if such a thing is possible—and my father, genial, affable, smiling audibly in every conversation, less and less credible in his supposed contentment as time goes by. I know his act, and most likely he knows I know it, but the game is still his. Who am I to question the gamemaster?

I ask him if everything is okay, so clearly a rewording of the question beneath—*What's wrong?*—that he cannot mistake its meaning. Yet he says everything is fine, fine, as tolerantly and earnestly as he would if he had cancer. Then, too, I think they are horrified we are living in Oklahoma City, however temporarily.

This is hard on Danielle, of course, because to hear me tell it, you'd think I'd been sired by robots, but her conversations back home are so short and superficial I find them positively painful to hear. In fact, as a rule, I do not eavesdrop, managing to find an errand to run or an appropriately noisy chore that will drown her out without preventing them from having their talk. Her relationship with Mr. Psychologist and Mrs. CPA, or the lack of it, I should say, gives me gratitude for the little bit of intimacy that remains between my parents and me.

It also fetches me up sharply when I complain to her. She's the wrong person to tell, and it crosses her face like a shadow whenever I am at all hard on my parents. Clearly, she feels, perhaps not envy, but something that approaches it. She never has to say a word to convey her meaning—an eyebrow slightly raised or an evasive glance brings me back in line.

And though I feel guiltily grateful, I resent the issue; it's as if her parents still drive a wedge between us, even in absentia. It's like being haunted by them and they aren't even dead. Mostly, I think I resent it because no one should have the power to separate her from me. It's ironic, too, since back in Connecticut, her parents would have tried to keep us apart if they'd ever gotten a clue about the real nature of the relationship. Now, many miles away, my parents' being relatively nice to me creates this blank spot that hovers between us like a bad habit neither wishes to discuss. Perhaps she's not envious, but merely sees me at my worst when I complain about my lot in life, and has little sympathy or ability to withhold judgment. In any case, we remain largely silent about it all, and whatever comes to the table will not come today.

But that's one small bump in the road, and most of the road is smooth for now. The days drift by, casting long friendly shadows on us, and spring turns to summer as we celebrate our third month of freedom, or the illusion of it, on the road.

Chapter 43

LIFE IN OKLAHOMA goes along smoothly, and we begin to prepare ourselves for our trip through Kansas and into Colorado. In order to accomplish this, our budget is so low that our sole recreational activities are long drives and hikes in the mountains. Oklahoma City is fairly industrialized, but local camping areas in the Wichita Mountains and the Tishomingo area provide a chance to explore and to get a little R & R. I know that not everyone appreciates nature, and I'm glad Danielle shares my appreciation.

Our favorite haunt is probably Devil's Den State Park, which is even farther south than the Wichita Mountains. Unlike the Quartz Mountain or Platt National parks, Devil's Den isn't a big area for camping. It has no accommodations, so if you're weird enough to camp out there, you'd be doing it illegally, and you'd definitely be roughing it. We like it because it is supremely creepy and "old West."

The Devil's Den is a cave area formed by boulders, and all the formations have names like something from a bad cowboy movie—Devil's Coffin, Witch's Tomb. Dead Man's Cave. On a more practical note, it's a great place to go rock-climbing without having to invest a lot of money in equipment. Closer to home, Red Rock Canyon State Park proves surprisingly picturesque, with high rock walls and huge, lovely old trees. In Connecticut you never notice rock formations, but here, each one is an event. Some of them look like they'd been dropped down on the flatlands right out of the sky.

We camp out at Red Rock on a weekend in early June. It is somewhat cool at night, but not enough to justify the army blankets. We're nervous about coyotes and bobcats, though the campfire will supposedly discourage their approach. We leave it burning low at night, big orange hunks of ember glowing like coals outside our new tent.

Inside, we are snug and warm, and the heavy zippers and flaps bring a sense of comfort and security. We are undoubtedly safe from any intruder unless they're human and well-armed. We have hunting knives in case one of us is attacked by an animal while heading out to our homemade privy in the middle of the night, but there's little reason to carry them. The park is as deserted as if we were the last people on earth.

Danielle's voice is low and regular, as if she's thinking out loud; not talking to another person at all. "The mountains were beautiful today."

"Yeah," I say.

"Sometimes I think I need the mountains. I've always loved the views from hills. That mountaintop today just made me feel something."

"Mm."

"I don't know how to describe it. I mean, it was uplifting and all that, but somehow it made me feel centered. Like I belonged there, almost like we were both part of a higher order—the mountain and me. And you." Her hand reaches out and covers mine. "Do you know what I mean?"

"I think so." I yawn suddenly loudly. "We all belonged there. Me, you, and the mountain. Is that it?"

"Yeah. Like we fit with the scheme of things in a way I hadn't felt before. I can't explain it." Her hand loosens up and rests lightly on my own.

"I think I know what you mean."

Her voice brightens. "Really?"

"I think so. Like when you and I were on the beach in Florida. I think we were out on Sanibel Island."

"Oh, Sanibel…."

"As a matter of fact, I'm sure that's where it was. I had this feeling of connectedness while we were on the beach."

"You knew you belonged."

"I belonged."

We lie in repose, her hand so light on my own that for a moment I trick myself into thinking I feel her pulse. Perhaps I do, and its cadence perfectly matches my own. She says nothing. I wrestle with the urge to speak again, but remain silent. I have come to enjoy the long silences, like when we glide down the road in the big white van and feel that comfortable feeling of contentment, as if we really were that couple, married for years, who long ago left off trying to entertain each other and are content to just *be*.

"I feel that way here," she says.

"Mm?"

"Don't you?"

I realize I have receded into that dreamy twilight state between waking and sleeping where dreams seem real, and reality dreamlike. "I'm sorry. What were you saying? I think I was starting to doze off."

"I was just saying that I feel the same way here tonight. Belongingness."

"Hmm." I turn sideways into her, my leg over hers. I am wide awake now. "You belong here. With me."

I feel her smiling by the way she exhales. "So it's not so much a matter of place as who you're with," she says.

"Mm-hm." I snuggle down next to her, nestling my cheek in the hollow of her shoulderblade. "As long as you're with me, you're right where you belong."

She laughs outright. "Wow, you sound like my ex-boyfriend."

I hold back a chuckle. "No, no, *he* was possessive. I think he was always a little surprised, somehow, that you didn't come with an owner's manual."

She laughs again, and I feel her shake her head. "He wasn't that bad."

"Are you kidding? He's probably in therapy right now, trying to work out all the issues about being left for another woman. I'm sure it wounded his vanity more than a little."

She seems to think about it. "No doubt, he was blown away." She sighs. "Poor James."

I pull my leg up across hers. "Well, he gets no sympathy from me."

"Come here," she says, and kisses me. In the dark I see the silhouette of her smile as she pulls back from me. "We really are living a dream, aren't we?" she whispers.

"This is no dream," I whisper back. "This is real."

She leans back into me, kissing my earlobe, neck, shoulder, her mouth hot and urgent. Outside, the fire burns low, a faint orange glow like candlelight from a distance, hazy with romance. She has me going now, my body ringing with electricity, and when I bring my tongue down her torso, pausing to kiss her breasts and abdomen in slow descent, her skin responds to the touch like the strings of a violin, yearning upward against my mouth, singing as she sighs soft and low. This is no dream, I think. This is no dream.

Chapter 44

THE NEXT MORNING, we explore Red Rock Canyon State Park. I decide a rock climb is in order, and we agree that early afternoon is best. So we have an early lunch and wander around for an hour, postponing the climb. It doesn't matter much that the sky is clouding up, or that the wind is blowing sand in the air in little handfuls, like sea spray. We're more concerned with making sure that we have limbered up properly and have allowed lunch to settle in our stomachs. Already we've gone on rock-climbing expeditions in baking midday sun, in pouring rain, both extremes that could only be surpassed today if it started to snow or if a tornado blew through the campground and carried us away.

We find a high rock wall that looks sufficiently imposing and get our gear in order. Danielle is not fond of rappelling, but we can't find an area where we can climb up one side and down the other without using a lot of rope. We have a bewildering array of spring-loaded camming devices, which to a casual observer would look like links in a chain, along with a rack of stoppers, chocks, and carabiners, or "biners," as we call them. For today, they should suffice, says Danielle. Still, the wind is picking up a bit, and that has me a little concerned. I take our entire supply of coated rope from the big white van and pack it up with the other gear.

We bring other standard equipment to the wall, of course, but not necessarily for immediate use. This type of climbing is known as multi-pitch climbing, which is just climbing a rock face taller than our rope is long, and so we will be rappelling: anchoring a piece of climbing equipment in a crack or crevice, usually a hexcentric (hex-shaped chock to be wedged in) or a "friend" (same basic purpose), then propelling ourselves down in fits and starts. This is different from the common practice of belaying—in belaying, you hold the rope in such a way that if your partner slips, it won't turn into an actual fall. In rappelling, the belay option is not there, because you have only one anchor, and must depend upon it entirely when you make your first leap backwards and rappel. In the olden days you would wrap the rope around your body, usually under one leg, in order to accomplish any rappelling; in modern rappelling, you can use a friction device called a figure-eight descender which the rope passes through, thereby avoiding friction burns on your hands or other body parts. You see this in the movies sometimes, usually looking like it's sticking out of the climber, around the midsection. From a distance, it reminds me of a big version of those pull-tab things on old soda cans.

While I pack up this gear, Danielle slips on her windsuit, a lightweight jacket like the old-fashioned windbreaker except not as warm, and made from some space age water-repellent fiber. I have only an old sweatshirt, but then, I am probably used to roughing it a little more than she is.

High on the rock, the dull wind roars in my ears, like the sound of a seashell only amplified. Each piece of equipment, as it finds its seat in a crack or crevice, sounds tinny and thin in the gust that presses us to the wall. We are facing northwest, and the wind is mainly blowing north, so it feels more friend than foe.

And yet, Danielle is uneasy. I hear her below me, calling up minute directions.

Be careful of that ledge.

Make sure that's secured enough for you.

Watch your foot.

At length, I'm irritated, as obvious caring and concern begin to sound like a matronly nagging. "Do you want to head back?" I call down.

She sidesteps the question. "I'm just worried about the wind."

"Do you want to head back?" I repeat, a little louder.

"No," she calls. But she sounds unconvinced.

We continue laboring up the wall in silence.

"I'm just a little concerned it might get worse."

I look down, no doubt unable to conceal my annoyance. With feigned patience, I call down, "We can go back if you want to. Or you can go back." The words catch on my tongue, and I hear how inconsiderate they sound.

She looks up at me, her expression understandably aggrieved. "Thanks a lot."

"Look, I just meant we can go either way," I call. "I can go back, or you can. Or we can keep going. It doesn't matter either way to me." And again, that overwhelming compulsion to take care of her feelings. Why do I always do this?

"Okay," she says, "let's keep going."

I sigh and resist the temptation to shake my head before turning my gaze from her, back to the rock. For a moment, I am overcome with guilt. How can I feel so strongly she is stampeding on my nerves after lying in her arms last night in such fullness and wonder? I feel the tug of remorse. I'm certain that, if I had a compact to take out and look into, I would see my face as haggard and discomposed as if I'd seen someone injured or killed—like the man on the highway on the road to Ohio, the man with the blanket whose face of terror made me go pale.

This provides food for thought on the long climb up. It strikes me as ironic that I feel so out of place today after last night's talk of belongingness. I face the fact that I'm not having a good day so far, and realize I can choose to start over right now. I take a deep breath, let it go, and when I call down again, it's with a smile in my voice. "How's the wind down there now?"

"Okay." A pause. "Maybe a little better."

I work on the cam in my left hand for a moment before replying, pulling the rope taut. "Yeah, it feels a little lighter up here, too. I think it's dying down."

As if in response, the breezes stir up, die down, then increase exponentially. All I can think is, *I spoke too soon*, as the wind gusts probably from twenty up to twenty-five, twenty-seven, twenty-nine, thirty, thirty-three.

Before it can get much worse, she calls up again: "Did you do that?"

I laugh. "Yeah, I prayed for a challenge. Talk about good turnaround from God, huh?"

Her laugh is muffled. "Should we keep going as we are, or do anything different?" she shouts back up, her voice small as the wind blows stronger still.

I have to think about it. I haven't done this long, and I'm no expert, but it seems to me we ought to stay as close to the rock as possible. Any temptation to use too much rope and swing back away from the rock face will have to be overruled by common sense, the swinging itself having possibly too much propulsion with the wind factor to be safe. A push could tear a stopper out of the wall and prove fatal to one or both of us.

"I think we should head back," I say.

We begin the laborious process of retracing our footsteps. I personally find it simpler and feel it safer to look for the same crevices and holes in the rock face on the way back down in this type of situation, so we attempt to do it that way. It takes longer than it would otherwise, and perhaps we would feel less anxiety if we just moved ourselves down faster, but I think of it as deferred gratification. Of course, in some places, we guess at the location of the last chock or stopper, but altogether we're being cautious, in spite of the wind getting stronger by the minute, thirty-eight, forty, forty-one.

Eventually, it relents, and Danielle likely breathes a sigh of relief at about the same time as my own, I look down and see her windsuit ballooning out from the wind like a sail, and when she looks up into my eyes I see that even if the momentary slowing of the wind brought her a modicum of relief she is nonetheless frightened, our eyes meet in that long suspension of sense and sound like a dream state that makes every scrape and clink of equipment sound far away and detached, as if none of it had anything to do with us, with our lives in their tenuous hold on the face of this rock, and as the wind picks up even more, I hear her cry *Jana*, and I look down saying, *I know hang on*, and she gets a chance to pause there on the wall, her face turned toward the west and the wind blowing even harder now, as if it meant to nail us to the rock and keep us suspended in our respective places although there's no need, we're not going anywhere, not for the moment anyway, and if we have to speak again, it's only to encourage each other, *Hold on*, and when I call down to her that we can wait until it dies down before we move again, I hear her tiny voice reply *I love you*, I laugh a little nervously, in spite of myself and in spite of the shriek of the wind, my sweatshirt flapping out around the middle of my waist and the hand on the carabiner feeling almost arthritic with fear yet slippery from sweat, it's all so surreal, something from some ridiculous action movie, and I half expect to hear bad music in the distance, the soundtrack of our lives thundering across the plain in mockery, I realize that the flapping sound like the sound of a helicopter is the fluttering of Danielle's windsuit below me, until at last it begins to abate, the clouds above us glowering down in that slow suspiration, and we begin to move again, slowly, tentatively, like soldiers in a minefield.

Clink and scrape. Clink and scrape and the tap-tap of the next anchor. We move in silence, afraid to breathe another word about the wind. Each piece of equipment, as it finds its seat in a crack or crevice, sounds tinny and thin. Clink and scrape. Clink and scrape.

The wind holds steady now, probably thirty miles an hour or so, which isn't all that bad, unless you happen to be high on a rock face like we are. We stay slow and steady in order to keep pace with it and with each other. Each time I glance down, I see Danielle making small progress, moving in fits and starts, with the timidity of a novice.

It will not be until much later that I understand how the stopper comes loose from the crevice she is using. All I hear is a barely audible scraping and a muffled thud that is drowned out, almost before it can happen, by Danielle's cry of *Jana.* I see her scrabbling for a handhold like someone with no rope whatever might do in a fall, and my heart bounds with terror as I watch the rope and its small hexcentric chock float outward and beyond her. It falls like a primitive weapon until the hex bounces off the wall below with a sickening clack, and I see her body flattened against the wall like Spiderwoman, one toe still searching in vain for a toehold.

She does not remember to call up *Belay,* the proper command on a wall in this type of crisis, but I know that's what she needs, the sound of my name floating up again in muffled supplication. *Hold on,* I cry as my shaking hands set up the figure-eight descender for a long rappel down past her where I can set up a belay, which is itself a major change in climbing strategy from our original climbing plan but must be employed in this kind of critical situation. Now she has begun to cry, she has had enough, first the wind and now this, she knows one or both of us may die. I know I have to make sure not to screw up on my rappel, it has to be nice and straight and not too fast, the wind factor still frightens me, yet somehow I am in the kind of mental overdrive, like being on autopilot, that a crisis demands, I even see the whole situation, the shape of the wall beneath us, with terrible clarity and calm, she waits, holds on, as I rappel down to her, and instead of bypassing her, I stop to let her hold me, tie rope around her waist to alleviate the terror of falling, and her whole body shakes like some kind of seizure, she refuses to open her eyes, and her frame trembles so badly in this paroxysm of terror that in order to make the situation as steady and safe as possible, I rappel down past her and hammer the hex-centric into another crevice so that even if she fell, she would be suspended in midair and not in any danger of hitting the ground, and now I set up a belay as I'd planned originally, and we work her down the wall slow and steady, and even though she slips and stumbles on toeholds and gets hurt several times from banging her shins and hands and one shoulder against the wall, we know she is not in danger of an actual freefall, and that seems to be enough.

Getting her to the doctor is a whole other matter. I take her into the van when, after what seems an eternity, our feet touch ground. And even though I too am shaky and exhausted, I dress her wounds as best I can with hydrogen peroxide and gauze from our emergency kit. One ankle is pretty badly banged up, pink flesh torn open so that it takes a Herculean effort to peel back the clinging bloody sock and she curses me and a few other people too as I perform the act of cleansing and binding up the area. But she's clearheaded enough to apologize right away and explain that she didn't really mean to curse *me*, after all.

I drive us back to town, wondering where we can go on a Saturday afternoon since we have to find a place that will accept the insurance plan provided by Don Pepé's restaurant. We opt for a little walk-in clinic that happens to be close to where we currently live. I have to admit to myself, silently of course, that I have my doubts about the need for further examination, but we have to make sure there are no broken bones, I suppose. Besides, some of her abrasions may need to be cleaned better to avoid infection, and I'm no Florence Nightingale.

A nurse practitioner enters the exam room with the doctor—they've graciously allowed me to sit with Danielle awaiting their arrival instead of forcing me to read old magazines in the musty waiting room—and since the situation is under control, the nurse leaves Danielle to the doctor, while I look on in silence.

"Where were you climbing?" the doctor asks.

"Red Rock," we answer in unison.

The doctor—middle-aged, dark hair, wire frame glasses—glances up, bemused. "Hm, there's an echo in here."

Danielle chuckles. "Yeah, we decided it was a nice enough day for it. At that point, it looked like it was going to be mostly sunny. Even the wind wasn't too noticeable at first."

I concur. "It's true. We would never have known."

He doesn't reply at first, and I realize he is clearing out the big gouge on her ankle, where obviously I have missed some dirt or sand. After a moment, he says idly, "I'm surprised you're not out doing something with your boyfriends on a day like this."

"Oh. Ah, well, you know." There's a brief, awkward pause as I force a laugh.

Danielle looks at me, then the doctor, then back at me.

"Hm?" He glances up, impassive, not getting it. Then a look passes between him and Danielle and somehow he knows, he does get it. He drops his eyes back to her ankle, visibly embarrassed. He sneaks a glance at me, as if to confirm what he has just realized, then back down to the ankle. "Ha. Well, anyway," he says with studied indifference and lets it trail off, a moment of unspoken revelation.

Danielle glances momentarily at me again, just like the doctor, then looks away, and now no one is looking at anyone else, but I can feel Danielle's embarrassment. I begin chattering away, hoping to relax all three of us, and in that moment I remember the day of the yard sale, Danielle and my father and me in the kitchen. "I tried to clean that spot on her ankle as best I could," I say, "but I don't have any training in this, so...."

Before long, we all relax into meaningless medical small talk about preventing infections and such, then the doctor manages to segue into practical advice for Danielle on her minor abrasions.

Bound and dressed, she takes her wounds back outside with a slight bow and a thank you.

"God, that was embarrassing," she says as soon as we're out in daylight.

"Why was it so embarrassing, anyway? I mean, I was embarrassed, too, but I don't get it. Why couldn't we have just told him we're dykes, for God's sake?"

"I don't know, I mean, uh, we didn't *have* to, he seemed to catch on all on his own, didn't he?"

"Well, yeah. I was mostly embarrassed for him. Like he was thinking, *Oh, shit, major faux pas.* Foot in mouth disease."

"Exactly. It wouldn't have been fun or funny to just announce it like you did with old Heckle and Jeckle at the truck stop. He probably would have been twice as embarrassed."

"No doubt. You know, it's too bad, because it's not a big deal. I mean, I'm sure he would have been like, *Hey, that's cool.* We have to stop worrying so much about other people's feelings in those situations."

"Like parents, for instance?"

"Well, that's not what I meant, but as a matter of fact, yeah. I mean, are we gonna live our lives, or not? You know?"

"I don't know, Jana. I don't think my parents are ready yet. It's not like we've been living together for years. Couldn't we just, y'know, see if they figure it out and give them a little more time to pick up on it? I don't mean lie...I just mean not tell them yet."

"Oh, I'm not suggesting we burst their bubble." We are standing outside the van, sunlight coming down through a break in the clouds. "I'm only saying that, if they ask questions, I think we should give them honest answers. Direct, honest answers."

She opens the door of the van and climbs in gingerly. "I guess you're better with direct answers than I am."

"Maybe that's why you like me so much." I flash her a wicked smile and see her relax.

"Oh, absolutely. You're a joy to be around." She laughs sharply.

I walk to the other side of the van, and call across the hood to her as I unlock my door. "Hey, at least people know where I'm coming from, right?"

"You've got a point," she says. "I wouldn't exactly say you're the in-your-face type, but I don't have any doubts as to whether you'd declare your sexual orientation to anyone who cared to know."

"Like Heckle and Jeckle?"

"Yeah, or like that doctor. I wouldn't have been the least bit surprised if you'd just looked at him and said, *Doc, we're a couple.*"

"Well, but I wouldn't have done it for shock value. It would have been strictly informational." I smile.

"I don't know about that. You're so outrageous sometimes."

"Me!? You're the one who started making out with me in downtown Dallas in front of two old ladies."

She cracks up.

"And remember that little scene at The Burning Brassiere?"

"Oh, no," she says. "That was all you. The day you found out you were the lead article in *The Alternative Voice?*"

It all comes rushing back, the shock, the outrage, pride, anger, embarrassment all rolled into one. "Wow, yeah, I was really beside myself, wasn't I?"

"Beside yourself? You were positively *manic.* Now, I wasn't exactly in the closet there myself, not completely. I remember very distinctly holding your hand across the table, right there in public."

"Hmm." I reach over to her hand, taking the cue. "There for me in my hour of need."

"That's right."

We ride a moment in silence. At length she says, "You realize you saved my life today?" Her tone has changed.

"Well...."

"Jana. There's no room for humility here. I really owe you my life." She says it quietly, looking down.

"What can I say to that? I mean, it's not like you wouldn't have done the same."

"But that situation never presented itself. The situation that presented itself was you saved my life."

I grin, a little uncomfortable with the direction the conversation has taken. "Well, what do you think I'm going to do next, ask you to swear allegiance of some sort?"

She bursts into laughter. "Yes, yes," she shouts, still laughing, "to pledge my undying gratitude and devote my life to you!" She leans back against me, her face smiling upside-down above my right shoulder.

"You're nuts. Thank you for not taking it too seriously."

"Thank you for saving my life, O powerful one —"

"Oh, cut it out."

"— to whom I owe eternal devotion and love —"

"Stop it."

"— and absolute obedience —"

"Heeeyy, now you're talking."

She squeals with laughter and delivers a series of little slaps to my arm. "You're a brute," she says. "Monstrous."

I laugh at her, and she kisses my hand loudly as the van rolls down the highway toward a big red sunset.

Chapter 45

NOT LONG AFTERWARD, we prepare to leave Oklahoma City.

Of all the relocations on our westward trail, including the northern and southern-tending parts, this is what I'd call the most "considered." What we do, really, is calculate every item's expense thoroughly until we know we have the funds, we know the van is in good enough shape to take us to Colorado, we know we won't have to face a three or four week stopover somewhere else to make another temporary livelihood before continuing on. As it stands, we've been in Oklahoma almost a month and a half, and have lived like nuns in order to accumulate sufficient cash and supplies. Now we prepare to leave Oklahoma behind.

Something has been building in me all along, and I feel it rise even higher as we pack up on our last night in this place. I thought I'd feel a sense of relief when I quit my job at the WATS Bank, and instead I just feel a cessation of activity, but this other thing still stands there. I don't know what it is, but something keeps me from sharing it with Danielle, and I'm strangely bright-eyed and alert, hypervigilant, on this last night.

It's as if I'd gotten another jolt of adrenalin like the one I got on that rock wall, and everything seems magnified, overly clear, like I'm in some emotional overdrive. Part of me is tempted to consider it another aspect of my inevitable drive to find contentment on the road, but another part fears that something is terribly wrong, like my intuition is actually behind the unsettled feeling, a red flag of some kind. And so I remain silent, hoping to solve the puzzle on my own.

Danielle lowers the last of a small bookcase's worth of books into a cardboard box—we have, sadly, had to sell a portion of our little paperback collections in order to lighten the van's load. She turns to me with a vague melancholy in her eyes.

"You look kind of…reflective," I say.

She sighs. "Did I ever tell you about the time my mother threw out the old seventy-eights?"

"I don't think so."

She pulls another box next to the book box and perches on it, one hand on her leg. "This is a sad story."

I smile, then turn appropriately serious. "Go ahead," I say

She clears her face of all expression, like an actress preparing to deliver a monologue.

"When I was seven, my mom and dad had a lot of old seventy-eight RPM records that they gave me. A fair amount of it was just goofy stuff—Spike Jones records, songs from old shows like *Guys and Dolls*. Some of it, though, was great. Jazz from the thirties, pieces from classic operas…all sorts of things. Anyway, I kept all this paraphernalia in the attic with this little record player. I had to keep it all up there because they didn't want me cluttering up my room. There was some other pretty neat stuff up there, too, like this old lamp my grandparents had owned, and a real sewing machine from probably the twenties or thirties. It was my home away from home, a little sanctuary.

"Well, they didn't know I went up there on sort of a semi-regular basis, because I only went up to play records when nobody was home. And it was brutally hot and humid in summer, which I could take for an hour at most, and uncomfortably cold in the winter—so uncomfortable I usually didn't go up there in the winter at all. So this stuff accumulated some dust, and when my parents decided to clean out the attic one year —"

"Oh, no…."

"Oh, yes: the records were gone, the record player was gone. Even the lamp. I knew nothing about it, because I wasn't always in on these little family decisions, and of course, my mother had forgotten all about giving me that stuff. She and dad thought it was just a bunch of junk. They hadn't even thought 'yard sale.'"

"That's horrible."

"Yeah, so I felt like I'd been robbed. I climbed up there and this whole little world that I'd created was gone."

"What'd you do? Just cry?"

"Not at first. My first reaction was complete denial. I truly couldn't believe it. I looked all through the rest of the boxes for my stuff. I never found it." She pauses. "Looking at these books made me think of that, 'cause it was a little sad parting with some of those. I think we kept all the best ones, though."

She smiles, a touch of bravery in her expression, as if I am seeing some shadow of the brave smile on the face of the seven-year-old who's just discovered all her seventy-eights gone. Her eyes flick down and away.

I nod. "Yeah. We kept all the best ones."

We pack and pack. Something unnameable still builds in me, and I try to think about something, anything, else. There's some kind of finality to all this packing, more than just leaving another stop behind. I'm tempted to think it's that we've been in Oklahoma longer than elsewhere, but then my mind keeps returning to that intuitive thought that something is gravely amiss. Certainly I have a grim, undeniable dissatisfaction with the way things have gone— our hopes of finding real jobs with real pay being dashed again and again; the grind of relative poverty taking some of the romance out of the trip; the big scare on the rock-climbing expedition. Yet my mind can't help straying back to that ambiguous red flag, like a toothache your tongue keeps worrying in spite of the inevitable pain.

But the next morning it's another day, and I shake it off. Big sunbeams pour down into the van and a cool morning breeze makes me feel we are at the start of a brand new adventure, a whole new era dawning. It's not just a new day, but a new beginning, another chance at life, success, dream-fulfillment.

Picking up 35 North to head into Wichita is a funny feeling. We were on 35 North when we first headed into Oklahoma City, but we have yet to go this far north on the highway. Watching our city disappear from the big side mirror, I realize it truly was just a stopover—in spite of Don Pepé, in spite of the scare at Red Rock Canyon, in spite of restlessness and unnamed fears, just another chapter in our lives, like Tallahassee, or Akron, Ohio.

Chapter 46

THE JUNE NIGHT is cool, and we sit by the side of a creek in eastern Colorado. We've been through Kansas, traveling north on 35 to Wichita, where the highway veers drastically east unless you switch over to the 235 loop by the airport, a loop that forms a ring around the city before continuing north as 135, up to Salina. From there, we go west on 70, mile after mile after mile, until after perhaps 250 miles, the Colorado border comes into view.

And now we've made it, not quite to Pike's Peak, but at least into Colorado. The drive from Salina to the border having been a good four hours, we are content to rest here in this park for a while, eating sandwiches and drinking iced tea like vagabond picnickers.

Danielle kicks a pebble into the brook. "Where's the Coleman stove?" she asks.

"I think it's packed in the box with the lanterns and all that." Our camping equipment box. "You want to have a little cookout?"

"I don't know." She seems far away. "I was just thinking maybe we should camp out here. Is this a state park?"

"I'm not sure."

"What's the map say?" She has been driving, and obviously has no desire to consult the atlas. We have fallen into our old roles, she being the driver only as long as I am navigator. I know how she is when she gets like this. As long as she drives, she will not want to do anything else, and one can hardly blame her. When I drive I, too, prefer to do nothing else. Still, she seems unusually cranky, as if the drive from Salina has been tedious. No doubt it has.

"Well, the map says *State Park* here." I show her with my finger. "So presumably this is part of it. We could camp out here, but we'd probably be doing it illegally."

"Let's wander down the trail over yonder." She points. "If we can find a nice clearing, we'll leave it behind without a scrap of anything changed. No one will ever know we were here."

This is true. Camping with Danielle is like camping with the head forest ranger: she'll leave no sign of having been on a campsite. I've seen her fluff up areas of trampled grass as if they were pillows, treat wildflowers like personal houseplants, and cover up a sandy campfire site with enough displaced dirt and leaves that it looks better than before our arrival.

We park the van in a place well hidden from the road, and unload: tent, cooler, Coleman stove, lanterns. The area looks promising enough that, even if we don't find a clearing in the woods, we can still count on a meadow, or a spot close to the creek. Danielle is characteristically silent, the reverent hush that overtakes her out in the forest, and the silence makes her seem even more remote. Suddenly, out here in this peaceful landscape, we are worlds apart.

"I'm going to scout around for some firewood."

She nods, then cocks her head. "Why do you need firewood? We have the Coleman."

"Well, for later. Even if we don't use it for cooking, it's gonna be chilly tonight. We don't want to be scavenging the forest floor in the dark, right?"

She looks at me, nods laconically. For an instant it seems she is just going to nod and turn away without actually replying, and this irritates me. But then she says, "You're right," and smiles.

I have a sensation almost of relief. I think about our not-so-distant adventure on the rock wall. Losing her seems more unthinkable now than ever.

We set up camp and prepare a site for the fire. Although it's nighttime by our watches, it will still be light for at least another hour or two, not dark enough for a fire. So we go for a short hike. On our way up the trail we fall into a silence so deep it makes our breathing sound more audible than it probably is, and as the rhythms of our footfall become even, like the steps of one person instead of two, I feel almost alone. Were it not for the constant sight of her bright yellow sweatshirt in front of me, I'd probably forget she was there.

I notice her breathing is exactly as loud and regular as mine, she inhales and exhales just as long as me, and for a moment, I wonder absurdly if she's doing it on purpose. But when I fall out of sync, she doesn't notice. I feel as if I ought to break the silence, but the things in my head are not things I would ordinarily say. They are small-talk comments on the weather, on flora and fauna, and they ring hollow in my mind. I stay silent.

Down and down the trail we go, into a wooded bottomland so deep and piney it seems inevitable it will turn swampy before long. But just as we get to the point where I am expecting to see skunk cabbage like I might in Connecticut, the trail winds uphill into an area nearly blackened with trees. The sky overhead is almost shut out, the silence on us now so profound and complete I no longer even hear her breathing or the sound of our footfall. There is nothing but the sound of my own breathing locked inside my head, my ears blocked up like I'm descending from a great height.

Eventually, we reach what we decide will have to be the half-way point, and agree to take a breather. Sitting beneath a tall pine branchless up to its uppermost reaches, we talk about the external things of the evening: the beautiful weather, sixty-five degrees according to the radio, this wild, stately landscape cradling us in its silence; all the topics I would have scorned just a moment before. And yet there's a strange comfort in these things, as if we were not so much reduced to small talk as elevated to it—again, like some long-married couple we've lapsed from the courtly need to be charming and interesting all the time, or the young person's burning compulsion to discuss "deep" subjects, into a kind of mutual contract to just go with the flow. We have learned to relax. We have mellowed, and I think again of our long silences in the van.

"This place reminds me a little of one of the campgrounds in the Norfolk area," she says. "Did I ever take you there with me?"

"What was it called?"

"I forget. It's right up near the Massachusetts border, northeast Connecticut. There's a waterfall…."

"Don't think so. Doesn't ring a bell."

There is a silence. We smile. Then we stop smiling. I hear myself say, "What are we going to do in Colorado?"

"Well," she says, reaching for the backpack, "let's see." She rifles through some of her things. But already I have seen by a gesture of hers, some slight movement of the shoulder, that she knows what my question really meant.

She begins to read. "*At 14,110 feet, Pike's Peak is one of the tallest and most well-known mountains in the country. Discovered by Zebulon Pike in —*"

"Zebulon? *Zebulon?*"

She laughs. "Yup. That's what it says. Let's see, where was I? Blah blah blah. Okay, listen to this: *Dominating the landscape, it was a common reference point for Indians and Conquistadors. The Pike's Peak Highway, which winds its way to the top, is a nineteen-mile road providing many picturesque and panoramic views, whether from your car or on foot.* On foot, Jesus, who would be up there on foot?"

"I guess they mean if you step out of your car for a moment."

"Ah. Well, all right, in that case."

"Or you're a mountain climber."

"Yeah, right." She laughs. "Don't remind me."

"Okay, other than Pike's Peak, what are we going to do?"

Her eyes meet mine, then slide away. "There's lots to do, it just depends on what strikes our fancy." She flips through the guide, and I tell myself *Just let it go*. When she starts to read again, I work hard to pay attention.

Something is building, though, and I don't know what it is. There's this wound I'm aware of only in the most hazy and nebulous way, the way you are aware of a car about to pass you when it hangs in your blind spot at sixty miles an hour, the sound through your window like some strange aural illusion.

I don't know what name to give this wound, but I think of it as a sunspot, because I suspect it will ultimately shed light on something for me. On some agonized, feral level, I am sure it has to do with my mother or father, maybe both, and the thought that the examination of a wound in me might provide the need to slam my parents in one way or another makes me backpedal so fast that, before long, I am thinking of my childhood in the most saccharine terms possible: the Monkees, the Partridge Family, every mop-topped bunch of smiling morons imaginable is suddenly lifted from that early seventies era and transported to the forefront of my consciousness. You'd think I'd never been yelled at in my life. You'd think I'd lived on the set of H.R. Pufnstuf.

All this, of course, I discuss with Danielle only in the most roundabout terms. Our more superficial conversations may touch on it, but only in form, not content (*Did you ever see that episode of Nancy Drew where Nancy…?*), and supposedly none of it ever has the slightest bearing on our present situation. But part of me—not the part that is aware of the wound so much as what I would call the Internal Devil's Advocate—wants to draw a straight line between the wound itself and this strange blind spot between Danielle and me, between the sunspot and the realm of shadows. Some temptress in me wants to demonstrate with unimpeachable logic that there's a connection there as incontrovertible as ABC and 1-2-3 (and, as if to create some kind of wacky nostalgic diversion, my mind responds to the suggestion with a phrase from The Jackson Five, drowning the dark implication with handclaps and a pop melody that once appeared on a record that actually came with your breakfast cereal).

But it may just be that that old issue of my parents being comparatively decent to me—compared to Danielle's, that is—fails to divide us irrevocably, fails to drive a wedge between us that could destroy the connection we have. In fact, it may just be that my self-defeating little ego cannot stand to see me happy. It may just be that the sound of her small, muffled voice on that rock wall calling up *I love you* was stronger than any blind spot that might hover between us. And so I suspect that whatever is happening here is more about *me* than about *us*, that whatever this thing is, it will only be able to declare itself as my own in the end.

We head back down the trail. Before long, our fire burns low and orange, the Coleman stove provides rustic dinners for us, and our lanterns are aswarm with moths like porchlights on the Fourth of July. Silence falls on this little cradle in the hills. We're far enough from the highway that the sound of traffic fails to reach us. We sit by the fire side by side like honeymooners, and the moon hangs low in the sky, and we are happy.

And yet that night, long after she has fallen asleep, I lie like a stone in my sleeping bag, stark raving wide awake.

Chapter 47

PIKE'S PEAK. LATE June, an incredible day. We take the nine-teen-mile road to its logical conclusion, the highest spot on the mountain.

The afternoon sun hangs in the sky, although neither of us could say exactly what time it is—our watches are packed away. But none of that matters here. Only the mountain matters.

A great breeze is blowing west as we face the eastern vista, and my hair is flying behind me like a banner as I look down and across the unfathomable distances, the view from 14,000 feet, the sheer immensity of it all. The summer moon is still visible, and I stand on the summit of the mountain with Danielle, windswept, sunlit, blood singing in my ears, the earth pulsing gently beneath—time-less, deeper than bone, deeper than marrow, deeper than all songs, mother earth, father sun, sister moon, all bound inexplicably up with this wild wind, stars, trees, vistas of sunsets, canyons and chasms, rivers, the sea....

I sit down on the rock, this part of the mountaintop itself being nearly all rock. Little pools of water from the last rain lie in the hollows, and I can see a fine silt in the bottom, which makes the water go cloudy when I put a stick into one and idly stir it around. Birds chirrup in the distance. The sun grows warmer, hot on my neck despite cooling breezes, and I glance up to where it towers in the sky almost midway between its eastern and western arc, no clouds to diminish its power.

Only to the north can we see clouds, huge flat grey-bottomed clouds with white caps that go all down the sky, as far as the horizon. Many of them are banked together, so that their effect is picturesque, evoking not so much cotton or mashed potatoes or indeed anything other than what they are: clouds, cirrus clouds or nimbus clouds, maybe, but undoubtedly the kind of clouds that only shimmer in a cerulean sky on a perfect summer afternoon. They go endlessly into the distance, like reflections of reflections, and I think of when a child holds a mirror up to another mirror and sees an inexhaustible infinity of mirrors, a geometric hat trick suggesting endless possibilities.

In the past two days we've gone from our state park campground to an official campsite just north of Larkspur called Devil's Head, visited a place called Cripple Creek—*just like that song by The Band*, Danielle says—and then gone up to Pike's Peak. They have a thing called the Cog Railway that also goes to the summit, but we suspected it would be filled almost exclusively with tourists and decided to pass. Even if few locals come up here, I imagined they would take the nineteen-mile road, and sure enough, we did see a Colorado plate on an oncoming car as we headed up the mountain road.

It's so beautiful here. Part of me feels like I'm on another planet, and part of me feels at home here, as if I was destined to see this. Never in my life have I been on a pinnacle so high that I could literally see for hundreds of miles, and the realization of my own relative size really awes me. More than the Mississippi. I feel humbled in such a wonderful way, if that makes sense. And we really can see as far as they said we could. Maybe even to New Mexico, that slender band of lavender a hundred miles to the south.

Heading down the mountain is sad. My ears keep popping and popping, like they did in the dark pine-filled cradle we camped in our first night here, and we chew gum to alleviate the sensation. I'm almost defiantly unwilling to descend, the air up there like distilled water, but I know it's just a stopover. You can't live on the edge of the Grand Canyon, either, however much you like it there.

Probably the saddest thing about going back is knowing that the main part of this leg of the trip is over now for Danielle; everything from here is literally "downhill." Of course she's chattering a mile a minute about it, but I know we'll only return maybe once before we leave for California.

I look out the window at the scenery going by and I feel a sense of finality. I don't quite know why. We're still so unsettled: we haven't found a new place to stay, haven't really decided on jobs. Haven't really decided where to touch down. Do we go into Colorado Springs? Do we head to Denver? Aspen? So many questions without answers, and my need to resolve these things, map everything out, clamors for resolution.

I know we need work. I know we need money. The reserves are dwindling fast, and the role I find myself taking on—the accountant, the financial planner, the "banker" of the family—forces me to take a long cold look at what there is, and what there could or should be. We need money, and that means work, and the uncertainty of what we'll find here has me rattled.

Of course, Oklahoma was no picnic. The WATS Room job was so-so at best, and Danielle's hours at the restaurant were predictably horrible, but we had just gotten into enough of a routine that it felt comfortable. Life on the road has lost its romance for me and become just another series of challenges. The trick must be to find rhythm in the chaos, a way of remaining interested without becoming too burned out by the constant changes.

For now, we head into Colorado Springs. This whole area is such a neat place to explore that we cannot resist it, but we have to resist the temptation to spend money. I find it especially difficult when we reach a place called the Garden of the Gods Trading Post.

I have a weakness for collectibles, and this place is chockablock with the kind of treasures I've always been gaga for—handpainted Native American pottery, sandpaintings and lithographs, figurines, jewelry, traditional rugs, anything and everything you could want for decorating an apartment in eclectic, multicultural tones. I've already acquired, in my travels, Kenyan wood sculptures, vases from Nairobi, an Eskimo wall hanging, a dreamcatcher. Now that I see so much beautiful work from virtually every southwestern tribe, Pueblo, Comanche, Ute, all in one place, my mind goes into information overload. I actually become anxiety-ridden, knowing I'd like so many of these things and can't have them. But Danielle talks me into buying a pair of turquoise-inlaid earrings, and I feel I have a tangible memory of the day when I walk away from the place.

Once we leave the Garden of the Gods Trading Post, of course, we have to go to its namesake, two blocks over, and now we become embarrassed. We truly are doing the touristy thing. The Garden of the Gods is spectacular, though, so no regrets. Here, the red sandstone rock formations are even more resplendent than anything we saw in Oklahoma, some appearing to defy gravity and others, the more typically eroded configurations, simply monolithic. They seem alive, almost, as if they hold some primal secret in their ancient silence, some healing power, and bear our scrutiny with the detachment of an ocean, not because they have to bear it. I think of Stonehenge, and I imagine it must be the same.

Chapter 48

I SUPPOSE THERE'S always been a fair amount of navel-gazing among lesbians, just as there is within any marginalized group, but personally I've never been cursed with the habit of morbid introspection. So it comes as quite a surprise when I find myself thinking about me in relation to Danielle, me in relation to my parents, and me in relation to Kiddie Korner Child Care Center, all within the same basic time frame. I haven't been this self-absorbed since I sat in the offices of John Wagner, Psy.D.

Something happened up there on old Pike's Peak, like all the uncertainty and discomfort came to a head, and a little bubble of peace and fortitude suddenly floated out of me and into the sky. Of course, I felt better only for a short time, then the inevitable disappointment as we made our slow descent down the nineteen-mile road. But something happened, and I feel like a fog has lifted from my consciousness. I have become more concerned about my relations with others—not just Danielle or my parents, but former employers, acquaintances, like Tillie Jones, Harmony Stone, Wendy Simpson, even the seemingly insignificant Sybil Gerard. Just as I wanted to leave them all on the beaches of Florida, I find my mind now seeking them out, the way a divining rod seeks water or mineral deposits, more instinct than intent. The desire to resolve, understand, or even make restitution if necessary, makes me stop and think.

I don't take the time to explain this to Danielle until we decide to look for work in Colorado Springs and set up house there. One thing bothering me is the lack of finality in so many of the peripheral relationships I left behind, the Harmony Stones and Standing Free Ibsens and Tillie Joneses. There's no sense of closure, and I said goodbye to so few. Only my close friends, like Roxanne, were definitely aware of the trip I'm on now.

Obviously, there was no big sensation in the press when my hearing fell through, so no one had a reason to be particularly well-informed as to my whereabouts. I talk to my parents periodically, but I never get a report that so-and-so was asking for me. In fact, I can't help asking myself whether or not this is actually homesickness, and I'll admit, it gives me pause.

I was never what you'd call a poster child for Connecticut Tourism—I always thought the place pretty much sucks, as a matter of fact, unless you happen to be extremely wealthy—so it surprises me I might even consider missing the place, let alone thinking the word *homesick*. But I decide eventually that I'm not homesick. I miss some of the people, but not the place, and in fact what's really bothering me is something else, this mysterious other thing building in me: a dawning realization that maybe all this is a pipe dream, and what I'm looking for has been inside me all along, not on the banks of the Mississippi or the mountains of Colorado.

This strikes me one night while on the phone with my parents, who, as usual, are telling me that they have no news, nothing out of the ordinary. When Danielle comes in and waves to me from across the room—one of those weird, dreamy moments when you see things with extreme clarity—it seems to kick in, like someone just flipped a switch. I see the train of events, our trek to Ohio, down to Florida, up to Georgia, Mississippi, Texas, Oklahoma, then the projected trip through Colorado and out to California, and suddenly it all seems pointless behavior. Well, not pointless, exactly, but not the solution it promised to be.

I get distracted for a moment from the conversation with my parents, a few *oohs* and *ahs* at something they're saying about a new car, then end the phonecall prematurely. I know I have to talk to Danielle about this.

"So what's up with Mom and Dad?" she says as I enter the bedroom. She's gone back to a pile of laundry after walking in and waving.

"Not much." I feel dazed. I've reached a point where I need to do something, but don't actually know what I'm doing. I sit down on the bed.

"Same old, same old." She grins, and I almost lose the meaning of what she's saying.

"Right. Listen, Dan, can I talk to you for a minute?"

The grin widens. "Who else is there to talk to here?" She studies my face and turns serious. "What's wrong? Did something happen at home?"

"No, no." But the word *home* sounds strange, especially given what I'm about to say.

"Tell me." She puts down the laundry and comes around to my side of the bed.

"Do you remember when we had our conversation about what we were going to do in Colorado? After we'd really gotten here and seen Pike's Peak and all that?"

"Yeah, you asked me about what we'd do *after* Pike's Peak, and I started talking about a bunch of tourist attractions. We never got into anything about work."

"I think I know why I was asking you all of that." She is sitting next to me now, and I avoid her eyes.

"Why?"

"I think I need to go back to Connecticut."

There is a pause, and then again she asks, "Why?" The tone of voice is different, as in, why would you want to do a thing like that?

Another long silence. "I don't know. Something tells me I have to get back there. I don't mean forever, necessarily, but at least for a while."

"Something tells you."

"Yes."

"Well, what is it? What do you need to do there that you haven't already done?" Her tone is strained.

"I'm not sure. It's a feeling I have —"

"Oh, God, your famous intu*ition*." She pushes herself to her feet with one hand. "Jesus, can't we at least have some direction together? Something we agree on? This whole thing wasn't my idea —"

"I know, I know, look, calm down," I say. "I'm not saying we can't ever go to California, I'm just—I just need to get home. It's like—you know how elephants know when it's time to die, how they go wherever it is they go, then they die when they get there?"

She gives me a dry look. "You trying to tell me you're gonna go home to die?"

Suddenly we burst into laughter together. "No, and I'm not an elephant, either."

"Well, nice analogy anyway." She pauses. "Goddamn."

"I know. I don't really even want to go back. It's just—I don't know, it's something I need to do. I don't know why, I really don't."

She looks at me, nodding, then stops. There is a long silence, as if we're both searching for resolution in each other's eyes, seeking answers and only finding the same questions. Then she looks down and quietly says, "How soon?"

"I don't know. Maybe a couple days." She makes a muffled sound, and I hurry on. "We can't stay too long on the money we have, or we'd never make it back. We'd have to start working, and work for weeks."

"Do we have enough to get back without any problems?"

I do a rapid calculation. "If we do it pretty quickly."

She sighs. "Are you leveling with me on this? There's nothing going on with your parents?"

"No. They haven't said a word."

"Nothing's happening there?"

"Nothing."

"What did they say about you coming back?"

"I haven't even mentioned it to them."

"But you just talked to them. When did you decide on all this?"

"I don't think I completely realized it until right now, when you came in and waved at me from across the room."

She looks dismayed. "Well, shit, how about if I retrace my footsteps?" She stands and backs away, doing everything backwards, waving again. I can't help laughing, although for some reason I am on the brink of tears.

"Couldn't we take a couple days to think this through?" she continues. "I mean, you know how it is with all these empty-nesters. They miss the kids at first, sure, but after a couple months… hell, I'm not sure my parents would even *want* me living with them again. Not this soon, anyway."

"We can stay together. Look for a place. I don't want to move back with Mom and Dad either."

"But Jana, think about the job market there. We'd be lucky if we could get into Burger Heaven, at this point."

"Let's take the couple days to think it through. Take your suggestion."

"What's today? Tuesday." She checks her watch absentmindedly. "How about Friday?"

"How about we plan to leave Friday, but we use some time tomorrow and Thursday to look at the logistics?"

"That's thinking it through?"

"Well, I mean we'll include that. We'll spend time thinking about it, or talking about it, or whatever. And if we haven't changed our minds while we're packing up these boxes, then we'll split Friday."

Danielle looks away from me, her eyes resting first on one box, then another, and another. Two-thirds of what we own is still packed. One hand sits on her hip, the other is suspended in midair: a gesture of futility, the cliché of throwing in the towel, of "you win." But I don't want to *win*.

I approach her and touch the outstretched hand. "Listen, it doesn't have to be forever. Just for a little while. Until I see whatever it is I need to see."

She looks at me, looks into my eyes so deep it is like a touch, like two souls touching. I feel myself almost cringe inside, the moment is so intimate. Then the look recedes and hardens into determination. Simple and unadorned. A look I know well.

"I'm gonna trust you on this one, but the next time I have an off-the-wall sounding idea, you're gonna have to cut *me* some slack."

It's not a request, and in my tenuous position I can hardly presume to disagree. "Of course," I says in a whisper.

She's silent again, and she still looks troubled.

"What's wrong?"

She looks back around at all the boxes. "I don't know if I can face the idea of packing up all those boxes again."

I can't help but laugh. "Well, most of them are still packed."

She shakes her head.

"Besides, it's not like we've established ourselves here. We're…."

"Drifters?"

"Uh—basically, yeah, I guess."

We both crack up, and I move forward into her arms. The tension in the room dissolves finally, as if it were a real, palpable thing, only waiting for us to touch before it had the opportunity to disappear.

"What am I gonna do with you?" she says into my ear.

I don't have an answer, but I feel somehow that some part of whatever's been building in me has just lifted.

Chapter 49

I GUESS TO say I know next to nothing about Missouri before I go there would be an understatement. I haven't even heard of the Ozarks before, although the name sounds familiar—something about a country band—and I don't know any of the names of the St. Louis teams—something to do with birds—but I want to see some of it on the way back east. So, after going across Kansas and into Kansas City, we head down south a little, toward Springfield, to check out this "Ozark National Scenic Riverways" area. I'm a sucker for anything scenic, my appetite primed by Pike's Peak, the mighty Mississippi, and funky rock formations. Now I have a constant craving for novelty and for the picturesque, and Danielle is willing to oblige if we can camp out. So we aim the big white van toward something called the Mark Twain National Forest, which I personally find an irresistible name, and off we go.

There's nothing terribly bizarre or ominous in this region, from what I see: no Devil's Den rock sculptures or astonishing hot springs. No Grand Canyons. But there's something comfortable and enticing about the hills and high limestone cliffs, something that beckons us to enter deeper and deeper into the heart of the wilderness until we get to a point where, were it not for the route we are on, we would imagine ourselves hundreds of miles from civilization.

I'm not anxious to go exploring after we set up camp. Certainly there are a couple of hours of daylight remaining, but I am preoccupied, and not for any reason I can bring up for discussion. My uncertainty about arriving in Connecticut looking for work, *again*, and for a place to live, *again*, continues to haunt the days, leaving me unsatisfied and edgy—almost frightened. By now, my parents know I'll be returning, and they are more pleased than I expected. In fact, they sounded delighted.

But Danielle's parents apparently gave her a lukewarm reception. This causes me some anguish on her behalf, not just because of them, but because *I* am dragging her back there, where she will be, if not unwelcome, merely tolerated. Or so it seems.

She comes back to the campsite with a bundle of firewood after having volunteered to look for kindling while I arrange a circle of stones for the fire. She looks at me and smiles without saying anything. These are the times I like best, like those quiet moments in the van when our silences say more than words, like our campout in the eastern part of Colorado. I lift a stone and watch the insects beneath it scatter among the clods of displaced soil.

"What are you thinking about?" she asks.

I have to search for an answer. "Connecticut. All this." I motion toward our environs.

"This is a nice spot, isn't it?" More a statement than a question.

"Mm-hm."

"You've never been to Missouri before, have you?"

"No," I say.

"And here we are in Missouri."

I smile.

"Except, you know, they pronounce it *Missoura*."

"They do?"

She pretends to think about it. "Yup. I've heard it. *Missoura*."

"*Missoura*."

"Yeah, you've gotta say it real loose and casual, the way you'd say —"

"*Missippi.*"

She cracks up. "Exactly!"

I start to laugh myself, remembering how we both heard that pronunciation when we were in Mississippi.

"Missoura," we say in unison. And laugh again.

"Why is that so funny to us, do you suppose?"

She looks at me under that shock of blonde hair. "It's because it's so laidback and casual. And we're a couple of hyper northeasterners."

"Yankees," I say, and again we laugh. There was a discussion about this when we were in Florida. The Yankees, Danielle likes to say, are a baseball team.

We are silent, then she chuckles again. "Yankees." She shakes her head.

"What precipitated that conversation, anyway?"

"I don't know," she says. "It seems like it was months ago. I don't even remember where we were."

"Well, it *was* months ago. We were in Florida, I remember that much. Probably in April."

"Yeah, so two months or so."

"Right. I think we'd been talking to some guy from a southern state. One of the few people we met who actually moved to Florida from a southern state."

"As opposed to a New England or Midwest state! That's right. God, we should go back *there* instead of Connecticut."

"I know." I smile guiltily. "We can, eventually. There's no law saying we have to stay in Connecticut. But I've got to get back there for at least a little while."

"It's gonna be interesting," she says. "Do you think we'll spend much time looking up old acquaintances?"

"Like who? Wendy Simpson?"

She bursts into laughter. "Yeah, right. Barbara Helms."

"Please. I'd rather eat lead paint."

"Seriously, though, who else is there to spend time with, other than each other? And our parents?"

"Well, Roxanne, I guess. If she's around."

"Yeah, that makes sense." She ponders it. "Maybe some of the old gang at the Burning Brassiere."

"The good ol' Burning Bra, yeah. Remember that night you got up there and —"

"Sang *The Pop Song?*" She starts to laugh again. "Oh, God. That was wild." She sings: "*So they sat like statuettes/And studied both their silhouettes/And felt like they were marionettes —*"

"*And probably they were right,*" I chime in.

"My knees were shaking."

"You sounded so good. You could do the nightclubs in Hartford."

We begin to slow dance around the campsite, as if we were on a ballroom floor. "Imagine it," she says, taking the lead in our little tango. "Imagine me doing open mike night at some of those places. I mean, as an act. I'd have to learn the guitar."

"And I could be your roadie!"

"Oh, no," she says, putting her cheek against mine. "No, that would never do. You're my biggest fan. I can't have you working for me." She lowers her voice to a whisper: "I'll just make sure you get a backstage pass."

"A backstage pass…at the Burning Brassiere?"

She laughs. "Hm, I see what you mean. Okay, then, a table up front. With flowers on it."

"That's more like it."

Round and round the campfire we dance, and the sky overhead grows darker and colder. A little breeze kicks up from the east, ruffling our hair.

"Maybe we'd better find those jackets of ours," she whispers.

"Okay," I whisper. "Hey—why are we whispering?"

We have separated for an instant, but now she steps back and puts her arms around my shoulders, her nose almost touching mine.

"Because," she whispers, "it's *more magical* that way." And flounces off, like some crazy laughing nymph in a waking dream.

Chapter 50

THE CURRENT RIVER flows from the southeast corner of Missouri all the way down into Arkansas, fed by great underground springs that interlace the entire region. Many of these originate from the bases of high limestone cliffs, and consequently, a trip downriver will most likely yield a view of caverns only accessible by water. One of these caverns is at Round Spring and, according to our guidebook, features picturesque stalactites and stalagmites. The spring closest to Van Buren, where we are, is simply called Big Spring, several miles' hike from our campsite.

We hike along the riverside on a trail blazed in the eighteenth century by Native Americans who came west in a fruitless search for a place white men would not venture. Our guide, a tanned, grey-haired woman named Sonya, tells us all about it. This is full summer in Missouri, the verdant banks of the Current River dotted with lavender clusters of primrose, blazing star, sweet William. We see abundant evidence of nearby springs, large and small, some streaming out from high walls and others, our guide points out, bubbling up from the riverbed itself. The sky above is blue and arid white, a midsummer drought sky, and we hear cicadas all day long among the dense thickets and on the high, sparsely covered banks of the river.

The view of Big Spring itself is the axis on which our whole scenic tour turns. Truly monumental in sheer size and power, the spring typifies all that is majestic in this region's natural beauty: giant trees, abundant flora and fauna, and the spring itself, churning out from its great bluff with the force of two rivers into the Current River, almost forbidding, except that it seems friendly, benevolent. We watch it a long time, not at all anxious to move on. Eventually, we trot down along the trail to catch up with the guide, who has wandered ahead of us.

The Big Spring hike feels like a milestone for me. I can't help thinking of it that way. All along this journey I can mark milestones, all of them in nature. I run down the list in my mind: beaches of southwest Florida, Mississippi River, bluebonnet fields of Texas, stone sculptures of Oklahoma, Pike's Peak in Colorado, and now the great springs of southern Missouri. All have given me, somehow, the sense of a larger scheme of things and a still-undefined impression of how I fit in that scheme. At the same time, each grandiloquent wonder—especially Pike's Peak—makes me acutely aware of my own size, my relative insignificance, and I'm not sure I like that much. Nonetheless, I wouldn't have traded a moment of it.

That night, we sleep the sleep of the dead. After a whole day's hiking, we both feel drained, exhausted in body and spirit, yet somehow coasting on a warm high, the byproduct of a long stretch of serious physical exertion. Undoubtedly, we will both be sore in the morning, but for now it's a relief to sit in this luxuriant breeze and ride the endorphin-flow.

The main part of the trip is certainly over now, in spite of the fact that we still have several big states to drive through. I can't escape the surreal sense that we're just returning home after a vacation, though it's hardly been that. We've been gone for months, have played out countless bizarre scenarios and half-baked fantasies, lived whole separate sections of our lives, our employment histories, our relationship. Yet I feel like we'll be returning to a musty-smelling house with a few stale perishables in the kitchen and a week's worth of newspapers on the front step.

The feeling grows stronger the next morning as we leave. Something about this area of Missouri is so welcoming and calming that to leave it behind is almost like departing from some warm, womblike place. As we drive down the road, a bittersweet yearning unlike anything I've experienced before rises in me, somehow anxious and peaceful and elegiac all at the same time.

We have a hard time getting ourselves excited about cruising down any of the long stretches between Missouri and Ohio after having experienced the scenic Ozarks, so we decide to go shopping in Indianapolis. We can crash in Indiana until late, spend the night, or a majority of it, anyway, heading through Ohio, Pennsylvania, and so on. I love driving on the highway at night, love that green dashboard glow, the awesome silences from big sleeping cities as we pass them, and spotlights from airports searching out banks of clouds in the sky. Most of all, I love having Danielle beside me as we fly down the highway, sprawled across her seat, her face childlike in sleep, wisps of her hair lifting occasionally and flowing in the breeze from the open window, only to drop again when we pass another car or truck.

It's a long trek across Ohio and a hell of a long trek across Pennsylvania—though not as long as it actually seems. I think of the people I may see back in Connecticut, particularly after my conversation with Danielle back at the campsite. I can't help wondering whether I'll find that any of them seem different after this very full six-month period. Will they find me different? Have I changed much? I look the same, though my hair is just a little longer, and I have a tan, but beyond that, how much difference could all those experiences really make? I can only imagine.

Cruising down the great highway, I think of Harmony Stone and her brother Stan, Steve Torres, Roxanne. People from the Burning Brassiere. John Wagner. Their faces float back with remarkable clarity—it's that kind of night—when everything looks clear and clean and all the cobwebs seem to have been swept out of my mind. It has all been so hectic, moving again, traveling, meeting new people.

Only now do I feel relaxed, calm and levelheaded, here on this darkened highway with Danielle dozing by my side and the radio turned way down, moonlight gleaming on the big white van, high clouds scudding across the sky. Only now do I feel some relief in those familiar faces flickering through my mind like images on a curtain, faces from what seems like so long ago, that may or may not come to mean anything to me in the days to come. I wonder if my journey will seem like a failure to some of them, and I wonder how I'll come to view it in the coming months myself.

Will I look back and say it was just a pipe dream, or view it all as a valuable life experience that gave me perspective? Will it really become a steppingstone to better things? Will I just use the information I gathered, the knowledge I gained, for some future decision about where I want to live? For surely, after all that, I do not want to go back to my hometown and actually *stay* there indefinitely.

I glance out the window at the leaves on passing trees, knowing that soon they'll be turning and falling, and the beaches of Florida beckon to me from across the miles, an old lover calling me home. But we are Connecticut-bound, that is where we have to go, I know. I can't say what unfinished business awaits me, but the intuition that I have to return is stronger than ever, and fills me with secret dread.

I stop in Allentown to refuel, and Danielle stirs in her sleep, muttering softly. Neon signs in the gas station parking lot mingle with the station's fluorescent glare in a harsh grey light that shines down into the van. Danielle does not close her eyes completely in sleep sometimes. Her eyes look eerily vacant, as if she were blind. I touch her hair—her face is so innocent and pale in that cold white light—and a chill runs down my back.

I decide I need to get something to drink, and I lock her in while I'm gone, shutting the door softly. I cannot help glancing back uneasily at the van as I walk across the parking lot and into the store to pay for my soda and gas. She's my precious one, God knows. I don't know how I ever lived without her, or how I could now. It is just that unthinkable.

When I return she's awake, sitting straight up in the seat, as if the silence shocked her into awareness. She smiles when I open the van door, her eyes questioning. "Where are we?" she asks after I hop in.

"Allentown, Pennsylvania." I take a sip of my soda.

She points to it. "None for me?"

"You were asleep." I hand it to her. "I didn't know what kind you wanted."

"So I guess I should thank you for not waking me." She gives me her mischievous grin.

"You want me to go back in and buy you one?"

"No, that's okay." She takes a swig and hands it back, then stretches herself across my side of the seat, curling her arms across my knees and resting her head in my lap. "Let's find a motel somewhere with a nice big bed and room service. And cable."

I laugh. "What do you think this is, some kind of yuppie tour of America? We're drifters, remember?"

"Right, I forgot." She shakes with laughter. "Drifters. That cracks me up."

"Well, you're just easily amused."

"Yes, that's true. I suppose I am." She pauses. "Actually, I guess I'd say we really *are* drifters, too, if it weren't for the fact that we have a destination. We certainly have wandered around a lot. Kentucky, Tennessee, Georgia, Florida."

"Mississippi, Texas…."

"Oklahoma."

"Kansas. Missouri. Pennsylvania." I find myself imitating her hypnotic monotone.

"Right, where we are now. What are we forgetting? Ohio?"

"Louisiana. Alabama."

"Oh, yeah," she says.

"Colorado."

Her tone brightens. "Of course. The best one of all." She shifts in my lap, her cheek against my leg.

"I still prefer Florida." I press my head back against the seat and close my eyes, forgetting that we are at a gas station. After a long silence, punctuated only by the sound of traffic on the freeway, she pulls herself up to eye level with me, propping herself up on one elbow and kissing me, kissing my neck, earlobe, cheek, forehead and mouth. Something about it is especially sweet, and it draws me in like the tide. I wrap myself around her as if we were kissing for the first time and I wanted to make an impression.

Before long, she is drawing her fingertips down the long line of my spine, and our lips part as she returns to my neck, ear, collarbone and shoulder. I hear a sigh escape my lips, but it's as if it comes from somewhere else, from someone else, somewhere outside myself. She goes down further, planting soft guileless kisses on my bosom, down to the solar plexus and then the hips, returning to kiss each breast, then down again to the thighs.

I run my fingers through her hair, my head back and eyes closed and, as she drags her cheek across my upper thigh, the sensation so sweet and irresistible, I can't help playing along. I rise to meet her as she presses down with her fingers like some schoolgirl trying to make it with her girlfriend in a backseat parking lot, and only when I have completely forgotten about everything on earth except the touch of her hands and the feel of her hair do I lean my head to one side and crack my eyes open just enough to let the light in. In that moment, I see the face of the man and hear the knock of his knuckles against the door.

At first, I do not scream but merely open my eyes and mouth like someone about to be executed. I hold Danielle's head and hands in place as if my life depended on it, and then, right when the man mouths the phrase, "Excuse me, miss, are you through using this pump?" I scream bloody hell and hold Danielle in place even more firmly, if such a thing is possible. The guy jumps back from the van with a look that's a cross between someone who's just been burned by the hot flame of a blowtorch and the sheepish expression of someone who has just scared a complete stranger into paralysis.

"I'm sorry, miss," he's saying as I roll down the window, "I just wanted to —"

"You scared the shit out of me!" I shout, half-hysterical and knowing I am not in the right, but not wanting to let him off the hook, either.

"I'm sorry," he says, "really sorry. I just wanted to use that pump, and I didn't know if you were asleep or sick, or if…if you were all right." Visibly appalled, he grovels as if he knows he has done something unforgivable.

"No," I say mechanically. "I'm not sick, and I'm not asleep, thank you very much. I'll move my vehicle right now."

"Thank you, miss. I'm really —"

I hold up a hand for silence. "No problem," I say curtly. "Have a good night." I begin rolling up the window.

"You too," he says, but I lose the end of it as the window closes and I put the van in gear. In my lap, Danielle is shaking with laughter.

"Oh, stop it, you." I give her a little slap on the shoulder.

"My God, I think you gave me whiplash," she says. "Ouch. Oh, that was too funny." And she laughs and laughs. "Did he see me? Did he know?"

"No, I don't think so." I swing the big white van onto the

highway. "I doubt it. Although who knows what he thought, because I probably looked like I was in mid-orgasm."

She snorts, and I smack her again on the shoulder, which probably hurts my fingertips more than anything else. "You can get up now. We're well out of sight."

"No, I think I'll stay here and continue where I left off," she says. "Maybe you can cause a few accidents with that facial expression you were just describing." She bursts into uncontrollable laughter.

"You little wench. C'mon, get up."

"Oh, okay, I'll get up. But I'm not gonna like it!" She smacks her lips loudly against my cheek, the kind of kiss meant for unpleasant old uncles or grandmothers who smell of liniment.

I can't help smiling. "You're a nut."

"You bet."

"That really wasn't funny, you know. That poor guy almost gave me a cardiac arrest."

"It was funny," she says. "Trust me. It'll be funny in a week. You'll look back on it and laugh."

"I doubt it."

"Okay, maybe a month. I swear to God, when you grabbed me and clamped down on the top of my head like that and screamed, I thought a cop had just poked his face in the window. I thought we were going to be taken to the freaking Allentown police department for lewd and lascivious behavior in public. What a scream. I wish I knew what was going on in that poor guy's mind right now."

"He's probably just leaving the gas station, and damn glad to get out of there."

She laughs again, harder than before. "You were so funny: *you scared the shit out of me!*"

"Ha. Ha."

"I'm sorry. I'm sure I *would* have had a cardiac arrest if it'd been me. In fact, the more I think about it, you handled it pretty damn well, considering the circumstances."

"Well, thanks, but I don't feel like I handled it at all. Look, I'm *still* shaking." I hold out a trembling hand.

"Wow, you are. Ma poor petit bebé," she says, a parody of a French accent, and leans over, pouting. But instead of another smack on the cheek, she only leans her head against my shoulder momentarily, a kind of nuzzle, then shrugs and sighs. "Ah, life is full of travails," she says in the same accent.

For some reason, this actually gets me to crack up.

She sits back, looking relieved, proud of her work. "So, where are we going next?"

"Well, we're just outside of Allentown, so from here it's about an hour and a half to Newark."

She makes a face. "Newark. Isn't that the place that smells?"

"I'm not sure. Every time I've ever been through New Jersey, I've had to go through this section that smelled like a cross between rotten eggs and a broken septic tank. I'm not sure if that's actually Newark, or just someplace near it."

"Doesn't sound appealing."

"I've gotta admit, I haven't exactly been looking forward to it. I mean, if you think about it, we've been through some fairly poor places on this trip, but a lot of those were more rural."

"Oh yeah."

"So, you know, it's gonna be kind of like culture shock for us going past these real inner city areas. Even parts of Connecticut on I-95 are pretty bleak, from what I recall."

"Well, we didn't take 95 originally. We took 84 west toward Danbury."

"I remember. I haven't been on 95 for a couple years, that's what I'm saying. I think some parts are pretty grim."

"Oh."

At that, we hunker down like birds in a storm and push ourselves through it as far as possible. We only make a few sounds of disapproval when we smell New Jersey's sewage treatment centers, or whatever the hell they are, and look at each other as if to say, "Dear God, it's worse than we thought it would be." We continue into Connecticut via 95 which, sure enough, leaves me with the impression that we're entering a barren wasteland with bombed-out factories whose few remaining windows are dark with grime, especially near Bridgeport, which has probably one of the worst poverty levels in the nation. We see it in the cold light of dawn, as we approach our old hometown. The half-dead cities with their warm, cracked sidewalks that are already beginning to steam, even though the August sun hasn't yet risen. A lone car or truck idles in an occasional sidestreet, earlier than the rest of the people on the day shift, and huge black crows perch on telephone wires like ravens in some medieval tapestry. When we've passed the old cities and are rapidly approaching familiar territory, I feel relieved, hot, cranky, and overtired, but also grateful to be where I will be soon.

I pull the van into my parents' driveway at quarter to six in the morning and shut off the engine. Here we are. This is home, such as it is.

My parents are still in bed. Ever since he took early retirement, my father stopped getting up at six, and he is more likely to sleep in all morning, even though it's a Tuesday. My mother will not have to be in the office before eight, so probably she will not be up until six-thirty or seven. Danielle waits in the van while I go in to check out the scene. My old key looks strange in my hand, grown foreign from long disuse. I feel like a visitor with "key privileges" as I turn the doorknob.

Inside, the house is silent as a monastery, and bears minor signs of change: new lamps, a picture or two replaced by new ones I don't much like, some furniture rearranged. The old grandfather clock is still stuck on eleven forty-five. There's a smell to the place I have never noticed until now, even when I went away to college, the smell of a lived-in house, an oddly romantic odor that may belong mostly to my parents' possessions, or maybe just to the air they have breathed in and out in this cool house with its musty old air conditioner and steamed-up windows. In any case, it calls up a whole range of memories, images and associations, and for a moment I stand rooted to the spot, lost in reverie.

I sneak back out, closing and locking the door behind me and feeling slightly guilty somehow, as if I had broken in.

Danielle leans out the passenger window, nonplussed. "What's up?"

I whisper, needlessly. "Still asleep."

"Ah." She nods, but I can see that she is just as tired as me and does not actually understand.

"I don't want to be sitting there in the kitchen when one of them comes out," I explain. "They're liable to have a massive coronary."

"They know we're gonna be here, though, right?"

"Yes and no. I didn't give them a specific time or day."

"Ah." She nods again mechanically. "Can we catch a nap somewhere? Or do you want to go for coffee? I'm gonna need to do one or the other."

"Let's get coffee and then come back in like half an hour."
She yawns. "Cool."

I can tell she doesn't care, her tone that inevitable non-voice she and I both develop whenever we go for a full day or two without sleep. I feel the same—I'd just as soon hole up in a cheapo motel at this point, I'm so hideously exhausted—and the part of me that is permanently connected to her shimmers with empathy. Also, I love the fact that she is so easygoing. I know she would say *cool* just as readily to a catnap, and my exhaustion and raw nerves make me disproportionately grateful. If I wasn't so tired, I'd probably find it funny.

We drive to Petersens' Café for breakfast, and we are surprised to see so few cars in the lot.

"Place is dead, huh?"

I nod. "Yeah. Must not be much of a 'breakfast town' anymore."

She chuckles under her breath. "Like we've been gone *so long.*"

"Well, you know."

We walk in at three minutes after six. The first customers of the day.

"Hi, what can I get you this morning? Coffees to start?" Her name is Rosie, fortyish with black hair, and I remember her, but she clearly does not remember me. She looks at us like we're nuts to be already out at this hour, especially on a summer day. Like we should be sleeping off a drunk or something.

"Coffee would be great."

Danielle nods agreement. Rosie leaves us menus and goes to fetch the coffee, and when we look across the table, we start to laugh. We *are* kind of nuts to be up at this hour, but only because we've been awake almost a full day already, and the end is nowhere in sight—unless we can't help crashing before dinnertime.

We order pancakes and waffles and muffins and juice, and I decide I really don't give a rat's ass whether I gain a couple pounds or a bit of acne from this. I'm just going to enjoy it.

We eat like horses—both surprised, I think, at how famished we actually are—then settle back with another pot of coffee, decaf this time, since the caffeinated stuff has given us both a bad case of jitters. By the time I check my watch, it's after seven, and I realize that now we're likely to miss Mom if we don't get back soon. I feel slightly remorseful at how little this would bother me—it would be nice to spend some time alone with good ol' Dad, especially on first returning—but I make the effort to get us back in a timely fashion nonetheless.

Danielle yawns and yawns on the way back, and it's contagious. Part of me wants to just crawl into bed and sleep off the big all-nighter, caffeine or no caffeine. I could sleep for years. But I know as soon as my head hit the pillow, I'd realize I'm too tired for sleep.

When we arrive, my mom is eating breakfast and Dad is still in bed, as I expected.

"Thank God you made it!" she says, hugging us both in an uncharacteristic display of emotion.

We cringe back a bit, sheepishly, returning her affection as warmly as possible while trying not to act too embarrassed. I have never known my mother to be a morning person, and this sudden infusion of energy really rocks her. When the excitement subsides, and she has asked the expected share of superfluous questions—"Did you have a safe trip? What am I saying, of course you had a safe trip, you're here!"—she sits back with her coffee, looking haggard, and fetches a sigh.

"Well, anyway," she says, "you're both all right, right?"

"We're *fine*, ma." I begin to feel cranky again.

She sips her coffee. "Your father's not up to par." Her eyes slide away from mine.

"What's wrong? Cold, flu?"

"I don't know. He sleeps all the time. Not *all* the time, but always late. Sometimes I call from work at ten o'clock and he's still in bed."

I can't help smiling. "You sound jealous, Mom. I don't know, ever since he took early retirement…."

"Tell me about it." She rolls her eyes. "Jealous, schmealous, I just wish he'd get up and *do* something. It's no good, this early retirement. It's like he's been lethargic for a month now. Maybe more. I didn't say anything on the phone, because I know how you worry."

"I don't worry."

"You do too. You're like two peas in a pod." She turns to Danielle, "Isn't she just like him? You tell me."

"Don't put her in the middle," I say, smiling.

"She's been around us long enough. She knows the score."

I shake my head at her. Danielle just laughs, not answering.

"Well, anyway," says Mom, "like I said, this early retirement's no good. All he wants to do is sit around listening to old records. Or golf. What kind of activity is that, golf?"

"Well, at least he's getting *some* exercise."

She grunts, then sips her coffee. "Sure. Walking from the car to the golf cart." She continues to downgrade the whole early retirement concept, and while she talks, my mind drifts off. I think about my dad sitting and listening to records, and the picture in my mind makes me think of Danielle in her parents' attic listening to old seventy-eights, before they threw them away. I glance from my mom to her, and notice that her eyes are shining unnaturally bright, though she looks tired.

When I sense an opening, I say, "Not to change the subject, Mom, but did you by any chance happen to rent out my old room?"

She pulls a face. "Of course not."

"Because I think we may be in need of a little nap. I don't know about Danielle, but it was a long night."

"Make yourselves comfortable." She gestures to Danielle. "You two can both go right ahead if you want, don't mind me. I'm just going to clean up my dishes here and be on my way." She rises.

Danielle nods. "Okay."

"You may want to lock yourselves in, or my husband the late sleeper is likely to disturb you in about three hours." She clanks her cup and saucer in the sink, as if the mere thought of it irritates her.

"Okay, Mom." I stand and hug her again, perfunctory. I realize that she is actually suggesting, though not in so many words, that Danielle and I go ahead and sleep together just as we normally would. This feels like a real breakthrough—the acceptance, resignation, whatever it is—and I have a surge of gratitude, just as I had a bit of sentimentality about Danielle being so easygoing a short while ago. I know I am overtired and emotional, but I feel what I feel, and my eyes get clouded.

"It's good to be back," I say. But, swallowing the little lump in my throat, I turn casual again. "And don't worry, we won't be moving back home."

We all laugh, and Mom says, "I gotta go." With a peck on the cheek, she shoos us upstairs.

Danielle and I lie in my creaky bed with its cool musty sheets and the old mattress with the lumpy center, and I feel a sense of vertigo, as if I were drugged. I am so tired that, each time I close my eyes and let my head and neck relax, I feel as if I am falling through an endless, timeless place, as in dreams when we fly over fields and rivers. I heave a long sigh, wrapping my arms around Danielle's midsection, and try to ride it out.

Chapter 51

WHEN I WAKE, the room is cool and quiet, and Danielle's breathing is soft beside me. Something feels resolved. And in spite of the fact that I could not say what that something might be, and in spite of the fact that I don't intend to stay and didn't even want to be here in the first place, I am glad to be back.

Until I try to move. Then—and I take a while before I even try it—I find myself stiff and sore from the long ride and the long awkward sleep, as if I'd been riding a horse for three days. Everything aches: neck, shoulders, back, arms, legs. I can even feel a headache coming on as my pulse pounds into my skull like the dull booming sound that signals the beginning of a hangover. I decide to postpone moving for as long as possible and search for a position as comfortable as the one I was in a moment before. But to no avail.

Every movement, each slight adjustment I make to accommodate an ache or pain, yields new discomfort elsewhere. It's like being trapped in an old and worn-out body, and for one bleak moment, I wonder if this is what elderly people have to deal with every morning. I try to think about something else.

Danielle's breathing is slow and regular, and part of me resents her blissful slumber. I realize right away that this is the kind of pure black comedy that makes for amusing stories, and I'm just conscious enough to know that, like the "peeper" at the gas station, this will all seem funny someday. But I also know it will not be anytime soon.

I wonder if she will feel anywhere near as lousy as I do upon awakening. For her sake, I sincerely hope not, but I have my doubts. And now the comedy continues as I realize that even the most delicate and painstaking attempt to slide out of bed is apt to rouse her, and that eventually, I'll have to risk it—not only because I am in pain, but also because I have to go to the bathroom.

Squeezing myself out of bed is undoubtedly the most ridiculous-looking and uncomfortable thing I will have to do all day, and it's quite a complex procedure, but somehow I manage it without waking her or wetting the bed. I crawl to the door and stand, my knees stiff and creaky, then lurch down the hall to the little half bath next to the old computer room, inordinately proud of escaping without waking her.

When I walk into the kitchen downstairs, I am surprised to see Dad not only home, but calmly making breakfast for us.

"Hi, honey. Welcome back."

"Hi, Dad." We exchange a hug and kiss. "How long have you known we were back?"

His smile is complacent. "I looked in on you about two hours ago. Snug as two bugs in a rug." Behind the counter he looks like a man at home in the kitchen, the sense of peace in the room almost surreal.

"How did you know to look for us?" I ask.

"Well, the big white van was a clue."

I see it behind him through the window. "Oh yeah." I smile at this sleepy lack of clarity. "I'm not too wide awake, I guess."

"Guess not." He smiles again. "Nice van, by the way."

"Oh." I sniff a little. "Yeah, we got rid of the Malibu. This made a lot more sense than the trailer after a while."

"Well, you made it here safe and sound. That's all that matters." He comes around my side of the counter to give me another quick peck on the cheek and a ruffling of my hair, then begins hurriedly scooping food onto plates. "Why don't you run up and get Danielle for some chow?"

I hesitate. "I don't know if I should wake her just yet."

"Ah, I'm sure she'll be fine."

I arch an eyebrow. "I don't know, Dad, you've never seen her when she gets up."

"You want *me* to get her?"

"You?" I'm appalled by the prospect.

Before I can say anything else, he barks, "Danielle! Breakfast!" Loud and clear, with no hesitation. This is not the man my mother described earlier, lethargic and purposeless.

I can't help laughing and shaking my head at him, but he just keeps that complacent smile on his face…like he's going to start whistling *I-know-something-you-don't-know*. There's a lull in the conversation while we both wait for a response from upstairs. To be honest, I expect nothing, but he's obviously waiting. The smile fades, but his eyebrows remain raised, and I don't doubt he is still amused by his little stunt. He busies himself behind the counter, wiping it off, putting things away, a whirlwind of meaningless activity. And sure enough, much to my surprise Danielle's voice floats down the stairs.

"Jana?"

"I'm down here."

"I thought I heard my name."

"You did," my dad calls up loudly, still in that teasing tone of voice he always adopts when he's in this mode. "Welcome back to Connecticut," he goes on. "Breakfast's on the table."

"Hi, Mr. Odessi," she says.

I see as she tiptoes down the stairs, one hand clutching her bathrobe, that she is still too affected by Rosie Petersen's fabulous greasy pancakes and muffins to even contemplate eating. Her eyes meet mine in a desperate plea to be excused somehow, but I can only shrug helplessly.

"I don't know, Dad. She doesn't look too hungry."

"Ah, come on now," he says. "*Mangia, mangia*! Put some meat on your bones." He pulls up a chair with his own place setting, sausage, eggs and toast, along with juice and coffee—what my mom calls The Cholesterol Special. He slathers butter on the toast like it's some kind of religious ceremony, and Danielle pales at the sight.

"Could I just have a little cereal, maybe?" she asks meekly. "I'm really not all that hungry."

"Oh, you're not afraid of my cooking, are you? Honey," he turns to me, "tell her what a good chef I am."

"Fabulous," I say with dripping sarcasm, though it actually is true.

"Jana!" He looks at me in dismay. "Really, now, c'mon, tell the truth." He takes a bite, making noises of contentment.

Danielle laughs in spite of herself. "Honest, Mr. Odessi, I believe you," she tells him. "I'm just not that hungry."

"Neither one of us are, Dad. We ate earlier at Petersens' Café."

He looks at each of us, trying to read our eyes. "Well, okay," he says, smirking again. "What about you, honey? You'll have some?"

"Maybe just a little," I say to appease him.

"Jeez, have you two both gone on diets since you've been gone?" He puts down his knife and fork for a moment, looking dismayed again. "I mean, I'm not the only one around here who eats nice big meals, am I?"

There is a silence, and Danielle and I both seem to shrug within it.

Dad laughs dryly. "Ho boy, we're not going to be one of those *dour* households, now, are we? That sort of thing may be de rigeur on the island of Dobu, but the isle of Odessi has sparkling wit and sangfroid as basic prerequisites." He slurps his juice noisily, enjoying himself. "You know," he says expansively, sitting back with his fork poised in midair, "in *my* day we used to eat three square meals every day of the week. These kids today…some of them used to come into my Intro to Anthro class at eight-thirty in the morning with a can of Pepsi. That was their breakfast. A fucking Pepsi!" He takes another big forkful. "Unbelievable."

Danielle and I sit and smile at him and at each other. I am thinking I can't remember him ever swearing like that, while Danielle just looks like she hopes he gets so carried away he'll forget about the cereal.

"I know *some* of them don't eat at all," he says. "Not breakfast, anyway. Most important meal of the day. But with some of 'em, it's just a weight thing." His eyes look far away, as if he's talking more to himself, or to a group or class, than to Danielle and me. He does that sometimes. "It's not really a weight thing, though, if the person doesn't have a weight problem. It's more a diet issue than an actual weight issue. But the ones who drink a Pepsi for breakfast, what the hell good is that?" He shudders and takes another mouthful of food. "Might as well eat a candy bar, for Christ's sake, at least it's solid food. Well, solid, anyway."

He shakes his head, ornery, still abstracted, and in a flash, I see what my mother meant. It's not that he's gone senile, or become the sluggish armchair retiree. It's just that he has changed, become more himself, his personality set more in bedrock than before. Everything, the expansiveness, the abstracted manner, the twenty-five-thousand-dollar words, even the forceful curse, are so *Dad*.

It shows me how much of my own personality still remains unformed, malleable, and I wonder what my mother sees in all this. Is it possible her character is still not fully formed even at her age, and that that's what bothers her? Does she see him fossilizing? It's a disturbing thought. I never thought of people in their forties or fifties going through a transitional stage, but I realize now that every age can be transitional. He is going through one, she is, we all are. Danielle, too. I look from one to the other, and I suddenly feel tired.

It feels so weird to be here. In Connecticut. Part of me knows that this is home, this old house with its condensation on window sills and its silent grandfather clock. But part of me also knows I truly have become more than this, that I am home in name only.

Dad and Danielle talk about the trip, how far we went, and I think about how far we've come. The thoughts of Harmony Stone, Standing Free Ibsen, John Wagner, all those faces dance across the landscape of my mind like friendly ghosts, and a sudden chill overtakes me as I wonder what's still to come.

As if on cue, my father turns his glance to me and asks, "Your mother say anything to you about your case?" He only refers to the Kiddie Korner Child Care Center situation as *the case.*

"No, why?" The question catches me off guard.

"With the center," he says for clarity.

"Kiddie Korner. No, she didn't mention them. Why, did they call or something? What's up?"

"Oh, nothing, nothing. Just wondered if she'd mentioned it." He looks down sheepishly. He is a bad liar, and I see he's hiding something, though obviously not bad news.

"What?" I get up and go over to him. "What do you mean?" I rock back and forth on his leg with one hand like I did when I was a little girl. "Wha-a-a-at? C'mon, tell me. They offer me my job back? Full restitution and awesome benes? Company car?"

"No, no." He laughs. "Are you kidding?"

"Well, what, then?"

He looks back and forth between her and me, the way I have just done with the two of them. "I wasn't supposed to bring this up."

"But…?"

He hesitates. "If you want to, you have the opportunity to go to Superior Court."

"What do you mean?"

"Remember your mother telling you about an attorney in Hartford named John Hailey?"

"No...."

"John Hailey used to go to school with your mother's boss's daughter. Anyway—now, remember, I'm not supposed to be telling you any of this—"

"Okay, okay."

"— It's supposed to be a surprise. Anyway, this John Hailey expressed an interest in the case, and he seemed to feel it was worth pursuing, so we spent some time talking to him. The upshot of the whole thing is, if you want to go after these guys, Hailey is the guy to do it, and, ah, we'll take care of the legal fees for you. Your mother and me." He smiles briefly, almost formally.

For a long while, I do not respond at all. I sit in silence and look from him to Danielle and back. The emotional wave hits me with such a confused jumble of fear, surprise, gratitude, and happiness, that I just stare. "I don't know what to say," I tell him finally.

"Think about it," he answers, getting up to clear his place. "And have some chow while you're thinking. For God's sake."

We laugh at his serious tone and he arches an eyebrow. "Listen," he goes on, "I'm going to go play nine holes while it's still sunny out. Based on the weather forecast, it may be the only opportunity I have all week."

"But Dad," I fumble, dismayed by the change of subject. "I don't know what to think about all this. I mean court, this lawyer...." I stand up.

"Just think about it," he says from behind the counter. "You don't have to make a decision right away. But do me a favor: *please* act surprised when your mother tells you, or I'll never hear the end of it."

All three of us smile, knowing it is true.

"Anyway, I'm off to the club. I'll clean this mess up when I come back. If you don't want to eat any of it, go ahead and put it in the fridge and I can nuke it tomorrow morning."

"Okay, Dad. Thanks."

"You bet." He comes back around our side of the counter. "Welcome back, kids." He gives each of us a peck on the cheek. "See ya later."

"Bye," we say in unison.

He grabs the golf bag and clubs, closes the door, and we sit in the silent kitchen, alone with our thoughts and the smell of eggs and sausage.

"I hope you don't mind, but I'm gonna go back to bed," Danielle says. "I know it'll screw up my sleep cycle, but I'm just too wiped to do anything."

I am still thinking about the case, but her words snap me out of it. "I think I'll go back to bed myself," I say. "I don't know if I'll sleep, but I'll join you anyway. Do you mind if I set the alarm for later this afternoon?"

"Not at all."

We climb back up the stairs after putting away the breakfast things, and within ten minutes she falls silent. But I'm too preoccupied now, just as I predicted, and I can't shut off my mind for even a minute. It races down hallways of possibility, corridors of maybe and what if. Kiddie Korner Child Care Center again. I cannot fathom that I may pick up that thread of my life again so readily. Already it seems like another lifetime.

Within minutes, Danielle's breathing grows slow and regular again, and we're back where we were a short time ago. I cannot help sighing. But I also know that I can get away with sneaking back out of bed again and not being terribly concerned about waking her, since she has already had a good long nap.

She does not stir when I move, and I cross the room to where an old tape player sits among books and magazines and find a Duke Ellington tape I neglected to take on the trip. I put on the first song, the volume appropriately low: *Prelude to A Kiss*. It sounds like the last slow dance at the end of an evening in a smoky jazz club. I climb back into bed slowly and cautiously, close my eyes, and the world spins.

Kiddie Korner. I can hardly think about it without my breathing getting shallower and my neck and shoulders growing tense. I cannot help but think of Barbara Helms, Wendy Simpson, the lawyers, all of them, the whole series of scenes playing back in my mind like flashbacks in some bad made-for-TV movie. *Do you recognize this document, Ms. Odessi?* Aauugh!

And maybe because I've been off gallivanting with Danielle all this time, I think about Dad. How often I've taken him for granted, and how great he is. Of course, I've always thought of him as this eccentric little guy, mildly disappointed at never having a son and not particularly hip or flashy; not the kind of dad you show off to your friends. But he is so solid and steady; he's always there. He had to deal with a lot of shit over the years, and Mom did too: the asthma episodes, my tomboyish phase when I worked on cars and spent free periods in wood shop, listening to my horrible saxophone playing when I first started.

And the way he just offers to pay for a lawyer like he's buying me a pair of nylons, for God's sake. I feel humbled, tired and humbled. And because I am so tired, tears well in my eyes, just thinking about how fortunate I am, before I fall asleep.

I awake much much later, surprised not only by the fact that I have slept at all, but also the length of time, the sun low in the sky now, the hottest part of the day past. I am surprised, too, to discover Danielle gone, and when I turn over and feel the cool blank sheet beside me, I am disappointed by it even before I wonder where she is.

I creep downstairs to find her sitting on the couch with her knees up under her chin, gazing languidly out into the sunlit yard. I curl up on the couch next to her, and we are silent. There is nothing to say. She knows as well as I do that I'll be going to court soon.

Chapter 52

MY DECISION TO go to court does not ease my transition back into life in good old Connecticut. In fact, I can't imagine anything more stressful than preparing for the big case, and at certain moments, I wonder if I've lost my mind completely, just like when Danielle and I prepared for our pseudo-cross-country jaunt. But I have faith it will all work out for the best, that everything happens for a reason.

Still, it is hard. John Hailey and I don't hit it off, for one. He is the kind of prematurely-older-looking attorney who strikes me as driven to accomplishments and prestige by some deep-seated insecurity or need for approval, hidden behind a strained reserve that borders on condescension. *Butter wouldn't melt in his mouth*, my grandmother would have said. He seems hesitant and mildly impatient with some of my initial questions, running a hand over his sleek black hair like a boy at a party trying to look casual, nodding smartly before replying.

Perhaps the rednecks in Oklahoma and Mississippi have given me less tolerance for the patrician prima donna types, or perhaps I'm just overly sensitive. But I feel confident that homophobia is not an issue here, so I'm not aware of what else could be bothering me like this nagging feeling I have about Hailey. For the moment, I resign myself to believing he and I probably rub each other the wrong way just because he's a sleek, rich, complacent attorney and I'm a struggling middle-class radical lesbian chick with an ax to grind and some rough edges after six months of travel.

"What about the pink slip?" he asks me in the course of our interminable first meeting.

"What *about* the pink slip?" I ask, puzzled.

"Do you still have your original copy?"

"*I* don't know." I say it testily. "I mean, I don't exactly have any desire to see the goddamn thing again." I laugh dryly.

He sighs, looking bitterly impatient but also swelled with pride for maintaining such marvelous reserve. "Do you know whether you have any copy at all?" he says neutrally. He leans back in the chair with an affable forced smile, perhaps wondering how someone could possibly *not know* whether an item is presently in their possession.

"No, I really don't know whether I still have my copy, to be perfectly honest with you. I haven't been here for the past six months, and all that stuff is in storage."

He sits up again, all business. "Okay, I'm going to need you to look for that." His eyes avoid mine. "Also, anything you have in your own records from the center. Anything at all, absolutely anything: promotional literature, timesheets, pay stubs…anything and everything. Okay?"

I glare with undisguised malice at his dictatorial tone, yet when he finishes speaking, I find myself reflecting back the same forced pleasant look he has just given me. I realize I have to be nice to him; he's on my side and, for better or worse, I have to be nice to him. *For better or worse. My God, it's like a marriage.* At moments like this, I am grateful to be a lesbian. I don't dislike men, but if I did, I wouldn't want this guy to be the representative of the gender coming to the table to win me over.

The chess game of cooperation and competition goes on throughout our conference, like we're gaming for power and the stakes are merely our own recognition, or the failure thereof, of certain customs and social mores vis-à-vis the attorney/client relationship. By the time we're finished, I'm baffled by it all. Am I just being paranoid? Hypersensitive? Am I reading him correctly, or is it possible that the excessive reserve and clipped, formal tone are just byproducts of too much time alone with books and briefs? Maybe there's even some gender or class thing I'm wrestling with? Whatever the case, for practical purposes, my solution is inevitably this: unless he comes up with some really screwball idea, he's the lawyer, so he's the boss. I'll have to live with the lack of chemistry and listen to his suggestions.

I feel sure of one other thing. I'm on the right path here, regardless of the "lack of compelling evidentiary documentation." Sure, it's my word against theirs, but I have one great thing going for me. I'm right. No matter what happens, I won't have to tell anyone anything other than the truth. And won't people know, just by looking at and listening to me, that I'm telling the truth?

I think back to my experience at the original hearing, the whole business with the press and a story forgotten in a day or two at most, the third column on page thirteen of some local newspaper. I presume the actual court case will generate little or no publicity, although I may be kidding myself. I wonder how I'd handle a slew of local TV and newspaper reporters. Possibly not all that well. I've been in such seclusion with Danielle these past months that things like controversy, publicity, and the spotlight do not sound like they belong in my life. They aren't part of the plan. My life is supposed to be quiet, sane, unexamined, or unexamined by strangers, at any rate. And the thought of a bunch of strangers sifting through the minutiae of my life is like the thought of someone picking through my trash. It makes me wince.

I'm sitting talking to my old friend Roxanne about all this stuff one day when I get a call on the other line..

"Hello?"

"Jana." My mom.

"Hi! Are you at work?"

"Jana, it's your father."

My heart freezes in my chest. "What?"

"He was on the golf course —"

"Is he all right? Mom, tell me he's all right." Her tone is like a death knell in my ear.

"He's had an attack. They don't know if it was a heart attack or a stroke."

"My God, Mom, where is he?"

"On his way to St. Agnes. They got an ambulance."

"Where can I meet you? Where are you?"

"I'm still at work," she says numbly. "They called me here."

"I can meet you at the hospital in twenty minutes."

"Okay."

"It's gonna be all right, Mom."

"I'll meet you out in front. Twenty minutes."

"All right, Mom. I love you."

"Okay. Goodbye."

I click off of that line and run to the door. I can hear Roxanne on the other line saying, "Jana? Jana?"

Call me later, I think, then run back in spite of myself and tell her I have to go: no explanation. Tears come after I hang up the second time, and I hear myself saying *shit* over and over again under my breath. But it's like someone else saying it, like an out-of-body experience. *I am in shock*, I think. I'm in shock, Mom is in shock, we're all in shock.

Outside, the world is blinding bright and difficult to withstand, an achingly beautiful day, the kind of day that hurts when you're suddenly faced with death. Not death, I tell myself, but disaster, anyway. Not death or disaster, I say as I start up the van. An attack. An attack, whatever that means. Stroke, maybe, but not necessarily. Christ, it could be gas, I tell myself, but I have to admit that gas probably doesn't send people to the hospital unconscious in an ambulance.

Then I realize I don't know whether he was unconscious. I don't think my mother even told me. Not her fault, either, I didn't ask, but what if he is unconscious?

No, I say. No, it's okay. It's going to be all right. I tell myself it's going to be all right, over and over. It becomes a mantra as I tap my left foot anxiously on the floor at traffic light after traffic light, trying to concentrate on the road, focusing on the drive itself so I don't have an accident—that's the last thing we need right now—and the red lights are so long, the drivers seem so slow, it's midafternoon, not even close to rush hour, and where are all these people coming from? They are going so damned slow I can't stand it, and even in the midst of the noise in my head and the honking of cars and the sound of the radio, I feel sure he is dead, will die, and the feeling is so big and scary that I can hardly see the traffic signals through the blur.

When I pull up to the emergency room entrance, I realize I won't be able to park here before I find my mother. I drive frantically toward the visitors lot, grab the first spot I find, then race to the emergency room, where I discover that my mother has yet to arrive. Now I have to wait, and in the state I'm in, waiting is not my forte. There's a nurse here to deal with me, and she's clearly unsympathetic to my anguish, which seems amplified in proportion to her apathy. She's a clipboard nurse, one who sits outside the operating room with a clipboard and dictates policy, but is never involved in any actual procedures.

"I'm afraid we can't let anyone in until after the doctors have finished with him," she says to my anxious query. The word *finished* is like a gong on my awareness.

"Is he at least alive? Is he conscious?"

"I'm sorry," she says, "I don't know. I'm sorry. You'll just have to wait." But clearly, she is more sorry about having to deal with me than anything else. She has likely seen too much. Too much death, too many distraught daughters, anxious husbands, heartbroken mothers. I wait at the entrance, so Mom cannot help but find me when she arrives. I have worked myself into such a frenzy of suspense that the only thing I can think of, for some reason, is the old expression "on tenterhooks." That's how I feel, waiting, *I am on tenterhooks.*

That, and a picture in my mind of my dad and I in his workshop when I was a kid, doing some sort of woodburning project. The image comes into my mind with an appalling and ominous clarity, as if to assert itself as one I must always remember, my dad at his best. The thought makes me rebel against possibilities. I *know* it's just a single memory, and that we'll make many more together. We have to, he can't go now, not yet. Not now.

Mom arrives. We commiserate. After an eternity, the doctors come out, tell us he's stable, we can see him momentarily. I stand looking out through the big tinted glass window, over the roof of a parking garage where cars are parked in neat rows, across the valley to where trees are bowing and nodding placidly in the summer wind. From here, they look like a ripple of air is passing across a green field, like soft hair rippling and swaying. My jaw clenches, and a dull persistent ache radiates out from my face to my neck, shoulders and back, the tension in my solar plexus undeniable.

"Ette," my father says softly from the bed as we enter, his nickname for "Ethel." Though he is smiling, he looks scared somehow, and older, too, if that's possible in so short a time—the prematurely white hair whiter, or perhaps only a darkening in his face.

We have only a minute. "What are you two doing out here on the golf course?" he asks, pretending to be serious.

My mother laughs silently, smoothing back his hair, pain in her eyes. She shakes her head.

"You gave us such a scare."

"Myself too," he says.

"Dad." I step forward. "Dad, you're gonna be all right." Before he has a chance to respond, I break down, sobbing, clutching his arm. I feel my mother tense up, cold with feigned calm.

"Honey," he says in the hesitant, ineffectual way I know well.

I'm overcome with emotion, unable to speak. I hold my breath, a hollow feeling in my chest, and tears burning on my cheeks like marks of shame.

"We have to go," my mother say stolidly. "Don't get yourself excited." This, to my father. "We'll be back tonight to see if they can get you out of ICU. Okay?"

"Okay," he whispers, scarcely audible. He squeezes my hand and forces a shadow of a smile. "Take it easy, tiger."

"Be back later."

"All right."

My mom kisses him goodbye on the cheek.

I hear him say, "I love you," as she bends down to him.

"We love you too, Thomas," she says.

I have never heard her call him that, and I wonder whether it is something reserved for intimate moments, like so many things.

For an instant, I think of Danielle, standing in that room in Colorado surrounded by boxes, one hand in the air in resignation. And the question *why* in my mind, the look between us like the look my parents exchange here in this cold hospital room so lacking in intimacy, clinical and impersonal. Incongruous, to be sure. Yet it appears that my mind must wander in this state, lost in this swirl of fear and raw confusion.

I hold the frame of the door, waiting for Mom to walk out before me.

With her face composed and expressionless, she says, "You're going to have to keep yourself in check in front of him for the time being, or it could be fatal." The words ring crisply in the bright sunshine of the corridor.

Fatal. She is right, of course. And the realization that she, too, is numb with fear softens me, puts me back to a place of empathy. I yearn toward her in that moment, an abandoned infant wanting to be loved. I want to hold her, and to be held, but the distances between us are immeasurable. We are in different time zones. On different planets. That hasn't changed, though it seems as if everything else is turned upside down.

We drive home in our separate vehicles. She's taking the rest of the day off, of course, and I have to go back to the want ads. It feels so strange to see her in my rearview mirror in the middle of the afternoon, the feeling of some warped holiday, that inevitable accompaniment of emergencies and sick days. I feel no guilty pleasure in this one, though, only a sense of surreal. And in my mirror, I see her unguarded, her face as sad and serious as someone with a wound that cannot be healed. She has had a hard life, I think to myself, in spite of what I sometimes think. I know this is the truth.

At home, we are silent, and withdraw into our own places. I call Danielle to tell her what's happened, but she must be out with her parents somewhere. No answer. Every rattle of a cup on a saucer, every rustle of paper or clothing resounds through the house with morbid clarity. There's no comfort here, no cozy familiarity. Even the sound of water running through the pipes is an enemy. I sit in an armchair and try to read, but my vision comes back again and again to the same old paragraph. At last, the telephone rings.

They tell my mother he is stable, and I think, What the hell does that mean? Didn't they say that before? What was he when we left, then, if not stable? Critical? It seems to me they don't let people in to see critical patients, but maybe my memory fails me there. *Stable.* As soon as my mother hangs up the phone, I am on her with the questions.

"Apparently, he's about the same," she confirms. Her tone is so flat it is almost glacial.

"But is he all right? Did they say when he'd be out, can we see him?"

"We can go back tonight during visiting hours," she says wearily, plopping down on a chair. "They didn't say when they could release him. I didn't ask." She closes her eyes.

"Do you want me to make us some dinner, or are you not going to be able to eat?"

"Go ahead and make whatever you want. I'm going to take a nap." She pauses. "I'll eat. Probably."

"Okay."

"Wake me at four if I'm not up."

"All right."

I take the hint and leave the room. After a moment or two of suspended silence, I hear her shut her bedroom door.

Now it is truly quiet, and the morbid clarity of everyday sounds is replaced with morbid silence. Even the occasional squeak on a floorboard when I walk down the hall to my old bedroom sounds ominously muffled, as if the whole house were wrapped in fiberglass insulation. I can hear the clock ticking from behind my mother's closed bedroom door, a sound I would ordinarily never hear even in quiet moments. Everything is heightened, yet dead.

I sit in my room, and now I am at last able to read something, but I don't have the patience to stay focused on one thing, so I keep putting things down and picking up others. First, I try a chapter in a mystery I'm reading called *Shanghai,* then an article in *L* magazine, then a different magazine, then another, then back to the want ads, until I find myself reading some incomprehensible news column on the Bosnian Serbs. I throw the paper across the room in mid-sentence, and the tears stream down my face like rain on a windshield.

Crying brings only a little relief. For one, I cannot help wondering why it is, exactly, that I cry only now. But even as my mind races down the list of possibilities, a measure of tranquility wells up in me that promises to carry me through tonight at least, if not tomorrow. The feeling remains as I poke around the kitchen in search of something easy for dinner. The microwaveable stuff in the freezer looks unpromising, but I don't find much in the fridge for a fast meal, so I decide to cook some brown rice and veggies. I know Mom will grumble a little, but the food will be wholesome and filling, and we will surely feel somewhat better before heading back to the hospital. Besides, I have forty-five minutes to kill, so the hell with it: brown rice it is.

The action of cooking—boiling water, cleaning and chopping up vegetables—soothes me, and helps me sustain this ragged vestige of peace. Considering what has happened, I feel remarkably well. But something inside rebels, and before long, I've done all the cleanup I can, and nothing remains but to wait for the food to be ready, so again, I have nothing to do. My heart sinks as I imagine the inevitable drive up the long driveway to the hospital, the chilly nurse, the uncertainty—and my father's blighted figure on the bed, conscious or unconscious, quiet or active, but irrevocably changed.

I have to shake off the thought, the possibilities of worst-case scenarios. I still have ten minutes left before I have to wake Mom, but after five spent looking through yet another magazine, I decide to wake her early. Ordinarily she would linger an extra ten minutes, but she gets up immediately. The crisis seems to have given her energy—not the restful kind that comes from a place of strength, but the kind people get from staying up all night, drinking too much coffee, working too long without rest. The kind they get from grief.

"I wanted to talk to you," she says at dinner, after the initial grumbles about meatless meals. "About your father."

I nod silently.

"God forbid anything should happen, but if it does…." Her voice trails off. "I want to make sure we're prepared for anything." She stabs a flower of broccoli with her fork.

"He's gonna be okay, Mom," I say, but I hear the quaver in my voice.

"I hope so, honey. I hope so, too. But he might not, you know. There comes a certain point in your life when you have to start thinking about…making plans."

"Mom, don't talk like this."

"Well, it's not easy to approach, no matter how you look at it. I don't like to think about the possibility either. But if it comes to it, we have to. Your grandparents are all gone, and of course, your cousins aren't any help with family matters—they can barely help themselves—so it's really just you and me."

In my present state of mind, her tone sounds so ominous that I hang on every word, my mind racing with disconnected ideas about insurance policies, funerals, wills, powers of attorney, anything I've ever heard and read about death in all its sterilized modern artifice. None of it makes any real sense to me; it's like I'm seeing a scrambled database scrolling past my line of vision, and the tired confusion I feel makes tears well up in my eyes. My stomach aches.

She looks up from her plate suddenly, and sees all. "I'm sorry, honey," she says. "I'm so sorry." And in that instant, when we both cry and she comes to my side of the table to hold me and stands there with her arms around my neck and my face against her belly, I tell her I am scared, and she says, "I know, I am too. I am too."

The ride to the hospital is long and quiet. Outside the air-conditioned car, sunlight shines across the city from the far horizon, winking from the spaces between passing buildings. I am so drained now from the grief compacted into the last few hours that I feel quite calm, my heartbeat slow and regular, like after a period of meditation. A dull persistent ache sits at the base of my neck, but beyond that, I am at peace, yawning lazily behind my hand. My mother, hearing me, yawns too.

When she has parked the car in the visitor's lot, we walk through gauzy sunlight up the long slow incline to the ER unit. Although we walk at a reasonable pace, it seems unnaturally fast, probably because we have just eaten dinner. Mom says nothing, but her single sigh says it all, as far as I'm concerned. We obviously would prefer to be home, and to have him home with us.

I am thinking, as we walk into the main lobby, that all of this has brought me strangely closer to my parents in a short time. At least, I feel it. The fact that I'm thinking of the house itself as home is an indication, having just a short time ago discovered it no longer really felt like home. Here I am, picturing Mom and Dad and me all cozy and snuggly at home like it's this idyllic vision, and all because I just want him alive, I don't want him to die. I don't know whether to see this as tragic or inspiring, and am too tired to lose what little serenity I have, so I decide not to consider it at all.

But when we actually enter the room, and I see him on the flat white hospital bed, everything changes again. I want to say hello casually and quietly, but the words stick in my throat. I can only smile and tiptoe into the room as if I'm trying not to wake him, though he's clearly wide awake, waiting for us.

He looks up, smiles weakly. "Hey, darlin'."

I give him a little wave, still unable to speak. He turns his gaze slowly toward my mother, searching her eyes for an answer and apparently finding it. Then the eyes close.

When he opens them again, there's a change. Something is happening, and the heart monitor beside the bed reflects it. We close in on him instinctively, anxious, and my mother says, "Tom?"

He reaches out for each of us with both hands, his whole frame shaking. I tremble at the look in his eyes as he stares up into my face, gripping my left wrist with his right hand and holding it so tight I almost fear it may break. "Sweetheart," he says hoarsely.

"Sh-shh," my mother whispers. She smoothes his hair with her free hand. "Don't make a fuss, you'll get too excited."

But there are tears in his eyes, and he wants to say something; needs to say it. "Darling," he says, "I'm sorry —"

"You don't have anything to be sorry about," I say. "It's okay. It's going to be okay."

But he insists, shaking his head as if to fight off some invisible force trying to hold him in place, or pull him away from us. "No, no," he says. "Listen. I'm sorry…sorry I was such a lousy father —"

"Stop," I plead, "that's not true."

"Shhh, Thomas," my mother says.

"I was." He holds up a hand for silence, while the one gripping my wrist tightens. "I never said I loved you. I nev—I never said I ac-accepted y—" He stops, gasping for air, shaking. In that moment, he is ancient, a palsied old man, and for the first time in my life I see, really see, his mortality. I go numb.

"Shh, Dad, please," I say over my mother's protestations. "Please. I love you, Dad. You've always done the best for me. I don't blame you for anything."

A sudden chill seizes me, and tears spring to my eyes. I choke them back and lay a hand atop the one my father has slid down my wrist. He shakes like mad and smiles up at me, and I see a light in his eyes blaze up and then ebb away. He says just one word, "Ette"—his nickname for my mother—and then he closes his eyes.

There's a scene: nurses, medics rushing around, jolts to the chest. But nothing remains. He is gone, the way people are sometimes, never to be revived.

Chapter 53

I SIT IN the car, numb beyond numbness. My ears ring. He's gone. I saw it all, saw how they tried, and now there's nothing left to do but mourn.

Feeling nothing but the anxious turbulence of the change itself, the loss irremediable and incomprehensible, I wonder when the hammer of rage will pound me down. I wonder when the next flood of tears will be, and I imagine the funeral. Almost as soon as I think the word *funeral,* I want to deny it. And almost that soon, the numbness evaporates, the tears come, hot down my cheeks, my head no longer clear.

At last my mother steps into the car, and by that time, I have nearly recovered. She looks troubled, though I'm not sure a stranger would see it, but beyond that, she is all business. Part of me wishes she would be dreamy and pious the way a religious person might be, saying, *He looked so peaceful. It was beautiful. I felt the hand of God.*

Instead, she says, "I don't know how we're going to make all these arrangements in the next twenty-four hours, but I'll need you to make some phone calls for me."

I am not surprised, yet somehow it still hurts, temporarily shattering the numbness.

"I'll call all the relatives," she continues, "but I'm going to need time to clean the house, and you can call around to some of the local places and see about catering for after the funeral. I'll be damned if I'm going to spend three hours making salami-and-cheese-on-crackers platters or chopping up carrots and celery. I'll have to sit down when we get home and put together a list of calls you can make after I've notified all the relatives. He had so damned many cousins...."

She goes on in this vein for a while—complaining about the relatives, anxiously anticipating the flurry of activity—until I grow numb again, not quite the numbness of grief for my father, but more a general deficit of feeling, a kind of hollowness in my chest. Somehow, even though the sun is setting now and spreading out across the hills, everything looks grey. The car's interior itself seems to have dulled. My breathing grows shallow.

I try to think about something else, the role I must play in my court case, the posture I must assume, or the job search or Danielle; anything but the crisis at hand. The thought of Danielle is a glimmer of light, a speck in the darkness, but I know that, even when I call her later tonight to tell her what's happened, the shock itself will create a momentary gulf between us, with predictable formalities and expressions of sympathy. It won't be until we actually connect in person that she can give me the comfort I need.

And yet, when I finally do make that phone call—later than I'd anticipated, and only after a tense conversation with mom about relatives—it's more of a relief than I could ever have imagined to hear Danielle's voice breaking, saying, *Oh, Jana, I'm so sorry*, and to cry myself, weep unabashedly into the telephone. She insists on coming over in spite of the lateness of the hour, and I can hardly refuse, although Mom is nearly ready for bed. Danielle and I will have to leave the house in order to be able to have any kind of meaningful dialogue.

I flash back to when I was a teenager, comforting my friend Lois the night *her* father died, walking along with her with the wind turning leaves on the trees upside down just before a thunderstorm.

Everything tonight is so similar as Danielle and I walk along: the darkness, big leaden clouds above us, the summertime setting. Is this all there is? Is this what life's supposed to be? Girls mourning their fathers in summer thunderstorms, big raindrops falling around them like bullets? Sitting in stale damp rooms reading magazines, staring at the spines of books?

I see my father's eyes again, the tears when he was about to tell me he loved me—was it really the first time?—and the brief flame that blazed up and died just before he went. I feel as utterly desolate as if God has just left the universe, slamming shut a door that echoes all across the universe.

Chapter 54

THE WAKE AND funeral pass without incident. I am dead to what happens around me, as if I am merely dreaming—more so, since even my least-remembered nightmares make me feel *something*. But in this bad dream, this parade of starchy men in flamboyant suits and powdered elderly women smelling of perfume or liniment, I am like a figure in the dream itself, not the dreamer, shadowy and insubstantial. Even when he is lowered into the ground, and I know without a doubt the finality of goodbye, I feel nothing. I am nothing, we are all ashes, the day is ash, the sky, the trees. Everything.

Then the long, slow, gentle incline on the ride home, the one I have ridden down hundreds and hundreds of times, a panoramic view of the town rising up to meet the eye like an early painting of colonial New England. Always as familiar to me as the façade of our house—comforting, sweet, and gentle—today, it registers blankly in my mind as we descend, the hills and valleys and the old churches with their spires reaching into the sky dismal and prosaic.

On the car radio station, they are playing some horrible old country song about mamas letting their babies grow up to be cowboys, and my jaw clenches in anger. Old house, old churches, old song; everything is old now, or dead. Dead.

The word resounds in my mind like the refrain of a playground taunt I used to hear when I was a girl, about me and somebody else up in a tree. How can he be dead? And how can she drive this car in her composed measureless silence down this dark grey road, with eyes dry and clear as marbles? I remember what she said to me at dinner that night—how there comes a point in life when you have to make plans—and I think, *She knew.* We both knew, but neither of us said a word. How could we have known, and why did we say nothing?

Ah, God, I want to tear my hair out. I want to reach over and grab her by the throat. I want wailing and gnashing of teeth.

Nothing happens, of course. The long incline levels out after a time, and before I know it we are easing the big sedan into the driveway, pulling in behind my white van, trailed by the long caravan of relatives, semi-familiar friends of the family, colleagues of my father's. Danielle. She and I will sit across from each other, knowing that if we were straight we would be sitting on the sofa holding hands like a couple of high school kids. The charade is degrading, however necessary it is that we avoid shocking older folks in the crowd.

To compensate, we busy ourselves in the kitchen with drinks for people—many of whom will be tanked in no time—and we talk about trivial things, sticking carefully to the past. Oklahoma City and cafés in Ybor and tourism in Tuscaloosa. Anything remote. It almost works, too.

When we return to the living room, two elderly women plant themselves on either side of me on the sofa—old friends of the family, Mom says, someone's cousin's aunts or something—and they pat my hands with expressions of genuine sympathy and assure me that my father is in a better place. They would be a comfort to me were it not for the fact of their own imminent mortality, but just as I realize this, they begin saying the worst things I could have imagined after a funeral.

"He looked good, didn't he?" says the one to my left.

"Oh yes," the other says across me. "Very distinguished."

Good? I think. Distinguished? I don't know if I can be that objective, having just seen him alive, kissed him, cried over his body when the life went out of it.

"It's such a shame. And he was so *young*. How old was he, dear?"

"Fifty," I say numbly. "Or fifty-one, I forget."

"Only fifty-one," she says, confused by my uncertainty. "At least you were able to be with him when he went."

"Yes," I say. "That's true."

Another pat on the hand.

There is a long pause, interrupted only by the voice of an old man in a long-backed chair haranguing the ashen-faced teenager facing him. "You kids today don't have to do any of that," he is saying. "You don't have to even think of it."

The kid nods resignedly, looking trapped.

Danielle comes to the rescue. "Do you want me to bring out more chips and dip?" she asks sweetly. Our eyes meet.

I stand. "I'll go and see what else there is."

"I'll come with." Her tone is all empathy, but her eyes register, *Let's get the hell out of this*. She takes my arm and we walk into the kitchen.

"Oh my God," I say under my breath as we ease our way through the crowd.

"Did you catch any of what was going on next to *me*?" she asks in the same undertone.

"No."

"Did you notice that kid on my left with the red hair? In front of the three people sitting in the folding chairs?"

"Yeah. They're all cousins."

"They're currently being entertained by the red-haired kid, who is talking to them in some sort of made-up kids' language."

"Oh, brother."

"And the couple on my right —"

"With the noisy kids?"

"— Are trying to teach their kids manners, yes, although they've obviously gotten too late of a start for anything other than long-term therapy to be an option."

I almost laugh. A ghost of a laugh, really. "I can't believe she actually said, *He looked good, didn't he?* He didn't look good. He's *dead.* He looked dead." I feel the pressure of her fingers on my arm.

"I know," she says. "I know."

"I mean, Christ…." For some reason, I expect her to interject again, and when she says nothing, I glance at her. She has a stricken look on her face, and I know it's time to shut up. "Hey," I say in a lightened tone, "do you think, if we bring out a lot of salsa and tortilla chips and stuff, they'll all stuff their faces and do less yakking?"

"I don't think old ladies are too big on chips and salsa." She smiles demurely.

"You're right. Why don't we just pour them some scotch?"

We explode into laughter, inappropriately loud and painful. In my own ears, it sounds like the laughter of the damned. Despairing, on the verge of nervous collapse. Disapproving eyes flicker on us inadvertently and flick away, embarrassed. Fake smiles.

My mother, across the kitchen in a deep discussion with a man who looks like a priest, seems not to have heard. I collect bowls of chips and condiments from the counter with the painful self-consciousness of an adolescent, smiling that obliging non-smile where the upper lip disappears inside the lower. The sound of voices around us rises back up again, falls, then rises higher still.

We return. Our places wait for us like guest-of-honor chairs, conspicuous, and there's nothing for it now but to take them. I can read Danielle's little smile of chagrin from across the way as clearly as if she was trying to flaunt it, and for a moment, I wonder if anyone else sees it. But of course, one glance around the room tells the story: the octogenarians flanking me are again bearing down with liquid, sympathetic eyes, and the old man beside them still drones on to his adolescent hostage. The red-headed linguist is in full feather, and I can hear him perfectly above the crowd's murmur, *Mub-eye scub-ool ub-iz ub-in Wub-est Hub-art-fub-ord*, as his audience giggles appropriately. Next to Danielle, in front of the overflowing coffee table, the harried couple whose kids run them like puppeteers are squandering their last ounces of patience.

The whole scene is like some bad Memorial Day get-together with drunken in-laws, wayward teenagers screwing in the upstairs bedrooms, firecrackers set off randomly, squalling babies, and green gelatin salad. It dawns on me that it is all too tacky and too loud, and that I will retreat—after another half hour, just to make it look good—with a fictional headache, to the quiet sanctuary of my bedroom. There, surrounded by books and boxes, I can safely say, *No one belongs in here unless I say so.*

The scene gives me an uncomfortable awareness about money, too. I don't know what any of these relatives do for a living, but I have always known in a hazy sort of way that my father made more than them. Not that we've ever been rich, but when I think back on family gatherings of my childhood, I realize that most of the extended family were only a paycheck or two away from becoming poor white trash. I think about the kitchens of their modest homes, underdecorated livingrooms with threadbare carpets, mangy dogs, scraggly cats—not squalor, exactly, but much lower in class than we ever were—and as I look around our antiseptic livingroom, with its Steinway and oriental vases, I see how precariously the relatives are perched on their folding chairs, as if they want to hover above the deep pile carpeting, afraid to soil it with their shoes, afraid of breaking something valuable.

I feel a surge of shame and pity for the class-consciousness we all have and cannot avoid, the unofficial caste system that no American ever seems to directly confront, or even acknowledge.

What could I possibly do to make these near-strangers more comfortable or, more accurately, less uncomfortable? And why do I feel such a vague distaste for their obtuse conversation, their narrow lives and questionable manners? They really are just *not* my type, they're not my people. And the old cliché drifts into my head: you can choose your friends, but you can't choose your relatives.

It's strange. I never finished college, I'm not exactly wealthy, and I'm no Miss Manners, either, as far as that goes. Most of what I've learned I taught myself, reading on my own with no guidance, no instruction. Yet I feel self-consciously proper and overrefined with these people around me.

The line of eye contact, the kinship, with Danielle seems to straighten and grow taut. And I think how we are frighteningly obsessed with images in this culture—our own images in particular—and how we favor form over substance almost ubiquitously. The thought makes me utterly weary. Fortunately, my last half hour before the Great Escape to my bed and my pillows goes fairly quickly, and before long, I'm alone in the darkness of my room.

Not for long, however. My mother comes in, concerned. I reassure her—feeling guilty for the dishonesty—that it's just a headache. She draws the curtains and presses cool lips to my forehead, her face expressionless. She goes.

I have only just settled back again among the heap of pillows when I hear a faint tapping at the door. Danielle. I tell her to come in. She tiptoes across the room like someone entering a sickroom, but looking slightly mischievous. "Hey," she whispers.

"Hi."

She sits on the bed beside me. "You're okay, right?" It is almost a statement.

"Yeah. I think you get the drift."

She laughs softly. "Oh, yeah. You'll be glad to know the redheaded kid finally ran out of steam."

"Good." I smile and close my eyes. "I hope he gets laryngitis." I look up again.

Her eyebrows arch. "Real life ain't that way." She bends forward at the waist, stretching across me and laying her cheek on my breast, facing away from me. I reach one hand out to touch the down at the nape of her neck.

She sighs, then the room grows quiet. "You know what I miss?"

I sit up a little, and she lifts her head, turns over to look at me. "No," I say, "what do you miss?"

"Life on the road with you. The excitement. Everything here is so white bread."

I can't restrain my smile. "We'll go again. After all this with my dad is over. And court."

"Don't lose sight of that," she says, turning serious. She sits up in the bed. "I know your father wouldn't have wanted —"

"Shh." I put one finger to her lips. "I know."

"I'm sorry," she says. She kisses my finger. "I love you." She gets up, kisses me softly on the mouth, and goes to the door. "Get some sleep," she says. "I'll see if I can keep the hounds at bay."

I smile again. "Thanks."

She closes the door, and I face the silence again. Life is terribly difficult sometimes, I think, and then I find myself thinking, *I can't believe he's gone.* I close my eyes. *Gone.* The room is dark, even darker with my eyes closed, and all I can think is: *Gone.*

Chapter 55

TWO WEEKS PASS, a time of quiet introspection, of store-bought salads on dinnerware, and long, sad silences that rise like smoke to the ceiling and permeate each room in turn. The insurance money is marginal, enough to cover funeral and hospital bills, and what remains goes into Treasury bonds or something. My mother tells me how it is, her tone resigned. Almost as if none of it mattered, nothing mattered, just the long grey road stretched out ahead of her, promising only loneliness and death.

The realization that I cannot lift her out of her torpor propels me back to my case with the center. I also get a job in the meantime—nothing very mentally taxing, just basic clerical work at a mortgage company—and it begins to look like Danielle and I will be stuck here for longer than expected. Without my mother's knowledge, I call Steve Torres at SCHRO to tell him about the thing with the lawyer, John Hailey, and he encourages me to pursue the case. Two weeks after my father's funeral, I broach the subject to my mother, asking as casually as I can if she would mind my calling Hailey.

"Why do *you* need to call him?" she asks.

The question throws me, and right away I feel defensive. "Well, I don't. I mean, would you prefer to be the one?"

She makes a vague gesture of futility. "Oh, I don't know. I don't even think we can afford it now, to tell you the truth. Your father…." She lets it trail off.

"Well, then, I'll pay. Or we can split the difference. Whatever you want to do."

She twists her mouth into a sarcastic grimace. "*You'll* pay," she says, "right. On what you're making, you think you're going to be able to afford *Hailey*?" She shakes her head and I feel anger rise in my throat, but I swallow it, not wanting an argument.

"Or we split the difference," I say casually, "like I said. Whatever you want. And I can pay you rent, too, if I have to."

"Trust me, honey, if you paid one third of the legal fees you wouldn't be able to pay any rent on top of it." She sips her coffee.

I wait silently, like I am brooding over what the other options might be. I hate this dependence, the financial issue, and the way I have learned to let her lord it over me. My fate subject to her whims.

"*I'll* take it up with Hailey," she says at great length. "If he can't do it, maybe someone else can. Who knows, he may give us a discount." She smiles wryly.

A day passes. Then two, then three. A week. Reluctant to resurrect the topic, I am steeling myself for it anyway when she says at dinnertime, "I talked to Hailey today."

"What?" She's said it so casually, I'm unsure whether I understood.

"Hailey. I called his office on my lunch hour. I had some time." She picks at her mixed vegetables absently.

"And you talked to *him*? Not his secretary?"

"Mm-hm. He remembered the case. He's very busy now, but I might be able to interest him in it again if I can feel confident you'll cooperate."

I feel my color rise. "What do you mean?"

She looks up from her plate. "He said you were 'singularly uncooperative.' Those were his exact words. Now," she continues, folding her napkin in her lap, "he did laugh about it, since he was talking to your mother. But he doesn't exactly throw around words. Do you know what he was talking about? I certainly never heard anything from you."

"Well, he was kind of an asshole, Mom."

She blanches. "Excuse me?"

"Sorry. He was rude, though. He insisted on me getting him my original pink slip. I don't even know if I still have it, but if I do, I sure as hell wouldn't know exactly where it is. He looked at me like I was some kind of idiot when I told him that." I shake my head, aware of the thinness of this defense. "I mean, I thought to myself, 'Didn't *he* ever move?'"

She makes a gesture of acquiescence, an *oh-okay* face. "When was this, about three weeks ago? Right before your father?" She will not say *died*.

I nod.

"Well, he wasn't over-anxious to follow up on the case. Like I said. But maybe I can persuade him. Just give me some reassurance you'll really cooperate. Asshole or not."

I smile at her. "Of course."

She seems to relax a little, though the look in her eyes makes me feel like I have to drop the grin pretty quickly.

That night, toward morning, I dream that my father is standing by the foot of my bed. In my dream, I am asleep, and then I wake suddenly, feeling his presence. Out loud I say, *Dad?* Then open my eyes. But he just stands with his hands clasped behind his back, smiling, with that faraway look he used to get during a lecture. I smile back. We smile that way for a long time, till eventually it occurs to me to wonder, in the vague way that dreamers do, what is going on. I want to ask him something, but cannot remember what, and then I wake—this time, for real—alone in my room, the objects around me as plain and immovable as the frame of the closet door. A part of me almost gasps with the suddenness of awakening, and yet another part cannot help but question whether it was more than a dream. But, of course, that's impossible.

I lie in the dark, picturing his smiling face. I cannot recall it completely now, although—or maybe it is *because*—I am fully wide awake. I realize with dismay that I am beginning to forget him. I almost sit upright in bed at the thought. I want to say, *No*, it's too soon to be moving away from him.

Guilt seizes me like a great hand around my ribcage. It's all a payback, I think, some big cosmic retribution for being a bad daughter, leaving the nest too soon, neglecting them. I think of the missed opportunities, times I could have called or written…like him, with his chances to say *I love you*. And although I want to cry again, I smile at this first attempt to forgive myself. We *all* did the best we could. I even feel a little better, just knowing that it's true.

I am awake now, fully awake, although the darkness in the room tells me it's cloudy outside. In my mind's eye, I see us in that hospital room. I feel again the hands on my wrist, the shaking frame, the look in his eyes. I even hear him saying my mother's name, that little retching sound that could have been nothing more than a death rattle but was undoubtedly *Ette*, and I realize that, in reality, the whole thing was beautiful. His last word was his wife's name.

And though God knows she isn't perfect, my heart yearns toward her. How she must have loved him! I try to imagine what it must be like for her now, and discover that, of course, I cannot know. Somehow the pain of her loss, the vastness of it compared to mine—and mine is deep—lends her a new aura in my mind. I feel greater respect for her.

I think of her gestures—the motions of resignation, the futile hand in the air, the shrug of her shoulders—and at last I know. Not her pain, but something about what it is in scale, in the scheme of things. It would have been easier, I think, to lose me. And I remember in my youth, how I used to wonder how she ended up with him, what strange quirk of romance or chemistry propelled her into the arms of this man who was always just…there.

Another wave of remorse rolls over me as I acknowledge his many merits: his humor, his incisive mind, gentleness, reliability, steadiness of purpose. His quiet strength. He didn't *have* to be exciting and sexy, glamorous, or dynamic. He was a great man, a beautiful man, and I wish I'd let him know that more often.

I think back—now that the floodgates have opened, and I can't return to sleep, so memories pour out of nowhere for the first time in years—and remember him being with me in the hospital when I had asthma attacks, and how we used to spend time together on those crazy woodworking projects of mine. He actually used to tell me he sold some of the junk I made to friends of his, though I suspect he just gave them away and took the money out of his own pocket. I think about how he wandered around the music store, absently fingering the keys on tubas and trombones the day I labored over the task of picking out my first saxophone.

Now I know that what Danielle almost said to me about my father is true: he would not have wanted me to let the case go, to roll over and die. He would have wanted me to fight. And I feel scared, more scared than I did before the hearing at SCHRO. Lying in the dark, my heart pounds harder at the thought of what may await me. I'm not sure I'm up for the job, but I'm sure I need to tackle it.

Chapter 56

IN THE MEANTIME, working at the mortgage company proves to be more taxing than I had anticipated, no pun intended. I'm mostly just dealing with an old and outdated system that will nonetheless probably still be there a hundred years from now. In the file room, miles of files line the walls like books in a library, and most of what I do is make copies of files or file copies of various documents—mortgages, disbursement authorizations, appraisals.

But as time goes by, my familiarity with various areas of the business grows more obvious, and the level of difficulty rises. I discover words like *subrogation* and *remonumentation*, and what the "HUD" is, and how to read a credit report. The list goes on and on. The questions go from, "Jana, are you familiar with such-and-such?" to "Could you pull this report and fax it to Chicago today before three?" And so, even though the mental strain remains manageable, my emotional stress goes up and up, and I come home each night at six feeling bruised, too drained to deal with the case, and barely able to space out in front of the TV with Danielle.

But since we are on a low budget, we do just that, and the early fall becomes a time of avid film criticism. We rent movies all the critics praised—*My Left Foot, Schindler's List, Sophie's Choice*—and watch them with the eyes of critics, lavishing praise here, finding fault there. We seek out the bizarre and the obscure: Stanley

Kubrick's *Barry Lyndon*, films by the infamous Leni Riefenstahl, classic Hitchcock. For a while, we even watch nothing but films with subtitles, just to see if we can stand it. But eventually we both become glutted, like someone who has eaten too much chocolate, and it's time to do something else.

So we go back to Elizabeth Park. Late summer and early fall are beautiful there, and of course, memories besiege us. Here we first spawned the plan to go cross-country, wandering among the heavy-laden arbors, making excited plans. Here we walked on open mike night at The Burning Brassiere, when Danielle got up and sang. And tonight, we are just here in peace and quiet, wondering what's next. The calm before the storm.

"What did your mom say about the case?"

I walk on silently for a moment, looking straight ahead. "She talked to Hailey. Trying to get him to pursue it."

"Is it still pending? I mean, is there like a deadline?"

"The date hasn't arrived yet. You know how the system is, always plenty of time to prepare."

"Yeah, but the closer the date, the tougher it would be to prepare, right?"

"Sure. I don't think the center even plans to have to appear. At least, no one's said anything about it."

"It's Hailey's job to notify them?"

"His office, yeah. I guess."

She takes my hand. Although we are alone, I still feel an element of risk letting her do that here, in staid old West Hartford. But I don't care. I retain the hand. It swings in time with mine as we walk along.

"What about Mom? Is she gonna pay?"

I do a quick calculation in silence. What exactly is this going to cost me, anyway? I haven't really thought it through. "Well," I say, "I'm going to pay *some* of the legal expenses. I don't really know what the bill will be."

"Think he'll give your mom a deal?"

"I don't know." I sigh. "I hope so. He's kind of a—I don't know. I don't like him."

"So I gathered."

"It's not so much that I mind him being arrogant. I mean, I guess that's not terribly surprising. I just don't like the way he acts like he's doing you a favor by having a conversation with you."

"But in your case, he really *is* doing you a favor, isn't he?"

"That's what bothers me."

She looks at me out of the corner of her eye and laughs. Then shrugs. "Well?"

I can't help smirking, but then I shrug, too. "Oh, I know. It's just—you know what I mean. You know how some people just act like they're God's gift?"

"You mean like my ex-boyfriend?"

"Worse. Much worse."

"Worse than James?"

"Much *much* worse. This guy makes James look like Mr. Humility."

"Jesus. That's scary. No wonder you told your mom he was an asshole."

My jaw drops. "Did I tell you that?"

"No, your mom did."

"*What?*"

"I called the other day, and we got to talking. As a matter of fact, the questions you just answered were about the only ones I had left."

"You brat. Why didn't you tell me you talked to Mom?"

"Research purposes. I'm experimenting."

I look at her again, swinging our hands to and fro between us. "You really are nuts, you know that?"

"Why not? One of us has to be. You're so stable."

"Yeah, right!" We both laugh at that.

"Anyway, I forgot all about it until now," she says. "And since we were talking about Hailey...."

We fall silent again. She is walking me beneath bowers of primroses, beside rows of orchids and tulips. In the distance, the sun spreads crimson light across the late afternoon sky, and I feel dreamy and drugged, all sensation narrowed to the two omnipotent ones, sight and touch. Everything else is filtered out except for my hand and hers, swinging in the idle air, and that soft light painted on the horizon.

"You know," I say, "I do believe that if it weren't for you, I'd never be able to make it through this thing."

We stop beneath a cascade of roses, pause as if standing at an altar.

"You know," she says, "I do believe you just might be right about that," and my smile meets hers.

Hailey's office. A dark wood-paneled room, books lining the walls like soldiers at attention. A giant old-fashioned desk, walnut or mahogany, stands in the center, with dark red leather chairs, big windows overlooking West Hartford center, a glass ashtray on an ornate metal stand, clean and new-looking, but probably forty or fifty years old. On the crystal coffee table, a stack of mail threatens to topple: *Wall Street Journal,* invitations to seminars, *Fortune* magazine.

He strides in quickly but softly to meet me, shutting the door behind him and walking over to where I have waited, biding my time with a copy of *American Business Journal,* my eyes glazing over as I struggle through an article on no-load mutual funds. We stand and greet each other formally, like strangers. Then he sits down behind the desk.

"I've been going through the materials I've gathered from the people at SCHRO, and of course from you, and I'm wondering if there's anything you may have forgotten about that I should know?

Anything misplaced or misfiled? Any people in our little cast of characters who we still need to look up?"

"Who do you have in the cast of characters?" I ask.

He names them.

When he gets to Tillie's name, I interrupt. "She'd be afraid to lose her job for telling the truth. She'll never testify."

He shakes his head, dismissive. "Of course she'll testify. She gets a subpoena just like everyone else."

"Even so, there's no guarantee she'd tell the truth."

"You think she'd perjure herself simply because of a piece of circumstantial evidence?"

I shake my head. "*I* don't know," I say testily. "My suspicion is that she would."

"Tell me again about the conversation she supposedly had with Barbara Helms."

I tell him.

"And that's all of it?" he asks when I have finished.

"That's it. And what if she gets subpoenaed but never shows up?"

"Then she's in contempt of court." Again he sounds like an impatient professor lecturing a dunce.

I remain silent. We sit like that for a few long moments, looking at each other, until I realize he is looking not at me but through me, far beyond the horizon, his mind working. I look away.

"Well," he says at length. "You realize this could be over in a day?"

"Sure. I don't have a bunch of witnesses lined up. Besides, they've got that bozo Kahn defending her. Isn't he supposed to be a big-time corporate hotshot?"

He looks surprised, but smiles. I don't recall having seen him smile before, not ever. Then he says something which surprises even me. "We'll beat him."

Anxious to change the subject—I don't want to get my hopes up too much, especially since I still don't trust this man—I ask another question. "Will there be any other lawyers for the defense, like there were at the hearing?"

"There are two other attorneys on the defense team," he says, lapsing back into formality, "and you probably noticed them at the hearing. One of them is a woman named Grisette, I don't recall her first name, and the other is a guy named Al Nulty. I don't believe either of them will do any cross-examination. So, for practical purposes, their role is strictly administrative. And psychological."

"What about you? Do you have somebody else?"

He looks impatient, but the answer is level. "My partner, William Demas. But again, his function is strictly administrative, just like on their end. You'll meet him beforehand."

"What happens if you get sick? Does he take over?"

"I don't get sick." His expression is deadly serious.

"Okay," I say, my color rising. I feel like saying, *Well, what if something happens to you, a car accident or something?* But I'm too uncomfortable now to press the issue. The hell with it, I decide. He'll be there.

"Anything else to cover?" he asks. It sounds more like a statement than a question.

"Will I see you again before the trial?"

He looks at me, and I am unable to read his expression. I realize at that instant how truly impossible it is to see beyond his external appearance, and I think to myself, *Damn*, he's got to be a great lawyer, it's like masks behind masks. Because of the way this strikes me, I cannot help smiling the moment after he answers: "Not unless you have to."

We're still staring at each other, and I know he is weighing something, looking *into* me in a way that is almost offensive in its penetration. He drums his fingers on the desktop idly, while my own fingers twirl a lock of hair round and round. At last, I break the now uncomfortable silence by standing—somewhat formally—and thanking him, shaking hands, and walking out of the office.

Back home, later on, I have time to reflect on the meeting, and I wonder, What really drives this guy? Part of me thinks he must have something to use that he's not telling me, while another part must content itself with standing back and wondering if he just likes a challenge. Did he say *We'll beat him* with such equanimity, even arrogance, merely because he's determined to do it? I can't figure it out, and of course *thinking* about it drives me crazy even more than trying to predict the outcome. So eventually, I try to cut it out by going to bed.

But I do not sleep. The trial is still three long weeks away, but tonight I'm as wide awake and nervous as if it were tomorrow. I go over every detail of the meeting with Hailey in my mind, I see again, with miserable clarity, the most pointless details—the ornate ashtray, *Fortune* magazine, Hailey's fingers drumming the desktop—and I realize how closely my state of mind resembles the pre-hearing jitters I had months ago, when I watched the court monitor sip her coffee out of its disposable cup and gazed at the microphones in their cold metal stands. I imagine myself staring down Barbara Helms or James Kahn or even Wendy Simpson, and I know that I'm scared, and that this fear too shall pass, but not now. Not tonight.

Chapter 57

TWO DAYS LATER, I'm walking down Main Street in downtown Hartford. As I approach the Gold Building, I see two figures coming toward me on the sidewalk. They look strangely familiar, a man and woman, both under fifty. Dark hair. From a distance, they look like they could be a couple or a brother and sister. Somehow, the man's gait, with its almost comic firmness, and the florid excess of the woman's outfit, awakens a recollection from long ago, and I have time to wonder why before they get close enough for me to recognize Standing Free Ibsen and Harmony Stone.

Two instant impulses spring up to battle each other. The first—the desire to greet them like long-lost cousins—is defused by the second, an impulse to turn tail and run like hell. A third desire comes to mind: that the sidewalk open up and swallow me right here, so I won't have to make a decision.

Of course, they are engaged in an animated conversation—or, more correctly, Stan is involved in an animated monologue, while Harmony appears to listen—so it's possible they'll pass by without even seeing me. But I know guilt will seize me if I allow this to happen, and in that instant of realization, I hail them like someone trying to flag a New York City taxicab. I feel my grimace tighten into a smile, and I know that, just like the tea party where I first met Barbara Helms, I will be able to grin through it all.

When they see who I am, and I hear their exclamations and see their faces, I know it will at least be tolerable. Apparently, they are so shocked and delighted to see someone who, for all they knew, had vanished into the great black hole of the city, that they come at me like *I'm* the long lost cousin.

"I can't believe it," says Harmony, releasing me from her embrace. "We were just talking about you a couple of weeks ago." She points back and forth from Stan to herself, shaking her head. "Not Stan and me. My husband, Fred. Do you remember Fred?"

"I don't think I met him." I smile. Then I remember the whole thing with greater clarity. No, I didn't meet him.

"Yeah," she says, "we were talking about Kiddie Korner, and I was saying something about you, I think. Anyway, how *are* you?"

"Okay, and you?"

"Fine, fine."

Stan steps forward to shake my hand. "Nice to see you again."

"You too. Stan, right?"

He beams, pleasantly surprised. "Right." After he shakes my hand, he puts his hands behind his back, standing like a military man "at ease," quietly attentive while Harmony and I exchange compliments. I notice his whole manner has changed, or is different than what I remember, at least. He has a look of confidence and strength, but in repose now, he's lost the old shifty-eyed nervousness. His eyes are clear and lively, and he radiates calm good health the way an avid runner or swimmer might. "We were just on our way to do some shopping," Harmony says. "There isn't much left in Hartford anymore, but we figured we'd look for some winter clothes for Stan at the Civic Center shops."

"I just came back from New Mexico," he says, by way of explanation.

"What were you doing there?" I ask.

He pauses. "Are you familiar with the Mescalero Apaches?"

"I can't say that I am. Is it a New Mexican tribe?"

"They live on a reservation south of Albuquerque. About a hundred and twenty miles away." His voice is low and even, and in spite of the noise and traffic around us, it lulls me into a kind of trance. "The federal government," he says, "has started to conspire with private utility companies to develop nuclear dumping grounds on Native lands. I went out there to join the local anti-nuke lobbying group, which was started by a Mescalero Apache, to protest Department Of Energy proposals. Everything is up in the air now." He smiles politely, accompanying the gesture with a slight shrug.

"Do I understand you correctly that the federal government wants to dump nuclear waste on Indian reservations?" I ask.

He shrugs. "Well, they would like to develop a so-called 'temporary' storage site for spent radioactive fuel, then eventually approve a permanent site…God knows where."

"That's horrible. How can they do it?"

He smiles ruefully. "Money. The Mescaleros are very poor. Money talks, bullshit walks, you know."

"You mean the Feds are actually paying them to accept this stuff?"

"No. The utilities would put up the money, actually, although the Federals have paid the Mescaleros' tribal council a lot of money to study the proposals. They are actually bringing this waste down on their own backs, like a plague of locusts or something."

I notice a lilt in his voice, a kind of creeping accent, and I realize he sounds a little like he's Latino—no doubt the influence of where he has been. For a moment, I stand there squirming, thinking about what he's just said. It's an uncomfortable thing to consider, but what do I say? Finally I opt for repetition. "That truly is horrible."

"Well, fortunately most of the tribe is opposed to placing a nuclear dump on this land. It is frightening, though, to think that some of the least populous places in Nevada, New Mexico, or who-knows-where, may soon be contaminated for centuries." He brightens suddenly, an artificial change of subject. "So, tell us about you. What's happening *here*?"

I know he means Connecticut, Hartford, the world of Kiddie Korner and kids, but I have already told them I am no longer working there, and my desire to discuss the case is at an all-time low. "I'm doing some clerical stuff for work. Nothing major."

Harmony asks, "Do you see any of the old gang from Kiddie Korner? Your old supervisor, what was her name? Tillie?"

"No, I haven't seen any of them lately," I say, thinking that will change soon. But I can see that they obviously know nothing about my case. "What about you?" I ask in an attempt to move on. "Do you see any of the other parents? Carlos Pareja, all those guys?"

"Carlos is moving to Chicago," says Harmony, pronouncing the *ch* like in *chick*: a little impersonation of Carlos, who is Puerto Rican.

"Wow," I say, "I didn't know that."

She continues on about him—she knows him from stopping to buy a juice from his cart every day—and while she talks, my mind drifts back to Kiddie Korner. I am looking at her, glancing at Stan periodically, smiling and making little sounds of interest or assent, but I am thinking about insurance forms, kids peeing their pants on their first day, Barbara Helms (*I think it's time we ended this relationship*), mornings when sunlight slanted down into the Day Room, making even the most prosaic scene look sublime, and days shortly after they fired me when I felt I'd left something truly special behind: a hectic time in my life, a time of great stresses and small rewards, but through the filter of nostalgia, it looks serene and beautiful. That's the problem with this era, I think, this instant nostalgia for yesterday that gets shorter in time with every generation. People in their thirties reminisce about their twenties, people in their twenties reminisce about their teens…where will it end? With pre-schoolers?

The thought draws my lips up into a smile, and I realize then that Harmony is still telling me a sad story about Carlos Pareja, the sacrifices he makes raising his daughter and the necessity of the move to Chicago. I frown appropriately. It is too bad, I tell her, about Carlos.

Later, driving back down Main Street, I turn reflective as the sun shines off the Gold Building and down across my face. I can see Carlos, his perennial turquoise T-shirt and gleaming sneakers, and I remember Harmony and Frederick's child on his belly among rows and rows of toy soldiers, the flag on the wall behind him. So many other pictures from back then drift through my mind like half-remembered images of dreams, and in this dreamy state, I drive unthinking back to my mother's house with its clipped green lawn, its well-kept bushes and newly-painted mailbox.

I think of the long slow incline leading down to our house, the one we had to ride down after the funeral, and how, until that after-noon, it always gave me that little lift of comfort and familiarity. I know that somehow an era of my life has come and gone, a stage is ending soon. Perhaps it already has.

That night I get a call from Lois Densmore. I know it's been at least seven years since I've seen her, because I was seventeen at the time, and when I went to school we lost touch—writing less and less often, until we no longer wrote at all.

"Hello, may I speak with Jana?"

"Who's calling, please?" I say, my stock response when I don't know the voice.

"Lois Densmore."

"Oh my God."

"Jana?"

"I can't *believe* it!" I hear my voice go up a full register with each syllable.

"Well, I guess you remember who I am, then?"

"Remember! My God, how are you?" My tone stays embarrassingly loud and enthusiastic.

"Good, good."

"I had no idea whether you were even living in Connecticut."

"Well, I wasn't, for a while," she says.

"But now you are."

"For an indefinite period, at this point, yeah."

"I can't believe it's really *you*, what are you doing?"

"Well, I'm in school again."

"Did you get your degree?"

"Not yet. Well, yes and no. I got an associate's degree at Bensonhurst Community College, but now I'm doing pre-law."

"Good for you. Do you like it?"

"It's fascinating, believe it or not. But…well, I don't love all of it, but it's what I want to be doing, so —"

"That's great."

"And it's given me the opportunity to meet some really interesting people."

"No doubt. So where are you calling from? Where is Bensonhurst Community College?"

"It's down in Milford. But I'm not living there anymore, actually. I'm living in New Haven until further notice. I have a couple weeks off, and I ended up coming here to Hartford with some friends."

"So you're in Hartford now! Cool."

"Yeah, and the funny thing is, I don't know anyone here anymore. That's why I took a chance on *your* old phone number."

"Same old number, hasn't changed. Mom and I are still here."

There is a pause, very brief, while she weighs a question. I answer it for her, whatever it may have been. "My dad passed away recently."

"Oh, *no.*"

"Just a couple weeks ago, in fact."

"Oh, Jana, I'm so sorry."

"It's okay," I say, still awkward with the need to respond to sympathy. "It was kind of touch-and-go for us there for a couple of days, but we're okay. Mom's a trooper." I force a smile, then realize there's no need to smile over the phone.

"Jana, I'm so sorry," she repeats. "I don't know what to say."

"It's really okay. You don't have to say anything." I realize at that moment that, if we were still close, she would already know she doesn't, and I feel a small ache in my heart at the passage of time. "Tell me about law school," I urge; a blatant change of subject.

She responds tactfully, tells me about the pre-law program, the attempts to prepare for LSATs—no amount of preparation, she says, can be sufficient—and the fear of not finding a job after law school.

I commiserate. "My schooling definitely hasn't proven very applicable to the real world, for whatever that's worth," I tell her. "Of course, it was only two years, but most of it was geared toward music, whereas my work experience in the past few years has mostly been with kids."

She asks me about the daycare situation in Connecticut, and I tell her the whole Kiddie Korner saga—complete with asides about Carlos and Harmony—which brings me to a tangent about the strange coincidence of running into Harmony and Stan, which in turn brings us to the coincidence of Lois herself calling me this very same night. She is impressed with the strangeness of it.

"Listen," she says. "I know it's short notice, and you probably already have plans, but is there any chance you could break away for, like, an hour tonight? Just for coffee? Say yes."

"Actually, I was going to spend the night at home obsessing about my trial. The big countdown has begun: eighteen days. So it would be great to get out of myself for a little while, and it would definitely be great to see you."

"All right. Where and when?"

"That's what I was just going to ask you."

We laugh.

"Well, where in Hartford are you?" I ask.

She describes the area, a neighborhood on the north end where we do not want to hang out, and she agrees to my suggestion, The Burning Brassiere, since she's never been. After hanging up, I don't know what to make of my tumult of feelings. After all, even today I think of her, on some level, as my first true love, cliché or not. I decide after a short time to just forget everything until I actually see her, and go with the flow.

Of course, I think of Danielle, and how this would look to her. Like a date? Like cheating? But no, Lois truly is nothing more than an old friend. Still, I can't escape the feeling I might be doing something wrong, something that could at least be misinterpreted.

I don't quite recognize her when she first walks into The Burning Bra. She always had hair that hung down her back, long blonde hair with a beautiful sheen and straightness to it: like honeyed sunlight, like spun gold, like any hackneyed phrase you could use to describe it. But she wears it short now, like Danielle's, only different—a bob cut, radically different from the old Lois.

"Look at you," I say, as we hug. "You look so…great."

"And so do you." She steps back, and for a moment, we seem to size each other up, then something in her face closes like a door, although she is still smiling. "I like what you've done with your hair," she says.

"Oh, thanks," I laugh.

We sit down, and out of the corner of my eye, I see our server making a beeline for us. I pat my hair self-consciously. "We'll have to talk about it later," I say.

"Are you ready to order?" the young woman asks.

Since Lois has in fact never been here, she scans the menu, while I order my usual mocha mint cappuccino. As she peruses the coffees and smoothies and old-fashioned sodas, I have a long silence in which to reflect on how she looks, acts, "feels" to me.

That something in her face that closed like a door is still there—it might even be more correct to say that whatever had been open remains closed—and I ponder this while she scans the menu. I think of recent encounters with others: John Hailey, and Harmony and Stan. This is almost like that. We do not really know each other, not today anyway; it's like a business meeting, and it shows.

"Tell me more about law school," I say when she has ordered.

"It's pretty much what you would expect, actually," she says brightly. "A *lot* of reading. Some of it is a little hard to stay interested in, but since I have a real investment in it, I do okay."

"I've been thinking about lawyers a lot lately, with my case coming up so soon. It seems like every time I turn around, there's another lawyer: mine, Kiddie Korner's…and now you."

"Well, I'm not a lawyer yet, that's for sure. But so far, everything I've done makes me feel like I'm going in the right direction."

We talk in this vein for a while, but that sentence sticks with me: *everything I've done makes me feel like I'm going in the right direction.* I wish I could say that that was true of my life. So much of what I've experienced has seemed like a stopover, a tangent, uncertainty about where to go or what to do next. We all buy into this notion of a clear direct line from the age of eighteen to the grave, but real life just isn't that way, and I'm sure Lois is in the minority. Pretty sure, anyway.

After we run through the topics of law school and my court case, I tell her about my travels with Danielle. I'm on my second mocha mint cappuccino when I get around to asking her what I've wanted somehow to ask all night.

"So, did you really come to Hartford and call me just to get together for coffee?"

She looks at me quizzically. "Why not?" She smiles. "I thought it would be good to see you again, and it definitely is. I mean, what the hell."

"Well, it's just—I don't know, I haven't seen you in years, and you *are* here with other friends. Why me?"

"You were one of the first people to come to mind."

I am sitting with my elbow on the table, my chin resting on my palm. I feel content, yet nervous. "I guess what I'm asking is whether you were thinking of, you know, of way back when?"

She smiles, a hard-to-read smile, almost indulgent. "We were *kids*, Jana. For me, it was a phase, experimentation. I have boyfriends now. Not right this second, actually," and she laughs, "but yeah, I have. I think it's great the way it's worked for you, with Danielle and all, but no. Not me."

I nod, understanding, yet sad somehow, happy and sad at the same time, if that's possible. Happy for me and sad for her, a little, or so I think, but who knows? Maybe it's simply that yearning I felt earlier tonight, that ache at the passage of time. To think that I feel it at my age. What will it be like when I'm forty or fifty? Will I be like those old greasers from the fifties, with their potbellied wives and their fifty-seven Chevys? Or, even worse, like some goofy hippie with a tie-dyed rocking chair and bells on my walker?

I shudder just thinking about it: me at eighty, shuffling down some dim hallway with an old flannel shirt and faded jeans with holes in them, an eyebrow ring in my grey eyebrow, Pearl Jam playing on my little headset. But no, I wouldn't be caught dead doing that. I might have a poster of Sandra Bullock on the wall, but that would be my limit.

Lois is still talking about her "bisexual" phase, such as it was, but I am only half-listening. I am thinking about the innumerable paths we all tread, the strange ways the lives of strangers intersect, sometimes briefly and sometimes for a long time, but then the inevitable moving on, until at last we all come to know we only have ourselves. When it comes down to it, I am the only one who will never leave me, so I need to make damn sure I know how to be good company for myself.

She's talking about her boyfriend now, the most recent ex-boyfriend, that is—one of the many future lawyers of corporate America—and I find myself thinking, God, how many lawyers do we need? She could have been anything, I'll bet: a classical guitarist, maybe, an architect, a university professor. As it is, she's planning a law career, so who am I to judge that? On the other hand, she still has time to change her mind.

Everything I've done makes me feel like I'm going in the right direction, she said. It seems impossible, but then, how does anyone choose? Just look at some of the politicians out there. Is their path that much different from a mafia don or embezzler? Do they all feel like they're going in the right direction too, and that their ideological rivals are all going hopelessly astray? I wonder, and I wonder, too, what it must be like to live in a world of black and white, where abortion is always wrong, where gays and lesbians are all speeding to the place with the fire and brimstone.

Mostly, I wonder what it must be like for Lois, so sure of where she's going and how to get there. I wonder if she sees it all as a game, a series of obstacles to overcome, or if it is as serious as war, a kind of strategizing where the stakes are career, livelihood and life itself. I can't imagine what her priorities are now, whether money, a luxury car and a palatial home, or just the pure desire to help people, to right wrongs. In any case, I feel she has changed irrevocably, and that ache in my heart at the passage of time is no doubt connected more to her than to any nostalgia of my own.

Of course, we talk of other things, and the conversation turns from ex-boyfriends to current events, to the good old days with my buddy Leon, and so on. But the night ends prematurely—I have to go home early, I say—and we part on warm terms with promises to write and so forth, but knowing it will never happen.

Back home, sitting beside my bed in the old blue rocking chair, reading a book, I find I can't stop thinking about her. Summer is truly gone now, the way it always goes in New England: cold and dark and depressing days are coming. And I think of Lois, the way she was always somehow mixed up with the dream in my head of the woman on the beach, and I feel the night grow a little bit darker.

Chapter 58

THE NIGHT BEFORE the trial, I have a terrible nightmare about Danielle and the huge rock wall we tried to climb in Red Rock Canyon State Park. It's as real as it was that day, and twice as bad. We climb the wall, looking up occasionally at the endless face looming down on us, a mountain of rock, and the wind howls louder and harder until my hearing is lost in the roar and my eyes dim with tears. But still we climb. I look down to where she is laboring, struggling to follow me up this implacable mountain face, her windsuit billowing out behind her the way it did that day, but worse. And this time, when she falls I cannot catch her. The rope is stuck by a stopper in a crevice far below me, and she is trapped in the wind, clinging only to the rope, nowhere to go and nothing to grip. As I struggle down the rock wall, backtracking as fast as I can, I hear her voice, *Jana, Jana,* she can hold out only so long, and my heart is booming when her last cry reaches my ears like a call from miles and miles away and she begins to fall.

Up in my bed like a rocket, wide awake and gasping, a diver coming up from heavy water. After a moment I realize she's not dead. I am alive, my mother and Danielle are alive. Only my father is dead. My forehead is wet.

I do not feel it is going to be a good day.

My mother is at work today and so is Danielle, out of necessity. They've been with me as much as possible, down to this last
day, and now I'll be on my own. The case will not be heard until
ten o'clock, and so, even getting up at eight after my mother has
left for work, I still have plenty of time to shower, eat breakfast,
ponder my fate.

At 8:30, the phone rings. I wander over to it, not expecting
much, probably a salesman.

"Hello?"

"Yes, I'm trying to locate Jana Odessi?"

"This is she."

"Ms. Odessi, this is the judge's clerk, Tanya Winston. I'm just
calling to confirm that your case will be heard this morning at ten
sharp."

I hesitate. "Yes. Is there a problem?"

"No, this is normal procedure. We have to call to remind you
and confirm the time."

"I'll be there," I say.

We say goodbye and hang up, and I feel somehow warmed
by the call. It feels special, like "how considerate," even though I
know it's just procedure.

Still, I don't want to think about any of it until I get there.
Part of me would like to take the bus to the courthouse, just so I
could read the paper, and presumably keep my mind off the case
for a while. But I know I have to drive. I cannot put that much
responsibility into the hands of public transportation authorities.
So I ease the good old van out into the street at what feels like
an ungodly hour and drive across town to what is euphemistically
called Superior Court.

The building is high and square and flatter across the top
than you would expect. No spires or gold domes, no arches, just
functional. The kind of building that will probably never inspire

anything better than a low level malaise, which is what it gives me this morning.

I climb out of the big white van with the same sensation I had as a child when my parents got me up at four o'clock in the morning to go on vacation, that strange all-nighter feeling of no sleep and something vaguely exciting to look forward to, knowing it's going to be an unusual day. Only this is the adult version, so I also have an upset stomach, and various aches and pains. I am not a morning person.

I walk into the courtroom half an hour early. The janitor is the only one here, and my stomach is immediately more upset than the moment before. I'd expected—always a mistake, having expectations—that I'd find at least a couple people…not necessarily lawyers, but clerical people, a stenographer; someone.

The aisle between the rows of benches is impossibly long, like walking between church pews toward an altar, except that we have The Bench instead of an altar. I feel like a four-year-old, totally dwarfed by this entire situation, and my first impulse is to turn and run right back out that door and never come back again. Of course, I know more than anything that I want to try to beat this thing somehow. I want to win. And yet my first impulse in times of crisis and confrontation and horrible uncertainty has always been to run, to retreat to some comfortable womblike hiding place where I can rest and regroup, think things through.

So now I am thinking I don't want to be in this, I don't want any of this, I want out. But don't I want to be an example, too? Don't I need to at least stand up and be counted, to have my rights defended?

I remember a woman from *The Alternative Voice* who accosted me in the hallway of the old SCHRO building and said, "Never again," when she touched my arm. I knew what it meant: never again, the cry of Holocaust survivors. They saw their brothers and sisters, mothers and fathers, taken to the gas chambers. They saw their closest friends and relatives spat on, shot like dogs, because of who and what they were. And this battle cry had been taken up by my gay and lesbian brothers and sisters, and no priest, no jury, no army should prevent me from standing up and saying, with my head held high, "Never again."

I'm ready.

I kneel on the floor of the first bench like I'm actually in the front row in church. I think of my dad and I pray. I don't know if the janitor notices any of what I'm doing, because my eyes are closed, and honestly, I don't even care. When you get to the point where I am, you don't worry about false pride anymore, and all that matters is acceptance: acceptance of the situation, of the outcome, whatever it may be, and, regardless of the outcome, of myself.

When I open my eyes, the room is quiet and I am alone. I slide back up onto the bench and sit for a long moment before I wonder when other people will join me. Soon there are a couple of older women testing microphones, and they talk idly while they set up, stopping occasionally to take a drink of coffee or hitch up an uncooperative stocking.

If they've noticed me, they've given no sign, and it occurs to me to ponder whether I'm a common sight—the plaintiff, half an hour early, waiting breathlessly for the trial. In any case, they do me no harm, and appear content to leave me to my own thoughts. I could be a homeless wanderer stopping in to cool off in the air conditioning and sit on a comfortable seat for a moment, and they probably wouldn't even see the dirty trenchcoat and baggy sweat-pants, the bags of bottles and cans.

The place doesn't fill up the way I expected, and after a few blank minutes of watching the setup procedure, I begin to feel concern about who exactly will show up. In my mind, I see Steve Torres and Wilson Carr, but I presume no one from SCHRO actu-ally took enough interest in the case to follow up on it as observers. As it is, they'd be at work now, so of course it makes no sense to even consider any of them appearing. No, the major players will be the other people I see in my mind's eye: Barbara Helms, James Kahn, and Hailey. I cannot imagine Barbara's testimony, what it might entail, but I expect her to be as breezy and unruffled as if she were plucking a tulip from a flower garden; much as she was when she said, *I think it's time we ended this relationship.*

Time moves too slowly now, just as the morning of my first hearing at the SCHRO office, when I sat in that room, feeling an overwhelming mixture of anger, anxiety, and fear, and my heart thudded so loudly I thought—cliché as it sounds—that other people in the room could hear it. I see everything in this courtroom today just as I did then, with a heightened, morbid clarity. It's a hallucinatory view of reality, I know, but here it is again just the same. Every microphone wire along the floor looks as black and cold as a snake, and the scuffed toe of my left pump looks as though I'd punted a brick across a schoolyard. The janitor, who has moved his bucket and mop into the hallway outside, seems to linger idly over a newly-wetted spot for no particular reason.

Hailey is the first person to arrive, thank God. He's as cool as ever, but his eyes gleam as if he is very high on the adrenalin rush of rehearsing his opening argument. The impeccably tailored grey suit and red and black tie with perfect symmetrical squares are conservative but dignified. Completely anal. He speaks to me very quickly in a low voice about procedure.

"Okay, the judge for this case is a guy named Karl Blankenship, a very serious old man who is so conservative it may scare you, but I want you to know about that up front because I don't want you to be scared or put off. I've known old Blankenship for years, and your saving grace is the fact that he's an absolute pillar in the community. He couldn't be bought off by Kiddie Korner, or anyone else, for a million dollars, so assuming things go well, which they will, he'll almost inevitably be working in our favor from word one. When he asks for opening statements, I'm going to hammer away at the fact that Barbara Helms' lawyer spoke entirely on her behalf during the whole thing at the commission, and basically set her up as the evil lesbian-baiting right-winger and you as the innocent-and-not-even-vindictive victim. It would almost help if you batted your eyes a lot, since old Blankenship has a soft spot for young women, but since you're a lesbian, it's a pretty bad idea. What you *should* do is just look downcast, sad, meek. Maintain your composure at all costs, and for God's sake, don't act tough or angry. There's definitely no need to show Blankenship your strong side. Impress on him the idea that you are here only because you want to do the right thing and not out of a sense of vengeance, and he'll be putty in your hands.

"If you do lose your composure, make it look like it's out of fear, timidity, frustration, the sadness and suffering you've endured…whatever. Your integrity is on the line, and if you show anger or rage, you will fuck it up royally—excuse me, screw it up royally—and the old man will close up in front of your eyes like a book. Kahn will attack your integrity again and again, and your job is to not feed into that. Answer his questions directly, keep your answers short, especially on the yes-and-no type questions… oh, and call him sir, they love that shit. Obviously, the judge is 'Your Honor,' but if you give me and Kahn a lot of *Yessir-Nosir*, you'll have old Blankenship eating out of your hand. Christ, am I using a lot of clichés today or what? It must be thinking about that goddamn Kahn, but don't worry, I always get like this, and once I get into a good rhythm, it'll be fine, the whole room will be mesmerized."

He sips his coffee, grinning almost moronically. He is so good, and knows he is so good, that he can't wait to show it off. You're a self-centered egomaniacal prick, I think, and am I ever glad I've got you for this case.

People file in: jurors, lined up in two rows like ducks in a carnival shooting gallery. They all look at me expressionlessly and look away. Kahn and Barbara Helms come in with the other two lawyers, the silent twosome from the SCHRO hearings—a bearded man of indeterminate age and a blonde of about forty or so, who looks like she may have put on some weight these past several months.

Seeing Barbara again is the weirdest sensation. I feel a curious detachment from her, almost compassion. For a moment, I can't help thinking she looks like she has been cryogenically frozen then thawed out just for the trial. If she was cool and frosty before, she is the Ice Queen now. Her face looks like she applied a mask of makeup to it that would crack if she registered the slightest emotion.

It's eerie, those eyes in that mask, pale and cool, but dead somehow, as if all human feeling had been extinguished long ago. I wonder whether there's still a person somewhere beneath that magisterial calm who cares about other people, who has fears and struggles, misplaced affections. It is hard to imagine.

Hailey shuffles paperwork and studies his notes, and I am left to observe all this in the cold silence—cold not just because of the Ice Queen, but because the air conditioning has been cranked too high. My anxiety combines with that to make my fingers feel like I can barely move them. Eventually, the silence gives way to a low murmur, the kind you might hear in a church fifteen or twenty minutes before the service, except that it grows louder and louder until I realize that the room has nearly filled up. This time, instead of press people, we have friends of friends, family members of jurors, Kiddie Korner parents. I don't know who they are. But none of them are friends or family of mine, and I can't help a bleak recognition of how alone I feel. I'm not the one on trial, but it still sort of feels like I am.

To break the tension, I lean over toward Hailey and whisper in his ear. "Shouldn't we be doing something?"

He draws back a little, as if my breath in his ear is slightly repugnant. "Not really," he says in a low voice. "I'm ready. Are you ready?"

I honestly don't know. "About as ready as I'll ever be, I guess."

"Think about something else if you can," he suggests. "Something that will keep you calm." He gestures in the air, encompassing the whole scene with a wave of his hand: "Forget all this." He pats my hand mechanically.

Probably I look at him like he's either an idiot or a complete nutcase, because he quickly looks away after meeting my gaze, clearly unnerved by whatever it is I'm showing. At this point, it might be hostility. I wouldn't even know it.

This worries me, this sudden painful inability to be anything other than an open book. I hope it will work in my favor, because of my honesty, but what he said about showing no anger or rage has me worried, and instead of thinking about some harmless and irrelevant topic, as he suggests—the weather, or national news—I worry that little bit of uncertainty like a dog with a bone. My fingers are so numb and cold now they could easily snap off like twigs, and I long for a few moments in the sun to warm them up.

But no, I'm trapped here. I rub my hands together like someone before a fire, no doubt creating the false impression that I actually relish my position. And I sit back in my chair, arms folded across my chest.

The defensive posture gets Hailey's attention, and he looks at me briefly—at my chest, actually, but not in an ogling manner; more like a doctor—and when he leans over, he gives me his best paternal smile and says, "Relax. We're going to do just fine."

Somehow, his phony benevolence calms me, even though I can see right through it. His energy so clearly radiates from the adrenalin rush of getting off on himself that I'd have to be an imbecile not to know better. And yet, the appearance of control and mastery is so complete, and he wears it so much like a second skin, that it actually makes me feel more confident. Self-centered egomaniacal prick or not, he has something that helps me in its own strange, obnoxious way.

I begin to relent. He's right, I tell myself, just relax. Don't fight him. Go with the flow.

I remember the moment in the SCHRO hearing when Wilson Carr asked me why I thought I'd been fired, how stunned and suspicious I felt. I need to avoid that kind of reaction today, need to rein in my impulse to show fear, mistrust, anger, rage. Hailey will probably pull some stuff here that makes Wilson Carr look like an archbishop, and I have to make sure I look composed if people start shouting objections and throwing tantrums. I am not on trial.

I repeat in my head, *I am not on trial.*

At this moment, the Honorable Karl Blankenship walks in, an old man with thin white hair and a thin white face.

The court monitor says, "All rise," and we do, and she introduces the jury to us. Karl Blankenship nods bleakly and tells us all to be seated. The court monitor tells him the case number and he nods again.

Then attorney Kahn stands to distinguish himself from the rest of the defense team and says, "Good morning, Your Honor."

"Good morning." Another bleak nod.

"For the record, I'm Attorney James A. Kahn, K-a-h-n. I represent the Kiddie Korner Child Care Center, and the board of trustees thereof, itself represented by Ms. Barbara Helms, who is seated to my right today."

Kahn bows a little, elegantly, and inclines his head toward Barbara Helms.

Then, to my surprise, Hailey speaks. "Your Honor, good morning. John Augustus Hailey, representing Ms. Jana Odessi, who is seated here beside me."

Yeesh, I think. Augustus. And to augment my discomfort he pats my hand gently. A calculated move, but it looks and feels as genuine and spontaneous as can be. I cringe inside and smile weakly.

Now that we have established who's who and what's what, and we have seen that the judge's look is bleak and my smile is weak, I feel as though I could use a few moments of silence. But before I have time to collect my thoughts, Kahn begins, with a great shuffling of papers, to elucidate his argument for the court. He makes quite a long statement that covers the points I have already heard all too clearly at SCHRO—lack of evidentiary documentation, the question of motive, the clarity of existing legislation, and on and on. I realize that, in addition to his eloquence, Kahn has a talent for making the eyes of jurors glaze over, and I wonder how long he will hammer away before their attention wanes. I have to admit it's disturbing to think that, by the time Hailey begins his opening statement, the jurors may be nodding off.

As Kahn winds up his opening, it strikes me that his tone is patronizing, and of course, it is at my expense. I feel myself change color when he hits the climactic moment. "Your Honor, we intend to demonstrate that the plaintiff has, in point of fact, no case whatsoever; that the alleged discrimination was simply all in her imagination." He pauses for effect, the words dripping with phony goodwill. "Understandably so, of course."

"Objection, Your Honor," Hailey says suddenly.

Karl Blankenship swivels his chair. "Mr. Hailey?"

"Your Honor, at the risk of sounding pedantic, I find it unlikely that the defense can presume to demonstrate what is or is not in my client's imagination."

He seems to think about it. "Sustained." Another swivel of the chair. "Mr. Kahn?"

Kahn smiles indulgently. "Your Honor, my intent here is only to convey that the plaintiff has made a mistake, that there's no empirical evidence to back the prosecution's assertions. Of course it is an understandable mistake—based on paranoia, perhaps, which is understandable in itself, given the plaintiff's lifestyle."

"*Objection*," Hailey says with a bang of the fist. "This is hardly congruous, Your Honor, to the ordinary protocol of this procedure."

"Sustained." He turns to the court monitor. "Strike the above remarks from the record." Another swivel. "Mr. Kahn, you have concluded your opening remarks?"

"Yes, Your Honor."

"I'll ask you to please conduct yourself in a manner congruous to the protocol of a court of law. I trust you'll be able to oblige?"

"Yes, Your Honor."

"Very well. Mr. Hailey, your opening remarks."

"Your Honor —" he nods "— ladies and gentlemen of the jury —" another nod "— today you will be asked to begin the process of determining whether the Kiddie Korner Child Care Center wrongly terminated Ms. Jana Odessi last March the third. You will need to evaluate some subtle pieces of evidence and listen to some subtle testimony. Remember that my client was, we believe, terminated from her position because the center wanted to avoid the ensuing controversy if Ms. Odessi's sexual orientation became known to parents whose children might have been under her supervision.

"I ask you to please bear in mind that the only person here who will say with confidence that discriminatory practices were at work here, other than myself, is my client, Ms. Jana Odessi. No one ran to her to console her after she was fired. No one witnessed any overt discrimination. No one responded to my investigative work by saying, 'Oh yes, Mr. Hailey, I'll testify on Jana's behalf. I'm sure she was a victim of discrimination.' Believe me when I say it is truly *their* word against hers.

"So why are we here today? What makes us think we even have a case?" He suddenly smiles, a broad, confident smile. "I'll tell you.

I have heard the whole story from my client, in her own words, and I am sure she's telling the truth. Not just her *perception* of what happened, but what actually happened. You'll hear the story, including the fact that Barbara Helms, who fired Jana, failed to testify in her own behalf at the initial hearing at the State Commission on Human Rights and Opportunities, and instead allowed her *attorney*—Mr. James Kahn, who has already spoken to you—to speak for her entirely.

"This is not simply a matter of financial compensation or of reparation for the emotional distress my client has suffered as a result of her termination. It's a matter of right and wrong; a moral issue, if you will. I ask you all to listen carefully to each person who testifies, and to examine carefully each piece of evidence. Of course, the defense will try to persuade you that the evidence is not there, but it is. And I feel confident that, in the end, you will all do the right thing."

At this moment, a man in a blue silk suit enters the room, walking briskly, yet trying to be unobtrusive. I do not recognize him, but when he approaches our table and sits down with a short whispered apology to Hailey, I realize he must be William Demas, Hailey's law partner. Hailey is about to sit down when he comes in, so presumably the interruption has no effect on the opening argument. I try to keep my face expressionless as I glance around the room, and what I see tells me nothing. The jury members' faces register nothing, the judge is impassive, and James Kahn is studying his cufflinks with apparent disinterest.

"Mr. Kahn, your first witness," says the judge.

"Your Honor, the defense would like to call to the bench Taylor Marks, board of directors member, Kiddie Korner Child Care Center."

The judge nods. Taylor Marks rises, an elderly man, glaucous and nondescript. He takes the stand.

"Mr. Marks, you are a member of the board of directors at the Kiddie Korner Child Care Center?"

"Yes."

"How long have you known Barbara Helms?"

"Twenty-six years."

"How would you describe her character?"

"Exemplary."

And so on. Kahn lays it on thick for what seems like a very long time with the same type of self-serving pap, obviously laying the groundwork for the unassailable argument that Barbara Helms' character is above reproach. I try not to gag, and look straight ahead into the core of the big black microphone.

When Kahn has finished questioning this "witness"—Witness to what? I have to ask myself—Judge Blankenship turns to Hailey. "Mr. Hailey?"

He looks bored and says, "No questions, Your Honor."

"Your witness."

"At this time, I would like to call to the stand my client, Jana Odessi."

I am only mildly surprised he didn't question the board of directors guy, but this really floors me. I find myself thinking, Already? Everything looks scary and surreal as I stand with a heavy heart and walk cautiously toward the front of the room.

"You swear to tell the truth, the whole truth, and nothing but the truth, so help you God?"

"I do." Just like a goddamn wedding vow.

Okay, I say. It's not a trick. Method to his madness. Get it over with, establish the integrity before Kahn has a chance to attack it. Put me at ease somehow. Maybe.

"Ms. Odessi, you were hired by Kiddie Korner in December according to this document, and terminated the following March. Is that correct?"

"Yes, sir." I remember to say *sir*. My spirits rise exactly one iota.

"The court will please consider this document Exhibit One. It shows both the dates of hiring and firing."

The court is willing to note it.

"At the risk of being redundant, I would also like the court to examine Exhibit Two, Ms. Odessi's job application. Ms. Odessi, would you please read the fine print at the bottom of page four of this document?"

I read the fine print: equal opportunity employer, etc., etc., no discrimination on the basis of blah blah blah, etc., etc., including race, disability or sexual orientation.

"What was the result of your interview at the center? How did you feel about job security, relative to the fact that you were still in your probationary period?"

"I can't say I felt any extra security. I don't think the job market is very secure at all."

"How did you feel about your relationship with Barbara Helms? Were you comfortable with her?"

I look at Barbara's blank, level gaze. I'm sure my eyes narrow. "I never had a problem." I avert my gaze, and after this, I will have to avoid looking at her.

"What about the relationship with Tillie Jones, your immediate supervisor? Did you ever suspect that they might have some sort of hidden agenda, something designed —"

"Objection," Kahn says suddenly. "Speculation."

"Sustained." A swivel of the chair. "Counsel?"

"How did you feel about Ms. Jones? Did you like her? Trust her?"

"Yessir."

"Did you feel she was a person of integrity?"

"Yessir."

"What would you say if I told you that, besides Barbara Helms, Ms. Tillie Jones was most likely the only person who could have any insight into the reasons for your termination? And what if I were to tell you also," he says, turning from me and toward the jury, pure showmanship, "what if I were to tell you also that Tillie Jones received a subpoena from my office *four days* ago, and not only failed to respond, but failed to appear here today?"

I wait, unsure whether he expects some sort of answer. He does not.

"Ms. Odessi, will you please tell the court whether you see Ms. Tillie Jones anywhere here in this room today?"

"No, sir, I do not."

"Your Honor," he says, "in light of the fact that this witness for the prosecution is presently in contempt of court for failure to appear—and she very well may be a witness for the defense as well—I would like to request a thirty-minute recess to avail ourselves of the opportunity to try one last time to contact this witness."

The judge seems to weigh it. "Very well, the court will adjourn for thirty minutes. However, I want to see you, Mr. Hailey, and you, Mr. Kahn, in my chambers."

Hailey's partner, Demas, gets up and heads for the door as the other two attorneys follow Karl Blankenship back to his chambers.

So now I sit here alone again, just as I did before Hailey's arrival, only this time I'm alone in a room full of people. Barbara Helms leans over to speak to the woman, Grisette, or whatever the hell her name is, and up front, the court monitor adjusts microphones and rewinds the tape, while all around us, people stand, flip cigarettes out, and head for the exits. I want to go, too—I don't smoke, but I'd like to escape from this room—yet I dread having to either mingle with other people or, worse, wander around the periphery of the crowd like some kind of leper.

I drum my fingers on the table, then realize that probably makes me look nervous, so I stop. I smile obligingly at no one, that half-smile reserved for moments when we want to look harmless but still somewhat hip. I can't seem to find anything to do with my hands. Since drumming on the table is out, I spend these few moments of desolation picking at my clothes, patting my hair, and shuffling papers on the table as if in preparation for something.

At last, Demas returns. He has his own version of the half-smile, and I know what he's going to tell me.

"Tillie wasn't home."

"I know."

He sits down, looks at me quizzically. "You know?" His voice is low and gentle.

"I could tell by the look on your face: the bearer of bad news."

He smiles. "In ancient times, they really used to kill the messenger. I'm glad you're not an Egyptian queen."

"Nope, not me. I have a couple friends who are queens, though." I laugh at my own joke, and he shakes his head at me, still smiling.

"Don't worry about Tillie," he says. "We won't need her to win. Just a diversionary tactic."

The low murmur of his voice puts me at ease. "Do you have something else up your sleeves that Hailey's just not telling me about?"

"You remember Wendy Simpson?"

"Sure I remember her. She's a fucking idiot."

He smiles. "We've got *her.*"

"As a witness!?" My blood pressure skyrockets.

"Don't worry, don't worry," he croons. "Let's just say her credibility is pretty questionable. Are you familiar with the concept of a 'hostile' witness?"

"Ah." I slow my breathing. "Like a reverse psychology thing—using her to make the defense look bad?"

"Something like that." He pats my hand, the way Hailey did a little while ago. "Don't worry, it'll be fine."

"I hope so. Christ, I thought she'd be a witness for the defense."

"Kahn will give her the cross. It won't matter. *You* probably know that better than anyone, since you know her."

"I hope so." I look into his eyes, trying unsuccessfully to read him just like Hailey. His quiet restraint serves as a good antidote to Hailey's conceit, yet I can't help wondering how much of it is just personal style.

The half hour passes faster than I expected. Kahn and Hailey come back, Blankenship lines them up, and before long they are back in their respective places. I return to the witness stand rubbing my hands together in the cold air conditioning.

"Ms. Odessi, who was the first person at the center in whom you confided your sexuality?"

"Tillie Jones."

"Was there anyone else you may have told?"

"No, sir."

He looks puzzled. "Are you certain that Tillie was the only person you told? Didn't you at least mention it to *any* other co-workers?"

I look across the room, and sure enough, there she is. I don't know how I didn't notice her before, unless she just came in during the break: our lovely Wendy.

"Yes, sir, I forgot. There was one other person."

"Is she in this room today?"

"Yessir."

"Be so good as to point her out to the court, Ms. Odessi."

I do. "Wendy Simpson."

"Ms. Simpson, would you mind standing, please? Thank you. Your Honor, I have no further questions at this time, and would like to request the opportunity to question Ms. Wendy Simpson."

"A strange request, counselor," says the judge. "Mr. Kahn, would you care to cross-examine the plaintiff at this time?"

"Not at this time, Your Honor."

"Very well." He swivels again. "Ms. Odessi, you may step down. Mr. Kahn, would you care to forfeit your next witness to the prosecution, or do you have a witness you'd like to question at this time?"

"Your Honor, I don't wish to forfeit my next witness, but thank you for asking all the same." He smiles ironically, drawing laughter from the jury. "Your Honor, I'd like to call to the stand Ms. Barbara Helms."

I am already in my seat by this time, but I'm sure my eyes blaze at the sound of the name. I look up at her briefly, then down.

Hailey leans in and says, "Relax. Think of her as someone who's just been released from a mental hospital. Think compassion. We can't afford to have you get pissed."

"Sorry," I whisper. "Do you think you can get anything out of her?"

He smiles. "She's not a problem. Don't worry. It'll be fine." Demas' words just a moment ago.

"Okay," I say, sitting back. But I don't believe it.

"Ms. Helms, how would you describe your position at Kiddie Korner Child Care Center?"

"I'm the Director. I oversee all marketing and public relations aspects of the center, as well as the actual day-to-day operations."

"And what is the center's policy on discrimination?"

"We're an equal opportunity employer."

"Which means that you do not discriminate on the basis of race, gender, religion, physical or mental disability, age, national origin, marital status or sexual orientation. Is that correct?"

"Yes, it is. I would also include prior criminal conviction and mental disorder in that definition." She's cool as dry ice.

"Very good. Now, it's been demonstrated by the prosecution that you signed off on a pink slip for Jana Odessi citing the reason for her termination as 'failure to meet company expectations.' Would you elaborate on that?"

She turns toward the jury. "Ms. Odessi was very enthusiastic with the children, and most of them seemed to like her. However, we felt she didn't truly embody the type of image we want to project, and that she wasn't able to *connect* with parents on the same level as our other employees. Also, she did make a couple of unauthorized visits to parents' homes."

I turn pale. "Nobody ever told me that was a problem!" I say before I can stop myself.

"Ms. Odessi, please," the judge says. "If you cannot restrain yourself, I'm going to have to find you in contempt of court."

"Sorry," I mumble, cursing myself inwardly. This is exactly what I wanted to avoid. I do not look at Hailey, but I feel his eyes, the tension between us like a horde of yellowjackets.

On and on the questions go. Before long, Barbara has managed to make me sound like an uncouth, socially maladjusted young creature headed for trouble, while painting herself as the great earth mother. I try not to grimace.

"Ms. Helms, is there any question in your mind," Kahn winds up, "of any possible wrongdoing by *any*one in the center in the termination of Jana Odessi?"

"No, there isn't."

"Thank you. Your Honor, I have no further questions at this time." He smiles his urbane smile, clicks his heels together like an SS officer, and returns to his seat.

"Ms. Helms." Hailey stands, walks in a little circle, like he is stalking her. "Ms. Helms, tell me about Paul and Jeanette Robeson." My stomach leaps, but I remain calm. The ace up his sleeve?

"What about Paul and Jeanette Robeson?" she asks.

Hailey doesn't buy the nonchalance. "Who are they?" he snaps. "And what's their relation to the center?"

"They're a couple of prominent members of the community. Their daughter, Ashley, is one of our children at the center. But I don't —"

"Thank you very much, Ms. Helms. That answers the question sufficiently. Tell me," and now his smile is most sinister, "what was their impression of Jana Odessi?"

"Objection," says Kahn. "Speculation."

"Sustained. Mr. Hailey?"

"Fair enough," he says. "I'll be more direct. Ms. Helms, did Paul or Jeanette Robeson ever complain to you about Ms. Odessi's sexual preference?"

She looks nonplussed. "No, Mr. Kahn, I can't say that they did."

"You *can't* say, or you *won't* say?"

"Objection!"

"Sustained. Counselor, badgering the witness isn't going to win points either with myself or this jury. Is there some relevance to this line of questioning that you'd like to share with the court?"

"Your Honor, I would like to establish a clear line of events between the Robesons and my client. At the moment, only my client herself can vouch for any animosity that these 'prominent' members of the community may have had for her, since Ms. Helms seems to be suffering from some pretty severe amnesia regarding this issue."

"All right, all right. Enough. You can continue, but —" he turns to the court monitor "— strike the above remarks from the record."

She nods.

Blankenship sighs.

"Ms. Helms, have you ever had any conversations, either with Paul or Jeanette Robeson, or with other parents at the center, regarding the sexual preference *or* sexual activities of any of your employees?"

"No, I have not."

He stops, looks dryly at her. "A little while ago, I noted the conspicuous absence of one of your employees here in court today—Ms. Tillie Jones. Do you know where she is?"

"No."

"Any idea why she would be in contempt of court? We did subpoena her."

"I don't vouch for my employees' whereabouts. Maybe she had a hair appointment."

There is a tinkle of laughter, but Hailey just looks bored and says, "Maybe so, maybe so." He seems to think about going on, then changes his mind. "Your Honor, I don't see any point in continuing to question this witness, but I would still like to call to the witness stand Ms. Wendy Simpson."

"Very well. Ms. Helms?" She takes the cue and steps down.

Wendy Simpson is sworn in.

"Ms. Simpson," Hailey says and smiles, "when did you first meet the plaintiff?"

"The what?"

He keeps up the forced grin. "When did you first meet Ms. Odessi—Jana?"

The baubles and bangles clatter. "Um, I don't know exactly. I think it was on her first day."

"All right. Ms. Simpson, have you ever spoken to anyone at the center about Ms. Odessi's sexuality?"

"What do you mean?"

"Have you ever discussed it?"

"If you mean have I ever talked about her sex life, no. The answer is no."

"Have you spoken to anyone about her sexual orientation?"

"Like how do you mean?"

"Ms. Simpson, please just answer the question yes or no," says the judge.

She looks around shiftily, her eyes lighting on Barbara, then darting away. Her reliability is so obviously questionable that even

Blankenship's eyebrows are raised. "I told Tillie about it," she says in a voice like a girl's.

"Would you please remind the court who Tillie is?" He turns to the jury with a look that says, *Watch this.*

"My supervisor."

"Tillie Jones, your supervisor, and Jana's, when she was there. Correct?"

"Yes."

"And what did Tillie—your supervisor—say to you about Ms. Odessi's sexual preference?"

"Objection," Kahn says suddenly. "The phrase is sexual *orientation*, not preference."

"Overruled," says Blankenship. "Ms. Simpson, you may answer the question."

"I don't know," she says, looking confused and a little awed. "I don't remember."

"Well, do you remember any of the substance of your conversation with—it is Tillie Jones, isn't that correct?" Hailey's voice is heavy with sarcasm, and he sounds completely condescending.

Kahn objects again, and says, "Badgering the witness."

"Overruled," says Blankenship, clearly irritated. "Counsel is unlikely to badger his own witness. Answer the question please, Ms. Simpson."

"I'm sorry," she says. "What was the question?"

Blankenship sighs, and a murmur of amusement runs through the crowd.

Hailey begins again patiently. "Tell us the substance of your conversation with Tillie Jones. What did you say to her, and what did she say to you, to the best of your recollection?"

She tosses her hair. "Well, I was upset when I came in, because I'd had a little, um…a little argument with Jana—with Ms. Odessi."

"An argument?"

"Well, not really an argument. I thought she was rude to me."

"Do you remember what she said?"

"Yes."

"Would you please tell the court what it was?"

"She used a word that I don't like to use."

"For the record, Ms. Simpson, will you tell us what she said?"

"She told me she was a lesbian."

"The word *lesbian* is a rude word?"

"Objection," Kahn says. "The witness did not say that *lesbian* is a rude word."

"I'm going to let it stand. However —" he swivels toward Hailey "— would you mind couching your language in more direct terms, Mr. Hailey?"

"Certainly, Your Honor. Ms. Simpson, do you feel that *lesbian* is a rude word?"

"No. And that wasn't the word, either." She twirls her hair with one finger.

"What word did Ms. Odessi use? You can tell us."

She squirms. "She said she was a dyke."

"A dyke." Weighty pause. "Very well. To return to the subject of Tillie Jones. Tell us about your conversation with her."

"Well, I was upset when I came in, like I said before. And I told her about the conversation I had with Jana—with Ms. Odessi."

"You told her Jana was a dyke."

"I didn't put it like *that*."

"You said, 'Jana's a lesbian.'"

"I told her Jana told me she was a lesbian."

"And what action did she take?"

"I don't know, she just said she'd keep us apart for a while, I guess. She didn't seem to think it was a problem."

"Why do you say that? Did she say something to you to indicate that?"

"I think she said it wasn't an 'employment issue,' or something. I don't remember, it was a long time ago."

"Do you know how long it was after your conversation that Jana was terminated?"

"No."

"Did anyone say anything to you about it? Did you have any indication that she might be losing her job?"

"No."

"And did you talk to anyone else at the center about it?"

She appears to consider it. "No," she says.

"No further questions."

"Mr. Kahn?" the judge says.

"Thank you, Your Honor." He stands and approaches the bench while Hailey sits down with a look of disgust.

What's happening? I write on a notepad in front of me. *What's wrong?*

She's lying. She talked to Barbara after Tillie.

I take the pen back. *Can we salvage it?*

Don't worry, he writes. *I expected her to be a hostile witness. A little surprised she perjured herself, though.*

Again I take the pen back, and this time I just underline my own words: Can we salvage it?

He nods, his lips pursed. He still looks confident, but now I feel doubtful. He is listening to Kahn.

"And how long would you say you've known Ms. Odessi?"

"How long have I known her?"

"Yes."

"I don't know, just since when she was at the center. I mean, she was only there like three months or something. I haven't seen her since then."

"How would you describe her psychological condition at the time she was there?"

"Objection." Hailey jumps up. "Is the witness qualified to make psychological evaluations?"

"Sustained." He swivels. "Ms. Simpson, I take it you are not a psychologist?"

"No, sir."

"Fair enough. Mr. Kahn?"

He smiles. "I beg your pardon, Your Honor. Ms. Simpson, were you ever aware of Jana Odessi's being in therapy of any sort?"

"Objection. Relevance?"

"Your Honor, I'm merely trying to establish whether the witness is aware of any mental problems the plaintiff may have had."

"Objection sustained," he says wearily. "Continue." Then, as if remembering, "Strike the above from the record."

"Have you ever heard of a Dr. John Wagner?" Kahn asks.

"*Objection.* Your Honor…?" Hailey is almost whining in protest. Then, as a postscript, he adds, "This is absurd."

"Sustained again. Mr. Kahn, you are in danger of being in contempt of court. Ms. Simpson, you are to disregard the question."

"Okay," she says quietly.

I am ready to explode. I know I've gone from white to red at the mention of John Wagner, but just as I am about to burst, I think of Tillie—what would she do in my situation?—and as if the very thought of her has opened some inexplicable magic door in the wall of reality, here she is, Tillie herself, walking down the long aisle between the courtroom benches as if she belongs here.

She is expressionless, dressed like a parishioner at Sunday services, and her footsteps echo, my eyes widening automatically as the shock of her sudden presence pounds in my chest wildly, and I gulp from my water glass, trying to look composed, but the effort costs me a dreadful amount of energy and I have to wipe perspiration from my forehead as casually as I possibly can while the long breath of anticipatory wonder flows out across the room in its low suspiration and all eyes turn upon her.

"What is this?" Judge Blankenship is saying, and, "Who is this woman? Order in the court." He bangs the gavel, but already Wendy is saying, "It's Tillie," and the jurors are leaning and whispering to each other and poking elbows into ribs while Blankenship pounds away. "Order. Order! Ma'am, please be seated," he says. "Is your name Tillie Jones?"

"Yes, sir," she says in a voice barely audible. "Yes, Your Honor."

He frowns. "You're late. All right, then —" he swivels back to Kahn "— you may proceed."

Tillie sits down quietly, and Kahn continues on, but he is visibly rattled. The interruption seems to have irritated him, and he asks Wendy nothing more of substance: no objections from Hailey, no admonitory comments from Blankenship.

Before long, Hailey stands and says, "Your Honor, the prosecution would like to call Ms. Tillie Jones to the stand."

Kahn gets up immediately. "Your Honor, I object to this witness giving testimony, on the grounds that defense has had no opportunity to prepare cross-examination."

"Objection overruled, Mr. Kahn. Mr. Hailey did subpoena the witness. If Ms. Jones had failed to appear at all today, she would have been in contempt of court."

"But Your Honor —"

"Mr. Kahn, I'm going to find *you* in contempt if you don't sit yourself down while the prosecution questions Ms. Jones. Mr. Hailey, you may proceed."

They swear her in.

"Ms. Jones, what is your position at the Kiddie Korner Child Care Center?"

"I'm a supervisor."

"And you have been responsible for supervising at least two people here in court today, Wendy Simpson, and the plaintiff, Jana Odessi. Is that correct?"

"Yes, sir."

"Is there anyone else presently in the courtroom whom you supervise or have supervised? Take a look around."

She does. "No, sir," she says.

"Very good. Now, Ms. Jones, I want you to think back to last March, when Ms. Odessi was terminated. Do you recall that incident?"

"Yes, sir. Very well." She looks down.

"Prior to this incident, you had had a discussion with Wendy Simpson about Jana Odessi's sexuality, a discussion which has already been mentioned here today. Do you recall the discussion to which I'm referring?"

"Yes, I do."

"We've already heard Ms. Simpson's testimony, but just for the record, would you give a summary of what was said?"

She folds her hands in her lap. "Wendy was upset because of a confrontation with Jana. She told me Jana had told *her* that she, Jana, was a lesbian. She said, 'What are we going to do?' I said I would keep them on different schedules as much as possible until we had an opportunity to sit down together and work some things out, but I also said it was a non-issue. I said it was not, in my view, a work issue or a safety issue. That's what I recall."

"And since she apparently got no satisfaction out of talking to you, do you think she went over your head?"

"Objection," says Kahn. "Speculation."

"Sustained."

"Your Honor," says Hailey, "with your permission, I'd like to rephrase the question."

Blankenship sighs. "Go for it, counselor." He looks dryly at the court, and a few people titter nervously.

"Ms. Jones, after Wendy spoke with you, are you aware of anyone else in the center having had a similar conversation with her?"

"Barbara Helms."

This causes a sensation, and Blankenship has to bang the gavel for order. Wendy's perjury is in the light.

"Really?" Hailey smiles. "Did Barbara Helms herself tell you about this?"

"Yes, she did."

"Would you recall *that* conversation for the court?"

Another brief moment of anticipation as she lets a long breath out and the jury appears to take one in. And she begins to tell the story, telling things even I do not know, in her low even voice, her hands folded in her lap, her face expressionless.

"Barbara called me into her office to tell me there was a problem. The first part of it was that Jana was a lesbian. I already knew this, not only from Wendy Simpson, but from Jana herself. My response was that a secondhand report did not necessarily guarantee homosexuality. Then she told me about a couple, Paul and Jeanette Robeson—whom I had met with—and that they had seen Jana somewhere in public with another woman…kissing her. I don't know if you've already heard testimony about the Robesons today —" Hailey nods "— well, then, I'll just say that my response to this *second* half of the issue was that what we might have was a *perceived* problem. I didn't want to let my own personal view be known because, I have to admit, I didn't know whether my own job might be on the line."

"And what else happened?"

"I told Barbara I'd talk to Jana, but she said she'd take care of it."

"How?"

"I didn't know at that time. I never heard another word about it, but shortly thereafter, Jana was let go."

"Were you present at that incident?"

"The firing? Yes."

"And what was said?'

"Just what's on the pink slip: failure to meet company expectations. But when Barbara said that, Jana looked to me for clarification, and I gave her the most doubtful look I could, out of Barbara's sight. I wanted her to know it was not legitimate, in my opinion."

I glance at Barbara Helms: no expression, her eyes averted.

"And were there any other conversations between you and Barbara Helms regarding this matter?"

"Yes."

Barbara looks up.

"Would you recall them for the court, please?"

"Barbara telephoned me late one night at home. This was long after the firing. The center had offered a conciliation agreement, and Jana rejected it. When Barbara telephoned me that night, I knew right away something was wrong. Her voice was different. But of course, I knew something was wrong if she was calling me at home…she never did that."

I look at Barbara again, and her face is a mask of fear and disbelief.

"What do you mean when you say that her voice was different?"

"She had been drinking."

"She had been *drinking*. And what did she say?"

"She was calling to tell me she would need my help. She said, 'The little dyke rejected the agreement.' She said, 'I may need you to go to bat for me.' I said I understood. She kept repeating herself and asking me if I understood. I told her I did."

"She said, 'The little dyke rejected the agreement?'"

I look at Barbara, and a fat teardrop is rolling down her cheek.

"Yes."

"Were those her exact words?"

She takes a long moment, weighing the impact. "Her exact words were, 'The little dyke rejected the goddamn agreement.'"

Chapter 59

WE ARE STANDING outside, looking at the midday patch of sunlight on the Gold Building, just Tillie and me. The others have gone, offering their congratulations or their stony silence.

I know if it hadn't been for Barbara Helms breaking down and crying, Tillie's testimony might not have meant much. But as it stands, it meant a lot. And I know they are going to appeal, but right now that doesn't mean shit, and I don't think it ever will. More than anything, Tillie's testimony means a lot to me.

We stand side by side, the sun warm on our backs.

"And so you managed to find victory," she says.

I smile a sidelong smile. "You managed to find me a victory."

She puts her arm around my shoulders, and I automatically do the same. "I told the truth," she says.

"Hailey really subpoenaed you, huh?"

"Oh yeah. He knew something was up from meeting with me. Though I held back on him, even then. I'm sorry. I just couldn't do it right away."

"And you went looking for a new job in the field before you decided to testify?"

"I went looking."

"You were able to find something pretty quickly?"

"No. But I made sure I was set up for a smooth transition into a new job by next week. A little C.Y.A."

For an instant, I misunderstand. "What?"

"Cover Your Ass."

I laugh. "So, you knew you'd have another job!"

"I sure wasn't planning on staying there after what I had to say today. Besides, it's a better job."

We both laugh.

"Oh, Tillie, I can't tell you how happy I am for you. You definitely deserve better."

"We all deserve better," she says. "Everyone."

The sun is bright now on the gold-domed Capitol Building, and we see it glinting in the light from all the way across town. A tiny bird—a sparrow or swallow, I can't tell which—lifts its song to the sky from the top of an elm beside us, then sails away into the updraft.

Want More!

I'm truly grateful to you for taking the time to read this novel. I hope it took you on a ride. It took me about seven years to complete, and is among the great accomplishments of my life.

If you'd like to read my other novels — each of which also took about seven years to complete — please visit my website at http://www.msahno.com/books. If you join my free email newsletter, you'll get news on upcoming events, along with my free e-book, Marketing for Authors.

For today's independent authors, book reviews are like currency. If you enjoyed this novel, please post a review of it on https://www.goodreads.com or https://www.amazon.com. If you email me to let me know that you've reviewed it, I'll send you a special bonus PDF of exclusive material.

Of course, if you liked the novel, I hope you'll recommend it to others and follow me on social media. You can follow me on Twitter at https://twitter.com/MikeSahno or like my Facebook page at https://www.facebook.com/sahnocomm. Thank you all.

- Mike

Acknowledgements

COUNTLESS INFLUENCES SHAPE an author's life and work, and space does not permit thank yous for all of them. But on some level or other I am gratefully indebted to the following people whether their help was inspirational, editorial, instructional, emotional, spiritual or all of the above: the lovely and wonderful Sunny Sotgaew Sahno, Bob Sahno, Evelyn Sahno, Cory Andrew, Lou Berkman, Don Booth, Geodie Baxter-Bowen, Xena Brown, Paul Bouyea, Martha Calligan, Michele Carrell, Bruce Cockburn, Janet Davidsen, Linda Rurka Dooley, Christie Bracciano, Jim Ellis, Tara Engstrom, Cha Gray, John Guzzardi, William Hanna, Lori Jewell, Gemma & Larry Kay, Tom Kelly, Mark & Elizabeth Leib, David J. Lipani, Virgil Mandanici, Joni Mitchell, Lyle & Caroline Mosier, Donna Murphy, Jennifer Nolen, Lorin Oberweger, Phil Ochs, Craig O'Neil, Angela Perkins, Fred Rezler, Liz Rosenberg, Ron Scott, Paul Stober, Sr. Marguerite Tarleton, Scott & Lauri Toler, Nick Vukasinovic, Ed Whittle, Dot Wilson, Brenda Windberg, Lisa Zackowski, Frank Zappa, Mike S., Rob D., Dick & Judy P., Brenda D., Kenny & Pat H., Ron B., Paul G., Kathi W., Eddie H. and Nancy A., the late Stan Geda and Jeremy Crowe, and above all, Mr. G.